Carol McGrath taugh
the state and private s
in Creative Writing
MPhil in English a   , ... she
developed her expertise on the Middle Ages.

Praise for *Mistress Cromwell*

'Step into the intimate world of Thomas Cromwell, as seen through the eyes of his wife Elizabeth.' **Anne O'Brien**

'A delicious frisson of danger slithers through every page of the book. Enthralling.' **Karen Maitland**

'A delicate and detailed portrayal, absolutely beautifully done. Captivating.' **Suzannah Dunn**

'Rich, vivid and immersive, an enthralling story of the turbulent Tudor era.' **Nicola Cornick**

Praise for the *Daughters of Hastings* trilogy

'Moving and vastly informative, a real page turner of a historical novel.' **Fay Weldon** on *The Handfasted Wife*

'Brings the 11th century alive . . . a wealth of well-researched detail.' **Historical Novel Society** on *The Swan-Daughter*

'A beautifully woven tale of an exiled princess's quest for happiness.' **Charlotte Betts** on *The Betrothed Sister*

'Like one of its own rich embroideries, cut from the cloth of history and stitched with strange and passionate lives.' **Emma Darwin** on *The Betrothed Sister*

Also by Carol McGrath

The She-Wolves trilogy
The Silken Rose

The Daughters of Hastings trilogy
The Betrothed Sister
The Swan-Daughter
The Handfasted Wife

MISTRESS CROMWELL

CAROL McGRATH

ACCENT

First published in Great Britain as *The Woman in the Shadows*
by Accent Press in 2017.

This paperback edition published in 2020 by Headline Accent
An imprint of HEADLINE PUBLISHING GROUP

5

Cataloguing in Publication Data is available from the British Library

ISBN 978 1 4722 8003 9

Printed and bound in Great Britain by Clays Ltd, Elcograf S.p.A.

MIX
Paper from
responsible sources
FSC® C104740

Headline's policy is to use papers that are natural, renewable and recyclable
products and made from wood grown in well-managed forests and other
controlled sources. The logging and manufacturing processes are expected
to conform to the environmental regulations of the country of origin.

HEADLINE PUBLISHING GROUP
An Hachette UK Company
Carmelite House
50 Victoria Embankment
London
EC4Y 0DZ

www.headline.co.uk
www.hachette.co.uk

For

Patrick

Midsummer's Eve

21st June 1526

IT IS A GLORIOUS DAY: the sky a spread of blue with the midsummer sun slowly rising towards its zenith. A sudden breeze blows through the boughs of the apple trees, causing leaves to shiver. On the other side of our garden wall, the monks of Austin Friars are at their morning prayers. A bell that peals the hour from St Peter's Broad Street gives way to chimes from a hundred London churches until, at last, they cease and for a moment there is only the hum of bees in my lavender beds.

From where I'm sitting in a shady arbour stitching a sleeve for Thomas' shirt I can see him tending his roses. Enjoy this moment, Lizzy, I think to myself, for in a heartbeat it will be gone. Enjoy watching Thomas taking advantage of a rare holiday, his sleeves rolled back, his shirt loose from his breeches, scattered with dirt like a peasant's smock, sweat pearling on his brow; my husband, Thomas Cromwell, who works so hard because he is determined to one day stand shoulder to shoulder with the greatest nobles in the land, so he says, and so I believe.

As if he senses me observing him, Thomas glances up from his work and pulls a linen cloth from his belt. 'We'll watch the guild marches from the river bank this evening,

Elizabeth,' he calls over, wiping his forehead. 'It'll be cooler there,' He leans on his spade and begins to dig again.

'Will it?' I say into the air, for he is not listening now.

I doubt it *will* be cooler by the river today. We'll be caught up in a press of people merrymaking. I find myself smiling. How our children love puppet shows that appear on the narrow, cramped streets all the way down to the river. Stages are already erected along the Cheape with tableaux from the Old Testament, and an angel and a devil will wander around the audience; the devil scaring the children, who love to be frightened more than they care for the angel's blessing.

Listen! Hear my girls now. Catch their excitement, their voices escaping from the opened windows above.

'What can I wear?' nine-year-old Annie cries.

'What can I wear?' echoes young Grace.

A coffer lid slams and their maid scolds, 'Hush now, children. You will disturb Gregory.'

Gregory is in the library, working at his letters. No sound escapes from that opened casement, though, without doubt, he would prefer to play outdoors on such a pleasant morning.

I draw my needle slowly in and out of the bleached linen cloth. They say Queen Catherine still embroiders shirts for King Henry, to whom she is devoted, though the pomegranate, her symbol and that of fruitfulness, has not helped her to bear fruit other than a daughter and this has brought about her misfortune and sadness. I am so fortunate to be blessed with my husband and children.

Later, we shall wend our way down to the ancient waterway that rolls through our city, watching our lives unfold, reminding us how life has its ebbs and flows, its truths and untruths, its sorrows and joys - and, yes, I too have known both great joy and profound sorrow, as I shall relate.

Part One

Wood Street

The Rose, it is a royal flower
The red or white, Shew his colour.
Both sweet and of like savour
All one they be
That day to see
It liketh well me.

Roses , a song for three voices
The Oxford Book of Medieval Verse

Chapter One

1513 Wood Street

BRANCHES OF ROSEMARY SLID from Tom Williams' funeral bier, scattering around the mourners' feet to be trampled into the tiles of the church nave, releasing the scent of remembrance. For a moment, it seemed as if the bier threatened to slope backwards. I let out a gasp of horror. Was it an ill omen? I stood still and my father, mother, sister and the long procession of merchants, their wives, and yeomen following behind me, stopped walking. With one adept movement, the six guildsmen adjusted its weight on their shoulders just in time, and righted it.

My husband had ever been a slight man. I wondered at that, because he had been a King's Yeoman of the Guard, a protector of the King's property. Surely this is a heavy man's job. Tom had been an agile swordsman, though it was sword-play that was to be his undoing. He died from a thrust through the chest on Monday and by Thursday he was wrapped in his shroud.

Tom's death had been an accident. The Tower yeomen had not used blunt swords for practice that day. It was a hot day and he drank too much ale on an empty stomach, which made him careless, and he'd been caught by a blade in his breast. It had pierced him through.

I smoothed down my dark overdress. With the sun slanting into the church's opened doorway the black bombazine took on a ghostly, silvery sheen. My breath felt trapped tight inside my chest as, again, I began to follow the bier through the great doorway of St Alban's Church along the pathway to the graveyard.

It had been raining but now the sun was out and, blinded by the bright June sunlight, I faltered on a loosened, slippery paving stone and almost tripped. Mother reached out and took my hand.

'Elizabeth, steady.'

Her voice was gentle. My younger sister, Joan, held my other hand.

By the graveside, my tears began to flow. I had never loved Tom Williams and had resented my marriage but I had become used to his quiet manner, his generosity, and to my position as one married into a respectable London family. At three and twenty, I was young to be a widow. Dabbing at my eyes with a soft linen cloth, I cried for his passing along with the other cloth merchants' wives who wept with me. He had sinned gravely and I despaired for his soul. He had not deserved to die.

Was he now truly at rest? If what the priests tell us is true, he will dwell long in purgatory. I must be strong and not give way to weeping. Wiping away my tears away with a linen handkerchief, I swallowed and distracted myself by scanning the gathering of merchants and merchants' wives, all familiar faces. A few moments later, my eye lighted on a new face amongst the mourners, a cloaked man standing a little apart under a yew tree. He was high-cheeked, of middle height and looked like a clerk, though wealthy enough to wear the best cloth. I noted the richness of his fur-trimmed hat and the lustre of his velvet cloak as he stepped forward to speak with

Father. Puzzled, I watched them as Mother adjusted her funeral hood, complaining how it pinched her ears.

Joan shook raindrops from her cloak and mumbled, 'Mother, I told you, you could have worn a simpler cap. I told you it was too tight.'

My forward younger sister was a trial to my mother, always knowing better than she.

The stranger nodded and, it seemed to me, discreetly stepped back into the shadow of the yew tree, just as the priest lifted his hand, his surplice hem caught by a breeze into a brief flutter and his raised arms in a flapping gesture making him seem like a strange dark bird, one you would see drawn on the border of a map.

The church bell tolled steadily as Tom was finally lowered into his last resting place. We said our Pater Noster as Father Luke committed my husband, sewn tightly into his linen shroud, onto the hay that lined his grave. As I glanced away, a tame blackbird began to hop about my skirts. Not wanting to tread on it, I moved too quickly, revealing a flash of crimson petticoat below my dark gown.

I tugged at my kirtle and gently shook it until the offending underskirt was once again hidden beneath the folds of my black gown. I knew that crimson was a colour forbidden to one of my humble rank, yet I could not resist wearing it. The soft, slippery silk had been left over from a length we had sold to a foreign merchant. Tom had given it to me as a New Year's gift. Today, I wanted the bright colour to temper the sombre mood that was drowning me, and why should I not? It was my own secret flaunting of the rules that contained our daily lives. Tom Williams had possessed a secret, a secret so dangerous it could never be spoken, and in the keeping of it I feared for his soul and for my own. Tom

7

had broken the rules and now he would receive God's judgement for his sin.

The priest signalled to me and I unpinned the posy of herbs I wore on my waist, and cast it on top of my husband's shroud. Others followed my lead until Tom's linen-wrapped body was concealed under a covering of laurel and rosemary.

Mother squeezed my hand. 'It's time to leave. Lizzy, speak, or do you wish your father to speak for you?'

'No, I shall thank them.'

I raised my head and turned towards the gathering. Through gaps in the mourners, I could see the patiently waiting band of parish poor who had led us through London's streets, pausing at every wayside cross to kneel and pray. I had not noticed the stench of poverty then, but now, a whiff of their staleness cut through the rain and the scent of damp earth, laurel, ivy and rosemary. I felt sorrow for them all. The world is cruel to the poor.

Joan lifted her black spice-filled pomander to her nose and said in too loud a voice. 'I am glad I do not live in the City.' A wimpled city matron standing near to us swivelled her head around and glowered at her.

'Be silent, Joan,' Mother said in a low, sharp tone. 'You may one day.'

I glared at my sixteen-year-old sister and whispered into her ear, 'Don't let the merchants' wives hear that sort of remark. They will think you proud.'

'I am proud,' she whispered back.

'Not today, Joan,' my mother snapped. 'Be silent. Your sister has to speak and be heard.'

Ignoring my sister, I turned towards the poor who were waiting by the church door and said, 'Thank you for coming today. Bread, cheese and ale will be served in the church.' I paused and added because Tom would need their prayers, 'Do not forget to say a last Pater Noster for my husband's soul. Your prayers will guide him into Heaven's blessed light.'

Their heads bowed with respect and gratitude, they went into the church, and my servants followed them through the door to distribute their funeral dole. How thankful they were for so little, I thought, tears filling my eyes again.

I drew breath and focused my attention on the cloth guildsmen and the yeomen by the graveside, 'Thank you for your vigil by my husband's bier this night past, for your candles, for your sorrow at his passing and for your prayers. You must all be hungry too. The funeral feast will be served in my hall.' They nodded their thanks but continued to pray.

My father smiled at me. I had spoken well. Glad the burial was over, though there was still the funeral feast to get through, I took my sister's hand in my own and hurried her along the path towards the graveyard gate with Mother just behind. I stopped to open the gate latch and glanced over my shoulder at those who were making ready to follow us. Some still knelt at the graveside, murmuring prayers. Others spoke with Father. They were merchants, good-wives, guildsmen and a knot of Tom's yeomen friends, red and gold uniforms flashing below their dark cloaks.

I glimpsed the blackbird again, hopping onto the ivy covering an ancient stone grave marker, pausing to study me with sharp, bright eyes. They say a blackbird can carry a dead person's soul. I shivered, despite the warmth of my garments and the midday sun.

My house stood close by, a tall building with a garden

that reached a long way back from the street. Its two overhanging floors held a number of upper chambers and attics. A wide alley along the side led to stables and a spacious gated yard, within which stood a warehouse where we kept the stores of woollen cloth we supplied for various monasteries in the City. Cloth rooms for finer fabrics were situated on the ground floor of the dwelling house.

We entered the great hall by the heavy street door. There, dining trestles were set in a horseshoe for the feast. I glanced through an open side door from the hall into my small parlour. It held a sense of emptiness now that the funeral bier had been removed. The tapers had been extinguished, leaving only black candlesticks, a pair of black gloves and a pile of mourning rings that lay in a basket by the bench.

I pulled the door closed, and stepped forward into the middle of the hall, ready to greet my guests. My father stood with me as, fussing, Mother and Joan checked the tables.

I could not help saying, 'All is as it should be, Mother. You needn't worry. Look, the only white on display is that of linen table cloths.'

'Yes my dear, but your funeral guests will judge us,' she said. 'Well, yes, I can see that your napkins are freshly laundered.'

I nodded. 'Meg has overseen all.'

The hangings that usually made the hall look welcoming were shrouded with thick black cloth. Mother swept over to the wall behind the high table and straightened a fall of black cloth so that not even a bright stitch on the hanging could show beneath it. Joan stood back with her arms folded and approved.

Hired servants were still in the process of setting out

borrowed pewter mugs for the funeral ale, plates of fowl, bread and savoury pies. Meg, my maid, led three kitchen servers along the trestles with dishes of meat and platters laden with fresh salad. For once Meg was clad tidily, in a dark kirtle with only one black, springing curl escaping her cap.

As she passed close to me, Meg whispered, 'Mistress Elizabeth, it will soon be over.'

'Thank you, Meg, for your concern,' I said, longing for the day to end.

As they flowed into the hall, mourners approached me with respectful words, and I noted that the stranger from the churchyard was amongst them. I had a strange feeling now that something about him felt familiar; his square jaw or the determined set of his shoulders. I was sure I had met him before. Perhaps it was just that he had purchased cloth from us in the past. He bowed to me and when Father introduced him as Master Cromwell, the gentleman said in a smooth, hushed voice, 'Mistress Williams, I am sorry for your loss.'

'Thank you, sir.'

He hesitated for a moment, as if he would say more, but closed his mouth again, bowed and then crossed the hall to speak to a group of local cloth merchants. Father took my arm and guided me to the high table. Everyone found places and Father Luke blessed the food and drink.

I had no appetite for the feast, though others clearly did as the pies and meats vanished from their platters with speed.

Crumbling a pasty on my plate, I found myself answering a visiting merchant's questions about Tom's death. He expressed his sorrow, excused himself and

11

turned to his neighbour. I heard him discuss his wool sales. Soon enough, I thought, I must think of my own business. Not today, not for a little time yet. Gerard Smith, my journeyman, was more than competent at managing things. I glanced along the trestles to where Smith, a small man around thirty and two, with sand-coloured hair and bright, kindly blue eyes, was seated with the apprentices. I hoped I could rely on him, because if I could not then Father would take over our cloth business himself.

For several hours, I spoke little and ate sparingly. Father went about the hall speaking with merchants. I wondered how I would manage but knew I must and would. A chair scraped beside me, jolting me out of my thoughts. I felt a light touch on my elbow and glanced up. The feast was ending. My merchant had left his place. Gone to the privy, no doubt. Instead, Father stood by my chair, with Master Cromwell by his side.

'Lizzy, Master Cromwell is my new cloth middle-man. He would like you to show him your bombazine cloth. He has admired your mourning gown.'

I started. This was nothing new. Father always employed different cloth middlemen to sell his fabrics to Flanders, thinking each one better than the last but today, at my husband's funeral, it was not seemly. Master Cromwell was watching me through eyes of an unusual shade, not quite blue or grey.

He bowed and said, 'Forgive me for staring, Mistress Williams, but you see I knew you as a child. Your father used our fulling mill in Putney.' He smiled at Father.

That was why he was familiar. I stared back, and in a moment or two I had recollected a tough, wicked little boy, some years older than I, who taught me to fish in the river with a string and a hook with a wriggling worm at the end of it.

'I do recollect you, Master Cromwell. We played together as children,' I said, feeling my mouth widen into a smile. 'Father sent your father our cloth to be washed, beaten, prepared and softened for sale. I remember climbing trees and stealing apples. You led me astray.'

'That was long ago. I am not that boy now, Mistress Williams.' His bulky frame seemed to shift uncomfortably.

'Nor I that girl.' I looked hard again at his face. The unruly child was utterly transformed into a smooth, sophisticated cloth merchant. 'I can see you no longer raid orchards for apples.'

I thought quickly. I would need a middleman. Aloud, I said, 'But my cloth, you want to view my fabrics now, sir? Today? Today of all days? Why?'

'Master Cromwell returns to Antwerp within a week, Lizzy. He can help you with cloth sales.' Father added quickly. 'In fact, Master Cromwell can help us both. He is working for the Merchant Adventurers, buying cloth for sale in Antwerp.'

I recognised that I needed this money as a matter of some urgency as, of late, we had not been doing as well as in previous years. I rose to my feet and said, 'Master Cromwell, it would be a pleasure, but to see my cloth you must come tomorrow.'

'Then, I shall come tomorrow, if I may.' He bowed low. 'Thank you for receiving me, Mistress Williams. I apologise for disturbing you on such a sorrowful day. Tomorrow morning at an hour before midday? Would this be suitable?'

'I shall be here to receive you.'

13

'God bless you, Mistress Williams,' he said quietly, then bowed again and took his leave.

When he had moved away, I glanced over to where my mother sat at the end of the table with Joan, thinking that if she had overheard she would object to any business broached by me at her son-in-law's funeral, but she was in conversation with Father Luke and I could see that he was listening closely to her. I smiled to myself. My mother was the beautiful, perfect hostess who could make everyone feel important. If only I was more like her; for I had no female friends, only Meg, the servant girl who grew up in our household, and very few male acquaintances.

'Elizabeth,' my father said, 'Your guests are leaving now. You must bid them God speed.'

I stood, neatly folded my hands and said aloud so all could hear me, 'May God guide you all safely home tonight. Thank you all for your care of me today.'

It was over. The interminable day was finished and tomorrow afternoon my family would return to Fulham and I would be on my own. My new life would begin. I determined that Thomas Cromwell would purchase as much of my cloth for sale as could be spared.

On the following day, the appointed hour arrived and after pleasantries were exchanged, I escorted Master Cromwell and Father to the storerooms. 'Master Cromwell,' I said, trying to make conversation as we walked along the passage. 'Where have you been these past years?'

'Abroad - Italy - learning the ways of business, banking, a little of the law and a bit of soldiering too, Mistress Williams.' His full mouth eased into a pleasant smile.

My father drew to a stop before the storeroom door. He held out his hand. 'The key, Lizzy?'

'Oh, a moment.' I returned along the dim corridor and entered the chilly parlour. Once inside, I felt a disturbance in the air, as if my husband's unhappy soul were watching me, hovering by the tall candlesticks that had guarded his bier. I hurriedly drew the storeroom key from the cupboard and ran from the darkened room as if its shadows were about to pursue me.

I opened the door and led us into a spacious chamber filled with shelves filled with fabrics and where summer light filled the room. Linen shone and gleamed; wools appeared soft and comforting; the new mixes of silk and linen seemed to glow with colour and texture. Father immediately took charge and led Master Cromwell forward. Fingering my cloth and moving his clearly experienced eye over the first ells of cloth that Father pulled out from the shelves along the wall, Thomas Cromwell chose the green bombazine to sell abroad as well as several lengths of fine worsted.

'I shall send for these tomorrow if it is not an intrusion on your time of sadness and prayer.'

'Thank you. I shall be here,' I said.

'And, I shall do my best to sell the fabrics, Mistress Williams. I set sail by Midsummer's Eve and should return in a month.' He touched my arm. At his familiar gesture, I drew back, but in my confusion my skirt caught on a wooden nail jutting from the shelf. As I tugged it loose, Master Cromwell glanced down. Fumbling nervously, I untangled my gown, praying that Father had not noticed the flash of crimson.

Thomas Cromwell had seen my forbidden underskirt, for he glanced down, mischievously raised an eyebrow and smiled at me. 'You have inherited a good trade, Mistress Williams. Who will help you now

15

that your husband has -' He broke off. I knew he was wondering, as had others, if my husband had been murdered or if his death was accidental. 'Now that he has passed,' he said with tact. 'How will you manage now?'

'I ran this business for a time after my father-in-law died of the bloody flux. When my husband had served the King, as a yeoman, I had to supervise the overseer, the apprentices and the cloth sales, all of it. I had to manage then and I shall manage now.'

'With my help, Lizzy,' Father said firmly, as he looked at me with piercing eyes from under bushy eyebrows.

'Of course, Father, indeed.' I thought of the day he had promised me away in marriage. He would have his eye on my business now. His face relaxed into a genial smile.

Thomas Cromwell's eyes darkened in the candlelight. I saw again that they were not exactly grey but rimmed with hazel, their centres brooding, and they changed colour as do agates.

'May I see if there is anything else?'

'Do,' I said.

Father shifted his bulk over to the shelves and pulled out my plainer cloth. Master Cromwell continued to study bolts of cloth as if he was measuring how much each was worth. He stopped by a roll of painted cloth Father had ignored, pulled it from its shelf and laid it out over a table until it revealed a carpet of golden stars scattered over a midnight-blue linen background.

His breath whistled through his teeth. 'Beautiful. Painted cloth can fetch a good price. And this painted cloth, well...I could sell it for you.'

'Oh,' said Father, raising his great eyebrows again;

he favoured plain cloth. 'You see profit in that?'

'I do.' Master Cromwell slid a long finger over the cloth. 'I certainly do.'

I moved to his side. 'That cloth is promised to Austin Friars.'

'What do the friars want with stars? Ah, of course, the Advent plays.' Master Cromwell was silent for a moment. 'Can you find more of this?'

Despite my desire to have nothing to do with painted cloth that my husband had purchased heaven only knew where, I said, 'Perhaps.'

'Well, then, Mistress Williams, fine painted cloth will sell in the courts of Europe. It is being used to ornament clothing these days. I shall make enquiries.' As he turned to me again, I felt the soft swish of his expensive cloak caress my hand as if a cat was purring against it. Father said that we would take an advance for me on my cloth today and the rest of the profit after it was sold. I liked this arrangement well. Most of all, I liked the fact that the merchant had addressed me, not Father, and had spoken to me as an equal.

Thomas Cromwell departed after the midday Angelus rang. When he kissed my hand, my fingers felt warm. My heart beat a little faster. He was a stranger, yet no stranger. The wild boy was now a handsome man, wealthy it seemed and not for the likes of me, a recent widow. I shrugged the thought away. For now on, I would sell cloth and continue to live quietly in life's shadows.

The following morning, Thomas Cromwell sent a wagon to collect the cloth. It was Midsummer's Eve, and I had hoped he would come himself, but he did not. Instead, his servant came and dealt with Smith. I faced a lonely midsummer. There would be no revels for me this year, for I would pass my Midsummer's Eve praying for the safe passage of my dead husband's soul, the husband who had been no husband to me.

The disastrous marriage to Tom Williams had been imposed on me four years earlier because Father claimed he always acted in my interests, and because, in turn, I had recognised that I had obligations and duties to my parent. I made the best of it I could, though I often wished I had never agreed to it.

Chapter Two

1509 Putney

I WAS A COWARD.

For I could not set myself against my father's wishes. A daughter could not. He called me into the little chamber off the hall on a chill February morning where a small fire was lit. After he had waved me to a stool close to the flame, I sat and waited for him to speak, wondering what merited this summons so early in the day. I had hoped that Father would suggest that I could help him in our cloth trade, because ever since he had spoken of trade with Flanders weeks earlier, I had prayed that he would include me in his new plans. I could read, write, count and keep ledgers up to date. I could negotiate and, importantly, I had an eye for colour. He often remarked on this.

Father coughed, folded his hands behind his back, looked at me earnestly and said, 'Lizzy, you are eighteen. It is time you were wed.'

This was not what I wanted to hear. I nearly fell off my stool, so great was my disappointment. I looked up at him, trying to hide my displeasure, blinked and nervously pinched the wool of my russet gown between finger and thumb. 'Is it, indeed, Father?'

'Yes, I have found you a husband.'

A chill gripped me. 'Who?'

'Tom Williams. A good family, cloth merchants, like us, only richer.' Father looked hopeful and said with meaning, 'He is an only son. Your mother has lost two children, boys.' He crossed himself. 'And there is only Harry who is busy with his estate in Surrey. I want to see you wed into cloth.'

'Well, I do know who Tom Williams is,' I burst out in a passion. 'I have seen the family at guild processions and I don't care for him and I am too young to wed.' My arms stubbornly folded themselves. They could not help it.

Father leaned down and kissed my forehead, loosed my arms and took my hands in his. 'We can afford a dowry and you are not too young, my child. Be reasonable, Lizzy. Tom Williams' father is an important member of the Drapers' Company. We spoke of you only yesterday. Look, he brought me that gift...as a token, a promise.' Father glanced up and pointed at a new painted cloth that hung on the wall above us. It showed Abraham's sacrifice which I now thought ominous. I looked away, refusing to praise it. He chose his next words carefully. 'One day Tom Williams will inherit the family fortune. They are wealthy drapers. Richard Williams will invest in my worsteds and fine wools. He is offering you, and our family, opportunity, don't you see? Will you agree, Lizzy?'

'No, I do not see, nor shall I agree,' I said.

I would not take this man Father was thrusting at me. I thought of children disturbing my happy existence. I thought of an end to my beloved studies.

Father reached for a chair and moved it around to face my stool. Sinking onto the cushioned seat, he leaned forward, his face so close to mine. His breath smelled of sweet peppermint. 'You will have a good home,' he said. 'Of course, since Master Williams is a King's yeoman you will have a most coveted position too. Our cloth business will be secure. They are well-connected.'

This was all about markets, not me, and I was the

sacrifice.

'Not as well-connected as we,' I said quickly, thinking of my mother's good connections with minor nobility. 'Mother needs me here. I help her with the household accounts, with embroidery, sewing and weaving. I had hoped to help you, too, Father, in the business.'

'Mercy will manage. You will not be lost to her. There are maids, plenty of those, to help and I have apprentices. The business is not for women.'

I snorted and frowned. The maids did not play the lute for my mother to sing in the evening dusk. As for business - better to be a cloth merchant than a cloth merchant's chattel. I fumed inside, anger eating me up.

Folding my hands in my lap, I tried to be still, but my soft blue woollen kirtle whispered as I restlessly moved my feet and strived hard to keep my voice even. 'I have learning, Father.' I shook my head. 'The Williamses will have no time for that.'

I thought of Tom Williams' ill, fragile mother with her yellowing pallor; the father who was bent and aged. Tom Williams, I truthfully did not know at all, but there was a quiet about him as silent as the falling snow. I imagined that as a King's yeoman, he moved with slow, thumping, marching feet, whereas I was small and quick.

My father looked weary and defeated. 'Won't you take him, Lizzy, take him for my sake, and, indeed, for your own? It is an excellent match. You will come to like him, love him perhaps.'

I would not take Tom Williams for my own sake. I began to form the words but I hesitated. What choice *did* I have? That was the truth of it and the lie. We daughters were given to believe we could refuse, but choice did not really exist for women like me. Love him! No. Like him, possibly.

As I hesitated, tears gathered in my dear father's eyes

21

and that was the moment I was lost. He had given me everything. Mother and I were clothed in fine wool and linens. He had indulged my love of learning and had me educated as he had my brother, as if I were a daughter of the King's court, rather than a middling merchant's female child.

February snow splattered the windows. A log on the fire hissed. For a heartbeat I looked into Father's watchful green eyes, so like my own, begging me to agree. As I considered my fate, a silence hung between us. I might, in time, find opportunity to help in the Williams' cloth trade since Richard and Agnes Williams were old. Maybe there were possibilities. And I would rule my own household. I made myself reconcile to the fact that there was no reason not to marry Tom Williams other than my contrary nature. People never married for love. Love belonged to stories such as King Arthur and Queen Guinevere. On that cold day, a hazy picture of Tom Williams formed in my head. He was just a slight, hazy line, muddied like water in the duck pond.

I inclined my head, and despite myself, my mouth formed the word, 'Yes'.

'Good,' Father said, patting my hand. 'I knew you would see sense, Lizzy.'

I met Tom Williams on my betrothal day, soon after I had agreed to marry him. I said my piece quietly, eyeing my betrothed with suspicion, as a harsh wind blew around our hall, upsetting buckets in the yard, rattling the gates, and shaking trees against the casement panes. Outside, dogs barked, hens squawked and cats yowled, but standing in my best grey woollen gown by the long table in our hall, I wore what was for many years to become my hall face. I smiled. I spoke politely to his mother, Agnes, a mild

22

woman, and to his father, the very serious master draper.

My father, delighted, beamed generously around the small gathered company and penned the marriage agreement with a flourish. I signed my name with confidence, proud that I could read and write. My betrothed slipped a betrothal ring of gold and sapphire onto my middle right finger. When he kissed me, I admit that I sensed his gentleness and kindness, but I felt distaste too.

During our four years of marriage, even though we shared a bed for most of those years, I lay with him only once, and that was on our wedding night.

Chapter Three

1514

FOUR YEARS ON, I was a cloth merchant's widow, without children to inherit the business, which no doubt the goodwives considered my fault, not his - though his mother, unknowing of the true way of things, kindly said it would happen in the fullness of time. My mother curiously never said a word. Now that Tom Williams was dead, if my household was to survive, I knew that I must become a cloth merchant myself, and I made a firm decision on the day Thomas Cromwell sent for my cloth that Father would not rule me again. Now that I had my once longed-for wish to be a merchant, I would make a success of my cloth business. It was indeed mine.

On the Midsummer's Eve after Tom's funeral, the servants wanted to join in the festivities, as had been their tradition in past years. I did not see any reason why they could not enjoy the holiday, even if I could not, so I suggested that Gerard Smith take the two apprentices and go out into the City streets to see the festivities.

Smith said, as he stood uncomfortably in my hall, bonnet in his hands, 'Are you sure, Mistress? We shall only be away for a short time. To see the guild companies march down by the river.'

'I am sure. Leave Toby to mind the shed. I shall give him another whole day off instead. He'll like that.'

'And you, Mistress?'

'Meg will stay with me and I shall sleep, Master

Gerard.' I swept my arm about the dark hangings. 'It has all tired me out.'

He nodded his sympathy but, not before I noticed the wistful glance he cast eighteen-year-old Meg's way. She glanced up and smiled at him. Yet, when my eyes lit on her again, her head had dropped once more over her sewing.

Demurely Meg continued to mend the shift that lay limply over her knee, as if butter would not melt in her pert mouth.

That Midsummer Eve I went to bed early and fell fast asleep as soon as my head touched my pillow.

Doors slamming. Shouting. Calls of fire. I sat up in bed, rubbing my eyes, hovering on the edge of sleep, in which I was dreaming of a boy with whom I had played long, long ago along the river bank in Fulham and who had sent a servant for my bombazine cloth.

I could see a shadowy figure beyond my bed curtains and immediately through my awakening state a deep fear gripped me. My heart began beating too fast against my ribs; my eyelids shot wider open. Someone was surely hovering about my chamber. I clutched the covers, closed my eyes again against the fast-moving apparition and tried to scream, but only a croak issued forth. I tried again. This time, my voice returned in a long roar.

It was only Meg who thrust her face through the half-opened bed curtains. Her night bonnet was askew on top of her dark wild curls and her face was creased into a hundred worry lines. She grabbed my arm and hissed, 'Mistress, hurry, there's a blaze.'

I sat up and began to swing my legs over the edge of the bed. 'By the Virgin and all her holy relics, the kitchen's not on fire is it?'

'No. Outside. It's the wool store.' She dragged the bed curtains wide open and pushed my cloak into my arms. 'Hurry, quick, no time to lose. Your cloak, your shoes!'

The church bell was ringing slowly, long haunting peals, signalling that there was fire in the neighbourhood. Jumping down from my high bed, I thrust past her and raced to the casement window. The full moon cast an eerie light that tried to squeeze through overhanging gabled buildings. Looking down into the narrow tunnel that was Wood Street, below the protruding casements, I saw my neighbours still dressed in their Midsummer revelling cloaks and masks, milling into the alley beside the house. Wreaths of dark smoke floated above their heads and over the leather buckets they clutched, drifting from behind my house out of the alley that led to the yard and my storage building. Two of Cripplegate's constables yelled at them to form an orderly chain. Already the line of neighbours stretched towards the conduit where Wood Street met Little Wood Street and buckets were being passed from person to person. Others raced past carrying pitchforks.

I spun around and ran from the room, not stopping to pull on slippers, into the chamber across the corridor, where I knelt on the window seat and threw open the shutters. The pungent smell of smoke immediately caught in my throat, causing me to step back. I drew my cloak over my nose and mouth and looked out into the garden and the yard. My warehouse was on fire. The mulberry tree in the garden blocked the true nature of the pandemonium beyond the garden but I could see pewter-coloured smoke rising. I could hear shouting, the crash of timbers, the hiss as water reached flames. My cloth was burning. I could smell it.

A gigantic flame jumped and licked up above

26

neighbouring rooftops. It glared at me, rising high above the garden wall like a great flowing dragon's breath of fire and smoke. I could see shadowy figures like sticks moving about the garden. I heard myself scream at the danger that threatened our very lives. We must stop the burning before it swallowed my stable as well as the storehouse and reached the wooden houses beyond. As I watched, more arching flickering flames grew large and diminished as water hissed on contact. A breath later, they reached up and lessened again as the fire fighters down in the yard attempted to quench them. All my hopes for my business were undone with those greedy flames. They would devour the woven wool for the monasteries that we had purchased in May, business that I desperately needed. A moment later and tiles from the roof came crashing down. I screamed again.

Meg pulled me away from the casement. 'Hurry.' She thrust my shoes at me. 'Out now, Mistress, out into the yard. If it spreads we will be trapped.'

I pulled the shoes on, reached up and fastened my cloak, fingers fumbling awkwardly at the neck button. My hair flying behind me in a mass of silvery curls, I ran down the staircase and out of the emptied house, Meg's frantic footsteps came clattering behind mine.

'Where are the servants?' I shouted once we reached the garden. 'Have they returned yet - from the revels? Is it after midnight?'

'Yes it is. In the yard; all the servants are outside. The apprentices and Gerard are trying to put out the fire.'

We exited the back entrance by the store rooms. The garden was filling with smoke and it was hot. We held our cloak edges up to our faces and coughed as we hurried past the herb beds and rounded the mulberry tree. We were quickly surrounded by drifting, stinking, dark clouds. The gate into the yard lay wide open. My household maids hung about it, helplessly holding hands, coughing, weeping and pulling their cloaks over noses and mouths. There was a great sudden cracking noise and sparks flying across the yard flew at them. In unison, they screamed. Little Bessie, only twelve years old, jumped up and down shaking them from her cloak, stamping them out on the cobbles, her fair hair flying everywhere. The flames licked up once again and a great heat blew around the yard and into the garden. My maidservants fell back against the wall almost knocking each other over in their hurry to escape the flying, hot embers.

'Get back, get back,' a voice yelled towards us. Its owner was invisible through the glowing cinders and clouds of smoke, but I recognised it as belonging to one of our parish wardens. There were the splashes of water spilling and shouts of, 'Get out of the way.'

The maids retreated into the garden, pushing through the gate, but instead of staying with them, I elbowed past the backwards flow, out through the gate, determined to see if my building could be saved, even if the cloth could not.

'Come back, Mistress,' Meg shouted at my back. Ignoring her, I shook my head and ploughed forward.

Water ran in thin rivulets through gaps in the stones to lick around my feet. I glimpsed the shadowy shapes of the apprentices leading my two whinnying horses from the stable into the alley, past a ghostly line of neighbours with pails who shouted, 'Hurry,' as they passed their buckets along.

The boys were safe. I heard their shouts of 'Make way,' as they led the stamping, snorting animals towards the alley.

I peered through acrid smoke that gathered about the yard, rising up in fat grey clouds, leaking through gaps in buildings, billowing up towards the moon and stars.

Meg was by my side again, pulling me back, crying, 'Mistress, come away.'

I shook her arm off and walked through the fire-fighters and neighbours and male servants, coughing and spluttering, stepping anxiously over hot embers, searching through the choking smoke, sweeping an arm across my forehead, mopping away the dripping sweat that was stinging my eyes, as I attempted to make a count of my remaining servants.

Toby was missing. Where was Cook?

I pushed through tight knots of neighbours searching for them. At last, I saw my cook. He was organising others with buckets of water as they attempted to quench the fire, but nowhere could I see Toby. Though they were containing the fire, tiles crashed onto the cobbles and smaller flames rose. Timbers collapsed. I jumped away from a descending tile as if a hobgoblin had leapt from the fiery building ready to seize me. There was another bang. Fire drops burst out at us yet again from the building's smouldering frame. I smelled my own singeing hair and reached up. The trailing end curls escaping my hood had been caught by a spark. I frantically beat out the burning and stuffed my hair back inside my cloak.

Another leaping malicious flame rose into a high pillar. The fire-fighters worked hard to quench it as helplessly I watched. For a moment as the flames were dying down and I could see inside the storehouse. What I had lost was illuminated by a strange rosy light; a heap of burning cloth, timbers and chests reduced to ash and embers of smouldering wood. Even a great dye cauldron, we rarely used, had melted into a pool of molten iron. Everything was destroyed. I cursed the Devil. I cursed Midsummer. I cursed the exhausted sleep that had rendered me insensible to the danger of fire. I stopped close of cursing God who had allowed this terrible thing to happen. I was too shocked to weep.

It was then, as I stood helplessly staring at the destruction of my goods, that a man's voice hissed into my ear, 'Sin never goes unpunished, widow.' I spun around but he was already vanishing into the smoke, hurrying away towards the alley. He had appeared by my side as a malicious shadow, and with an intake of breath he was gone. In that moment, I remembered my dead husband. Who here knew what he had been when living? God did - God did, and this destruction was our punishment, his and mine.

Those near me had not heard the shadow's words. They were focused on the ghastly spectacle before them, drawing back and forward, passing water to quench the last flames, not taking any notice of me, but someone *had* known whom I was. Someone had been watching for me.

Was I being punished for concealing my husband's sin? Were all my servants safe? Where was the watch boy? Roused by fear to action, I pushed through those standing near me, heard a few mutters of 'the widow' as I reached Gerard Smith. I caught hold of his loose shirt sleeve. 'Is everyone safe?' I shouted above the rumble of dying flames, the crackle of burning and sizzling of water.'

I still had not seen our watchman.

'Yes, mistress,' he shouted back. 'No one has burned though it may have been the intent.'

'How,' I said, helplessly, trying to keep anger from my voice. 'Where was Toby then? He was on guard duty tonight. Where is he?'

Smith shook his head, lifted a bucket, tossed water on the expiring flames, and when that was done, he looked at

30

me with anger on his blackened face. 'I know not, Mistress, nor do I care. The boy disobeyed my orders. We were out in the streets, me and the apprentice lads, watching the revellers return from the Smithfield bonfire. Someone could have raced down the alley and tossed a torch into the workshop.' He paused and shrugged. 'Toby must have followed us out earlier and left the building unguarded. This is the Devil's work.' He spat on the ground. Before he reached for a new bucket passed along the chain, he crossed himself. 'Get back, Mistress. It is no place for you. The master, yes - were he living. For a woman, no.'

Biting on a sharp retort, I drew back and stood by the garden gate with Meg and my household servants, swallowing my tears. I watched as my storeroom became a heap of burning timbers and charred roof tiles. At last, there was just a terrible heat left and smoke hanging over the yard, clinging to everything in its malodorous path. As a rosy dawn broke and I thanked my neighbours, I saw pity clothe their faces. One merchant said with candour, 'Someone wants your business, Mistress Williams.' He shook his head and added, 'You should think hard before going on by your own. Not work for a woman.'

'Many widowed women have their own businesses.'

'Sell up, Mistress. Get out if you are wise. Go back to your family.'

I set my shoulders squarely and said to my neighbour, 'Thank you for helping tonight. I shall rebuild. I have cloth that is selling abroad as we speak. Thank you, sir, for your concern'

He shook his head and sloped off.

If the survival of my business was threatened, I knew not from whence the threat came. I tasted salty blood tickle onto my tongue as I chewed my cheek. Tears sprang into my stinging eyes at last. The Company might not support me in my time of need. Many cloth merchants held a resentment of our long-standing business with abbeys in five wards including the great Austin Friars in Broad Street. There were, indeed, those who would wish me ill.

As I made my way back through the foul-smelling, smoky garden I pondered the fire's cause. Only Toby would know and Toby's disappearance was as much as mystery as that of those who had started it.

'Come, Mistress.' Meg gently took my arm. 'You need the tub. Thank the Lord for small mercies. We still have a roof over our heads.'

'It will take heaven to move and the stars to smile down on us,' I said. 'For we have lost the cloth for the abbeys and look, the garden is ruined too.'

'We have survived. The horses are safe, and we can save what we can from the garden. It looks worse than it is.'

'But Toby is gone. What if he burned to a cinder like the chests and the wool?'

'Maybe he was just afeared and ran, thinking he would be blamed.'

I shook my head. 'Maybe, but it seems unlikely.'

Toby never returned that night and he never came back the next night either. Nor was his body found in the ruined building once everything had cooled enough us to search there. I insisted that the constables made enquiries on my behalf, even offering a reward if Toby was found. The youth was pleasant and diligent; a kind, honourable boy who could use a sword. Something dreadful had occurred to make Toby run away, and it was not the fire, which, of course, was terrible enough.

'We must find my boy,' I said to the constable when

32

he called on us. Smith stood beside me, his countenance puzzled and still streaked with dirt.

'We shall discover the lad's whereabouts, Mistress,' the constable replied, his three chins wobbling. He stood in my office closet and drowned the cup of ale I had proffered, gobbets of foam hanging like droplets of sticky white sap from his little grey beard as he drained the cup. 'I must be going now. It was a long night,' he added.

Smith shook his head. 'I liked the lad. Trusted him.'

'Who knows what went through that lad's head. I shall send out the watch to find him. If he is alive, we shall discover him. He will not go unpunished.'

I shuddered at the thought of Toby's punishment if the ward decided on his guilt, and called for Meg to show the constable out.

After he had lumbered off, Smith shook his head, and sipped his ale thoughtfully. 'Toby is either well on the road out of the City or has vanished beyond the river to Southwark. The streets of Southwark was where the master discovered him. Mistress, but if he is in that place we'll never track him down.' He stared at the ledgers piled up on my desk. 'Best we think of how you can replace that woollen cloth before others take your trade.'

'I shall think of something,' I said and hurried from the office before I burst into tears of self-pity.

That night, I sat on my bed-cover, awake for hours thinking of what to do, realising that now I would have to borrow money. I had little coin in my coffers.

My thoughts uneasily leapt forward. What would Father do when he found out what had happened? I must send him word. Although perhaps he knew it already. Rumour spread faster than fires did in the City. I buried my head in my hands and wept again for what was lost - my husband, my cloth, my reeking garden, and Toby, because I was sure that it was not his fault and that something terrible had happened to him. I was fearful of a voice in the dark.

This would not do. I leaned my head against my bedpost and drew a deep breath. I wiped away my tears with my apron. This would not do. We would go on. I must.

Chapter Four

FATHER CAME TO SURVEY the damage, angry at the vanished watch boy, cursing the lost wool for the monasteries, nagging me to give up my plans to run the business. I stiffened my shoulders and said to him, same as I had told my neighbours, 'Father, I shall manage.'

'If you need me and you will when you face up to all this,' he replied sternly, impatiently batting at the air in the hall with his expansive arm, making me feel eighteen again, 'Send for me.'

'Thank you, Father. You should go now.' I showed him to the door myself. He was on his way to his premises on Cornhill that morning. Since he assumed that my coffers were filled, I did not enlighten him. The smell of smoke had dissipated somewhat, mingling with whiffs of lavender-scented soap, and since I was busy checking what stores we had left in the kitchen, I did not want him to linger. I needed to collect my thoughts. I needed time.

He threw one last glance around my hall before passing through the opened door. Susannah and Bessie, two of the maids, were bustling about with armfuls of linen to wash. 'I shall be back soon, my dear. Your mother worries about you, you know.'

'Yes, I'm sure, but no need for Mother to worry. We are putting everything to rights again.' I closed the door on him with a smile, wiped my hand over my forehead and sank onto a stool in the hall where, only a week before, trestles had been laden with food for a funeral feast. The thought spooled about and around my aching head. What *would* I do?

While I thought about procuring a loan, the maids scrubbed the house from top to bottom and washed our household linen with perfumed water to dispel the smell of smoke. There was no money for fresh linen, even for a cloth merchant. We would make do with what we had. I rolled up my sleeves and helped my maids to pound sheets in the copper kettle we set up in the kitchen beyond the hall.

The apprentices moved inside the house to share a rough, empty chamber on the third floor. They had previously slept in the storehouse. Gerard Smith kept to his cupboard-sized alcove in one of the indoor storerooms and guarded what remained of our cloth. He remained edgy and anxious for days following the fire. I watched from the upper floor window in the chamber adjoining my own as he disappeared into the yard, staying out for hours trying to salvage what wood he could from the ruined building. From there, my eyes followed him when he returned to the house with hunched shoulders, bent with despair. As the week after St John's Eve dragged on and there was no news, he became morose. He never said it, but I know he blamed himself for what had happened.

So many people depended on me now that finding a way to replace the cloth I had lost became urgent. All our nerves were on edge. Meg was snappy, the maids were hushed, Cook grumped about how he had to make ends meet on a pittance and I worried about how

I could feed them all.

A few weeks after the fire, I called my household together and told them that it was necessary to make economies. We began to live on vegetables, cabbages and purple carrots, those that had survived, supping on pottage every day, with fish on Friday and a little meat on Sundays.

Gentle June hurried into a sweating July. After Thomas Cromwell returned later that month, my father took charge of my share of the payment for my bombazine cloth. To my relief, this would be sufficient to run my household for a few more months, though it was not enough to replace the loss. I did not see Master Cromwell myself because once he delivered my money to Father, he immediately sailed back to Antwerp, and much as I had liked him, I was too worried about my business to mind. Since there was no spare money to buy new cloth, Father's solution was that I closed up my house, paid off my servants and returned home to Putney.

I ushered Father into the privacy of the closet and stood firm.

'Close up the house! It is my livelihood. To what end, Father?'

'Your security, Lizzy. You are young and pretty - when you smile - and despite what has happened here, I can make the business grow again, for us both. You will make another marriage soon, and the profits can provide your dowry.' I saw his expansive chest puff out and the linen of his shirt stretch. 'Are you practising your lute?' Tempted to burst into laughter at the absurdity of playing my lute at such a time or giving in to him, I shook my head. I took possession of Thomas Cromwell's silver and turned the keys in the five locks that opened my money coffer, hoping that Father, who was hovering by the window of my closet, would not notice how empty it was.

The coffer was a deceptively simple oak box which opened to show complicated mechanisms in the lid and sections for differing coins and promissory notes. Father was always distracted by its workings. The keys were secreted safely in a hidden part of my untidy chamber cupboard, in a little niche at the back that I had covered with a close fitting panel. I placed Master Cromwell's silver inside the chest and repressed a sigh because once summer ended I would need to replace it. I must purchase more cloth and feed my servants.

I drew breath and sighed. I stiffened my hands, which lingered on the chest. Eventually, I realised, I would have to ask Father for help and it may as well be now. He hovered by my shoulder, studying the box. Banging closed the lid and fiddling around locking the coffer gave myself another few moments' grace before I confessed to poverty. Taking a deep breath and exhaling it again, I looked up. His forehead had creased into a deep line above his nose between his eyes. They were filled with concern. Father had noticed my scarcity of coin.

'You have nothing, Lizzy. How do you eat?'

I folded my arms.

'We live on the produce from the garden - onions and cabbages, mostly, since the smoke ruined much of the herb garden and the salad. Cook is inventive. With economies, I can survive if the Company grants a loan on my behalf.' I paused, watching his forehead creased into furrows as he waited for me to finish. 'But, well ... I wonder, can you lend me enough to replace part of my ruined cloth? I must do so this very month. Otherwise I'll have to borrow from Zackary the Jew, or from the Company if they will lend - or both, if I must.'

There was silence. I broke it.

'I don't want the monastery trade to go elsewhere.'

He turned away from me and for a moment looked out at the garden. 'The Company only lends on rare occasions,' he said to the lead-framed window panes. 'The Jews, like Zackary, do lend but there will be a high interest. Sometimes Italians from Tuscany will lend, though they are accused of usury.'

'Then cover it for me, for my sake,' I said with reluctance. I did not remind him that I had married Tom Williams for his sake, though I thought it.

He turned to face me. 'It seems to me, Lizzy, that your husband was not doing as well as I thought, was he?'

'No, but not as badly as you now think either. Father, I simply need cloth to sell.'

He nodded. 'You should have said when I came before. Yes, I'll purchase the cloth for you at the Bartholomew Fair this month, but only on condition that if things worsen here you come home. You will not borrow from Zackary Bassett or the Italians.' He thought for a moment. 'Mercy ought to come and stay for a few weeks.' What he meant was she would come to persuade me to give up my cloth business, though he did not admit it. This would be the deal.

I shook my head. 'Father, I don't know that Mother would like it here at the moment; it still smells of smoke, and I shall be busy. You see, I must reassure the Abbots of St Nicholas and St Martins and the Prior of Austin Friars that we will have good woollen cloth for their novices by October. The others can wait.'

.'Smith can do all that for you.' He rapped my desk impatiently with his knuckles. 'Mercy will visit within a week and that is that.' He leaned over and laid a hand on my shoulder. I stood in front of the coffer as if I were guarding it, though I had so little to guard. 'You have had a difficult time. Mercy will help you set this house in order. That is my condition, Lizzy. I buy you cloth for the monasteries and Mercy spends a week here improving your mood.'

I knew that 'improving my mood' meant that my mother would persuade me to return home. I was determined that she would not. I smiled to myself for the first time in days. A new plan was forming in my head. I would be rich if it worked. If I sold the new stuffs that Thomas Cromwell had liked, light fabrics such as bombazines and perpetuanas, rather than sticking to broadcloths that Father favoured, I could redeem my fortunes. Aloud I said, 'Yes, Father. Now come and have some of my rabbit stew. Cook's son caught the rabbit in the woods beyond Moorgate.'

'Poaching, no good will come of that.' He glared at me as if *I* were the poacher.

Even so, Father sat down with me to dinner. I ushered him into the hall just as the mid-day Angelus bells were chiming throughout the City, and closer to at St Alban's Church where my Tom lay sleeping under his cover of earth and wilted rosemary.

'Your mother will visit, and maybe if you won't listen to me you will take heed of her advice,' he said, wiping goblets of gravy from his chin with a napkin.

40

'Well, then, Father, I had better have a chamber prepared for her. I look forward to it.' I dabbed my mouth with my own napkin and managed to smile.

Chapter Five

MOTHER ARRIVED A WEEK later with her travelling bag and her maid. Within a day she charmed my household with kindness and compliments. She bothered to enquire after the servants' well-being, to generously bestow special 'you are the only one who matters' smiles and, in turn, the servants went out of their way to win her approval.

'Susannah, I wonder, would you bring me my stitching, the new block work collar from my chamber. Thank you, my child.' And when Susannah returned to the parlour. 'That was most thoughtful.' Susannah adored Mother and I could see that Mother's own maid, Lettie, was all pins and scissors, possessive of her mistress, and jealous of those smiles towards other maids.

My mother helped me pack greengages and gooseberries into stone jars, to pickle onions, and to gather and dry parsley, sage and thyme, all that was left of my garden now. The lingering smoky smell vanished because the kitchen now smelled sweetly of herbs, vinegar and pickling spices.

I used two of Thomas Cromwell's shillings to purchase fish and meat. That week, we dined well and over dinner Mother's chatter gradually drew me into a happier state of mind. For a time she never spoke of the business, though every evening, for a short time, as she embroidered an altar cloth for a chantry, I poured over

42

ledgers trying to make sense of why we had made so little profit since Tom's father died. My husband had given money generously to the Church, made poor investments and had purchased new clothing he had not needed.

That week, I stopped worrying and life temporarily took on a semblance of normality. Later in the evenings I put the ledgers aside, and played my lute while Mother sang ballads in her soft enchanting voice. She entertained Meg and myself as she related stories of a cousin who was one of Queen Catherine's clerks.

'You know he has dined on swan,' she said. 'And on an orange-flavoured syllabub.'

'Oranges from Spain,' I said.

'Of course, and on figs too. He says they taste of nectar.'

'I cannot even imagine them.'

I relaxed as we gossiped, and longed to taste this orange syllabub. After all, Father was purchasing the monastery cloth for me at the Bartholomew Cloth Fair, and he had promised a small loan to tide me over. Maybe one day, I, too, could afford to purchase oranges from Spain.

My immediate concern dwelt on how well Smith was doing on his errands to the three big monasteries. I had dispatched him to finalise our long-established cloth deals, and I used a half angel to purchase sweetmeats and jellies as gifts for abbots and priors with whom we had previously done business. While I bottled gooseberries alongside Mother and Meg, trying to imagine the taste of oranges and figs, my mind was busy counting up my profit after I returned Father's share. I thought of ledgers that showed profit and not loss, of a coffer not empty but filled with more shillings and half angels.

Meg and Mother sorted out the linen cupboards and

chests that week, directing the maids to reorganise everything. I had considered clearing out Tom's neatly arranged clothing cupboard but until Mother came to stay, I had not been able to bring myself to attend to the task. The blackbird, which I was sure had followed me from the churchyard, had taken up residence in the garden where he dodged about, hopping up onto bushes whenever I passed, watching me even as I glanced out of the chamber window. Just like that annoying creature, Tom's gowns and tunics taunted me from his clothing pole, so that every time I contemplated the task, I had slammed closet doors closed again.

I liked to see order, though my own closet was never orderly. So, when, at dinner, Mother suggested sorting out clothing ready for me to emerge from my dark mourning, I suggested we instead clear out the clothing that had once belonged to Tom. 'You can take his long gowns away. They are of good worsted and trimmed, Mother.'

'Let us see, Elizabeth.' She laid down her knife and smiled at me.

'Father might like a hat.'

'Perhaps he would. Shall we look today?'

'Why not.' I would be glad to see those expensive clothes gone, to eradicate Tom's extravagance and cleanse my house of his memory. I did not expect it to be as upsetting a task as it turned out.

That afternoon, we climbed the narrow stairway to my late husband's chamber, hefting a great wicker basket up with us, ready to pack away the garments. I thumped the basket down on the rushes. After a brief hesitation, I opened up the large cupboard that closeted Tom Williams' clothing and shoes.

I turned back to my mother. 'I really should have done

44

this before you came. You have had to make room on that crowded rail for your own gowns and cloak.'

'Lettie did that, not me. Lizzy, remember that everything has its own time. It won't be easy to dispose of these goods. You will feel sad.' She smiled her lovely smile, and in that moment I was grateful for her help.

The chamber was a pleasant room with good furnishings - a light oak-wood cupboard, a beech-wood chest, a wash table on which stood a pretty china bowl, a high, curtained bed with a comfortable flock mattress, fine linen sheets lace-edged and covered with a counterpane on which a strange mythical half-man, half-deer was embroidered in bright silks. The armed chair where Mother chose to sit was a valuable oak chair, its arms engraved with a pattern of carved acanthus leaves. Tom had purchased it a year ago when the business was doing well. Mother leaned against its cushioned velvet back, watching me as I lifted shirts and hose from the chest and holding them up, examined them for moth holes. I pulled out hats that were baggy on top and trimmed with squirrel and held them up, too. Mother admired them all.

'Tom had exceptionally good taste, I'll say that,' she said as she reached out for a hat with a green velvet crown and a long curling feather that was dyed blue. She stroked the feather, set it aside and reached over to me for a second hat that was trimmed with rabbit fur. 'He did not spare the cost on clothing.' She looked approvingly at the black over-gown I was wearing. 'He allowed you fine cloth for your gowns also.'

'He was a merchant,' I said quickly, for Tom's kindness and generosity had not compensated for the unnatural marriage we had shared, and since I had discovered that he had emptied our coffer to purchase new clothes, I was angry. 'Tom cared about his clothing, when

45

he was not playing at being a yeoman in a red doublet.' I said evenly enough, and waved my hand at the hat. 'Keep the one with the fur trimming for Father. They both have large heads. Pity that Tom Williams was thin and Father is well…broad, otherwise the doublets would fit,' I added unkindly.

'Fat, you mean.' Mother tut-tutted across the crown of the rabbit-trimmed hat. 'Your father is too fond of sweet wines, rich red meats and sweetmeats. They will be his undoing, I fear.' She smiled indulgently as if Father were present.

'I hope his love of sweet things will not be his undoing. He should spend a week here in Wood Street. That would trim him down; we eat plenty of soups and cabbage stews here,' I said before I realised that I had relaxed my guard. She would realise that my generous table of this week was an exception, and I had no intention of giving her further excuse to press for my return to our Putney manor house. I fussed about the clothing pole and busied myself pulling out a linen shirt with buttons. It was old, worn into thin patches, past mending. I set it aside for the poor, thinking that I should remove the bone buttons first since they could be re-used.

'You do not have to live in such a way, nor do you have to hide your difficulties, Lizzy. Come home,' Mother leaned towards me clasping the furred hat, her face intense with concern. 'You always loved the manor house. I …'

I spun around and faced her, my face hot, 'I cannot, so do not ask me to. Examine your reasoning, Mother. Maybe, in truth, you want me to keep you company now that Joan is living with Alice and Harry. I enjoy your company, Mother, but I must remain here.'

She sighed. 'It is not just about companionship. I wish

you would reconsider, Lizzy. Joan is a trial and I am glad she is living in Surrey. You cannot stay here on your own.'

She placed the hat on the counterpane and sank down beside it. I held onto the shirt. 'I am not alone, as you well know, and I have responsibility towards my household here.'

'One day, you will have another husband. You are not safe here on your own with only servants and that man, Smith, to guard you. You are tired and you are often melancholy. What if you are attacked again, or the house is fired next time?'

'I do not expect a further attack.'

'Your father says that there are merchants who want your trade. He thinks one or even two of them had the fire set and others may be covering it up. He will take your cloth, your apprentices and your journeyman into the warehouse on Cornhill. It is a safe proposition. The profit will be set aside for your marriage.'

I shook my head. 'Next time, if there is a marriage, it will be one of my own choosing. That is my widow's right.'

'It may be your right, but you must allow your father to guide you.'

Stretching up to my full height, which was not all that much, I said, 'The business is enough for now, for I shall stay in Wood Street and move forwards with my life, not backwards.' I said it with a catch in my voice for, after all, four years ago I had not wanted to leave the manor in Putney. We were silent for a moment until I added quietly, 'I am not coming home. This is my home.'

'If you change your mind, we -'

'Thank you for your consideration, but I won't.'

I turned to the cupboard again and dragged out several heavily embroidered robes followed by plainer tunics of brown worsted. After I had made two heaps on the bed of good garments that my mother and the servants could use, I set aside older items of Tom Williams' linen and clothing into a third pile for the poor. The shirt with the bone buttons I had hesitated over. 'Mother, would you like the buttons?' I said determined to lighten the conversation.

Mother took her scissors from her belt purse and, taking the shirt from me, began to cut away the buttons.

I folded the best clothing in the basket for my mother. She could cut the tunics down and refashion them for my brother's children. Last of all, I lifted Tom's yeoman's uniform from the clothing pole and folded it into a chest, setting small bags of dried fennel into the red doublet and hose before wrapping both in linen. When I lifted his fine leather shoes and smelled the leather again, my tears flowed for him, my sensitivity at his demise so conflicted. I turned away and wiped at my eyes with my sleeve. Shaking my head, I bent down and lifted the shoes I had dropped by the bedpost, and tossed them into the basket. I scooped up the clothing from the bed and threw the garments on top of the shoes.

I heard Mother cross the chamber, and a heartbeat later, felt her fold me into her arms. 'There, there, sweeting,' she said to me soothingly as if I were still the vulnerable small girl who had too often cut herself in rough play with a fuller's son. 'Cry. It is best that you weep.'

I leaned into her embrace and wept, not, I think, because of what had been between Tom Williams and me, but for what could have been and what should have been and that which had never been.

'Holy Mother of God, Blessed Lady,' I repeated over and over, sobbing into my mother's breast. 'May his soul rest in peace.'

48

My mother let me go and fetched a cloth from the side table on which stood a washing bowl, dipped it in the cool water and gently, oh so softly, gave it into my hands.

She lowered her voice. 'I think I know why you could not love Tom Williams. He was a kind man, though I thought,' her voice was a whisper; 'I cannot speak it, for it is a great and terrible sin.'

I shook my head. 'Do not ever speak of it, Mother.' The rest, unspoken, continued to hang between us. Mother crossed herself and shook her head, but I knew she was grateful that I had kept silent all the years of my marriage, lest the truth caused us all disgrace. I could not speak of it for it made me think of Hell's fork-tailed devils stabbing at him with hot prongs, his flesh burning and stinking.

I wiped away my tears at length and glanced down at the piles of clothing. 'I shall send Meg up later to take away those old clothes. Smith will take them with him when he visits St Anselm's Priory. The rest are yours.'

'You could sell them, you know,' Mother said.

'I could, but I think you will make them over for my nephews. Father will be pleased with the hats, especially the one with the fur trim, and, well, do as you wish with the shoes.'

The day was close and Tom's chamber was oppressive, the atmosphere tense. I untied my cap and shook my hair until it fell about my face. 'Faery hair,' my father used to say when I was a child without cares, 'silver curls for a faery princess.' I did not feel light and faery-like now. 'I think, Mother, we could leave the rest of this to Meg. Let us pass an hour or so outside. The chamber is hot. I cannot remain in it.'

Mother nodded and piled the rest of the clothing in a basket for Meg, while I fetched straw hats from my chamber. I managed a smile.

'Those old things. Just what we need.' Mother said, smiling again at last, setting the hat I handed her on top of her wimple, its wide brim sheltering her face. Now she laughed. With her laughter, my mood lightened and I spontaneously kissed her cheek almost knocking her cap off. They say laughing is good for us. I am sure those wise women are right for I felt lighter because of it.

Descending the stairs, we took up our sewing bags from the parlour bench and, once outdoors, sat in the shade under the mulberry tree. In the cool of the garden, we sipped strawberry cordial and talked of Joan and Alice and Harry who would be haymaking in the country. Eventually, our conversation turned to the King's court which had set off on a summer progress and Mother, who, of course, prided herself on her court connections, told me how courageously Queen Catherine saved the North from the Scottish attack while King Henry was in France.

'Did she go north herself?' I asked.

'Of course not, but the kingdom was in her charge. She had to put her seal on all decisions her knights made.'

'She is clever and brave,' I said. 'Determined to win.'

'She did win. There was a battle at Flodden. Our army won, and I have heard that Queen Catherine has had the Scottish King's head. Cousin William says she was the real commander of Flodden while our King has been away fighting the French.' Her cap bobbed up and down enthusiastically as she spoke of Queen Catherine. 'She is a warrior queen.'

'Yes, but it is so sad that she lost her little prince,' I said. 'The King was devastated. Little Henry was only a few months old. He even held a joust in his honour.'

'She is with child again, I have heard, and they are hopeful.' Mother laid her cup on a bench and pulled her embroidery from its bag, the altar cloth for St Ursula's chantry, a beautiful fabric with a design of silver fishes, a wavy black sea and dark green silken reeds.

'God willing.' I crossed myself and sent a silent prayer up through the mulberry leaves to my saint.

I tucked my sewing in its bag, lifted my cup thoughtfully and drained it thinking that it was a shame that Tom Williams and I could never have a child because I would not permit it. For a moment I dozed, the sun caressing my back making me sleepy. Gradually my eyes opened again. I could hear the Wood Street birds chirruping. Mother was drawing her thread back through the linen cloth, making a dainty stitch on her silver fish. The bells of St Albans were ringing.

'Lizzie.' My mother leaned over her embroidery, speaking softly. 'Lizzie, the Vespers bells. I promised Father Luke we would attend service today.'

'Mother, sorry. I forgot.' I gathered my skirts, stood and lifted our cups from the low wooden table, scattering biscuit crumbs over the path. 'And after we return, I must attend to the books. You can sew in the parlour and Meg will keep you company. She has been making gooseberry syllabub today.'

'Meg always makes a perfect syllabub. She is light-handed with pastry too, but you should stay and embroider with us. Those books are all you think of, Lizzy.'

'It is what I must think of.' I glanced down at my ink-stained fingers. 'Now if we don't hurry, Father Luke will be disappointed. He will blame me for keeping you away.'

It was not a chore to attend Vespers with Mother. I enjoyed the haunting melodies of the plainchant and today, I longed for the peace of the colourful, cool church, where for a few moments after the Mass, I promised myself that I would empty my mind and pray.

51

It had been a difficult afternoon.

Within the hour, clicking my beads one by one, kneeling by an alcove altar to the blue-cloaked Virgin, I was whispering my prayers, earnestly hoping that the Madonna would guide me into a safe future of my own making. I thought of the queen and prayed for her too. Within the click and clack of the rosary beads, a long forgotten memory flashed into my mind.

Chapter Six

Midsummer's Eve, 1509

A LONG-AGO JUNE HERALDED the summer after my betrothal to Tom Williams and the eve of the King and Queen's coronation. Another long ago Midsummer's Eve.

I was in a state of high excitement since we were to watch the royal procession ride through the streets from the Tower to Westminster. Harry and his wife Alice had declined Father's invitation to join us in London. They preferred to spend their Midsummer on their tiny manor in Surrey, saying they could not leave the sheep, nor could they abandon the haymaking, not even for a King's holiday. Besides, the shepherds and cotters expected my brother to provide them with a feast. I thought how fortunate they were to watch the country bonfires and dance freely to the sound of fiddles. That just left Father, Mother, Joan and myself to be rowed from Putney to London Bridge as a glorious dawn broke on that summer morning.

Mother and I decorously arranged our skirts over the wherry bench. Mother's green and gold embroidered gown complimented my pink kirtle with its new rose-embroidered sleeves. 'We look like a tapestry illustrating a garden,' I remarked, as we made ourselves comfortable. Joan could not remain still and Father threatened that he would take her back and leave her in Putney. She behaved.

Mother smiled. 'All of London will appear as lovely as a garden today, Lizzy.'

I doubted this. There were too many poor people in the City. They would not wear embroidered sleeves or eat a fine dinner like the one in Meg's wicker basket.

Soon, we were passing by Chelsea where grand gardens sloped down to jetties on the riverside. Our oarsmen rowed us past high-reaching arches until, at last, we reached the Abbey at Westminster and the King's Hall close by. I peered hard over the busy river, trying to snatch a glimpse of the tapestries being laid out before the Abbey for the Queen and King to step upon tomorrow before they were crowned in the Abbey Nave. I saw nothing except the magnificent turreted church, but those gleaming spires felt so holy to me that I fancied angels hovered about the walls and entrance.

A great cheer swelled upwards from the river. 'God bless our King and Queen.' 'God give them health.' 'God bless the Rose and the Pomegranate'. I felt tears well in my eyes, while my mother dabbed at hers with a tiny lace-edged cloth. My father cried out across the boats, 'God bless us all. A new age is coming. '

'Amen,' other voices chorused, the sound of them echoing off the water.

We left our oarsmen at Drinkwater Wharf and from there followed Grasschurch Street towards Leadenhall Market.

There were cutpurses everywhere. I felt for the purse hanging from my belt, was relieved to find it still there and pushed it below my kirtle into the folds of my linen. When we reached the water conduit in the middle of the crossroads of Grass-Church and

Cornhill, we could see that though it was early yet, the City guildsmen were gathering in companies along Cheape Street, clad in their particular livery.

'Father, why are you not joining the cloth merchants?' I asked. It would be good for my father to be positioned amongst his fellows. Were women merchants permitted, *I* would have been there.

'My back would not stand the strain. They must wait for hours. But we shall take a look, Lizzy.' In spite of his mild tone, I could see that Father was annoyed that he was not amongst the cloth-makers.

'I need the chamber pot,' Joan protested.

Father turned to Meg and the servant boy. 'Take Joan with you. Go to the shop and tell Master William we shall be along soon. Make sure he does not allow anyone to position themselves before my building.'

Father waved the two servants and my sister past the conduit, which was transformed as it was smothered in white and red Tudor roses and fat golden pomegranates.

'Won't everyone be thirsty with all the waiting,' I remarked.

'Worth it,' Father said. 'Wine will flow from all the fountainheads tonight.'

The streets were swept clean. No animals dared foul the sweet-scented grasses that had been scattered with herbs and flowers. Painted cloths and tapestries of gold hung from casements, from awnings, from doorways; no wall on the Cheape had been left under-covered that day. As we wandered along, weaving through the gathering crowd, Father pointed out his favourites.

'Look at the red dragon! See that silver cock!' He beamed. 'Flames of fire, too. He will be a great and fiery king, I have no doubt. He will make England noble and powerful again. And he looks just like his grandfather Edward, a very handsome young man indeed, by all accounts.'

'I like the red and white rose and the crowned portcullis. It is gold thread.' I said.

'Look at the half rose, half pomegranate over there,' Mother exclaimed with delight.

We walked as far as St Paul's Church to see stalls occupied by virgins in white gowns holding up entangled branches of white wax. Priests stood patiently holding silver censers, to waft the King and Queen with incense as they passed.

'It is pure frankincense,' my father remarked and sneezed. When he had recovered himself, he added, 'They will have to wait another four hours. I hope those wax branches last.' He took my mother's arm and gently spun us round. 'Come, Mercy, I have seen enough. Lizzy, I heard your stomach growl a moment ago.'

It took ages to push our way through the gathering crowds back down Cheape Street to our shop. At last we were back at Cornhill and inside Father's cool warehouse, where our servants had set out our picnic dinner on a white cloth. Chattering, laughter, cheers and even cries of 'Stop thief' flew in through the opened casements, from which hung our best cloth alongside the large red rose made by my mother, sister and myself.

Our appliqué was fine work and we were proud of it because we had taken several weeks to stitch it. After we appraised our work, we drew up our chairs to the table and Father crossed himself. 'God bless our humble repast,' he said.

My excitement over the day did not stop me from falling greedily on our picnic dinner. I loved little pasties filled with meat. Cook had made these yesterday, and the pastry was still crisp. When I sank my teeth into one, gravy dribbled down my chin.

Mother frowned. 'Do not eat like a peasant, Elizabeth. You must show manners fitting a lady, now your wedding is almost upon us. Use your napkin.'

'*I* don't eat like a peasant,' Joan said primly.

'Just as well you do not. If you are finished eating, Joan, Meg will walk with you a little way along the street to see the hangings. Your mother and I wish to speak to your sister.'

'Yes, Father,' Joan said and slipped from her seat.

'Lizzy,' Father said, after Meg had hurried with Joan out and down the stairs. He wiped crumbs from his mouth with the back of his hand, 'I may as well tell you now. Your mother and I are agreed. No further delay. We must have you wed by Christmas.'

I dropped my pasty onto my plate, where it disintegrated into a mess of crust and gravy. Father's words had soured the day's happiness. He placed his ale cup on the table, folded his arms and announced happily that he had ordered a bolt of fine cloth from his weavers for my wedding gown. 'Blue like the Virgin's robes,' he enthused. 'the colour of cornflowers to compliment your eyes and your silver curls.' He sat back in his chair and added proudly, 'I shall give you a feast like none I have ever given before. It will be St Cecilia's feast day, the twenty-second day of November. We shall employ the best city musicians that I can afford.'

'Thank you, Father,' I said quietly and tried to listen to my mother's chatter as she talked to him about my wedding feast. It was as if I were not there.

'And your dowry will be an orchard. Of course, in return, the boy's father promises to invest in my cloth business.'

'Do you mean an orchard attached to our land?' There it was again, Father's own interests, but, at least I would have one of his apple orchards.

'Indeed, I do. I hope that one day you will move to Fulham from the City; better for the children.'

'I am sure.'

I could find no objection to my marriage, except that I did not love Tom Williams. Remembering his reluctant kiss, I closed my eyes. Love was a foolish, romantic notion. I whispered a prayer to St Elizabeth: 'Make me a good wife.'

I heard footsteps on the stairs and a moment afterwards the door opened. Joan and Meg were back. As Meg cleared away the remains of our picnic, an excited Joan gave us a detailed account of all she had seen.

By mid-afternoon, the heat slumped over the street below and the air thickened like soup. We delayed descending the rickety stairs to the street until we knew the procession was drawing close.

Horses clattered along the cobbles. I craned my neck to the left, peering to see them better. Two richly clothed gentlemen walked in front of the King's horse. Their hats were powdered with ermine and their robes were trimmed with the same expensive fur. One carried the King's hat, the other his cloak.

After this we had eyes only for our beautiful young King, so near my own age, dressed in crimson velvet furred with ermine. 'That jacket alone,' my father muttered from behind me, 'is worth a lifetime of dinners. His coat would feed London's poor for the rest of our days.'

The King's jacket was raised gold studded with jewels, diamonds, rubies, emeralds and great pearls, and he wore a gleaming baldrick. His horse sported trappings of gold damask. My heart throbbed within my ribs when he passed close by us. The women curtsied; my father raised his hat and bowed.

My mother rose from her curtsey and exclaimed, 'The man behind the King is Sir Thomas Brandon. Just look at the horse he is leading, and by a rein of silk!'

The master of the King's horse was clad in tissue embroidered with golden roses. I loved the fabrics. In the sun's rays, the rich materials glowed even more brightly. If I were my own mistress, I thought, I would sell such beautiful cloth as these courtiers wore.

As the procession of nobles and bishops moved on towards the display of the City companies, I spotted my betrothed in his gold and red uniform, amongst the yeomen following the King's procession. Tom Williams never looked my way that day, though he must have known we would be watching. He walked beside a handsome youth. I saw them exchange a smile, then an almost imperceptible touch. My heart plummeted.

Drums rolled. 'The Queen approaches,' a herald announced.

In that moment, I forgot Tom Williams. I forgot the King. My eyes were now only for Queen Catherine, seated on a litter borne by two white palfreys, draped in white cloth. Her satin dress floated about her. A silver coronet studded with jewels sat upon her magnificent auburn hair, which fell in coils past her waist, and for a moment I felt a twinge of envy.

The Queen was followed by a group of noblewomen apparelled in cloth of gold, tinsels, embroideries and velvets, driven in richly adorned chariots. I could not help but wonder what my life would be like if I could serve the Queen, if I could dwell in a palace...

At that moment, the sky darkened. A heavy cloud blotted out the sun and opened; rain showered down on the Queen's litter, halting the procession. Liveried guards drew the litter towards us. Others pushed us back into our shop front. Obediently, the white palfreys stood still. The Queen was sheltered from the rain under our huge awning.

We sank to our knees; common men and nobles alike knelt amongst the flower-strewn grasses on the street. All London bowed to their Queen and my mother almost prostrated herself. As I rose from my curtsey, my stomach churned again because the Queen was looking straight down at me. She spoke not a word but she smiled.

As quickly as it had started, the rain stopped and the sun came out. A cheer rose to meet the sun's rays as the procession slowly began to move again towards Cheape Street.

My father's eyes were glazed over.

'Oh, Father,' I gasped.

'Elizabeth, we have been greatly honoured this day.'

I knew it, but I also recognised that a Queen's smile was a transient thing. It mattered little, yet it mattered much. It mattered to us, her subjects and it was especially important to me. She seemed to me even then, so long ago, as a woman of great courage.

Her husband had been chosen for her and she looked
happy. Maybe, I thought that afternoon as she smiled,
I could be happy as well.

Chapter Seven

MOTHER RETURNED TO HER manor without me, and Father purchased broadcloth at the Bartholomew Cloth Fair, as well as the fabric for the monasteries. I was grateful. When I promised to repay his generosity, he opened his hands in an expansive gesture and shook his head.

'You are my elder daughter, are you not? You need help, my dear. I give it willingly.' A mysterious smile hovered about his whiskered mouth.

'Yes, Father,' I said and held my tongue, wondering why he was not renewing his attempts to persuade me home again and what the return for his generosity would now be. Perhaps I was too cynical and Mother had swayed him after all. Or maybe, and this was more likely, he had another husband in mind for me. If he did, I would be ready to challenge him.

'Please, stay for dinner. I have a chicken pie today, a pease pottage and newly baked bread..

He bustled into his cloak and set his new hat on his head. A feather nodded as he moved towards the doorway, as if to remind me that this extravagant hat had once belonged to my poor dead husband. 'I believe I must not, my dear. I have a middleman to see today.'

'Not Master Cromwell?'

'Not this time. Master Cromwell has vanished again.'

'Oh,' I said, and could not help feeling disappointment as he swept out.

Gerard Smith made all my deliveries that week, except for the cloth to Austin Friars. I told him not to visit the friars because I wanted to bring them the painted cloth myself. The Friary's beauty was well-known and, since Tom had dealt with the Prior before, I hoped to see something of this famous place where scholars gathered, often travelling there from far-flung countries, the lands of oranges and figs.

When the monasteries paid us, I paid my debt, pleased to see that there was now enough left over from the sale of the plain fabric to keep my household fed that winter. The rent on Wood Street was due by All Hallows' Eve and I knew that I must use the rest of Master Cromwell's silver for this. Simply, there would not be enough over to rebuild my much-needed woolshed unless I sold the remaining mixed cloth I kept in the attic storerooms and replaced it with even better cloth.

'Smith,' I said after I had recorded our gains in the ledgers. 'Where can I buy new draperies? You know, linen or wool and silk mixes.'

He thought for a moment, then beaming broadly said, 'There is always the Northampton Cloth Fair. Those fancy new cloths are woven up in Norfolk. They will be there aplenty, Mistress. They are in high demand.'

Meg looked up from her black work stitching. Her mouth was open and she shook her head so hard that her cap fell off her wayward curls and dropped into her lap. 'How can you think of it, Mistress? Master Wykes would not approve, nor your mother.' She clicked her tongue between her teeth. 'It is not right for a lady to travel to the cloth fairs.' Smith smiled at her, nodding his head. I had long suspected that he was sweet on her.

I stood up and spread my fingers on my desk. 'Meg,

they would have me back in Putney. Think on this. Where will my household be? I would have to close down my business and send you all away. So you see, I must go - and you will accompany me, as will Smith.'

That did it. She looked contrite, nodded, and picked up her needle again, concentrating small black cross stitches along the hem of the table napkin she was embroidering.

Smith watched her for a moment with admiring eyes, then said, 'We shall have the money from the Friary to reinvest. They always purchase the most cloth from us. And there is the painted cloth they ordered too. That will fetch a good price.' He rubbed his hands and grinned at me. I found myself smiling back.

October slid in quickly with tossing leaves, cooler air and crisp evenings. I arranged to deliver the painted cloth to the Friary along with bolts of broadcloth for new habits. On that day, I called my apprentices to help me. We packed the starry fabric into our wagon, along with bolts of plain brown woollen cloth. With Gerard Smith at the reins of our wagon, one apprentice boy and Meg, I set out to visit the Austin Friars.

Early morning dew coated the gateposts of the Guildhall, lacing the hedges with watery droplets, and water carriers and milkmaids shouted out their presence as we passed them. When a group of horsemen clip-clopped past us, Smith tugged the nag's reins, drawing the wagon to the side of the street. At that moment, a maid about to empty a bucket into the channel that ran like a hollowed-out bone of stone through the street's centre, called a warning from a casement set into the overhang above. We leaned away from the mess, almost upsetting our wagon.

'Be careful,' I snapped at Smith. 'Think of the cloth.'

He turned to me. 'Mistress, if you want to drive, take the reins. Happy I am to let you.'

Meg jerked her neck round, sharp as sticking pins. 'Gerard, you mind your tongue.'

I looked straight ahead, my eyes fixed on the street, but never spoke. For the moment, I was furious.

Pigs sauntered along the cobbles, snuffling through the discarded waste. A chattering queue formed outside a bake-house. The soothing smell of newly baked loaves escaped through its opened doors, but no sooner had Smith urged our nag on towards Throgmorton Street, than I was wrinkling my nose again. A band of night soil boys marched by, shovels hoisted over their shoulders, buckets over their arms. Meg unclipped a lavender ball from her kirtle belt, passed it to me and I held it to my nose, longing for the fresher air of the Friary.

We entered the Austin Friary from the gates at the junction of Throgmorton Street and Broad Street.

'Meg, straighten your cap. You need to look neat here,' I said, removing the pomander from my nose and handing it back to her, determined that we would make a good impression on the friars.

I cast a sideways look at Gerard Smith who looked sullen. 'You, Gerard, mind the wagon and water the horse.'

He mumbled something, clearly not pleased that I had deprived him of the honour of his annual delivery. No doubt, in the past he had been the recipient of a good dinner in the friary kitchens and he could take his leisure. This time I was in charge, which would explain the abrupt manner in which he had loaded the wagon and driven us here. He was still not used to a woman giving him orders despite his willingness to help me recover the business.

Without replying, he sent the boy, Barnaby, a bright

tow-haired lad, to fetch help to unload our cloth. A short time passed. We waited in silence. Even Meg was annoyed with me because I had told her to neaten herself up, I who could never keep my own cupboards tidy. Yet, to the world I appeared ordered. Her face was long and her lips pursed. I looked away and studied the buildings, deciding to ignore her petulance. The Friary was as magnificent as I had expected, with its handsome church and the well-kept gardens which could be glimpsed once we were inside the Friary's walls.

Friars, their habits flapping, came rushing across the courtyard to help us unload the wagon. Moments later they had hoisted our cloth over their shoulders. One, whom I assumed must be more senior than the others, stepped over to speak with me.

'Mistress Williams, our Prior wishes to converse with you today. He is in the North Cloister.' He turned to Smith. 'Welcome, Master Gerard, Friar Francis here will show you to the kitchen for refreshment as usual. You too, Mistress,' he said to Meg. 'The stable boys will water your horse. Bring the boy with you.'

At last, Smith smiled, his eyes twinkling and, turning to me, he spoke gently this time, his mood much improved. 'Mistress, you are surely honoured and, therefore, we your servants are also.'

I nodded and forgave him his earlier petulance.

'I have the painted cloth?' I said to the monk, pointing to the bolt of painted cloth that none of the friars had lifted.

'Prior Anthony wishes us to carry it straight to him.'

'I see.' I wondered if he was going to inform me that he would not do business with a woman cloth merchant.

Filled with anxiety, I followed the friars and the roll of painted cloth around the main cloister to the North

Cloister. Students and clergy purposefully bustled by us. Some of them looked foreign, Italian or perhaps Spanish. Their gowns were of fine wool and well-cut to flow about legs encased in colourful, close-fitting hose. Many Italians came to study at Austin Friars. It was renowned for scholarship and possessed a great library, with printed books as well as many very old decorated books painstakingly copied by generations of scriptorium monks.

Prior Anthony was seated on a stone bench. He stood up, putting down the little book he was reading and which he had held with long elegant hands. 'Ah, Mistress Williams, I wished to express my sorrow at Master Williams' death directly to you. A fencing accident, I heard.'

I nodded. 'During sword practice. He was a King's yeoman - sometimes.'

'I see. Only sometimes?'

'He was a reserve.' I did not want to speak of his accident further so I kept silent.

The Prior looked approvingly at my neat black kirtle, my white coif and the simple black cross on a silver chain that today I wore hanging over my bodice. A breeze caught my cloak and it flapped about me like a rook's wings as the Friars laid the cloth on the bench. I helped them open it up so Prior Anthony could see and appreciate the gleaming stars and the deep blue heavens that contained them.

He nodded appreciatively. 'Very good, Mistress Williams. I see you are intent on carrying on the cloth business.' He glanced up at me. 'Or are you just completing orders already promised? I hope you will continue our business.'

'I intend to continue the business. I have always kept the accounts, Prior Anthony.'

67

'That is very brave, and many widows do well carrying on their husbands' businesses.'

'I shall do my best to please. I have a competent journeyman and am training up two apprentices.'

Prior Anthony opened the roll a little further. 'Good,' he said.

As Thomas Cromwell had done some months past, he fingered the painted cloth. Remembering him, I felt a tug in my breast.

'I am very pleased with this.'

When he looked up, I noticed his eyes were of the deepest blue, as blue as the cloth he had just purchased for the Friary's Christmas plays.

'I shall send you payment later this week, for this and for the broadcloth.' He looked anxiously at me. 'But I don't like to think of you crossing to Wood Street with a bag of coin. I shall send it tomorrow with Friar Thomas.' He added, 'Accompanied by a guard.' He smiled. His was a kind generous smile and I liked him immediately. 'We cannot always trust to God's protection. The streets are dangerous.'

'Thank you, Prior Anthony.'

He raised an eyebrow as he saw me glance towards the book he had left lying on the bench. I possessed few books because, as I had suspected, my reading was not encouraged in the Williams household.

'You are interested in texts, Mistress Williams,' the Prior said. He lifted up the little book. I peered closely at it trying to decipher the words on its cover.

'This printed book is by Desiderius Erasmus of Antwerp. Have you heard of this scholar?'

'I had a Latin master as a girl. He said Master Erasmus wanted readers to think of the meaning of things.'

He looked at me with earnest eyes. 'This is true. You

68

are indeed educated. Once, Erasmus said, "When I get a little money I buy books; and if there is any left I buy food and clothes."'

'But if he is hungry he cannot concentrate,' I remarked, feeling my forehead crease as I thought about what I was saying. 'I mean if *I* were truly hungry, I could not think of books.'

'He has a hunger for the written word. We have many books in our library. This little book is a collection of Latin proverbs.' He placed the book in my hands. 'Take it.'

I handled it carefully as if it was a brittle leaf that could break if I breathed on it, and turned the page over. Glancing up at his earnest face, I said, 'It is wonderful, a printed book, just as the painted cloth is printed with tiny gleaming stars.'

'Indeed, my child, and as Erasmus says, "Give light and the darkness will disappear of itself." So, since you have brought me stars to light our Christmas plays, I would give you this book, Mistress Williams. Learn to question the world and find your own sense of light.' I felt that he had given me advice of great value and whispered my thanks. The Madonna had answered my prayer. She had sent me a good omen. I would thrive.

The Nonce bells suddenly began to ring, sending a beautiful sound around the cloister. It was joined by the bells of a hundred London churches and more.

'I must attend to the noonday service,' Prior Anthony said above the ringing bells, looking towards small groups of friars walking in the direction of the church. When he noticed a lone friar walking alone along the cloister pathway close to us, he called him over. 'Deliver Mistress Williams to her maid.' Turning to me he inclined his head and said, his voice slightly raised above the bells, 'Return one day,

69

Mistress Elizabeth. Next time I shall show you our library.'

'Thank you,' I replied, clutching the little book. 'Thank you for my book.'

As quickly as the bells rang, they stopped. I followed the friar and, in a strange way, as I held that little book to my breast, I felt as free as a bird of the air. It was unusual for a man, even a Prior, to care about a woman's education.

The following day I summoned Smith and the apprentices into the office behind my stores which looked out over the garden.

'The two of you,' I looked at my apprentices, 'and Master Smith here will be accompanying me to Cheape Street on St Luke's Day. We'll sell the rest of the cloth there, or as much of it as we can.' I had to suppress a smile as I struggled to be very firm. 'Gerard, you will organise a stall for me.' I lifted a sample of green woollen fabric from the top of my ledger. 'It's fine cloth. I intend to get as good a price for it as is possible. Before Christmastide, I shall buy new fabrics to replace the cloth we sell.' If I cleared most of this cloth on St Luke's Day we would travel to the Northampton November Fair.

Smith scratched his head through thinning yellow hair. 'If you insist, Mistress, but I think it dangerous for a ...'

I set my mouth as if it were carved of stone.

'Woman? That's what you mean to say, is it not?' I said. 'I know what I am about, so don't say it. You, yourself, said there would be new draperies at the Northampton Fair and to purchase them I shall need as much coin as we can gather up. Arrange a stall with the Drapers' Company. Make sure we have a cover and a good position.' My lanky apprentice boys looked amused. One began to giggle behind his fist. I glared at them.

'Between now and then, you boys will clean these storerooms. Make sure the cloth is parcelled with fennel and lavender to keep vermin off, and the bolts wrapped in linen. You have two days. If it is not done well, you will repeat the process until I am satisfied.'

'Yes Mistress,' they chorused with downcast eyes. Their faces reddened as they sloped off to do my bidding. Smith nodded, which I took to be assent, if not quite meant.

St Luke's Day dawned sunny with a nip in the air. I noted the cloudless sky, thankful that rain would not wet my fabrics.

We sold a little in the morning. Smith watched me closely as I negotiated with a Flanders middleman on a half-dozen bolts of kersies. For the first time since my husband died, I saw Smith throw a smile of admiration my way. By eleven o'clock a great number of bodies pushed through the stalls, women with servants and maids, flocks of dark-clothed priests, cloth men from all over Northern Europe, Flanders merchants, a few olive-skinned, richly dressed Italians, a band of nobility who looked too proud to buy anything. Nonetheless, they fingered the goods on display, turned to servants and, with a click of their fingers, ordered them to buy fine cloth from stalls close to mine. Other traders were not so kind.

A group of them close to my pitch watched me with critical eyes. As I sold cloth to a lady with a page, a young woman who looked as if she could be a maid at court, just the customer I needed to spread word of my new fabrics, I saw that the master traders looked at us as if we were small insects not worth their regard, whispering with raised eyebrows. From time to time, as they glanced my way heads came together as if in debate and I their subject. I squared

71

my shoulders and turned my back on them.

One sidled forward. I spun around crossly at his tap on my shoulder. He was the same merchant who had sat beside me months ago at Tom's funeral feast. I was about to greet him pleasantly, determined not to be belittled by him, but before I could speak, he pinched one of my draperies between finger and thumb, a fine linen and soft silk mix, lifted it, dropped it and remarked, 'Insubstantial, Mistress Williams, as thin of character as those who would chose to wear such poor fabric.' He seemed to ponder for a moment, stumpy finger against chin, almost but not quite mockingly. 'Your father has sense. Listen to him. He trades in good worsteds and sensible wool.' He looked from me to Smith and shook his grey head at him in a critical manner.

'No money in that fabric, Gerard, no worth.'

By association with me, whom they clearly saw an insubstantial woman, my journeyman was demeaned as well.

Smith muttered, 'We shall see, we shall see. She'll find out soon enough.' In that moment, I was angry both with Smith and at the trader. I coolly studied my journeyman.

'And so shall you, Smith.'

He had the grace to redden and say, 'I meant no ill, Mistress.'

'Show me loyalty,' I snapped once the trader had moved off.

Later, two senior guildsmen with long grey beards and walking sticks wandered through the market, examining the quality of the merchandise.

They lingered by my stall, looked over my cloth carefully, nodded and one said, 'A valiant effort, Mistress Williams.' I felt crosser than ever.

The other said, 'It is good to see you recovering from the fire. No word of the rogue who set it?'

'Which rogue, sir?' I said, trying to remain calm.

'The boy who guarded the store?' The guildsman snorted and looked at his companion, who frowned and shook his head as if to silence his friend.

My apprentices looked concerned. Smith raised a bushy eyebrow and was about to speak, but I spoke up, determined to stop whatever he might say.

'No, we have not heard of Toby's whereabouts, nor have we knowledge of who was responsible. Toby was not to blame. Why would he destroy his livelihood?'

'Perhaps he missed the master. Maybe it was grief.'

'Or jealousy?' the other said in a sly tone.

'If you hear anything, please inform me,' I said sharply and added, 'If that is all, I must continue selling my cloth. Excuse me, please, sirs.'

The guildsmen could find no real complaint with the quality I was selling, but they despised me. I was sure of it. When, or if, Toby returned I was sure that they would determine that he was guilty and my heart sank. I still suspected that he was innocent. The guildsmen bowed to me and moved away. Upset by their remarks, I busied myself with my cloth.

A band of children rushed through the stalls, grasping apple pies that oozed fruit over their hands, their sticky fingers moving dangerously near my carefully displayed fabric. I stood firmly in front of my cloth, glad of the apprentice, Wilfrid, who was wiry and cross-eyed. He lifted his hand to the boys and they skittered into the gathering crowd. We had, by now, opened all the linen covers so that the colours were displayed: dark blues, light blues, saffron yellows, browns and serge-green, less expensive fabric in good plain colours, easily dyed and popular with tradesmen's wives. As the cloth sold, I felt my spirits lifting. Smith persuaded passers-by to come and feel the quality, always taking care to give a detailed account of each ell of fabric - where it had come from, how fast the dye and how fine the weave.

The bolt of good, soft, dark green kersey had made me long for the oak woods of Putney when I had first discovered it. It was such a beautiful hue and texture that I had been tempted to save it for myself for a fine winter cloak lined with fleece. There might even be enough left to cover a new hood to set off my silvery hair and my sea-coloured eyes. Longing for new garments to wear once my period of mourning had ended, I had almost persuaded myself that I needed that new winter cloak, when I heard a voice beside me.

'Mistress, is this your cloth?' I glanced up.

'Yes, it is, sir.' I replied quickly and stood aside to allow the owner of this slick voice to look more closely at my fabrics.

I watched him as he fingered my cloth. He was tall man with eyes as brown as treacle, his hair dark and falling to curl under below his chin, hair on which he was wearing an expensive black woollen hat with velvet trim. I noted that his fine brown tunic was tapered, revealing a slender waist before it generously flowed into gathers to cover his hose at the knees. He trailed his hand delicately over my green wool, then the brown and back to the green kersey. Since the tunic he wore was trimmed with dark fox fur, I knew that he could well afford the cloth.

'May I assist you?' I ventured. 'Perhaps you need a new cloak? The brown broadcloth is very serviceable.'

His long fingers caressed the bolt of green wool. There was something possessive in the gesture that made me feel uneasy. 'This is much finer,' he said. 'How much?'

There went my green cloak. 'Two shillings for the ell.' I presented him with an inflated price, hoping he would decline. He frowned. I lowered my price slightly. He countered with another much lower price. I shook my head.

It was unfortunate that at that moment my father came wandering towards my stall, just as the finely dressed gentleman was examining the cloth, clearly looking for any fault that might make me further lower the price. I saw Father approaching with a scowl on his face. No doubt, I thought furiously, Smith had told Father where I was today.

The gentleman looked up and smiled broadly at Father. Father's scowl fled his countenance, for he had recognised the gentleman.

'Why, it's Henry Wykes. Greetings. I was on my way to Cornhill, but my attention was captured by this superb green wool. Look, is it not a wonderful shade? Such a fine and even dye.'

I stood back and folded my arms. How did Father know this person to whom I was quickly taking a dislike? When this customer opened his mouth I could see the teeth behind the smooth smiles that were frightening and piratical.

Father looked straight at me. If a look could have sliced me through, that one almost did, it was so sharp.

'This is my daughter, Master Northleach, and *I* purchased this cloth for her.'

I was irritated by Father's proprietary manner.

Smith stepped forward and said to Father, 'But Mistress Williams is selling it, Master Wykes,'

Father's mouth fell open. 'I am not sure I like to see my daughter here.' He glared at Smith. 'Surely you can do business for her, Smith?'

'She is more than competent, Master.'

Smith did not wait for Father to tell him he was bold, but turned to the customer. 'I think if you want that cloth, sir, you should close the deal. I see another interest already.'

My father and Master Northleach both followed the hand touching my cloth up to its owner's face. The merchant who owned it had the look of a Spaniard about him.

'How much for the green cloth?' the new customer asked, on seeing that our attention had shifted to him.

'It is not for sale.' Master Northleach said. His face had darkened and his teeth appeared to snap like a wolf's. He reached over and tapped the ell of cloth. 'This cloth is already spoken for. I shall give the merchant the price she asks.'

The Spaniard bowed politely and, backing off, moved to the next trestle.

As Father crossly looked on, Smith smiled and nodded, his thin yellow hair falling for a moment over his face. He swept it back with a flourish and winked at me. I increased my first price by two shillings.

The smoothly spoken man counted out the money and handed it to Gerard, who immediately secreted it in a purse. 'You strike a hard bargain, Mistress,' Master Northleach said, smiling with those great white teeth that looked as if they could snap off my very hand. 'Since you are such a pretty woman, I am happy to purchase. No doubt, I shall make up the difference when I sell your father's worsted in Bruges this winter.'

'You are a cloth man?' I said, shocked that my father had changed middlemen again, and to this smooth creature. Never had Father spoken of him before. Momentarily I wondered what had happened to Thomas

Cromwell. Even so, Father had more than one middleman. Once one completed a sale, another soon took his place.

'Your father and I are in business together, that of selling cloth - but this,' he tapped the bolt of green woollen fabric- 'I shall have made into a short cloak. Now, if you will excuse us.' He reached out an arm to guide Father away, the bolt of green cloth entrusted to a servant who wore an ancient padded jerkin splattered with a few rust-hued stains, as if it had once belonged to a soldier.

Father turned back. He glared again at Smith and said to me in a perfunctory manner, 'Elizabeth, I'll call on you later this week.' Conversing together, the cloth merchant and Father walked off towards Cornhill.

'If I may be so bold, Mistress Elizabeth,' Smith said in a low voice after they were lost amongst a seething crowd gathered by the conduit at the crossroads. 'I don't think your father should put his trust in that middleman. I've never seen him before at the cloth fairs. There's something about his manner that I cannot lay my finger on. It's too smooth.'

'Oh, Gerard, I know, but maybe we can't judge too quickly. Father, after all, as you believe, has so much experience with cloth.'

'Perhaps I'm wrong.' Smith shrugged his shoulders. He looked into my face, his eyes sincere. 'Mistress Elizabeth, I have underestimated you and I'm sorry for it.'

'Really,' I said sharply, though I felt we had crossed over from suspicion of each other to acceptance.

'You see, I was concerned, Mistress. I told your father you were here, and it is your father that I worry for now.'

'I'm relieved that you need have no concern for me, Smith,' I said. 'Neither should you worry about him. He's made a fortune selling abroad,' I added loyally, though I

77

did not like the new middleman one bit either.

'Yes, Mistress,' Smith replied, though his thoughtful face still betrayed his concern. He disguised it by swiftly accosting a customer and selling yet another bolt of woollen fabric. There was something about the new middleman that had unsettled me and I determined to speak about this to Father next he came to Wood Street.

Chapter Eight

MY APPRENTICES PROVED THOROUGH at cleaning, sorting and organising the storerooms. Two weeks later, just before All Hallows' Eve, I called them to the office and instructed them about the cloths I wished to purchase at the Northampton Cloth Fair.

I showed them samples of the new fabrics they must seek out, encouraging them gently to feel the textures and look at the colours, reminding them of sumptuary laws, the colours ordinary citizens were permitted to wear and those not permitted.

'Only the queen and king may wear purple. The nobility may wear -' I caught myself guiltily hesitating, 'scarlet. You, Barnaby, must wear browns, pale blues, forest greens, black and grey, and yellow. The nobility can wear a rich deep blue. Black is a most expensive cloth - the dye costly, multiple dyeing of woad or indigo, and the mordant is usually copperas. In Northampton we shall buy fine cloth in ordinary colours and sell it on for city wives. You'll watch out for velvet trim. That's allowed. I think a silversmith's wife would be delighted with yellow serge for a winter cloak. She may also trim it with fox fur but not ermine. That's for the rich.'

Barnaby glanced down at his pale blue tunic. 'It is as well that I like these colours, Mistress. They are honest colours.'

'True enough, blue for humility, but we'll ensure that

we have velvet and satin in many colours for trims. The colours will please many.' For a moment I thought wistfully of a gentleman who dressed plainly but was clearly wealthy enough to wear a whole cloak of soft black velvet. 'We are done for today,' I said.

At that moment, Meg came to see me. 'Mistress Elizabeth, your father is here to see you and he's with a companion.' She lowered her voice in a confidential manner. 'I don't know the gentleman with him but he's handsome, Mistress Elizabeth.' She fiddled coyly with one of her dark curls and straightened her cap.

I wondered just for a heartbeat if Father's companion could be Thomas Cromwell. My heart beat faster as I said, 'Barnaby, Wilfrid, go and find Master Smith. Tell him you are to spend an hour learning multiplication.' I removed my great linen apron and handed it to Meg. 'Serve my father and his friend hippocras and seed cakes, Meg.'

'I think your father called his companion Master Northleach. Shall I set out refreshments in the parlour or the hall?'

My heart screeched disappointment. It was as if, without warning, a poisonous snake had slithered over my threshold. My back stiffened. Detachment, I told myself. I would conceal my true feelings until I discovered Father's motives. I suspected these might not be to further my own interests. I had pushed Northleach to the recesses of thought since our first meeting and Father had not come to see me for a fortnight.

'I see. Serve them in the hall, not the parlour. I hardly know that man.' I hurried up to my chamber to change my white widow's wimple for a suitable hood and my dark work dress for the funeral black bombazine. I would not look shabby in front of the merchant, but in a small act of defiance, I mischievously wore my crimson petticoat.

Father would not manage me today, as I suspected would be his intent, and hoping that they would not stay long, I determined that, just in case they lingered, I would attend Vespers to make a timely end to Master Northleach's visit.

When I stepped down the staircase into the hall, Father and Master Northleach were seated comfortably on the velvet padded bench by the hearth, stretching leather-covered toes towards the warmth; Father's, I observed, a serviceable brown, but his companion's footwear was dyed green to match his mantle. As I approached, they hurried to their feet, too anxious, I noted. Father stretched his large hands out to gasp mine while Northleach made a polite bow. As he swept up again, I saw that his green short cloak was fashioned from my beautiful wool mix and clasped at the neck with a large gold pin. I swept an eye over the cloak but refused to remark on it. Instead, I bade them both sit, poured the hippocras that Meg had placed on a low table and offered them seed cakes along with linen napkins edged with black-work stitching. Taking the straight-backed chair opposite, I arranged my skirts so that my crimson underskirt did not creep below my bombazine gown.

'How is business?' I asked my father.

'Well enough, Lizzy. Master Northleach will take my kersies and medley cloth to the Bruges market.' He drew in a breath. 'This is one reason we are here. Do you wish to join my venture?'

'I can guarantee sales if you do, Mistress Williams,' Northleach said earnestly.

'I have little left to sell abroad as I sold very well in September, though I do intend purchasing more cloth at the Northampton Fair, but I have another middleman in mind for this cloth.' I smiled, wondering what the other reason for Northleach's visit could be, though I had my suspicions.

Open-mouthed, my father stared at me, shocked at my forthright manner. His cup tilted and golden drops of hippocras dribbled onto his lap. As he dabbed at the sticky drops with his napkin, I handed him a jug of water. 'If you are quick, Father, it will not stain.' He did not yet know about my plan or my intent to seek out Thomas Cromwell as my own middleman and I had wondered if I should even tell him. But now that it was revealed, I intended sticking to it.

'Elizabeth, did I hear correctly? You plan on travelling to the Northampton Cloth Fair in November? I forbid you.'

'Father, it is not your right to forbid me anything.'

At this, he puffed out his chest in the usual way when he was irritated, and looked flustered. 'You will be prey to cut-throats and thieves, never mind the weather. You have no wit, no care for your own safety, nor consideration for your mother's heart or mine.' He dramatically struck his breast with one hand, still clutching the napkin in the other. 'In November!' he repeated.

'I am taking Smith with me, the apprentices and Meg, too. She is worth two armed men.'

He dropped the napkin, stood up with the spring of a younger man and slammed the water jug back on the table. 'Two women on the roads! You cannot travel like this.' His face was as red as my petticoat.

Northleach flashed his large teeth, 'I can see Mistress Elizabeth is learning to look after her own interests. But your father is right. A lady should not be exposed to dangers such as the roads contain.'

'Indeed,' I said calmly to the merchant, curious as to where *his* interests in my affairs really lay. I turned back to father. 'Father, do sit down again. Finish your hippocras. I am going to the Cloth Fair. Nothing will stop me returning with new cloth.'

Father shook his head. 'The sooner you have a new husband the better, Elizabeth.'

Perhaps I imagined that in that moment Master Northleach looked at Father and shook his head and Father nodded, but I suspected not.

Master Northleach eased himself up from the bench, placed his cup on the table, and as if he was trying to calm troubled waters said, 'Mistress Elizabeth, I hear you have a fine garden. I wonder whether we could take a turn in it. I need fresh air.' He smiled, flashing those teeth again. 'If you wouldn't mind?'

His long, lean hand reached out to me.

'Do so, Elizabeth,' Father said, his face less fiery now. 'I must have a word with Smith.'

I rose and hurried to the door, ignoring Master Northleach's offer of his hand and called for Meg to accompany us into the garden. A boy came running from the kitchen to say that Meg was gone out to fetch milk from the dairy.

'Send me Susannah, or Bess,' I said. 'Tell her to bring a basket. She can pick herbs for the supper salad while I speak with Master Northleach.'

Northleach offered me his arm again and this time I took it.

'Five minutes, sir,' I said and looked at Father's pleased face. 'I am attending Vespers today.'

'I won't be long, Elizabeth, just long enough to make sure that Smith knows what you are doing.'

I extricated my arm from the elbow it was tucked into. 'No need, Father. Smith knows perfectly well that I am buying new cloth.'

His face lost its smile. 'There will be conditions, Elizabeth, if you are set on this.'

'What conditions?' How dare my father suggest conditions to me, but then there was that outstanding loan and I did not want to estrange him completely because, after all, despite his behaviour he was my father and doubtless meant well.

'Guards, wagons, safe accommodation.'

'Are you providing all this? Monastery common rooms will do for us.'

'We shall see. You may be trying to make a cloth merchant of yourself, Elizabeth, but you are still my daughter.' He managed to look disconcerted.

I smiled to myself. 'And a woman.' Those words he did not say though I knew my father, like most men, considered a woman a lesser being than a man and like Eve, open to temptation. At least he accepted that I was indeed going to Northampton. Relishing my small triumph, I confidently led Master Northleach along the passage from the hall just as Susannah, basket swinging by her side, joined us. Leaving my father at the storeroom door, we entered the garden by a small side entrance. The maid trailed behind us, her basket bumping against her kirtle.

Northleach stood, legs akimbo, and his greedy eyes surveyed the garden with admiration, not seeing the charred timbers of my burned-out warehouse building beyond the garden wall. 'It is a delight to find such well-kept gardens hidden behind the City dwellings.' He plucked rosemary from the bush and rubbed it between his long fingers. The sad smell of remembrance reminded me of Tom's funeral. He cast it lightly from his long fingers and turned to me with a flashing smile.

Susannah hurried off to busy herself amongst the

84

plants, snipping furiously with her scissors. The boy I employed to sweep the pathway was busy with a bundle of twigs, making piles of fallen leaves. Master Northleach glanced their way before making further comment.

'In the Low Countries where I have lived, there are many new plants these days.'

'Such as?' I asked, listening more closely now. I liked plants. This, I would hear. The colours dyers extracted from plants always fascinated me. Perhaps Northleach was more informed than I.

'Travellers have discovered a new thistle that, steeped in vinegar, might help toothache. It is also thought that drinking an infusion of this thistle can help with the sweating sickness.'

I was curious, since Tom Williams' mother had died of the sweat. Meg and I had needed to wash everything, absolutely every surface in the house, with lye soap and vinegar. The rooms smelled for days after her death. The sweat, an illness that haunted our city some years, was said to have come with our king's father's mercenaries from the continent, when he won the final battle in the cousins' war, and it was so rampant, it killed many too quickly.

'A humble thistle. Just imagine that it has such potency,' I said.

'It does, I believe.' He flashed his great teeth again. 'I like to travel, to discover new places.'

We had reached the mulberry tree, so we sat on the wooden bench. He stretched his arm along the back of the bench towards me. I slid along it, as far from my companion as I could manage. My original suspicions about his slippery character were correct. Looking down, I noticed a flash of pale yellow peeking up through the gap where the back of the bench joined its arm, which I leaned

85

on. Studying it for a moment as I thought of something to say to this stranger, I realised that an embroidery skein had dropped by the side of the bench and had worked its way into a rose bush growing beside it. I leaned over and plucked it up between finger and thumb and examined it. It was muddied and in a sorry state, but I would wash it later and it could be used again.

Master Northleach removed his arm from the back of the bench and glanced down at the thread in my hands. 'Silver thread. Though not as fine as your hair.'

I involuntarily touched my hood cap where I knew that my silvery hair neatly showed on my forehead. I looked around for Susannah. She was absorbed in her task but not far off, though, I hoped, out of earshot.

He was smiling yet again. I fancied his teeth were biting me. He edged closer. There was nowhere I could retreat now so I stared ahead, very obviously across the herb beds where Susannah was bent over her basket. She glanced up. I wished that Father would hurry outside and stared down at my hands as I turned the filmy silver thread over in my fingers.

Master Northleach reached over and touched my hand, making me freeze like a startled cat terrified of an advancing hound. I drew my fingers back and made a fuss of tucking the embroidery skein into my belt purse. As I moved, my household keys jangled. He drew back. 'I really do not mean to upset you, Mistress Williams, but I *do* have something to ask of you,' he said, his voice smooth as pressed linen.

I started. He did not frighten me, I decided, but he was like a slimy sea creature, an eel or a water snake, all in green, including the boots. He made me feel uncomfortable.

'Be brief,' I said and added with suitable forcefulness,

'Master Northleach, I've work to do today and intend to put fresh rosemary on my husband's grave when I attend Vespers.' I glanced over at Susannah. Her back was bent again as she gathered parsley. She moved along the path towards the rosemary bush. The boy who was sweeping the path looked over at us and then resumed his work. He was coming closer towards us, but paused by the wall to secure a pear tree I was training to grow against it. I took the moment to say to the merchant, 'What do you wish to say?'

Master Northleach folded one long arm over the other and looked straight at me. 'I am a wealthy man, Mistress Elizabeth. I own a dye works and a cloth business in Bruges. We are friends, your father and I, so you must call me Edward. It is after Saint Edward, Confessor. I know your name to be Elizabeth, John the Baptist's mother's name, and that, too, of King Henry's mother.'

I frowned. What a silly nonsense over names. I doubted Father could vouch for his Flanders dye works. Edward Northleach may have fooled my unsuspicious father but not me. I looked boldly at him and raised an eyebrow, waiting for the rest. He shifted even closer. I edged away. My right side was squashed up against the bench arm.

He moved slightly on seeing my discomfort. 'I just want ask you, Mistress Elizabeth, that when you are ready to wed again…' Lowering his voice, he murmured, 'You would -'

I knew it and did not give Master Northleach the chance to continue, nor would I call him Edward. 'No, Master Northleach, it is kind of you to offer but I do not intend to marry again, not you, nor anybody else.' I stood up and swept my hand along my skirt. 'Now if you will excuse me, I must attend Vespers.'

I called across the vegetable garden. 'Susannah, escort Master Northleach to my father. Tell him I am attending Vespers today. I shall take a few sprigs of rosemary. Leave the basket with Cook and fetch your cloak. You will accompany me, so tie up the rosemary for me and bring it with you.'

'Yes, Mistress.' She made a half-curtsey. Gathering up her basket, she sauntered towards us.

I allowed my bombazine to swish to show my impatience and hoped that the scarlet underskirt did not show below it. I drew myself up as tall and straight as I could.

Master Northleach, who was clearly surprised at my hasty response, rose and bowed again. 'Mistress Elizabeth, you will give me hope, of course?' He lifted my hand to his lips and kissed my fingers, one by one. I snatched them back before he reached the little finger. Susannah looked from the merchant to me, as her eyes widened. The boy, too, who was just within earshot threw us an interested glance. Susannah looked down at her feet.

'Master Northleach, I wish you well.'

Then he did something surprising. He lifted my hand again and pressed something into it. I opened my hand and stared down to where in my palm lay a fine silver chain and a cross with a tiny diamond set into it.

If it had not been a cross, I might have returned it immediately, but I could not resist appraising such a delicate piece, which was quite beautiful. I offered it back. 'I cannot accept this. It is very fine, and valuable.'

He shook his head. 'Just a token.' Tears seemed to gather in his eyes. 'I understand what it is to lose a loved one. It is a woman's piece, a mourning gift, and that is all. You see, my wife died some years ago. It belonged to her. Please do not offend me by refusing it.' He stepped to my other side. He was indeed light on his feet. 'I shall not bother you again. Forgive me.' In that moment I almost felt sorry for him.

Before I could return the mourning gift, he nodded briefly and followed the waiting, gibbous-eyed Susannah, who had observed all, leaving me alone on the path by the garden bench clutching the cross in my palm. I held it up and dangled it from my middle finger, allowing the sunlight to catch at the glittering diamond. It was fine and dainty, the chain and cross of good quality, the diamond perfect. Foolishly, I slipped it into my belt purse.

Later, as we hurried to Vespers, I recognised why I should have hurried after Master Northleach and returned the ornament to him. Gifts proffered with an offer of marriage were a suitor's way of sealing a betrothal. My acceptance could be misconstrued as a promise of future encounters, as, I remembered, such tokens often were intended. That evening I placed it at the bottom of my trinket box and, because Master Northleach did not return with further tokens, I chose to forget its existence.

Chapter Nine

Midsummer's Day, I526, The First Parlour

I FISH OUT THE DELICATE chain and cross from a beech-wood trinket box that has found its way into the first parlour. The diamond twinkles at me like a miniature star. I allow it to slither through my fingers, thinking that, one day, I must pass it to Grace. Yet, even though it is so beautiful, I should have rid myself of this unfortunate piece of my life long, long ago. My second Thomas wanted it returned to its owner but that never happened, and even though this gift was a mistake that bore misfortune, the cross does not feel malevolent. Perhaps, this is because it once belonged to the wife rather than to the husband. I return it to the casket where it creeps to the bottom and disappears, softly shut the lid and glance around my parlour.

All rests in its own true place here at Austin Friars - the clock, the tapestries, two arm-chairs by the fireplace, stuffed with embroidered cushions, and a collection of padded benches, a polished table where we can dine privately, and a tall cupboard with pewter plates displayed beside our Italian candlesticks. I pad over our grandest luxury, a Turkey carpet, to pat an embroidered cushion on Thomas' chair, and moving to the table, begin to rearrange a posy of rosemary, bay, feverdew and pinks, pinching the bay to release its fresh, almost woody perfume. The glass decanter that holds this confection of flowers was a present from one of Thomas' clients. Since it is chipped, I arrange herbs and flowers in it so as to conceal the chip and scent this spacious chamber. Just as everything in my life has over the years been shaken and tossed around like leaves in an autumn storm, the objects that belong to a past time have come to rest quietly and peacefully in this calm home of ours.

My eye dwells with pleasure upon a richly woven tapestry that depicts courtly life with its silken ladies and gentlemen setting off for a day's hunting. There are nobles whose elegant hawks sit obediently on leather-gloved hands, and rabbits and fawns peering out from the green and brown secret world of a dark, imagined forest. Ah, how many secrets does my hawk-loving husband guard for his silken smooth-faced Cardinal, a man I consider both dangerous and greedy? Yet, I, too, own a life filled with secrets belonging to my two husbands. I smile as I peer far into the threaded forest's leafy depths. Thomas purchased this piece in Antwerp last time he was there, shortly after our move to this home which we have called Austin Friars, for it had no other name and, after all, it nestles close to the Friary walls. And then my eyes close in on a pair of sparrow hawks hidden in the trees and I shudder.

Since my husband has been in the Cardinal's employ, he has discovered a love of falconry, a pleasure for noblemen. He would bring his birds inside though I have insisted that they stay out in mews so they can be trained by our falconer. You see, Thomas is rising in the world, to be able to afford such pastimes as hunting with birds, never mind the hoods, jesses and bells his two goshawks need as their furniture. He is aping the nobility, which I don't think at all wise, even though I admit I enjoy flying Elinor, my merlin, a gift from my husband.

'One day, I shall have a place at court,' Thomas

remarked only yesterday, after he returned from a long day with Cardinal Wolsey, during which they discussed the removal of further monastic gains into the Cardinal's possession. 'Thanks to the Cardinal's employ and all the other extra legal work I have acquired, we are becoming very wealthy, my love. I shall buy us manors outside the City. Land is security for our future, Lizzy.' His ever-changing eyes had turned a soft grey. 'Our son will be educated by the best tutors in the land.' He folded my hands into his. 'Our daughters must receive an education as do Thomas More's girls. And soon you, Elizabeth, will be a lady such as you see in that tapestry hanging up there.'

My reply reflected my unease with Thomas' lucrative employment in the Cardinal's household. With Thomas' help, the Cardinal is closing down a number of tiny monasteries and, though it is just a few, where will it end? I am sad about the closures, even though Cardinal Wolsey claims he will put the money gained to good; into the new colleges in Oxford and Lincoln that he is furnishing and which Thomas has helped him organise.

'Take care, my husband, outward appearances are not always as they seem amongst great folk,' I warn. 'There is a world of dissembling. The Cardinal will bring us trouble yet. Court is a dangerous place. Look at how the King had his dear friend the Duke of Buckingham executed some years ago, and he was a great noble.' I lower my voice. 'The King might yet turn against Wolsey and, with him, you too.'

'No, Lizzy. The Cardinal will not fall.'

'Mother tells me that there are dangerous men around King Henry's person. It is the Lady Anne who completely holds his attention now. Stay away from court.' I shook my head. 'Poor Queen Catherine. It is so

92

unjust. King Henry pays her so little attention.'

Thomas looked thoughtful. 'Hush, Lizzy, you speak treason. I work for the Cardinal, not the King,' he said. 'I am a servant, a lawyer. And doing well for us. I have investments. We are purchasing land.' He opened his arms expansively. 'We have this house. We have children. It is all for us, my love. I am no threat to the King. I am a mouse under his feet, and not even of noble blood.'

'Nor is the Cardinal of noble blood. This king will squash you both under those gilded shoes he wears.'

'Well, then, he is no threat to King Henry.'

'Buckingham was once King Henry's friend too. He is dead, head chopped from body.'

'He was too arrogant, too close by birth to a throne, Lizzy.'

'What a reason that was,' I said and turned my back on Thomas.

This morning, I peer out of the mullioned window and reflect on all that Thomas has given me. He loves his family, his sisters and his children. He is a kind, generous husband. When I watch him lean against the garden wall inspecting his work, it is so ordinary a moment I cannot imagine what lies concealed in the future for us all.

For a moment, I turn to study the painted cloth that hangs opposite the tapestry, staring at its red and white roses with silver centres. They are Tudor roses. It is dangerous to come too close to them. If only Thomas would listen to me and avoid court. I let a sigh escape because I discovered the rose hanging at the Northampton Fair, meaning to sell it on, but I never have. The painted cloth, like that silver cross, has remained with me ever since, such objects marking out my life's passage from then until now.

Northampton…I smile. It was my bid for freedom and

independence. I muse on the cloth business that I worked hard to save, and which brought us to our marriage.

We had a safer world then. The King was happy on his throne and he was loving with his queen. Thomas had not even met the Cardinal. He was a clever merchant and lawyer then, just beginning.

I lift the little jewel box and call for Bessie to take it to my bed chamber. It is time to join Meg in the kitchen because she has promised to help me make our special Midsummer's pie.

Chapter Ten

1513

FATHER CAME TO SAY GOODBYE but still he scolded me, nagging me like a goodwife berating an errant husband. 'Meg and Smith must stay by your side always. This venture is utter foolishness, but if you insist on this nonsense, Elizabeth, all I can do now is make sure that you and the coin and the goods are protected.' He shook his head. 'You rejected Edward Northleach and that was very foolish, my dear. He was most suitable, an excellent man. I ... I promised him that, that you would ma-marry him,' he stammered.

'What? My hand is not yours to promise. He is not even suitable, nor is he worthy.' I moved closer to Father and almost spat through my teeth. 'I will not be married again because you think marriage a *suitable* state for me.'

'Why did I breed such a wayward daughter? I pray daily that Joan has more sense.'

'Do not wed her off to Master Northleach either. She can do better when her time comes.'

I swept around to the chests that stood waiting in my hall and using the keys hanging from my belt, locked them.

Glancing up at Father who was still hovering about me, I said, 'Thank you for helping me purchase more cloth, and arranging inns for us, Father. I shall repay it all.'

The Northampton fair was as bustling as I had hoped. It was already busy as we rolled and clip-clopped through the busy narrow streets, under the overhangs of houses that stretched three and four storeys towards the sky that often was hardly visible. We took up residence at the Swan Inn. I was pleased to see that here Father, who was known in Northampton, had procured the best chamber available for myself and Meg, and a room for Smith and the apprentices. The guards slept in the carts in the stable and did not complain.

On the first day, I focused on selling the last of my woollen cloth, and on the second purchasing cloth. With Smith's help we accumulated valuable new draperies such as frisadoes, serges and bayes. I had enough and now all I needed to add was trims for gowns, sleeves and cloaks and anything else I thought I could afford.

Our last day dawned bright and chill with pink-edged clouds. Meg happily remained at the Swan with our guards and a wagon already packed with goods. We took one of the wagons and a gelding called Midnight, as dark a horse as his name suggested, and he was, as we discovered that day, black in nature as well as shade. I patted Bella, my grey palfrey, and gave her a windfall apple to munch. She nuzzled my hand and looked up at me with great, pleading eyes. 'Never mind, Bella,' I said. 'We shall be cantering south tomorrow. You'll get plenty of exercise then.'

We set out back to the Swan that evening, satisfied with our final purchases and, knowing the town better now, chose a shorter route that cut through a narrow cobbled lane behind the cloth hall. My apprentices were laden down with packages of velvet and satin trimmings. They trailed behind me while Smith wearily led Midnight, our frisky cart horse, forward.

'We have done well, Smith,' I called over to him as we turned into a dim, silent street, far from the bustle of the market.

'Aye, Mistress, we have,' he said. 'But did you really need the painted cloth?'

'Oh, yes,' I said with enthusiasm. 'The King's roses. An excellent purchase.' The roll of painted cloth, now tucked safely inside the covered wagon beside rolls of ordinary woollen fabric and ells of various new draperies, was decorated with tiny Tudor roses, an attractive, loyal pattern that might sell to one of Queen Catherine's ladies, or even to the Queen herself. I wondered if I needed sell it at all. It would brighten up my Wood Street parlour, and sweep away those gloomy lingering memories of Tom Williams' coffin which had sat there for three long days in June.

'We shall sell that, if not here, then to a Flanders merchant. They like painted cloth there, I hear.' As I spoke, I wistfully thought of one such merchant whom I feared was long lost to us but whom I hoped to find again.

'Mistress, it would be wise to sell it, though I noticed how much you like that cloth.'

'I do, Master Gerard. I very much like it.'

We were quite close to the inn when a gang of fast-moving apprentice boys came hurtling towards us. They appeared through a narrow arched entrance that led into a churchyard. My two apprentice boys shouted at them to stop. Midnight bellowed as Smith pulled hard on his reins, trying to avoid them.

They did not slow down. I moved into the side of

97

the lane, near Smith who had drawn the cart over to the side closest to the churchyard. I thought that that the youths only wanted passage along the street, not realising that the shouting, carousing band would deliberately barrel into my apprentice boys.

It happened quickly, like a sudden ice storm crashing down on us. Veering to the side the fast-moving gang knocked into Barnaby and Wilfrid, shoving them to the ground, so that our valuable linen-wrapped packages dropped and scattered over the cobbles. Several parcels burst open, disgorging precious gold threads, velvet ribbons, furs, and swatches of satin and silk. The band of youths stopped and laughed. My boys yelled curses up at them as they tried to scrabble for their broken packages.

Horrified, I stumbled forward, as Barnaby reached up and warned, 'Mistress, stay back.' Smith, who was trying to calm the rearing Midnight, swivelled about this way and that, tugging at the horse's bridle. He shouted, 'Get over by the wall, Mistress, lest the horse bolts.' The horse was pulling at him rather than the other way round. Then Midnight leapt up with a huge roar! I screamed and ran for the wall.

The gang jumped about like demons, deliberately and viciously causing havoc. There were six of them. We were outnumbered. One lad, taking advantage of the chaos, reached down, grabbed for the contents of an opened parcel, and stuffed its rich pickings into his jerkin. Barnaby attempted to scramble to his feet but slipped back again. Wilfrid was already up and shouting at two of the attackers who, following the other's lead, grabbed what trimmings they could shoved their gains into their clothing. All the while, they laughed wildly at my apprentices, jeering and provoking. 'Come on,' one taunted Wilfrid, raising his fists, prancing jerkily around my apprentice like a puppet disconnected from its cords. Wilfrid wielded a punch and brought the taunting lad down close to my feet.

I began to move forward, yelling for help.

Another apprentice appeared from the churchyard and flashed a knife in Wilfrid's direction. He whipped past me. I froze on the spot. Smith desperately held onto Midnight and called out above the taunts and the horse's neighing, 'Watch your back, Wilfrid.'

Barnaby managed to get to his feet and knock Wilfrid out of the way of the knife's thrust. It all happened as quickly as horsemen could gallop through a broken gateway after a siege.

The assailant raised the knife again. It glinted in the moonlight. I shouted, 'Look out.' But Barnaby fell back onto the ground with a thump, a steam of blood pouring from his head, having saved his friend only to be attacked himself. More knives were out, long sharp steel blades ready to do murder. Another assailant struck out, wounding Wilfrid in his hand. He began to dance around him, goading him to fight back, the raised knife teasing and taunting.

I screamed, 'Murder,' and, finding my legs could move, and my feet gain purchase on the slippery, muddy ground, I ran to Barnaby. One of the attackers knocked me to the ground. I crawled through the dirt and leaned back against the wall, winded. Clutching his damaged arm in his good hand, Wilfrid backed towards the cart where Smith was still unsuccessfully trying to control the horse. It reared up again with a great whinny, this time almost overturning the wagon.

Smith attempted to hold the horse's rope firm,

quieten Midnight, right the wagon and shout for help all at the same time. For a moment, my mouth closed and I looked on the scene as if it was a dream, bruised and frozen like an effigy in a church. I gathered my wits and rose to my feet. I tried to get to Barnaby again. I stumbled and fell again. Why had I worn such a cumbersome cloak? We were going to die in Northampton, in a lonely street behind the cloth hall. We needed our guards. Father was right. What had I been thinking of ordering them *all* to stay at the inn with Meg to guard the fabrics we had bought in the days before?

The attackers laughed at us. Four of them began to calmly gather up the spoils while the two others turning around, back to back, in a co-ordinated move, flashed their knives fearlessly at Smith, Midnight and Wilfrid in turn. Though the horse appeared momentarily calmer, Smith could not let him go.

The cloth hall's back door swung open. A large cloaked figure exited. He raced along the cobbles, waving a long sword and shouting like a berserker from ancient times, One of the assailants spun round to face him but the cloaked person pricked him with his short sword, kicked him in the knees, and in a flowing movement brought him to the ground. He held him down, the point of his sword against the youth's throat. I whispered thanks to the Virgin Mary whose blue-clad image rose out of the shadows on the wall by the church doorway. This dark-cloaked man was solid, tall and he was our rescuer.

'Jacob,' our saviour called over his shoulder as another tall figure emerged from the cloth hall, followed by a band of cloth men carrying short swords or cudgels. Outnumbered, the gang fled with ribbons and braid dropping in their wake. Racing past me, they flew along the cobbles into the churchyard, littering their way with my velvet trims as they raced around the squat church.

I found myself on the ground again, back leaning against the wall.

Our cloaked rescuer raced after them and caught one of them. His companions pursued the others around the church. He yanked the boy he held to his feet.

'Jack, take this creature into the Cloth Hall,' he shouted over to a large man dressed in a smith's apron who was helping Smith to steady Midnight. 'Send for the constable. He intended murder.' The lad yelped and protested his innocence. 'Shut your trap or I'll shut it for you,' the cloaked man clutched the lad with one hand and in a threatening manner lifted his sword with the other. The boy cowered.

'Aye, and the others?' said Jack.

'They'll be lucky to catch them.' He shook the lad. 'Take him inside and make him talk, Jack.'

As Jack dragged the yelping lad off, our rescuer hurried over the cobbles towards me. I looked up at him, tears streaming down my face. There was surprise and concern in his eyes.

'Mistress Williams? Can it really be you?' He pulled out a handkerchief from his cloak purse. He gently smoothed down my cloak and handed me the cloth. 'Here, take it, Mistress Elizabeth. I'll see to your boy. He is badly wounded.'

As he lifted me up, my legs began folding under me and I couldn't speak. I was baffled. Thomas Cromwell was our rescuer, a saviour sent by God to us. He steadied me and walked me the few steps to a stone bench inside the church yard. 'Sit. I'll help your people. Those little bastards were very quick, a ruthless gang. An alley beyond the church leads out of the town by a small postern gate. The river bank is thick with reeds. They'll be running through those down to a skiff and off before we can draw breath. With luck, the men who followed me out will catch them. They are armed. If those lads put up a fight, they are dead.'

I whispered, 'Why, for a few ribbons?'

'Even ribbons have a price. Now, take deep breaths.'

He hurried over to Barnaby who lay on his back, still and pale like a corpse. Wilfrid sank beside Barnaby, clutching his injured hand. I felt my breath become even again and rose to my feet again. I began to make my way towards them. Smith detached Midnight from the wagon and drew him up the street to the Cloth Hall, where he threw the rope around a hitching post beside the open door. Though Midnight continued to skitter about and whinny, he stopped rearing up.

'Steady now, boy,' Smith said softly, patting him. He left the horse and hurried to Barnaby's side.

But it was Thomas Cromwell who took charge of the broken boy. He listened to his chest. Whipping off his cloak, he wrapped Barnaby in it. He looked up and said, 'He'll live, but only if I get him to the Hospital of St John the Baptist.'

Wilfred was now on his feet again, collecting up broken parcels with his good hand, blood seeping into the linen wrappings. 'Leave them,' I shouted. Wilfrid dropped the parcels and limped over to Smith.

'I've seen you before.' Smith said to Master

Cromwell. He whistled through his teeth. 'At Master's funeral, and with the cloth we sold you. Will the boy live?'

Master Cromwell nodded. 'We'll see, Master Gerard. Take his head, cup your hands under it and hold it still as I lift him, very still. I'll take him. I'll bring him to the monks of St John. I have seen men die from a knock on the head such as this.'

Smith helped to place the unconscious Barnaby into Cromwell's solid arms. I felt helpless but I was not going to leave Barnaby. I was going to wherever Thomas Cromwell was taking him.

Cromwell commanded Smith, 'Guide your mistress and the other boy to the inn. Is it the Swan?'

'Yes, it's not far,' Smith said.

'Barnaby is my responsibility, I must come too.' When Smith hesitated, I added firmly, 'Master Gerard, gather what you can of my parcels and help Wilfrid back. Tell Meg to wash his hand. There is powder of willow bark in her satchel. Go.'

'Hurry, Mistress Elizabeth,' Thomas Cromwell was saying, urgency seeping into his voice. 'We must, if we are to save him.'

I was sure that The Hospital of St John the Baptist was close because I had noticed its arched main entrance as we had entered the town several days earlier. Setting off along the lane in the direction we had come from earlier, we followed yet another narrow dark alley and walked as fast as was possible. Master Cromwell was burdened with Barnaby's dead weight in his arms. He stopped at a small low door, half-opened onto the street, one of several mysterious, almost concealed entrances into the church of John the Baptist. 'The hospital lies behind,' he said.

I nodded. Barnaby never stirred.

We passed into the church's nave and through a quiet chapel into an alms house. Inmates glided past us wearing plain undyed woollen robes with black crosses stitched on their breasts. They bowed their heads respectfully.

It was so hushed, I thought I dare not speak. When Thomas Cromwell asked a friar for the Master and for a cot for Barnaby, the friar nodded and pointed across the hall to an arched doorway that led to the infirmary. 'Follow me,' he said softly.

We entered a long room with cots on which bodies lay. I could not discern if they were male or female or both. Some slept. Others started and mumbled words at us as we passed. The friar led us to an unoccupied mattress at the end of this hall. Thomas laid Barnaby on top of the bed's rough sheet and sent the friar for the master.

All around us were snores, moans, and groans. Now we had paused, I could smell excrement and the staleness of unwashed bodies. I did not want to leave Barnaby in this place and, once the friar had hurried away, I said, 'We can't leave him here. It is foul.'

'I know, but the master surgeon here is known for his skill with medicine, especially broken bones.'

As we waited, a large candle clock at our end of the hall marked the hours. It burned down a half notch before we observed the hospital's master apothecary, who was also a surgeon, enter the chamber. He approached us slowly, moving through the air as if he were an apparition and not a man. The atmosphere in the hall stilled as he appeared. He was a tall man in a white friar's habit, on which was stitched a large black cross. My sharp eye for fabrics noticed that his habit, unlike those that clothed the attendant friars and servants, was of the finest wool. On reaching us, he bowed and spoke quietly to Thomas, who gesturing towards Barnaby, explained what had happened.

'Mistress,' the surgeon said to me, with calm authority, after Thomas' exposition, 'we shall do what we can. First, I must stop pressure gathering in the head.'

He bent over Barnaby's prostrate form and lifted his eyelids, poked and prodded him. Barnaby breathed but never stirred. An assistant friar stood by with a reed basket that held various oddly shaped clay vessels. The surgeon selected several of these along with a cup. He placed them on the bench and gave the servant another instruction. Reaching into the basket again, the assistant selected a sharp instrument that looked like some sort of drill. When I realised what he was planning to do, I felt the blood drain from my face. Thomas caught me as I fell to the floor.

'Elizabeth, the surgeon of St John the Baptist is skilled. He will save the boy's life. Come away until it is done. There is a cloister outside that leads back into the chapel. We'll wait there.'

The surgeon glanced up at me and called for another friar to take us back to the chapel.

'The boy's heart is strong. He will live,' he said 'Leave him with me and pray for his recovery.'

'His name is Barnaby,' I said. 'Save him, Master Apothecary, and I promise you that I shall send your hospital a gift on this very day every year for the rest of my life.'

The master looked up at me. 'I said I would save him and I shall. By the morrow he will be recovering well. St Cecilia will be watching over him, I promise. Now go and pray for Barnaby's fast recovery.'

I realised as he referred to the saint which day the morrow was. It was St Cecilia's Day, the day on which four years earlier I had married Tom Williams, only two days before my name day. How strange, I reflected, as we left the hospital and entered the church's nave, that I was here, in this place, with Thomas Cromwell and my apprentice, on the eve of that anniversary.

I sank to my knees in the side chapel dedicated to the Virgin which the friar had led us to and prayed for Barnaby, counting the rosary beads that dangled from my waist. I repeated Pater Noster after Pater Noster and whispered prayers of my own. The gentle rhythm of counting calmed me. I paused, opened my eyes and glanced sideways, assuming that Thomas Cromwell was praying too, but he wasn't. His soft, brown-rimmed grey eyes were resting on my face. He was studying me..

He touched my arm, a feather-light touch. 'Forgive me, Mistress Elizabeth; excuse my boldness but your profile is one that the Antwerp artists would long to paint.' He reached his hand up and gently turned my face towards his. 'And, if I were a painter I would want to paint you as the Lady Mary up there.' He glanced up at the statue above us. 'At rest your face is perfectly serene, beautiful, and I had no idea of it before.'

I did not feel at all serene. 'You hardly know me, Master Cromwell,' I whispered. I held my breath and dropped my rosary. It clattered onto the tiles but I didn't stoop to retrieve it. Words came tumbling from my mouth. 'But, no one has ever called me beautiful before. Sir, you honour me. I do not deserve such.'

'Not even your husband? Surely he considered you so.' I glanced down at my hands and shook my head. He continued, 'Your face belongs to an intelligent woman. You said your own prayer. I can only suppose it comes from your heart, as, indeed, a prayer ought.'

I inclined my head. 'No, I should say the appropriate prayers from my book of the hours but I don't have it with me.'

'None the less, God will listen.'

At that, I stared up at him. In the candlelight his face was roguish and full of mischief. He reached out for my hand. I found myself slipping it into his. 'Just as a crimson underskirt is forgivable,' he whispered into my ear, 'so is much else about you.' He bent down, scooped up my rosary from the tiles and folded it into my hands. The jet beads gleamed in the candlelight.

The chapel door squeaked open. I peered over my shoulder. One of the pale-gowned friars was gliding towards us along the Nave, carrying a lamp. I released my hand and stood up, crossing myself. Thomas, following my lead, crossed himself decorously and stood by my side. As the friar came closer I saw that he was smiling.

'Good news. The boy is weak but he shall recover in the prior's house. It is pleasant. Come, I shall take you back.'

My face, I knew, showed my relief.

We entered a low thatched building close to the church and I saw that it resembled an old manor house, not unlike Father's house in Putney. We sat on a bench beside the central hearth in the hall. There, we waited until the master surgeon slipped out from behind a screen at the end of the room.

'You may see the boy now. He is sleeping but he will recover well. A fortnight here and your apprentice will be fit again.'

A fortnight was a long time to wait in Northampton.

As if he read my thoughts, Thomas laid his hand on my arm. 'Do not worry, Mistress Elizabeth. Barnaby can travel back to London with Jack and myself. He will be well-cared for by my servants. I have legal work here for the Merchant Adventurers. I am lodging at the Guild Hall, where Barnaby will be comfortable until our return to London.'

I thanked Thomas Cromwell, saying, 'I can never return your kindness.'

'No need. Seeing that you are reassured is enough.'

After we were satisfied that Barnaby was comfortable, Thomas Cromwell escorted me back to The Swan, the kindly friar walking in front of us carrying his lantern. I felt shy because of his words in the church and some unspoken sense that the air around us had subtly shifted, so never spoke, and for the most part we walked quietly together, encircled by the night's hush. When we reached the inn a torch was burning comfortingly in my chamber, directly above the street. I pointed up to it. 'Meg has waited up for me.'

'The best chamber, I see, Mistress Elizabeth.'

'Yes, Master Thomas, Father organised it.'

'He should, 'Thomas said. 'If he has a care for you.' He glanced down as I placed my foot on the outside staircase that led up to my chamber. 'No crimson petticoat today?' he added, a mischievous smile playing about his mouth.

108

'No, not today.'

He said softly, 'Goodnight, Elizabeth.' He lifted my gloved hand to his lips and lightly kissed it. I felt a tingle in my fingers as he released my hand. He moved back into the shadows to join the friar who waited to light his way home.

Meg had already opened the door from our chamber. I glanced over my shoulder. 'Goodnight,' I called to Thomas Cromwell's retreating back. He raised his hand and moved off into the night.

Chapter Eleven

THE RETURN JOURNEY TO London was uneventful, three nights of clip-clopping along Watling Street, bedding down in monastery rooms as we had on the way, glad that the weather remained crisp and fine. In the morning frost ferns edged the glass in my chamber windows but the frost did not lie.

I did not miss the secret smiles between Meg and Smith. She had tended to Wilfrid's wounds and, of course, he wanted to talk of his bravery and the attack to any who would listen. We were glad, at last, we trundled into the yard behind my house. The sad remnants of the small warehouse remained, since there was no money spare to rebuild it yet, so the cloth was all stored inside my house.

After a long day recording the newly purchased cloth in a ledger, I organised my stock anywhere I could, mostly above me in the attics where the apprentices could keep watch over it. I needed my bed. That first night of our return, thankful to be home, I climbed up onto my goose feather mattress, pulled the counterpane up to my chin, longing for rest and easy dreams, satisfied that I had arrived back in Wood Street with new cloth and without further misadventure.

A pounding on the outside door put paid to my rest. Hearing the porter draw back the hall door's enormous bolts, I climbed out of bed again, lifted my cloak off its hook, grasped hold of my night lantern, and opened my chamber door a crack. There were voices below in the hall. I slipped out and listened at the top of the stairway. I could not recognise them immediately, nor could I make out what was being said.

Before we had set off for Northampton, I had asked for a spy window to be inserted into the hall door. The servant on night duty was instructed to lift this up before opening my latches, yet tonight he had apparently allowed a stranger in.

Ducking back inside my chamber, I slipped a sharp dagger from below my pillow into my mantle pocket and lifted a lantern we kept lit just outside in the passage way. I heard the door below creak closed. I hurried down the stairway into the hall and threaded my way through my sleeping servants to the hall door. Just inside the porch, in a pool of weak rushlight, two of my servants were bending over a collapsing man who was gasping for breath.

'Fetch the mistress,' the door porter was saying. 'She will want to deal with this so-called knight, this traitor. He won't escape this time.'

There was a yelp from below a thatch of bright hair.

'She's here,' I said, lifting my lantern higher. 'What is going on?'

The figure groaned and looked up at me.

'Mistress, have pity,' he gasped before I could speak again and I knew that voice.

The porter had him by the shirt collar and was shaking him like a drowned water rat. 'Stop that, Dicken,' I ordered. 'You don't need to shake him.'

It was young Toby; not the handsome sword-waving Toby I had once known but a sad, bruised-face reflection of that boy. Though in my heart I knew he was not responsible for the Midsummer's Eve fire, I was as

111

furious as my servants that he could just turn up like this. He was in a terrible state but pity departed me and I accused him. 'My warehouse burned down and you have the nerve to return here. Were you responsible? Many think it *was* you, Toby.'

'Answer the mistress.' Another shake from Dicken.

Toby groaned, 'No, no, Mistress. It was not me. I did not cause the fire.'

'Did you not, Toby? It has taken you long enough to explain. Why should I listen to you now? You never raised the alarm and you ran away. You were our sword and you fled. You claimed to be a knight's son, a scion of the great de Bohun family.' I snorted. 'A true knight's son has courage. You possess none.'

The servant holding him shook him, emitting a growl like a hound with its parry, cruel and fearsome. 'Noble family, by the saints, 'tis a lie. What are we to do with him, Mistress? Send for the constable?'

I lifted my lantern higher. Toby's face was badly bruised, his left eye swollen. Something bad had occurred to bring him back on a freezing November night and I wanted to know what. I needed to discover what had occurred on the night of the fire. I recollected the shadowed man of that evening and the veiled threat. 'Bring him into my parlour before the whole house awakens. Fetch Meg. He's hurt. Before we call the constable, I want to find out the truth of what happened that night.' Already the sleeping servants were awake and mumbling.

'Go back to sleep,' I ordered. The four hall servants fell back onto their pallets again.

Toby was clearly very frightened. Blood had seeped through his tunic sleeve. He kept glancing over his shoulder as if there was a pursuit, even though the door was closed and bolted again. We bundled him into the parlour through the hall's side door. 'Tell Meg to fetch food. He looks half-starved, and bring me lavender water and cloth.' I almost felt sorry for Toby. Was he guilty? I still thought not. The servant hurried upstairs to the miniscule closet beside my chamber where Meg was, I suspected, exhausted after our journey and sleeping the sleep of the departed.

The lad slumped onto the settle by the dying fire, trembling with fear and shivering with cold. I threw a blanket around him then knelt by the fire and blew on the embers, coaxing it to flame and carefully adding kindling stick by stick from the hearth box. Toby never spoke. Soon, Dicken returned with water and cloth. 'Mistress Meg is on her way,' he said, taking a moment to glare at Toby.

'We near burned into cinders that night,' he spat. 'Because of you. You are only good for chains and a fire about you scorching as Hell. No mercy!'

'That's quite enough, Dicken.'

At least the fire had revived and now it burned merrily.

'Go then, Dicken, and make sure the door is bolted. Let no one else over my threshold tonight.'

Dicken scuttled off. 'He is dangerous, Mistress,' he threw back at me.

I lifted away the blanket, made Toby remove his filthy tunic and dabbed at his wounds with the soothing water. He bore my ministrations bravely. What was it about me that attracted overt malevolence to the boys in my service?

'They are flesh wounds and bruises,' I said as I wound a linen bandage around his injured arm. 'Nothing is broken. You have explaining to do.'

'I know,' he whispered.

I took the chair that had been my husband's and sat

down utterly exhausted. 'Talk.'

'Mistress, it was not me who torched the warehouse.'

'If not you, who was it? You were supposed to watch out for danger.'

This was followed by a rush of tears but I refused to be moved by them. 'Toby, where have you been?' I said sternly.

He shook his head, wiped his eyes and swallowed. 'South of the river. I was frightened so I ran, Mistress. I ran away because they were going to murder me. It was me they wanted, not the warehouse. The fire was an accident.' He took a long breath.

'I need to understand what happened. Who are they? Did you carelessly cause the fire, knock over a lantern?'

'No, I did not. They had been carrying torches. One was knocked over when they tried to hold me down and take my sword. Everything caught fire at once.'

'Who were they?'

'Mistress, they were holding on to me. I know not who they were but they called me a catamite, which I am not.' He paused. I crossed myself. 'They said they would take away my manhood and feed it to their dogs. They said they would gut me. When flames rose they never tried to kick them out. They dragged me out into the yard with them. There was then an explosion inside the warehouse and they loosened their hold on me. The explosion saved me. I shook them off and ran through the opened gate into the alley. I ran and ran until I found myself a hiding place in a backyard stable.' He stopped again.

'Go on,' I said, terrified now myself. Whoever they were they were out there, possibly watching my house, watching out for Toby. I needed to know the rest. I needed to know whether I was placed in danger too.

He swallowed and continued. 'I hid there until

daylight. I crossed the big bridge. I've been hiding in Southwark since, with the prostitutes, begging food, sweeping floor straw like I did before. I am no catamite.'

My hand flew to my mouth. But my husband had been... Would this secret never go away? Not even our servants knew what Tom Williams was. Again, I remembered the shadowy person who had whispered in my ear on the night of the fire. As Toby paused his tale, I found myself drawing my cloak protectively about me. Toby may not have been a catamite but they thought he was. They had attacked the wrong person because Toby was not my husband's lover. That person had never lived here. I never saw him, but I had known of him. He was a nobleman who lived at court and I had hated the way he had corrupted my husband years before we had wed. I did not want to know his name. It would bring accompanying shame to me. Tom's lover was powerful. Mine was a sham marriage but I could tell no one this. I could only pray to St Elizabeth to intercede to God for my soul's safety because of my concealment of this truth. I could only pray for forgiveness for my husband's sin. Even now I was guilty of harbouring this hideous sin and secret, because none of it must get about or I would be ruined. Toby was innocent but no one would believe him. My husband had taken such care of his secret life and was so protected by his noble lover that even Toby did not know the truth. I crossed myself again and said as evenly as I could, 'Why return here now?'

'Look at me, Mistress,' Toby was saying. 'I throw myself on your mercy. I upset a customer. He wanted what I would not give and when I refused he drew a knife, beat me and cut me. I have no food, nothing and I have nowhere else to go.'

'You ran away from us, Toby, and expect my protection?'

'I was outnumbered, Mistress Williams.'

I heard the door open. Meg appeared in the doorway, wrapped in her mantle, carrying ale and a bowl of last night's gruel. 'What is *he* doing here?' she said and shoved the bowl into his hands. She made to turn on her heel.

I lifted my hand to stop her. 'No, stay, Meg.' I sighed. We were going to have to do something about him. 'I don't want him upsetting my household. I have heard his tale and I don't want him turned away.'

Meg glared at him. 'A sorry night this is when he who is so cowardly that he betrays those who feed him comes back to cause trouble.'

I turned to Toby. 'The constable has searched throughout the Cripplegate Ward for you.' I shook my head and angrily folded my arms. 'Eat, Toby. I shall tell you what is going to happen.'

Meg tossed a log on the reviving fire and it blazed up. Toby gulped his food down as I thought of what to do with him. If the servants did not know already that he had returned, they would soon enough. Toby's story must not become servants' gossip.

'Did you see anything of those who attacked you that night, Toby? Features, height, clothing?'

He hung his head over his plate. 'One had a jagged scar on his face. It ran from his left ear down to his chin. I smelled his perfume too. It was expensive for I know it. I have smelled it in Church, the incense, I mean, the Frankincense.' He shuddered and I felt sorry for him.

'And?' I spoke quietly.

'Another had no hair on his head and he had eyes that

116

bulged out. He was the one who pulled my sword from me. He was strong.'

'How many?'

'Three, all cloaked. The third - I don't know. I never saw him. Good cloaks. Good weave; one was brown with velvet trim. The third I just don't much remember. He was small but sturdy.'

'Not poor then,' I said thoughtfully.

'No,' Toby said. 'Of middling height - strong too. I don't know who those men were - and I never want to see them again.'

'Where do your family dwell? My husband said you had been a ward and that you ran away. Are you really a knight's son?'

'A poor knight's son. Lincoln. They have a manor there. We dwell on De Bohun land. They are relatives, distant, though I bear the name, my father's name too.' He hung his head. 'Wrong side of the blanket, long ago.'

'Then you will return to Lincoln, as soon as I can arrange it, and never will you return.'

I turned to Meg who was standing beside me with her arms folded. She wore a fearsome look on her face. Her uncovered head was a wild mass of curls. 'Meg, tell Cook Toby is to sleep in the kitchen. He does not allow himself to be seen outside this house. We can tell the servants that he was frightened and not responsible for the fire. He ran away because he was attacked and fearful. Mostly this is true.'

I turned back to Toby. 'I do not think you were responsible for the fire, nor do I think that we shall get justice either for you. You can stay here until I can arrange your departure. It must be soon. You saw tonight what Dicken intends, given a chance.'

'To turn me over to the constables.' He sighed. 'Thank

you, Mistress.' After a moment's thought, his eyes filled with tears. 'My family won't want me either.'

'You *will* go to them none the less or I shall give you over to Dicken's kind of justice. I shall provide you with a purse of coins and a set of fresh clothes. As to what you say to them or how you behave with them, well, Toby, that is for you to decide over the coming few days.

Chapter Twelve

Springtime of the previous year

I COULD NOT FORGIVE TOM Williams for his betrayal of our marriage in such a sinful manner, but I had discovered a sense of repose in his Wood Street house. His mother had died from the sweating sickness in the spring of 1511 and, after her death, I was in charge of the day-to-day affairs of our household. I smiled at the merchants' wives, helped his father, kept the cloth ledgers for Tom and attended to business when he was away. Before Christmastide that year Richard Williams, too, sickened and died of the bloody flux. His death had caused me sadness, since I had grown fond of my father-in-law. I had nursed him and through his recent illness I had prayed hard to Our Lady for his recovery. My prayers were to no avail. In the end, his death was a relief because it ended his suffering.

Spring winds had blown the day Tom had brought Toby to our house, the sort of wind that rattles the window panes, that makes you glad to be inside and which promises to blow away the chill of winter frost and the endless fasting of Lent.

I sat in my parlour by the fire embroidering purple daisies on a napkin. My hands had constantly sought occupation since we had buried my husband's father just before Christmastide.

That winter, my husband had been excused his yeoman

119

duty so that he could put his business affairs in order. In the space of a year he had lost both mother and father. He had worked hard and purchased new cloth. Despite my anger at him, I admired this. Time was running out and he was anxious to return to his duties by Eastertide.

It was at this time that he employed Gerard Smith as his right-hand man. The apprentices liked Smith. They respected and looked up to him because he was already a journeyman. Although I kept the books, once Tom employed Gerard Smith, I had a little more time for myself. I did not have to nurse an aged father-in-law anymore, nor did I expect any more additions to our household. I was right on the first count and wrong about the second.

'Lizzy,' my husband blithely called through the parlour door that March afternoon, 'come and meet Toby, for he is as good with a sword as I, a young nobleman, no less, though without money to purchase steed or patron. When I return to my duties, Toby will guard the warehouse and run our errands. He's helping me with a roll of painted cloth right now. Come and see it, my dear. Do come and meet him.'

What now, I thought, feeling irritated, though I had no right to be annoyed; we needed a watch man, but what good would an impoverished nobleman be to us? We were cloth merchants. I tucked my petulance away, folded my sewing into my work basket, placed it on the shelf and followed Tom into the hall.

First of all, I noticed the gorgeous painted fabric, half-unrolled on the trestle, all silvered stars. Then my eyes beheld the golden-headed vision that was Toby.

The cloth that lay on the large trestle in the hall was the same starry fabric that I took to the Prior of Austin

120

Friars the following September. The fair-haired, blue-eyed, handsome youth of less than sixteen years was unrolling it. I beheld the loveliness of a night sky unfold as a beautiful boy solemnly opened it up. The lad was as lovely as the painted cloth. He wore a faded tunic and a gambeson. His impoverished state did not detract from his beauty and his wide eyes. I sighed to myself thinking, will I have to share my home with a new lover of my husband's? It must not be. If he dared this, I would make a great fuss. I would return to my father's house, no doubt never to wed again. If my husband kept his secret life away from me at least I could pretend a half-lived life, though I feared for my soul and for his. Yet, when Toby bowed low and smiled a genuine and very charming smile at me, and fetched me a padded stool to sit upon, I was almost won over by his manners - but not quite, not yet.

'The cloth is beautiful,' I said, trying not to be distracted by the boy's angelic face. 'Where shall we sell it?'

'One of the monasteries we sell woollen cloth to in autumn - you know, the wool for their novice's new habits. This painted cloth, the prior and his friars will like. They might use it as a hanging for the Christmastide plays.' Tom and Toby began to roll the cloth away. 'You are right, Elizabeth, it is very fine.' He turned to Toby. 'Now, since you are to stay, I shall introduce you to Master Smith, my journeyman.'

I returned to the parlour but could not concentrate on my sewing. My needle stabbed me and the daisies came out wrong and had to be unpicked. I kept wondering if the handsome youth was about to replace my husband's friend. When our supper of cheese and bread and buttermilk was served in the hall that evening, I noticed my husband smiling at Toby. The candlelight emphasised the boy's beauty and his young skin glowed. No, I thought, he must go. We are undone if this boy stays.

'He is not staying,' I told my husband later that evening in the privacy of the bedchamber he occupied, the one opposite my own, his clothing pole filled with beautiful, expensive garments; fancy hats stored with gorgeous shoes in his coffers. 'I will not permit such danger here. You sin, husband, but you will not bring this sin into our house.'

Tom Williams folded my hands into his own and held my look with earnest blue eyes. 'Elizabeth, Toby is not my lover, nor will he ever be so. I plighted my troth long ago to another.'

'And not me,' I muttered angrily.

'Oh, Elizabeth, I will say it over and over - I care for you deeply. You are my wife. I am not a true husband to you, and shall not pretend it is so, but I would never put our lives in jeopardy. Never, my dear, my sweet Lizzy. Understand this. You have given me your trust, and I care for you more than my life. I would give you children if you would let me.'

I bowed my head because he meant those words. It was I who had insisted that he moved into the chamber across the narrow passageway, and I certainly did not want him to share that other chamber with another, not Toby, not anyone. Nor did I wish to share my cold bed with Tom Williams either. I did not want his children. I did not want him. I remained his wife because I had no choice as I saw it. Disgrace was worse than an endangered soul. I often spent hours on my knees before the statue of the Virgin in St Alban's Church, begging intercession for my concealment and forgiveness for his sin, for his soul, praying that he would change his nature.

I said bitterly, 'I should never have wed with you, Tom Williams, but I shall keep your secret, just never bring it here to our home.' I turned to go, but stopped. 'Toby will bring trouble to this house. Send him away.'

'Listen.' He pulled me back and folded me close to his breast. He gently stroked my loosened hair - for he was a very gentle man - and whispered into my ear, 'Toby is not a threat to you or to me. You know I have long known another. We accept that our marriage is an arrangement, but, as I have often said, if you can share me, I am still willing to woo you. You never have allowed me this. Any time I made an advance you have shunned me, even when we shared a bed, and I would never force you.'

I pulled away from him. 'I cannot share you. I won't share you. Let it be enough that I keep your secret, that I have kept it for years from your mother and your father and from the servants. No one knows. They consider me barren,' I said bitterly. 'They pity me. Let it be so,' I said bitterly. 'They think I spend so much time on my knees because I pray for a child, but it is because I pray for your soul.'

He sank down onto his clothing coffer, his eyes brimming tears. I stared back at him. Our wedding night had been a disaster. I was a virgin before it and I remained so now. How could I allow him intimacy knowing what I had recognised on our wedding night, and on hearing the distraught confession he had whispered in my ear several nights later. He said then that he would never lie to me and he never had. That took courage, for the Church would condemn him as a heretic. He went against God's laws, and was neither holy nor pure. Some may ignore this unnatural state, but if he was discovered by priests such as the righteous Dominicans he would be castrated and executed. He was unnatural, Leviticus said so, but

Tom opined that that his love should neither be a questioned nor a judged matter.

He reached out to me again. 'Forgive me, Elizabeth. Forgive me, and let us make a child together.'

I shook my head. 'No, I prefer to be considered barren.'

'The Church would approve of a child.'

I, who had never wanted to wed and have children, often felt the loss now that I was married. Yet, I would not make one with Tom Williams. I doubted he was capable of the deed with me, as our marriage night had proved. How could I bear any renewed attempt with him, his awkwardness and fumbling? I shook my head and felt tears gather behind my eyes.

I recovered my equilibrium and said, turning back to face him, 'Where did you find Toby? Why is he here?'

'I was south of the river today delivering cloth to Mistress Worth. As you know, she has bought yellow wool for dresses for her girls, her geese, from us. Toby was employed sweeping floors. We fell to conversation. When I discovered that his father was a knight up in Lincoln and that he had run away, I could not leave him to a life of drudgery in Mistress Worth's stew pot. He is only fifteen but trained with a sword.'

I conceded. 'If I keep him, he must behave.'

'The maids will all love him. Give him a chance, Elizabeth. He is of no interest to me, not in that way.'

'I believe you, Tom,' I said after a long silence. 'He may stay, but if he is trouble you must return him to Mistress Worth.' I turned my back on him, closed the door and stepped into the narrow corridor between our chambers, shutting him out.

Tom was right and I was wrong.

Toby slept with the apprentices in a chamber attached

124

to the warehouse. They liked him. He performed sword tricks for them and fenced with Tom when he wanted to practice his own skills. Even so, Toby did not seem much of a guard to me. He simply was not much of a threat to anyone and was more useful chopping wood and running messages, mostly for Tom. He knew the City well.

The maids adored Toby from the moment of his arrival. Who would not? A painter's brush could not do him justice. Our slim young watchman had singular beauty. His face had perfect contours. He possessed wide, forget-me-not blue, dancing eyes, a straight nose, broad cheekbones and full red lips. Toby was petted and fawned upon by all and soon absorbed into my household. I, too, was glad of his antics, jokes and stories and, in time, he won me over with charm, manners and courtesies. That May he turned sixteen and on his name day we gave him a small celebration and a new jerkin, cloak and hose.

I was right. Toby had brought us trouble, though not of his own making. Someone had suspected the truth about my husband, and decided that Toby had similar desires. He could not stay.

Chapter Thirteen

1513

I CALLED MY SERVANTS together and informed them
that Toby was not responsible for the fire, inventing
a story about a feud that had existed in his past
before he had come into our household. He had been
attacked in June and attacked again last night. He
was guilty of not returning to us before but he had
been terrified. Since he was still in grave danger, he
would soon be leaving the household. I requested
their silence and expected their loyalty. Gerard Smith
glared at me when I made this pronouncement. He
told me that I should have turned Toby out but I said,
'No, I cannot.' Meg shook her head, glancing at
Smith as she did.

I knew the wisdom of my journeyman's concern
and I knew, too, that Toby must go and soon. I just
could not think of how I was to get him to Lincoln.
The apprentices and Gerard Smith might not keep
silent for long. Meg grunted at Toby. Cook tolerated
him. The other servants avoided him.

As this taxed me, and in addition to this new
crisis, I had to think of my business. There was to be
a cloth market in the Drapers' Guildhall before
Christmas and as a cloth merchant's widow, I would
be eligible to sell my cloth there. When I broached
this with Smith, he said that he would ready the cloth
and make sure of its value. He never spoke of Toby,

who had retreated to the kitchen and hid away there, spoiled by cook who had quickly forgiven him and the servant girls with whom he flirted outrageously, especially Bessie who was only twelve.

The opportunity to send Toby to Lincoln came from an unexpected quarter when Thomas Cromwell returned from Northampton with Barnaby. I received them in my parlour. Barnaby was paler but otherwise well. I sent him off to recount his adventures to the other apprentices and sent Meg to the kitchen for a jug of wine and cakes. When she returned, I suggested that for propriety's sake she remained and sewed at the other side of the chamber. Smiling, she settled herself on the bench below the window where she could stitch and watch the street at the same time, both occupations she enjoyed. Meg was working on a piece of saffron-coloured woollen cloth sewing sleeves for a new gown I was to wear when I would come out of mourning. I often thought Meg would make a good spy. She knew, too, how to guard her tongue.

Thomas Cromwell and I sat on either side of the fire place. After we had exchanged pleasantries, and I had thanked him again for his care of Barnaby, I told him about Toby. I had a feeling that he did not believe my story about a feud but that he was not going to question it either.

He placed his glass down on the table and began to pace the room. The logs crackled in the fire place. I sipped my wine. A log spat. I lifted a small fire brush and swept the myriad of sparks back into the fire. As Thomas never spoke but sat down in a chair by the fire, his hands folded under his chin deep in thought, I watched Meg make dainty stitches and waited. She was absorbed in her task and, ever the good servant, she was all but invisible when she chose.

At last Thomas spoke, 'Here is my suggestion. I know a cloth merchant who is travelling north of Lincoln to Boston, and the boy could journey north with him. But, Mistress Elizabeth, it might be best if I take Toby with me this afternoon. Since I arrived with one boy, it will not cause remark if I depart with one.' I felt a sense of gratitude and relief flow through me. This man had twice been my saviour.

'Thank you, sir.'

'Not sir, surely. Thomas, please.' He leaned forward holding my eyes with his cool grey look. 'May I call you Elizabeth?'

I nodded. 'You do already.' I smiled. As if he needed permission! 'Where do you lodge?' I added, thinking that it was in the City, and Toby would have to be concealed there.

'I am staying in Putney for now, in my father's tavern.'

'Your father's house?' I was surprised. I had thought he would lodge in the City.

I was even more astonished when he said, 'My father was in prison this year for cheating with ale and other crimes.' He rolled his grey eyes. 'My father won't change. He is a lout and a cheat, simple as that. He has not recovered his health. Now, he is dying. As you may know, because my mother died long ago, my sister, Cat, rules the household. Usually, I lodge in the City since I am studying the law. I help with cases that come to the attention of the Company of Merchant Adventurers.' He hesitated

128

and sighed deeply. 'I suppose it is blood ties that persuade me home. He is my father, after all.'

I murmured, 'And we forgive our fathers.' Louder I said, 'I am sorry for his ill-health.' I could see sorrow gather in Thomas' eyes. 'I am passing Christmastide in Putney at my father's manor house. You see, I promised Mother that I would come. Unfortunately, I fear *my* father will press me to allow him to direct my affairs.' Thomas Cromwell was watching me intently and with understanding in his eyes. I found that I wanted to tell him about my father and even all the burdensome things concerning my marriage because I had so long kept these events close to my heart. This man had a way about him that made you want to tell him things. He was a listener. The tale threatened to come out but I knew that must stop. I folded my hands in my lap and ceased talking.

Meg put her sewing down. 'Shall I fetch candles, Mistress Elizabeth? The day is fading and with it the light.'

This simple question was so normal, I felt a wash of relief flow through me. 'Thank you, Meg, and tell Toby to fetch his bundle and come here. He is leaving with Master Cromwell today.'

'Good.' I glared at her and with a swish of her kirtle she fled from the parlour.

Thomas leaned forward. 'You were speaking of your father, Elizabeth.'

I took a breath and said, 'My father thinks I must marry again. He found me a suitor. There is no place for a woman in the cloth business, so he says.'

'And you rejected the suitor?' He smiled. 'You seem to be managing very well, but perhaps I can help you to further success. After Christmastide, I return to

Antwerp. I could sell some of the cloth you purchased in Northampton for you.'

I felt a smile light up my face. 'I had hoped you would and I am grateful.'

'I have many contacts.' He paused, then said, 'May I look at your new cloth? I hope you will consider keeping the best for a new gown for your Christmastide. I think a deep burgundy is your colour.'

'I do have a deep burgundy amongst the new cloth.'

'To allow the petticoat to fade into obscurity.' He put on a very solemn face.

'Possibly,' I said.

Taking a lamp, I led him two flights of stairs to the attic where I had stored the best of the new cloth. Thomas fingered the ells of fabric as carefully as he had done months previously. He held the lantern higher. 'You have an expert eye.' He pulled out the burgundy, a patterned mixed cloth, and held it up as if he could see it already sewn into a gown. 'This would look lovely on *you*, Elizabeth.' He appraised me for a moment, his eyes moving down my person as if he had a sense of my exact measurements. 'Yes, it will be a gift.'

I knew that if I permitted it, he would send for this cloth and return it to me sewn into an elegant gown fit for a court lady. I shook my head. 'You must not. It is not seemly. I have my own tailor, Master Thomas.'

'I wish it was appropriate,' he said and laid down the bolt of cloth. 'But you are right. It is not so yet,' he said in his quiet voice.

I was confused as to what he had meant by 'yet.'

He looked around again, touching materials, looking closely with a practised eye until, finally, he came to the painted cloth covered with Tudor roses. He turned back the roll and peered closely. 'I am sure a courtier would delight in this.' He put it down too. 'I shall do my best for you.'

'Thank you, but I am keeping this for my parlour.'

He raised a quizzical eyebrow. 'Did I notice a small printed volume of Erasmus on the table in your parlour?'

'Yes, Prior Anthony from Austin Friars gave it to me.'

Thomas' grey eyes looked animated and in the lamp glow I saw that they were again hazel rimmed with grey, ever changing, the warm brown softening them. Today they seemed to contain flecks of green too, reminding me of woods on a gentle spring day. He reached over, took my hands and added, 'You once said that you can read and write?'

'Yes, I keep ledgers. I have always done that. The Prior of Austin Friars invited me to come and see their library, but, now, I haven't time for reading books.'

'That *is* a pity. Books provide windows into the soul and tease the imagination both.' He looked at me, thoughtfully now, and his face lit up to match the glow in his eyes, as if he suddenly had a brilliant thought. 'If you are in Putney would you permit me to visit you at Christmastide? We must talk of books and other things too, Mistress Elizabeth.'

'It would please me very much,' I said. 'Father will be happy to see you. He has been concerned for me since the fire in my storehouse. He will be pleased to know you are taking my cloth to the Low Countries for sale.'

Thomas allowed my hands to fall again. He looked thoughtful again. 'Elizabeth, have you idea who caused the fire that night?'

'No, Toby did say that one of the men who attacked him had a scar on his face and that he wore a brown mantle with velvet trim. He smelled of incense.'

'So perhaps not a feud.'

I slowly inclined my head. 'Maybe not.'

'Take precautions, Elizabeth. You are a widow with only servants to protect you. Most merchants with valuable goods would have an armed keep watch on their merchandise.'

I nodded. 'I do my best.'

'It may not be enough.' He lifted my hand to his lips and held it for a moment in his own finely manicured hand before letting it go. 'If you ever have need of me you must send for me.'

That afternoon, I discerned loyalty in Thomas Cromwell. He had travelled far, and had observed much that I did not understand. He understood things without speaking of them. Love is a slippery business. Love unrequited is destructive, but I could not help myself. I wanted love. The wise say marry as advised and love will follow. How could I believe this aphorism since I had not found it so in my own life? Knots gathered in my stomach when I was with him, telling me over and over that, simply, I was falling in love with him.

'We must fetch Toby,' I said, remembering uncomfortably that I was an unchaperoned woman.

'Indeed, Elizabeth, and I shall send for whatever you wish me to sell in Antwerp.'

I wished he would come himself.

Father would be pleased to hear I had a protector in Thomas Cromwell. Perhaps, now he would forget his obsession with Master Northleach, who was gone away to Flanders.

Chapter Fourteen

LIFE RESUMED NORMALITY DURING the week following Toby's departure. At the end of the week, Thomas Cromwell sent a covered wagon for the fabrics. His factor would sell them for him, he had said. Fortunately, I had enough time to have the new cloth passed for quality by the drapers' inspectors and it was stamped to clear it for sale. Smith took control of this, his mood pleasant now that Toby was gone. The rest of the new cloth I held onto for sale in the Drapers' Guildhall. I kept back my roll of painted cloth, deciding that I would not sell it until I must.

On the tenth day of December I set up my stall in the Guildhall. I was not the only merchant's widow to do so, though it was my cloth that won envious glances from other merchants. The same merchants who had been rude in September glared my way. As we were setting up, the two other widows came over swishing their practical though nondescript skirts over the tiled floor to examine my goods.

Running her hand over a length of grey serge, one said, 'Very good, Mistress Williams. It is pleasing to see you taking control of your business. Such fine cloth too. That fire last Midsummer was a terrible business. And just after your husband's funeral. If you need advice ask Widow Ponsenby.' She pointed to her ample bosom. 'That is me.'

Smiling, I thanked her for her concern.

The other, Mistress Argent, a mean-faced woman from lower Wood Street whom I recognised from my husband's funeral, was not so kind. Her remark, *Lucky indeed it is that you have a father to help you,* was unnecessary. She fingered my cloth in a dismissive manner and moved along the trestles to where Meg was setting out trims, lifted a strip of grey rabbit fur and dropped it onto the table again as if it could bite. 'Could be better and somewhat scrappy. I hope there are no forbidden furs here,' she said unkindly and quickly moved away. For a moment her words hurt. As if I would have ermine anyway.

Meg glared at her back. 'Ignore that one, Mistress.'

'I intend to. She is a bitter woman,' I replied and wore my most confident smile.

Smith nodded at Meg. 'Good to see sense in a woman,' he said.

I was still smiling when Barnaby looked up from his task of setting out ells of brown worsted and said, 'Look, Mistress, Master Cromwell is here today.' I glanced up and could not hide my delight at seeing him soon again. I had not dared to hope he would come. My mouth widened into a huge smile, a genuine one this time.

He affectionately cuffed Barnaby and asked me how I was doing.

'Very well, thank you, Master Cromwell,' I said, feeling colour rise into my cheeks. 'Have you come to buy cloth? You have already sent for more than enough of my fabrics. How can you take more?'

'Indeed, I might take a look around at what is on sale today.' He touched the ell of black kersey, pinching it even though he already knew its worth. 'I shall need a new cloak, myself, soon enough.' He lifted the cloth up to the thin December light and remarked, 'This is a good dye, Mistress Williams. Black is difficult. You have a discerning eye.'

'So you keep saying. Thank you, sir. I hope I do.' I set the cloth aside for him.

I thought he would move away after this, but he lingered. While Smith was engaged in conversation elsewhere, and Meg set out more trims, he leaned down and whispered, 'Toby is safe. He is already in Lincoln.'

'Thank you,' I said softly, thinking of how many times I had already found it necessary to thank Thomas Cromwell.

'I wonder, if later, we could have a private moment together?'

'Oh, yes, of course.' My heart started to beat faster as I relished the thought of moments alone with him. 'We can walk in the courtyard but Meg must accompany me, otherwise there will be talk amongst the Company.' I glanced around at the other drapers busily setting out their cloth and watching eagle-eyed for customers. One or two had looked our way, their eyebrows raised.

'Later then, Elizabeth. I know many of the merchants here, and would like to introduce you to those who belong to the Merchant Adventurers.'

'You are well-connected, Master Cromwell.'

'I am busy with legal work for the company as well as selling cloth.'

'You are most considerate.'

'And you need connections. Connections are everything in this world.'

I nodded my agreement with this, a fact I knew from my father and had seen for myself while Tom Williams lived. The better connected drapers were, the more successful they were too, so I was grateful that he was interested in me. Thomas Cromwell was not just helping me. He genuinely cared about what I wanted to achieve.

'Leave the selling to Smith and come with me,' he said.

As he led me about the hall, I realised that he knew everybody. Searchers, weight-checkers and foreign merchants bowed low to us, addressing him reverently by name as they passed. No searcher dared question me this time, I realised, remembering the comments they had tossed my way when I sold cloth on Cheape Street. The Merchant-Taylors' searchers, who in stern-faced manner approached my stall to examine the trims Meg had laid out, spoke with Thomas about his last journey to Antwerp. Without hesitation, Thomas smiled, made conversation and encouraged them to select fox fur, velvet and satin pieces. They made purchases. These would soon adorn the Christmas jackets and cloaks of their clients. 'Excellent quality,' they approved, nodding enthusiastically as they allowed silk ribbons to slither through their fingers and moved their hands in caresses over velvets.

I felt vindicated after Mistress Argent's unkind remark. As for that harridan, she was selling little and was already packing up her cloth to leave. She hurried past me, her four servants carrying her cloth, and in a bustling manner, swept from the hall as if she had more important business to conduct elsewhere.

With Thomas' introductions to merchants from the Adventurers, I sold all of the fabrics that he had not ear-marked for himself. I found myself glowing with satisfaction, thinking he had forgotten that he had wanted to speak privately with me, and not minding too much because I was so pleased with my sales. But once the church bells pealed the midday Angelus and the crowd began to thin, he whispered, 'Come out into the garden with me.'

I called over to Meg to leave the ribbons to the apprentices. 'Meg, Master Cromwell has important business to speak of with me in private. Please accompany us.'

Meg nodded and set aside the green and yellow ribbons she was plaiting to sell as purse decorations.

We left Smith and the apprentices showing the last ells of cloth to a lingering Hollander, and exited by a side door into the courtyard. We sought a quiet bench under a patch of grey sky, while Meg discreetly took a turn about the rectangular garden path. My heart sang with absolute joy, because there, in that peaceful spot, just after the Angelus bells stopped peeling, Thomas Cromwell gently took my hands, folding them into his own and asked me to allow him to seek my father's permission for our betrothal.

I glanced up at him, my eyes growing soft with desire. How I longed to discover what it was like to be desired by the man I wanted with all my being. For a moment I was shocked by my own musing. Could I be so fallen as to discover such carnal needs lay secretly amongst my thoughts?

I looked down at our clasped hands. 'I am my own mistress and can decide whom I wish to wed,' I said quietly.

'Then, Elizabeth, there is no hope for me?'

'Of course, I mean yes, there is every hope. I am a widow. You do not need my father's permission to marry me.'

'No, Elizabeth, I do not need his permission.' he turned my hands over and lifted my left palm to his lips. The sensation of the delicate touch floated through my

138

hand, my body and slid into my heart. 'Yet your father should bless our union and I do need his goodwill. Let us do this properly,' he said. 'Will you accept me? I know the answer but I need to hear you say it.'

'I accept you with all my heart, but, if my father should refuse?' An image of another merchant flitted through my head, one whom I had so recently refused, one to whom my father had clearly made promises concerning my future.

Thomas frowned. 'No one refuses me, and Elizabeth, know this, I love you with all my heart.' Although, he was not smiling, his eyes seemed to reflect my own deep longings, and I believed that he spoke with sincerity. Thomas Cromwell, persuasive and charming, would always make people see his point of view. Father might attempt to discuss other suitors' interest, men he considered were wealthier and better connected, but the result was a foregone conclusion. Thomas Cromwell would marry me because he willed it, because he loved me and because I loved him back.

I looked far into his penetrating grey eyes and discerned determination. 'I love you too, Thomas,' I said a moment later. 'It is my wish that we are betrothed.' I took a deep breath. 'However, there is something I have not told you, something important about my first marriage, and if we are to wed there should be no secrets between man and wife.' I felt choked, 'Something that could make you change your mind.'

'Not now, not here, Elizabeth.' He placed his finger on my lips. 'We shall not speak of it today. Nothing will deter me though I think I already know what you would say. Tom Williams is the past. Today is where a happier future begins; it will be yours and mine.'

The face that looked down on mine was inscrutable.

Either he did not want to hear it from me today, or he thought it unwise that I speak of it. We sat quietly for a minute, happy in each other's company, holding hands, savouring the moment as if it were about to be snatched away. A robin hopped amongst the fallen beech leaves that piled up by our bench and swiftly flew off again as if it was carrying our news far beyond the garden. A blackbird glossy and sleek strutted about my feet, jerking like a puppet dangling onto a miniature stage. He looked at me through his yellow eyes and seemed to incline his tiny head quizzically before hopping away to disappear behind a holly bush.

'Will you be in Antwerp often after we are married?' I asked breaking the silence, knowing that I would miss his absences much more than I had missed Tom Williams' odd and mysterious departures. Just like the blackbird, my first husband had been here one moment and gone the next, to hide behind a prickly cover.

'Sometimes, I shall be away sometimes, but, more often, I hope that I am here with you. I must remain in London working on legal matters. We shall set up our home in a different ward. It will be a new beginning, a larger house, where I can practice the law as well as continuing to send cloth abroad with agents. We can rent a warehouse by St Catherine's Dock. I have the space already and can increase it.'

It was all happening so quickly, but it did not take longer than the quiver of a butterfly wing for me to agree. 'I would like to move away from Wood Street. The lease on my house is up for renewal next summer. My mother wants me to return to Putney and join my business with Father's enterprises.' I looked up, filled with realisation, 'Thomas, maybe we still could join with him.' I felt myself smiling at him. With Thomas

140

by my side, Father could not bully me.

'Yes,' he said. 'But it will be a legal agreement. You have a brother in Surrey, so it's wise to protect your future interests.' He rose from the bench. 'Shall we go into the hall, my dear, dear Elizabeth, otherwise Gerard Smith will think I have abducted you.'

'I would not mind at all if you had,' I said allowing myself a giggle. Meg turned again and glanced over at us quizzically. How things of great significance been decided in the time it had taken Meg to walk twice about the paths. I called her over. I longed to confide my news in her, but decided not to, not before my family knew our intention.

Chapter Fifteen

SINCE FATHER WAS TO have his rebellious daughter safely wed after all, he was delighted. He insisted that we must be betrothed at Christmas and married by Midsummer. I think he thought that I might change my mind. Little did he know that I was in love! Changing my mind was now impossible. Thomas and I were destined for each other, and, I thought joyfully, by Christmastide, I could put away my widow's white wimple and leave off my mourning for Tom Williams.

Thomas eased himself down on his knees to receive my father's blessing, his cloak sweeping the rush matting of Father's closet. I knelt beside him, Guinevere to Tom's Launcelot, and felt pride in this eloquent yet humble man who had just asked my father for my hand.

'Thomas,' Father said, after we had both risen. 'Do you think that St Stephen's Day would be a suitable day to proclaim your betrothal?'

'The great Christmas pie, the wassail, the boy bishop, the mummers, the musicians. Your sisters and their husbands must come.' My mother said breathlessly as she clasped my hands, her utter joy unbridled. 'A summer wedding? What do you think, Lizzy?'

'Thomas sails to the Low Countries after Christmastide for business reasons. I think he must decide.

'Mistress Wykes, I would marry your daughter on the morrow, but summer it is.' Thomas took my hand in his

142

own. We stood smiling, delighted with each other.

My mother clasped her hands together. 'It is decided, and from now on, Master Cromwell, you must call me Mercy, for that is how I am named, and I shall call you Thomas.' She gave us her lovely smile and Father called for wine and almond biscuits to be served. 'We must send news to Surrey at once. Joan loves weddings.'

'Joan must be my maiden again,' I said.

'And you must meet my sisters,' Thomas said. He clapped his hand to his forehead. 'It is only two weeks away. I must tell them. They will be pleased. And, I must tell my poor foolish father.'

Before dinner hour on St Stephen's Day, Meg, Alice my sister-in-law, Joan my sister and I gathered by the great fireplace in our hall to await our guests. Mother appeared smiling through the arched kitchen doorway, flushed from supervising the slow baking of the great pie; a goose with a quail, pigeon and small hen squeezed inside each other, within a huge pastry coffin. I could smell spice from small sweet pies and as I inhaled the rich, deep scent of the wassail cup, I was reminded of my childhood Christmases. It was a joyful occasion, celebrated fully in my Wood Street house, though never as great an occasion as in my childhood home. As ever, despite the heat in the kitchen and the cooking, my mother remained as serene and unruffled as the Virgin depicted on our Church windows.

She wore her best gown, a blue wool overdress cut to reveal a paler kirtle with blue and rose sleeves which she had embroidered with golden acanthus leaves. Her cap sat daintily on neatly plaited hair that was as dark and glossy as a magpie's coat. My own waving, silver hair flowed loose, cascading to my waist in shining, silvery ringlets.

For modesty's sake, I wore a small blue and silver-embroidered cap tied with thin velvet ribbons under my chin. 'Will he like it?' I thought again and again, hardly able to contain my excitement, longing to see Thomas. Joan, always one to enjoy a celebration, wore creamy ribbons threaded through her dark plaits. One day, not so long off, I thought, Joan will have a husband and a gaggle of giggling babies. In Surrey she contentedly kept watch over my brother's children and she was happier than she had been at our parents' manor house.

'You look as lovely as the day you were betrothed to Tom Williams,' Mother remarked, kissing me on both of my cheeks. She held me back and nodded approvingly. 'Now, I wonder what surprises your father has arranged for us today.' I laughed, for Mother always said this exact thing on St Stephen's Day.

At our manor house, the day was always celebrated with mischief and fun. My eyes searched about the hall for Father but he had vanished with my brother after Mass that morning and had not yet returned. Behind us, the Yule log in the fireplace spluttered then glowed red, and the cauldron suspended from its hook above it smelled of roasted apples, beer, nutmeg, ginger and sugar. Joan peered into it and glanced up with mischievous dark eyes.

'Why don't we just taste the brew now?'

'You will wait until our guests arrive,' my mother said firmly.

My brother's four enthusiastic children came darting into the hall. Joan called them to her and they gathered about her, tugging her to the large mullioned window that looked towards the lane. I followed.

'Listen,' cried out nine-year-old Will. 'I hear bells and music coming up the lane. I saw Grandfather from the gallery window. You can't see from here, Joan. The boy bishop is leading Grandfather and my papa and Father Christopher.'

We hurried from the window to the door and peered out into the crisp snow. The sound of the wassailers drifted closer and closer, swirling around the great oaks that grew about the house. I could see the figures clearly now. Our guests were accompanied by musicians, my father and the boy bishop who was a chorister from the Church of All Saints in Fulham. I peered out at the procession but I could not see Thomas, nor could I see his two sisters. A small anxiety caught at me. What if he never came?

The crowd burst into the porch, shaking off snow from their boots. Gradually, they came in small groups into the hall. We greeted whom we could but were swept back by the great number of guests soon pressing towards the fire place and the great cauldron. The hall was full of laughter and music. More revellers arrived, kicking snow from their boots. The maids were kept busy, dipping into the cauldron with huge wooden dippers as they filled pewter cups with the frothy wassail punch we called lambs-wool and handed them out to the guests.

'About time,' Joan said with a toss of her beribboned dark plait. She chivvied the children over to an alcove saying, 'I promised them games, and they have a little performance to rehearse-for later.'

'Excellent lambs-wool, Mistress Wykes,' I heard our neighbours and relatives say to Mother as they sipped the hot foaming punch.

Moments later I felt Thomas at my side. He bowed over my hand and kissed it. He gestured behind him, to where a kindly-faced woman of around thirty years stood with a boy and her tall black-haired husband. 'Elizabeth, Mercy, meet my sister Cat, her husband,

Morgan - Richard, my nephew,' he was saying.

I had last seen Catherine at the Corpus Christi procession in May four years earlier, though we had never been formally introduced as we were today.

'I am pleased to meet you at last, Elizabeth.' She extended her hands and took both of mine in hers. I noticed how soft they were, so soft she might have slept with chicken-skin gloves covering them and maybe did. She spoke quietly to my mother who enthusiastically welcomed the family, her new relatives in waiting, into her hall.

'How is he, your father?' Mother enquired.

'Not well at all, I fear. He has a nurse all the time, day and night. He is slipping in and out of consciousness.' Cat crossed herself. 'I think, like St Edward, Confessor, he will depart this world before Epiphany. You must forgive us, Mistress Wykes, if we do not stay late.'

'I am sorry to hear of his illness. Perhaps we should have delayed the betrothal.'

'No, Mistress Wykes, not at all, for it is as well now as ever it would be. Father has given Thomas his blessing.'

Morgan Williams immediately stepped forward and, lightening the mood, said, 'Mistress Wykes, my brother-in-law is fortunate to be connected to your family, and -' He looked over at me and bowed, 'to be betrothed to one as fair of face as Mistress Elizabeth.'

I thanked him for his compliment and added that it was I who was fortunate to be betrothed to Master Thomas.

Morgan Williams bowed low again, his cloak swirling about his knees, 'May I be excused as I must speak with your father, Mistress Elizabeth?'

'Of course.'

'Allow me to bring you to him.' Mother said. 'I think he is speaking to Father Christopher. Come with me.'

146

Once my mother and Morgan Williams had mingled with the other guests, Cat took my hands. 'My thanks for such a warm greeting, Elizabeth, and soon, I hope you will be welcoming me as a sister to your own home, yours and Tom's. How fortunate we are that Tom will settle down with one as well-connected and as lovely as you.'

I knew then that Cat and I were to be firm friends. I loved her already. 'Thank you, Cat, and who is this?' I said, turning to the boy patiently standing by her side. He had the large family nose and grey eyes like both his mother and uncle. I guessed him to be around ten years of age. Morgan was a lawyer, Thomas was practising law. It occurred to me that this watching, quiet boy would also enter the profession.

'My son Richard.'

'I am pleased to meet you, Richard,' I said.

The boy bowed. 'Thank you, Mistress Elizabeth,' he said in a very grown-up, self-assured manner. Quick-eyed, he looked over my shoulder to where my brother's children were laughing over a game they were engaged with in the alcove that fronted my father's closet.

My eyes followed him. 'Join them. They are planning games and I think one might be a play. They will welcome another conspirator.'

Thomas affectionately threw an arm over his nephew's shoulders. 'Come, Richard. I shall introduce you to them.'

Moments later, the children were all laughing together.

'Do you have daughters too, Cat?' I queried.

'None living, not yet,' she said, but I caught a sigh in her voice. Her sad tone suggested that illness had stolen away at least one daughter.

'I am sorry,' I said and glanced across the hall. 'Who is that speaking to Thomas?'

'Morgan's brother, John. He is steward to Lord Scales.

147

We are honoured today that he has come to Thomas' betrothal.'

'Are your sister and Master Wellifield coming?'

'There she is. Eliza has come.' Cat pointed through the groups of guests to the door. 'Wearing the green cloak, speaking with that thin man with the tall blue hat.'

In the doorway stood a pretty woman in her late twenties, just a little older than Thomas. 'Is the man in the tall hat her husband?' I asked Cat. Eliza's husband was a busy sheep farmer, red-faced and rotund. As soon as I had said it, I knew he could not be the man wearing the blue hat and I wondered where he could be.

'No,' Cat said. 'He has not come.'

Eliza hurried towards us as if blown in by a storm. 'My goodness, Cat, people simply will not move out of the way. Their rudeness astounds me,' she said with a hint of discontent in her tone.

'It is Christmas after all,' Cat said quietly. 'Folks are celebrating today. They are happy that our brother is to be wed to one of our own community.'

Eliza Wellifield's green eyes ran up and down my person as if she was sizing up the value of my new burgundy gown. A moment later she said to Cat, 'Remind me of her name, sister.'

'Elizabeth, of course, sister, as you well know.'

She turned to me, her face supercilious. 'Well, Mistress Elizabeth, as well 'tis that I prefer to be called Eliza as we own the same name. Such an over-used name - Elizabeth - after the old queen. Wellifield could not come. You see, my husband is busy with his sheep and I am soon to have a child.' This was spoken dramatically as if the child's birth was imminent, which it clearly was not. 'Our father is dying so we shall not stay long.'

'I understand,' I said, trying to remain unruffled by her impatient, fussy manner.

Servants bustled about setting out platters on two long trestle tables ready for the dinner that was to follow. Eliza said not another word to me, only to excuse herself to join other women whom she knew. Cat apologised for her, saying that Wellifield treated her badly and she was resentful. I shook my head and said, 'I hope that she resolves what is making her unhappy.'

'She is lonely. Eliza longs for children, so perhaps the baby will make her content.'

We sipped our frothy drink and Cat told me about a beautiful Christmas lantern Morgan had purchased for her. We talked of small things until the boy bishop struck his staff on the floor rushes and the priest announced that it was time for Thomas and I to receive his blessing. My father led me forward to where Thomas was already waiting proudly in the centre of the room. Our family clerk handed us a document that confirmed properties we would own jointly once we were married. Father Christopher read it aloud. We would keep possession of the orchard granted to my first husband as my dowry. Further to this, my father granted us land in Chiswick and in Battersea. Once we were married, Thomas must confirm that I would take possession of a generous dower portion. My business was to be safeguarded by my husband during my lifetime.

The priest witnessed our signatures and blessed us both. Thomas' brother-in-law added his signature. My father signed and my brother, Harry, placed his signature below ours. Thomas slipped a betrothal ring, a gold band with a sapphire, onto my middle right finger. Father secreted the document in a sycamore-wood coffer he kept for family documents and sent it with his clerk for safe keeping in his closet.

Clapping his hands he said, 'Meat and ale on the table. Come, all of you, and fill up the benches.'

After Father spoke, Thomas kissed me on my mouth, and I felt the lingering sensation of that kiss all through St Stephen's feast.

'If this is the betrothal,' he said, 'the wedding will be sumptuous.'

'No,' I said. 'I want it to be quiet.'

'I agree to that, sweetheart,' he said and led me to our places at the table.

Later that evening, having eaten our fill of the Christmas pie, beef, mutton, and pork accompanied by sauces both savoury and fruit, spiced vegetable dishes, cheeses, fruit tarts and marzipan cakes, we chose young Richard as our lord of misrule and played games. We joined the children in blind man's buff, taking up their infectious laughter. We would not go to sleep until well past midnight.

'If this is our future,' Thomas whispered in my ear as he caught me in the game for a fourth time. 'I shall never want for another.'

'I hope not, Thomas,' I said, but I thought that as I said it, I saw a shadow cross his face. 'You are sure,' I said.

'I am as sure of my love for you as much as I can be sure of anything.'

Years later, I remembered these words.

That night in bed, after Joan's excited chatter had trailed into gentle snores, I lay awake. With Thomas Cromwell by my side, I need never fear danger again. For a moment, I recollected my first Tom and felt a creeping cold possess my limbs. I vowed to myself that I would now have the future I had never truly owned before. This time, nothing must disturb my heart's peace. No cruel gossip would touch our lives.

My mind turned to Edward Northleach. How fortunate I was that I had found love and not a charlatan. Yet, an anxious thought niggled. The merchant had not returned to England. He could not have, because if Father had already received his due from him, he surely would have mentioned it. In fact, I puzzled the fact that Father never referred to Northleach, but since I wanted nothing more to do with the middleman, I did not ask after him. Master Northleach would hear from others of my betrothal. He would forget me.

I thought happy thoughts until I finally drifted off into a contented sleep, listening to my sister snoring softly by my side.

Chapter Sixteen

Midsummer 1526, The Kitchen

THE EGG FOR THE midsummer tart slides out of my hand to break onto the floor tiles where yellow yolk pools into a viscous mess. A bevy of cook's boys rush to clean up this gluey puddle. The cooks look askance at me, and I realise they would rather Meg and I left the kitchen to them. Meg, is visiting us because she lives on Cornhill now. See how she is stirring up a bowl of preserved spiced fruit in the corner by the window. She glares at the cooks, who look away and attend to basting the leg of lamb the spit boy is turning.

Meg turns to me and remarks, 'An egg is smashed, Mistress Elizabeth. Mind you, we can't make a tart without breaking a few eggs. There will be some good out of it.'

I cannot think what she means. She is always repeating obscure sayings. She likes the sound of them rolling off her tongue.

'The only good I want today is pastry for the Midsummer tart,' I reply firmly, as I crack another egg, then another, and they plop neatly into the bowl to join with a half-dozen other egg yolks.

The Midsummer tart is not my recipe but my mother's, one that she inherited from her mother. Pastry cooks call it a Florentine. Its filling will be a thick plum and spiced fruit marmalade, and to finish, I shall lace it with bands of pastry and sugar comfits. The pastry is easy, since it is simply made from egg yolks, flour and cream, yet its crust will be so delicate that once cooked we could serve it up to Queen Catherine herself.

Instead, we have another visitor for dinner - Henry Vaughan, who is Thomas' agent in the Netherlands, a young man whom my husband wishes to thank for the wonderful globe he has sent to us, a ball painted with outlines of the countries of this world, its oceans and with peculiar creatures frolicking within them, a marvellous gift which fascinates our son and daughters. When I was a child the world was flat, so it was said in some circles, with Heaven above the skies and Hell beneath the earth. Now that it appears round, where is Heaven? What else will change?

The cooks are preparing a special dinner for our St John's Eve and Henry Vaughan, a great favourite with all our family, will stay to walk with us through the streets and watch the Midsummer pageants. I smile with pleasure at this thought as I carefully roll out pastry and wipe my hands on my apron. I ease my great sheet of pastry into the gigantic tart plate, a difficult thing to do which requires much patience. Once it is safely delivered to the plate, I stand back, pleased with my work. Now, the tart is almost ready to be filled with the marmalade, to receive its sculptured pastry decoration and be sprinkled with sugar before the cook bakes it.

The first time Thomas ate my mother's Midsummer tart was on our wedding day, and he enjoyed it so much then that I have made one every Midsummer since.

Chapter Seventeen

1514

BEFORE THOMAS DEPARTED FOR Flanders, his father was laid to rest in the churchyard of St Mary's in Putney. It was a sad occasion because, although Thomas had always found his father difficult, he insisted that he owed him familial respect and he provided a great funeral feast for his father's friends in Putney.

'Family matters,' he said on that chilly afternoon by his father's grave. 'You can always trust your family.'

'Indeed,' I replied, without genuine commitment, because I had not always trusted Father, nor Tom Williams either.

Thomas was a worldly man and he had a strong sense of whom he would trust. I had been so used to keeping my first husband's secret that I was inclined to trust very few. There were things you could not even tell your family.

After their father's death, Eliza, Thomas' sister, and her husband lived on in the Putney house owned by his family. Thomas was content to permit this. Wellifield had managed everything, the inn, the brewery and his flock of sheep. Their son, Christopher, was born that spring. On the few occasions I met Eliza after my betrothal, we had little to say to each other. Tom's sister talked boastfully of how she and Wellifield hoped for a company of sons to continue their great lineage. What lineage, I wondered to myself, thinking that, unlike my mother who was descended from minor nobility, they probably had no ancestry worth remark. I was quietly pleased that I rarely saw her. Cat, of course, was different. I enjoyed her company and she fast became the friend I had often wished for but never had.

Thomas' agent had sold my cloth in Antwerp for a generous price and when Thomas had returned to Flanders in 1514, he purchased a dozen ells of damask mixed with linen in various hues of lavender, rose and soft green. He sent the fabrics back to me along with a gift, one of many I received from him that spring. The first token of his love meant more to me than all the others - a pair of soft kidskin gloves wrapped in painted paper rather than linen, valuable paper that was stamped with gold angels along with a message - *To keep your hands warm until I can hold them again, my Elizabeth. May God and all his angels protect you, my dearest love.*

I owned many pairs of gloves and kept them with dried rose petals in a cedar-wood coffer. I had leather gloves for riding, others of canvas for gardening, every-day gloves knitted from fine dyed linen threads to match my various gowns, two pairs of silk knit gloves, and mittens to ward off the winter cold. I even had a pair made from fragile soft chicken-skin, to wear at night to keep my hands soft, though I rarely wore these. I held up Thomas' gift and admired the quality and the colour. They were dyed a soft rose and their scalloped cuffs were edged with silver flowers.

The messenger was returning to Antwerp within the week, so I asked him to carry a letter to Thomas. For two whole days, I thought long and hard as to what I could send Thomas as a token of my love. I searched the best goldsmiths' shops for a ring, but instead, after much searching, I found a poky little place in a narrow lane off the main thoroughfare where I purchased silver aglets for his clothing laces and gold beads for his cap. Of late, gentlemen were pinning gold baubles and semi-precious jewels onto the velvet that decorated the necks of their gowns as well as the fur trimming on their hats. Thomas would never buy such things for himself as he dressed plainly, though well, but a few of these tokens from me would not be ostentatious.

After I wrapped my gifts in velvet cloth, I wrote Thomas a letter describing my day-to-day life; how I had visited my mother and father on St Elizabeth's Day, my name day; how I skated on the ice because that winter of 1514 was bitter and the manor pond froze. Joan had returned to Surrey with Harry, Alice and their children.

Before she left she had said, 'I never shall return to live with our parents because Harry will help me to a good marriage.'

I had replied, 'I hope, Joan, in the event, our brother finds you a wealthy suitor and one that is not old.'

I thought this might bring a smile to Thomas' face.

Finally, I wrote that Cat, his sister, had come to visit, had skated with me on the pond in February and was well-liked by all my family.

Lent is hard to bear without you. I long to see you at my door wearing my tokens in the squirrel-fur trim on your bonnet.

Your Elizabeth.

Ribbons, girdles and bracelets of gold and silver set with semi-precious stones followed, and every time I opened a new parcel, cast the linen wrappings aside and called Meg to share my joy, my heart lifted and tilted towards Flanders and Thomas.

It was not just I who was greeting every dawn with joy that spring. Another surprise arrived when Meg flew in

156

my chamber one morning flushed and excited.

'Look what Gerard Smith has given me, Mistress Elizabeth.'

She lifted up a small cage with a songbird in it. 'May I keep it?'

I stared at the tiny fragile creature which tweeted its little melody up at me. 'Of course, Meg. Hang it in your chamber window.' Then I frowned at the cage. 'I hope Smith's intentions are honest, Meg.'

'Shame, Mistress, he is but a friend. The gift is by way of repayment for my stitching and mending for him. Marry not, not Gerard Smith.'

But she was blushing as rosy as the painted cage she was holding. I smiled as she left my chamber, the bird singing sweetly in its cage that rocked as she walked away with swaying hips.

That February, I sent Smith to sell the damask at the Drapers' Guildhall, though I set aside the length of rose damask mix for my wedding gown. Smith sold all of my cloth to a merchant tailor who created magnificent gowns for courtiers. Many court ladies preferred the lightness and the patterns that shot through the mixed fabrics to wools and linen. I was growing rich and a year had not passed since Tom Williams' death. I had succeeded in my desire to have a successful cloth business.

As I felt the clink of coin rattle into my coffer again, I congratulated myself that I could afford my own wedding feast. It would be held in my Wood Street house that June. My father was not as fortunate with his cloth sales as I. Master Northleach had not returned and by February Father insisted that he had been hoodwinked by a rogue. Northleach had disappeared just as surely as the villains who had attacked Toby, without trace, so I wrote to

Thomas asking him to find out what he could about the middleman.

Thomas returned briefly in March with gifts for us all: a length of soft green Spanish wool for my mother, a cloak trimmed with silver fox fur for my father. He gave me a printed Latin psalter with its pictures of the seasons touched with gold. From his cavernous leather travelling chest, he also produced a fashionable chain of gold studded with garnets for me to wear about my neck on my wedding day. In return, I gave him a ring, inscribed *Una in perpetuum*: together forever, a sentiment I hoped that he would always treasure.

On the evening of a visit to the Putney manor, he told Father that although he had inquired amongst the merchant adventurers in Antwerp, Bruges and Middleburg, all places where merchants traded, he had not been able to discover Edward Northleach's whereabouts. He had seen a record of the sale of Father's wool in Antwerp and even found out where Northleach had lodged during the previous autumn. The middleman then simply vanished.

'He left without paying his bills.' Thomas shook his head. 'The trail disappeared. I have a hunch he may be in France, though where, I cannot discover.'

'Scoundrel,' Father said angrily, the veins in his forehead swollen and his face as red as the flames in the hall hearth.

'Sir, I shall try harder to find out about him.'

'I would that you could, Thomas,' Father said. 'He has robbed me of a fortune.'

'I have to travel to Italy this month. Perhaps I can inquire on my travels.' He looked at us all in turn. There was a steely determination in his grey eyes.

I raised my eyebrows. 'That might help.' I took a deep

breath and asked, 'Why are you travelling to Italy before our wedding?'

'Money for our new house, for us, Lizzy. It is for profit, believe me, not for the sake of my soul nor for yours. I am employed by Cardinal Bainbridge as an agent in a mercantile case involving the Church because I speak Italian fluently.' He leaned forward. 'The task will be completed within a week. I have no desire to linger amongst the Holy Father's sycophants. Rome has turned away from truth and modest living. Cardinals take mistresses, install them in palaces, breed children and the Pope places all his own illegitimate off-spring in positions of authority. They live off the fat of the land. I am happy to take their silver.' He looked pleased.

I thought him cynical. The Holy Father was God's representative on earth. To complain about the Church and its cardinals was dangerous, especially in front of my parents, and the servants who hovered around the hall. 'Where will you stay?' I said aloud, determined to steer him to safer ground.

'In a monastery hostel, a humble abode, a pilgrim's hospice.' He pressed my hands into his. 'I shall return safely to you, and by midsummer: one month there, and another back on fast horses and with guards on equally fast horses, all armed and menacing. I promise it, Lizzy. Do not frown. It does not become you.' He leaned over and kissed me lightly on my mouth.

A few days later, we sat in a garden warmed by March sunshine that caused branch-shaped shadows to cross the path. Distant city sounds hummed, rang, and echoed beyond the garden walls. London with its great river, its pleasures, dangers and teeming life was placed safely outside of our lives. Behind my walls, with Thomas, I felt secluded and safe.

'You really will return to us by Midsummer?' I said holding his hand, still feeling concern for him.

'I am like a cat with nine lives. Rest assured that I shall come back to you. Our banns can still be called in June.'

I relaxed.

We would marry quietly in the Wood Street parish church and we would donate generously to it, so that the parish officers would approve our marriage. After all, Tom Williams would be only a year in his grave.

Despite my concern, I was, in truth, impressed by Thomas' mission. I longed to hear about Italy, its palaces, ancient buildings and beautiful paintings, for although I had no desire to travel myself, I was happy listening to others' tales of adventure in foreign lands. Thomas spoke often of distant places, of history and of great Greek and Roman thinkers, of the new learning he said was sweeping through Europe, the discovery of ancient Greek poetry, new translations of the Bible.

'We must explore, question and debate,' he would say.

I had no idea that the Bible we had was not a true translation and determined to educate myself further. To that end, I began to purchase books, printed copies that did not cost me a great fortune. My first treasure, discovered amongst the print stalls by St Paul's, was a fat copy of the *Canterbury Tales*. I read my books over and over in the years that followed. Stories from Ovid were my second purchase. I read my Ovid in secret and thought of Thomas.

Some long evenings, however, I read the *Canterbury Tales* to Meg, who all but swooned at the tales of wooing and laughed at the bawdy stories contained within its covers.

'I swear you are in love, Meg,' I teased.

160

'No, not I,' she said, but blushed and bent over her sewing.

I attended services in the parish church with renewed fervour, to pray with joy for Thomas' safe travel in Flanders, and I prayed sadly for the safety of Tom Williams' soul, always fancying that I saw devils torturing him. One May morning, Father Luke found me laying primroses on my first husband's grave. Feeling his close presence beside me, I glanced up.

He leaned over me and said, 'He will be in Heaven. He was a kind man and he would want you to remarry. When shall I call the banns for your new wedding?' He lifted my hand and looked upon my betrothal ring. 'It is a lovely gem, my child. I am glad to see you settled, Elizabeth. These are difficult times for a young woman. There were rumours concerning that fire in your storehouse last year. Now, with this marriage to Thomas Cromwell, you will put that sort of talk to rest. Time passes and people forget.'

'Rumours, Father Luke?' I said, startled by his words. 'Who is talking about the fire?'

I wondered, and even dared to hope that Father Luke could led us to the perpetrators. I had never considered this before because I was too afraid of the priest's criticism. I was never sure what he could have suspected about Tom Williams. What if the reason for the fire lay with my husband's sin? But kindly Father Luke was not prepared to say, even if he knew. I thought and prayed that he did not. I could not unburden myself of this terrible, sinful secret to him. I could not bear to do so. My holding the secret from the confessional was yet another sin but I could not help myself.

'Just talk. Even so, it is best for you to have a

161

protector.'

Holding my hand, he helped me stand. I swept the dust from the path off my skirt.

'As soon as Master Cromwell returns I shall announce the wedding banns,' he said. 'I take it he will be back from Rome in time!' he added, his voice softly reassuring.

'Yes. He is already on his return journey.'

Gathering up his cloak, Father Luke inclined his head and continued with a quick step past me along the path to the bell tower.

'Thank you, Father,' I called after him.

He gave me a backward wave and vanished into the church.

It would not be long now. I daily considered myself fortunate because love within a marriage was hard to discover. Love hid itself in shaded places, our marriages decided by parents and by duty, but I loved Thomas Cromwell with all my being and, that spring, I held my excitement to myself at this thought, in case our love was snatched away by fate.

I glanced about the hillocks that marked graves, and studied the trees that overhung them, looking for a sleek little blackbird, but he had gone. Tom Williams had loved in a shaded place. 'May his soul rest in peace,' I thought to myself. I whispered a Pater Noster for my first Tom, fingering the ebony rosary beads that dropped from my waist chain. My mind at peace, I picked up the empty basket and retraced my footsteps along the churchyard path to the Wood Street gate. Hopefully, that day, I had put Tom Williams and his secrets to rest.

Chapter Eighteen

THOMAS RETURNED TO ME by the first Sunday in June. On his arrival, he unrolled a painter's canvas to reveal a deep blue sky, a manger and the Holy Family clad in the garments of Italian nobles. The angels in their cerulean heaven were golden and white, happy, plump and pouting, so real that I felt they could fly with their gilded wings from their heavenly sky and hover around me.

'It is a gift for you to hang in our new home. I shall have a carpenter make a frame to hold it.'

I looked up from the painting. 'But, Thomas, a new home already! I thought we would live here for a while first.'

'No, since Rome, I have enough silver for us to move house. New beginnings start as soon as we are married,' he said, smiling. 'I have already taken a lease on a property. We need a spacious hall in which to entertain, and an office so I can see my clients in private. There are rooms for our apprentices, my clerks and a well-appointed parlour where you can hang this painting, or perhaps in our bedchamber to lull us into gentle acts of love.' His fingers lightly trailed over the cherubs. 'The new house is closer to the warehouse I am using, the one on St Catherine's dock.'

'Which street?'

'Fenchurch Street, not at all far from the Tower and the river. You will like it, Lizzy. We shall have enough

163

bedchambers for your father and mother to stay with us whenever they wish. We can move in after our wedding.'

'You have arranged all this quickly, Thomas, and without once asking my opinion.'

'The Boston aldermen paid me well for my legal work.' He looked pleased with himself as he said this. Thomas, I had discovered, was proud of his ability with languages and his astounding memory. 'I knew the property would come available and expressed my interest before setting out for Rome -'

'And you said nothing to me.'

'No, Lizzy, I hoped to surprise you. The fewer people who knew it was available the better.' His left eyebrow was quizzically raised and, for a moment, I wondered what else he was arranging.

'When can I see this new house?'

'Soon.'

Our wedding bans were called in the Wood Street parish church, over three Sundays. No one came forward saying I was unfit for marriage because I had protected a heretic. We would wed on Midsummer's Day. A week later we would remove to Fenchurch Street and I knew deep in my heart that I would not be sad to leave Wood Street.

Gossip has its own wings and they are not gilded and gentle as those in my painting, and they flap quickly. The Company men soon found out that I was marrying the clever merchant who did legal work for the Merchant Adventurers. Their wives, who had viewed me with suspicion, now hovered about me like clucking pigeons, greeting me in church and on the street. They liked a funeral or a wedding, or both in my case. They never spoke again of Tom Williams, so apparently I was no longer perceived as a widowed threat.

When Thomas and I had chosen Midsummer's morning for our wedding, we had been wise. I would not have a great merchant gathering descending upon my hall, taking over my wedding with their showy presence, profligate drinking and boisterous behaviour. The City drapers observed their own riotous Midsummer feast at the company's hall in St Swithin's Lane. Not only did I not want a big wedding, I didn't want to be fussed over by the wives from the Drapers' Company while their husbands accosted my female servants. My wedding would be conducted to my liking, with only family and Thomas' friends present. My cook and his assistants would provide a bridal cake and a feast for them and we would dance with dignity to pipes, tabors and the gentle sound of lutes.

On the appointed morning, my two young nephews, with rosemary pinned to their silken sleeves, led me to the church porch. Cat's son, Richard, headed the procession carrying before us my silver bridal cup festooned with colourful ribbons. On that blue midsummer's day, the sun beat down on us relentlessly. Though I wore my rose damask gown cut in a fashionable inverted open shape at the front, revealed my floating embroidered silk petticoat, and though the fabrics were light in weight, I felt myself perspiring because of my excitement, my undersleeves damp though scented with lavender.

The fanfare of bagpipes, pipes and tabors that followed us ceased playing. We had arrived at the Church door where Thomas was waiting with his sisters, their husbands and a small number of his friends. Joan was my only maiden that day. She stepped behind me, joyful in this duty which no doubt she considered a rehearsal for her own wedding, pleased that I had given her a new blue gown of soft light weight wool that complimented her dark eyes and loose hair. Joan had passed her sixteenth birthday in May, ever a spring child with a sunny disposition, but still young for marriage. Only the children of the great could afford to wed before their eighteenth year, unless there was reason for a hasty wedding. Although we were wealthy merchants, we were not great.

Father proudly stood by me as my dowry agreement was read aloud. A purse of coins which he produced from his cloak pocket was passed by one of my nephews to a priest to be distributed to the Parish poor. Thomas, who looked handsome in a grey, fur-trimmed gown placed a gold ring in a silver dish. After Father Luke blessed it and sprinkled it with Christ's holy water, Thomas placed it on my finger and once we were married, my heart soared with joy. I was now Elizabeth Cromwell. Hand in hand, we returned to the Wood Street house followed along the narrow street by my noise-some procession. As was the tradition, we had presented our guests with gifts of silk ribbons. That day, I received a multitude of pewter basins, decorated plate and embroidered linen for our new home in Fenchurch Street.

My wedding feast commenced with salads, roasted meats, pies and sauces. Thomas placed the finest cuts of beef and pork on my side of our shared plate. He served me with my cook's best sweet sauce of apples spiced with cinnamon, teasing me to eat as our hired musicians played their lutes, and sang love songs and ballads of the greenwoods that lay far beyond the City walls.

Between courses, Tom's friends came over to speak with me, all educated gentlemen, like Thomas; followers of the new learning. Later, Joan and I were introduced to a delightful young man called John Williamson, almost as handsome as Toby, with fair locks that waved onto his

166

collar and smiling eyes the colour of cornflowers.

After he returned to his place on the lower trestles, my sister continued to gaze over, clearly besotted by the beautiful youth. I whispered to her to stop staring his way so boldly.

'He smiled my way first,' she murmured.

'Even so, it is not becoming to stare at him, Joan.'

She raised her eyebrows at me and I determined to send her over to Mother on an errand and out of John's line of vision.

Before I could accomplish this, I was distracted when Thomas nudged my elbow. He introduced me to an old friend, Henry Sadler, who was a steward for Thomas Grey, the Marquess of Dorset, for whom my husband had done legal work. His son, tow-haired Ralph, only seven years old, was already a charming boy with twinkling blue eyes that seemed to study us all. Thomas had said to me before our wedding day that he would like to take Ralph Sadler into our household for his education - if I were willing. With an education, he would one day make Ralph into a clerk.

'Yes, it would be a pleasure,' I said smiling. I liked the boy on meeting him and was glad I had agreed to take him into our household.

Thomas' cousin Robert, who was the vicar of Battersea, came over to be introduced. I had no idea on my wedding day how significant this man would be for our future. I did, however, realise that it was important that he was impressed by me, because this cousin knew Thomas Wolsey, the King's most important advisor. I made conversation by asking him about this great man. I was very curious about the king's advisor, whom many citizen disliked because he was so pompous. 'Jumped-up,' they would say, 'fat and greedy, a butcher's boy made good.' I wondered at that. He had risen on his own merits, which I thought admirable at first, though then I did not know our future or how suspicious I would later become of this crimson silken-clad man.

That afternoon, I smiled when Cousin Robert, a small round balding man, leaned closer to me and said, 'Elizabeth, Thomas Wolsey is an extremely large man.' He widened his arms expansively. 'Though not as tall as our king who is six feet and two inches tall. He is devoted to King Henry and a great churchman. The queen likes him well enough, though, truth to say, she prefers Thomas More.' He lowered his voice and I felt my Thomas lean towards me to catch his words.

Cousin Robert said, 'I think my master will be a cardinal one of these days.'

'Good,' Thomas said in his quiet voice. 'We need an English cardinal, a man who will give his loyalty to our King when debating with the French and the Spanish. He will be an improvement on the Pope's men. I saw this only too clearly when I visited Rome this spring.'

Cousin Robert smiled as he popped a fat grape into his mouth. 'Perhaps I can introduce you, Cousin Thomas, that is, if you intend putting more time into legal matters than cloth matters.'

'Aye, yes, I do, Cousin Robert, now that my father-in-law will oversee our cloth interests.' Thomas patted my hand and smiled his most charming smile at me.

I started at this revelation. Thomas had never said that he had amalgamated our interests and my father had never mentioned a change in our business relationship. I looked straight into my husband's eyes and began to mouth, 'You never -'

He whispered into my ear, 'I have only just made this agreement, Lizzy. I meant to tell you later. It was what we

168

agreed. We should work with your father. It makes perfect sense.'

Cousin Robert looked quizzically at us.

'Yes, of course,' I said aloud, remembering my manners in front of Thomas' important cousin.

The puddings had arrived. I lifted a slice of Mother's midsummer tart from the passing platter and placed it on our shared plate. I did not want to upset Thomas, but for a moment I had uncomfortably wondered if the reason he had so swiftly sought my hand was to do with family connections and not for love's sake after all.

Cousin Robert was saying, 'Come and visit me in Battersea, Thomas, and I shall see what I can do for you. Bring your Elizabeth.'

My husband thanked him. In our world, patronage was everything. Thomas lifted my hand to his lips and kissed my fingers one by one. 'Lizzy,' he whispered once his cousin's attention turned to his neighbour. 'I will never make any decision that does not advance us. Trust me on it.'

I loved him, but I had a niggling sense that, although Thomas cared deeply about family, he would sacrifice my own independence if he felt it advantageous to do so. I had not wanted to join my business with Father's trade unless Thomas could watch over it. How could he watch Father if he took on more legal work? Yet, if Thomas became wealthy through his legal work, I reasoned, so would I. I swallowed my complaints. He was my husband and I must trust him. By the time the bridal cake appeared - a wonderful confection, a bridal crown, coated with marzipan and studied with little jellies fashioned as jewels - my good temper was restored, though I watched Cousin Robert cram marzipan into his mouth with suspicion. What if

169

Thomas worked for the Archbishop one day? Would it take him from my side?

Pipes and tabors opened the beats of dancing tunes. Servants dragged the trestles back to the walls. Guests sat in small groups on stools and benches. Children raced about the hall waving ribbons. The talk close to me became increasingly teasing and bawdy as more and more wine was poured. The Lincoln lawyer frowned as the women of our families opened the dancing with a stately pavan.

Thomas took my hand. 'Can you dance the gilliard?' I nodded. I had danced it at the feasts I had attended for Christmas celebrations at the Drapers' Guildhall. For a time, Father had allowed me a dancing master and, although I had not danced it for over a year, I thought I could remember the steps. We moved into the circle's centre to great stamping and clapping.

Thomas' face would alight with a warm glow when his interest was taken, especially when he found himself in good company, as he was on our wedding day. 'I'll never remember all your friends' names,' I whispered.

'Never mind that, for you will meet them all again and I shall remind you. Enjoy the dance, my sweeting.'

Thomas was a superb dancer and never failed to catch me as I made the leap. It was as I turned in the dance that I noticed my bold sister approach the handsome John Williamson, whom I had forgotten. She leaned towards him, her loose dark hair falling to conceal their faces. Moments later they were dancing near us. As my sister made graceful turns, her partner gazed into her eyes when he had captured her after a jump and his hands were encircling her tiny waist. When there was a pause in the dancing, he drew her to the side of the hall. Lutes struck up for the fedelta, another circular dance. Although it was impolite for a maiden to dance each dance with the same partner, Joan never moved from John Williamson's side.

I drew Thomas' attention to them.

'I hope she is back in Surrey the moment our wedding is over.'

'Why?'

'She is only past her sixteenth name day.'

'Not so young,' Thomas remarked with a sardonic smile.

'No,' I said thoughtfully.

In the Fedelta three couples work their way around in circles, dancing with all members of the opposite sex. We were six couples in two sets. To my relief my parents were in the other set, as were Joan and John. From the corner of my eye I saw my father frown at Joan, who had the grace to look chastened, and for the rest of the afternoon she allowed others to partner her, or sat obediently beside Mother and Father. As we turned again, my eye discovered the servants gathered in a group by the kitchen entrance. The apprentices were vying for the maids' attentions, especially favours from pretty blond-headed Bess. Meg was leaning into a foot-tapping Smith, who had thrown an arm about her waist. Not interested indeed. Nonsense.

Finally, we danced the branle, all of us who could stand in lines carefully passing lighted candles from person to person as we turned. It was a dance of love. I smiled through the candle flame at Tom and whispered 'I love you'. When he returned, 'Likewise, I thee.' I was showered with happiness.

After the candles were extinguished there was a lull in the dancing. This provided a rest period for the musicians, but not for us. Old stockings that had been saved for such occasions whipped us towards the hall door and so

Thomas and I were chased from the hall up the stairs to where a very flushed Meg was waiting at the top of the stairway for me. She ushered me through the doorway into my chamber but sent Thomas and his friends into the chamber that had been Tom Williams' room. My mother, Meg and Joan helped me remove my gown, my kirtle, my petticoat and linen. They eased a new nightgown over my head, untied the ribbons from my hair and brushed it until it fell onto my shoulders in a silvery cascade.

'Ready,' came the call from beyond the chamber. Mother nodded and Meg opened the door. The men burst in with Thomas in their midst only in his nightshirt. We were placed into my petal-strewn bed with gentle teasing, and Father Luke pushed forward and blessed us with his sprinkling of holy water. We dutifully sat up together and said our prayers. Through my half-opened eyes, I noticed a hint of cynicism play about my husband's mouth as he prayed. Was I married to an unbeliever?

Mother came to my side, bent down and whispered into my ear. 'This will be happier than before, my love. Rest well.' She handed us a goblet of malmsey to share.

I prayed that he had not heard her words. I was determined that I would not confess Tom Williams' sin, for I could not spoil what had been a perfect wedding with a less than perfect wedding night. As if Thomas knew my concern, he wooed me gently with soft kisses and gentle strokes until I could no longer bear it. And when he discovered the truth, all he said into my ear was, 'My lovely, sweet Elizabeth, of course I had suspected you were a virgin.' I felt tears welling up in my eyes. He placed a finger on my lips. 'Do not weep, my love, for I am glad of it. There is no need to explain. I know the world of men. I do not think God is an unforgiving God.'

As the candle's glow lit up his face, I saw passion stir

his grey eyes. 'Do not let us ever speak of it,' I said holding back my sobs. 'Let us both remember that this is our beginning. Promise me this, my Thomas, let us never lie to each other, never, from this day forth.'

Thomas had promised God's forgiveness, though he did not have that authority to make such a bold promise. I thought that He would send devils with spiky claws to torture Tom Williams before my first husband could ever enter Heaven's safety.

Thomas held me close in his arms, and we loved as if passion had never been known to mankind before. That night, I put Tom Williams behind me and felt as if we two were the subject of love's invention.

Part Two

Fenchurch Street

I love a flower of sweet odour
Marjoram gentle or sweet lavender
Columbine, gold of sweet flavour
Nay, nay let be
Is none of them that liketh me

Roses, a Song for Three Voices

Chapter Nineteen

Midsummer 1526, The Bedchamber

I GLANCE ABOUT THE large bedchamber I share with Thomas. The maids have tidied away my nightgown and Thomas' dressing robe, an embroidered garment of soft silk, purchased on his last journey to Italy, a second visit on behalf of the Boston aldermen. He revisited Rome in 1517 to renew their right to sell indulgences, and returned even more disillusioned by the clergy's profligate manner of living and with the sale of indulgences, which has caused such an uproar in some parts of the German Empire and with an evangelical called Martin Luther.

'But you do legal work for the Cardinal,' I pointed out every time he complained about the clergy. I add, 'People complain that Cardinal Wolsey is enriching his own coffers. Just look at the palace he has built on the river, the thousand servants he employs, the cooks, his food taster, the gold plate, the tapestries which hang in his many houses. He rides on an ass but it is covered with golden cloth, his hat carried before him on a golden cushion. The gossips say he is feared by all and loved by few. He sets himself up as greater than the king himself.'

Thomas claims that I rant on unnecessarily. 'The Cardinal is different. He is of the common people. He is not of noble blood as many of the Italian cardinals are. No, Lizzy, he has strived hard for everything he has achieved. Do not become a scold.'

'So you like him because he strived hard like yourself,

177

Thomas.' A hint of sarcasm creeps into my voice.

He looks serious and remarks, 'Like myself, indeed, and I intend to rise high too.'

There is no answer to this because I must live with his admiration for the Cardinal. I love my husband and I believe that he loves me too, though there was a time when I thought that I had lost his love. I bite my bottom lip and taste the trickle of my own blood as I remember this bitter betrayal, but I shall come to that shortly.

I understand how Thomas thinks. By our bed, he keeps a strange work scribed in Italian. This is not a printed book but a hand-copied codex titled *The Prince* by an Italian called Niccolo Machiavelli, a volume that he brought from Italy. Thomas has read me extracts from it, translating it as he reads, explaining how fate and destiny work. It makes me shudder to think that my gentle husband can be influenced by writing that tells men to carve out their own destiny, for this is what it does. Take for instance -

He who neglects what is done for what ought to be done, sooner effects his ruin than his preservation.

It is, Thomas says, about new princedoms like King Henry's, and ways of seeing how they work. 'A ruler must establish himself in defiance of customs.'

'Against the Pope's authority,' I parry. 'The Pope is our Holy Father and even a King must care for his soul and revere the Pope's spiritual authority,'

Tom raises an eyebrow and throws me a sharp look. 'Perhaps, it is wise for a prince to destroy powerful people if they threaten his authority, even a Pope.' He sets the codex to one side. 'Many think the Church needs reform, but they still care for their souls and for the Church's teachings.' He sighs. 'People are naturally resistant to reform and change. I would they could be guided in this matter by good and strong leaders.'

'Thomas, do not speak these things abroad,' I caution him.

He raises his eyebrows, tired of hearing my warning. 'As I keep telling you, I am no fool, Lizzy.'

Though I cannot complain to Thomas about Niccolo Machiavelli and be certain he will listen, I can take care for my own soul and, by humble example, urge him to have a care for his own. I pray daily for Queen Catherine, especially now that we often hear that the King is besotted with a new lady. I give generously to the poor, and I always speak well of the Church.

As these thoughts trouble my mind, my hands slide along the rich garments hanging on my clothing pole, searching for a gown to wear for our Midsummer's dinner. My eyes follow my collection of beautiful gowns until I catch sight of one I wore to the Drapers' Company's Midsummer Feast only a year after we had moved into the house at Fenchurch Street. The fabric is of softest yellow silk threads mixed with cotton. It is embroidered with golden flowers, and owns a matching overskirt cut in a V to show off a creamy underskirt. I lift it down and lay it on the bed and remember that I own a hood to compliment the gown. Thomas had similar material in his store on St Catherine's Wharf and, recently, he asked a haberdasher to use black velvet for the hood's newly fashionable curved frame and the yellow fabric for its fall.

I take the underskirt, figured in cream silk from my cupboard, and leaving it lying across the counterpane with the overdress, set out from my chamber to look for Bessie who will help me tie the laces for the sleeves and bodice.

Glancing down into the courtyard from the window at the top of our great staircase, I see Thomas and Ralph

Sadler carrying gardening tools into the shed. The youth is now taller than my husband. When I first wore the yellow and cream gown, Ralph had just joined our household and as a small boy, was not afraid of anything, certainly not thunder and lightning, even though that night of the Drapers' Company's Midsummer Feast, I had feared for him.

Chapter Twenty

1515

LOOSE TILES CLACKED ON city roofs as a sudden wind shook through the streets. The unseasonal storm blew up from the river, carrying with it the river's stink.

We returned from the Drapers' Midsummer Feast, struggling along St Swithin's Lane, clutching each other to steady our walk as a gale blew us forward. Smith held our covered lantern with one cloaked arm protectively about it, as if encircling a small child. Although first and second storey overhangs allowed some protection from the heavy rain, the journey from St Swithin's Lane to Fenchurch Street felt interminable. Little Ralph Sadler had joined our household earlier that week and I thought of him sleeping alone in his small chamber high up in the attic with this storm worrying at the rafters.

'Ralph will be so frightened. I should go to him when we get back.'

Thomas shook his head, rivulets of water running down his hood and his face. He lifted his hand from my elbow and tried to wipe the water away. 'The others will look after him.' He clutched my arm even more tightly. 'Stay close to the walls and try to stay dry.'

I was six months with child, and could not help feeling worried about a boy whose father had placed him in our care at such a tender age. He was only turned eight last month. I stoically pushed on through the wind and rain. Never in my lifetime, not before, nor since, has there been such a terrible Midsummer storm.

We had to sidestep buckets that clattered along the slippery cobbles and avoid the waste that spilled out of the central gutters. We passed others caught in the storm who flitted past like dark shades. More than once lightning leapt out at us like a Midsummer actor intending to surprise us. This year the usual festivities were cancelled. Rain lashed through my cloak drenching my new yellow gown, water seeped into my thin leather shoes and the candle in Smith's lantern shrank into a slender ghost of light, blowing out as we reached the courtyard of our Fenchurch Street house.

Gerard Smith banged on our great knocker. There was a rattle at the sliding window peep hole. The porter's large face emerged, red and fat-veined. I turned away on smelling his foul, ale-infused breath, noting that he had been celebrating his Midsummer alone rather than guarding the house. I determined to have words with Thomas about him. After all, it was Midsummer when my warehouse in Wood Street burned down. I had forgotten to be vigilant where our property is concerned and there were so often celebrations out on the streets involving fire- should they be May Day, All Hallows Eve or Midsummer Revels.

It was after nine by the time we reached home. The porter quickly drew back, slamming shut the peep hole and rattling keys. Moments later, too slow for my liking, two of his servants dragged the gate opened. Smith growled at them for their tardiness. We hurried through the yard hearing the restless neighing from our stable and the barking of our dogs from the hall. Meg pulled open the house door and ushered us inside.

'Sainted Mary, what a state you are in. Upstairs, Mistress Elizabeth. Now. Get you out of those wet clothes.'

We were drenched and dripping but safely home.

***

Thomas and Meg helped me upstairs. On the way up, when I mentioned the boy again, he told me to stop fussing and to have a care for my own needs.

Meg, remarked, 'I have heard that lightning could shock the unborn child. We must get you into bed at once.'

'Nonsense, an old gossip's tale,' I grumbled.

'That is a storm out there to beat all others and you should have a care, Mistress. There are all kinds of poisons in the air this summer.'

'So the drapers' goodwives were saying.' I removed my headdress and shook out my damp hair. Rubbing it viciously with a towel I said, 'A posset would help, Meg.'

Thomas sent Meg down to the kitchens for a filled kettle to warm my bed and a hot posset. He unlaced and helped me out of my over-gown as expertly as any experienced maidservant could manage. For a moment, I wondered at his expertise in this area of our lives.

He said, 'We should send for Mistress Webster in the morning since it is best to be sure all is well with you.' I instinctively drew my hands across my swollen stomach. Mrs Webster was the midwife, a plump and comely barber-surgeon's wife of good reputation. I liked her well enough but didn't think I needed her.

'Don't fuss, the child has quickened. That's all. My womb is not wandering about my body because of a bit of lightning, no matter Meg's concern. Nor do I intend catching a chill.'

He shook his head. 'You must take care from now on. You must rest. You are always rushing up to Cornhill to check on the cloth sales when your father and Smith can handle it all. Trust them.' A fine thing for him to say

183

when he rarely trusted anyone, and I knew he kept a close eye on the two clerks he employed to keep accounts.

I was about to say so when Meg bustled back into our chamber with an egg and milk posset. Thomas gently took the posset and gave it into my hands. She placed a warm stone jar into my bed to warm the sheets. Thomas sat on a stool and rubbed my feet until I had finished sipping the frothy drink, while Meg lifted the empty cup from my hand, grumbling that I should be in bed forthwith. He rose from his stool, nodded and said he would work in his closet for a few hours. 'I shall leave you in Meg's care, Lizzy, but if there is a problem we must send for Jane Webster immediately. Do you hear me, Meg?'

I shook my head; Thomas' concern for my well-being bordered on obsession.

'Yes, Master,' Meg said, concern plastered over her face.

I felt the last flicker of energy fade as Meg helped me into a warm linen nightgown and into my bed. I glanced at my yellow dress and its sodden silken petticoat where it was drying out over my clothing chest. 'I shall never be able to wear that gown again.'

Meg lifted the petticoat up and examined the damp, fragile material. 'Yes, you will, Mistress. I can clean it of mud and you will never think it had been damaged. Your cloak protected it well enough.' She drew her hand over the petticoat. 'Only a small rent and I can mend that. Even a queen would not discard such lovely figured silk.'

'Meg, can you see that young Ralph is not afraid of the storm?'

'I doubt that child is afraid of anything or anyone and certainly not a storm.' Meg filled her arms with my discarded linen. 'Sleep well, Mistress. Shall I draw the bed curtains?'

'Leave them open.'

Though the storm raged outside, hammering at our gates, our chamber felt warm and safe. Stretching out on the feather mattress, I fell into a deep sleep and never heard Thomas come to bed.

When I awoke, Thomas was climbing down the bed step. The Italian coverlet lay in a green, gleaming, satin heap on the floor. It was the sea. Our bed was an island. Sunbeams slanted in through the window glass. The sudden storm was over.

'Are you well, Lizzy?' Thomas looked down on me, his bed cap askew.

I laughed, reached up and straightened it. 'It would seem so; no need to send for Mistress Webster. My womb is not terrified by a crack of lightning nor is your daughter.' I was sure we would safely have our child by the feast of St Michael and intuition told me that we were having a girl.

'That is a relief.' He reached for the fresh hose Meg had laid out for him.

'Are you staying at home today?' I asked Thomas, as I watched him dress.

'No, I have to visit a widow in Bishopsgate. She is in a dispute over land.'

'Where is her land?' I pulled myself up against the pillows, interested.

'Surrey. I may go down later in the week and stay with your brother. I could take John Williamson with me. He is proving helpful.'

'My sister would like that,' I said, amused, thinking that Joan would be delighted if John stayed with them on Henry's manor. 'This widow, is she young?'

'I believe you are jealous, wife.' He looked me in the

eye. I glanced away. He was sharp; his look too penetrating.

'No, not at all. I just wondered.' Truth was, I felt ungainly and feelings of insecurity churned about in my stomach. I loved him too much, but for all his gregariousness around our close friends, he could be aloof, difficult to reach, close about his business and his true thoughts difficult to read.

'She is not in the first flush of youth,' he said, glancing up at me, his eyes twinkling as he worked his charm. 'You, my Lizzy, are the most handsome widow-wife in all London. I would never look at another.' He reached over and patted my belly. 'Now...' he lifted the coverlet from the floor and draped it over my shoulders, 'I shall take dinner with your father at the Guildhall. You must rest today.'

'I have fabrics to make into a book. The mayor's wife is coming to look at the fabric samples next week.'

'Good, Mistress Butler is an excellent connection for us, but, Lizzy, no garden work. Leave that to the gardener.' Thomas hummed as he drew the black leather laces of his boots through the eyelets.

'Thomas?'

'Yes?'

'Remind Father about the wool for the Religious Houses. I don't want us to lose that trade.'

'Lizzy, don't worry about such things.'

I almost spoiled our moment of domestic happiness with a protest, bit my lower lip and drew back a sharp retort just in time. I had never been happy that he allowed Father to run our business. I felt increasingly unnecessary to our joint venture, since I was usually occupied in the still room, in the dairy making cheeses, in my parlour stitching black work on nightgowns or collars, or supervising the cook's endeavours with dinner. I had taken to making pattern books to show clients now. It was a task I thoroughly enjoyed and one that had helped the new cloth gather sales.

He leaned down to kiss me. 'I must go. Meg will come up to you. What would you like her to bring you?'

I felt ravenous and, for the moment, privileged at the thought of breaking my fast in bed like a great lady. 'Warm buttermilk and soft rolls with honey, if she pleases.'

''Tis done!' He winked at me as he opened the latch to our chamber door and I nestled back into the covers listening to his step tripping down the stairway towards the great chamber. I loved to hear his tread. I loved him so much, I would not spoil that for the whole world of London and its great swirling river. I put my mind to making up a new book of samples in preparation for Mistress Butler's visit. Father had sent me swatches of our new materials and they waited my attention in the parlour.

Chapter Twenty-one

MISTRESS BUTLER, A PRETTY, dimple-faced, fair-haired woman, called on me the following week accompanied by her mother and her mother's friend. My samples book of material mixes was ready. Inside a pair of covers, I had pasted small swatches of fabrics, along with descriptions, onto vellum. As I waited, I passed the morning teaching young Ralph his Latin reading.

The boy was then, and is now, years later, quite brilliant. He read well and had quickly absorbed the few Latin verbs I was teaching him. Soon, young Ralph would have more vocabulary than I, and Thomas was already seeking a teacher for him from amongst the tutors his Cousin Robert knew. Ralph Sadler not only needed Latin and Greek, but also adding and subtracting figures if he was to be a useful legal assistant.

As I heard approaching footsteps in the passage, I closed the primer and laid it on the table. 'Now, Ralph, run along to Barnaby. He'll take you with him to the warehouse this afternoon. When you return I want you to give me an account of all the cloth you have seen there, and I want to know how many rolls of each kind you have counted in our stock. He will show you, so pay attention to all he says.'

Ralph nodded obediently. The door was flung opened by one of my servants. He scurried towards the ladies who stood waiting for me in the doorway. 'Bow to the gentlewomen,' I reminded him. 'Remember your manners.'

'Yes, Mistress, he said, stopped and made such a perfect little bow he drew a smile from Mistress Joanna, the mayor's wife, who moved aside to allow him by. Mistress Joanna's mother, Annette Harrison, and her friend, a cross-faced woman whom I had not met before but knew to be a widow of this parish, Margaret Watt, scowled at the boy's retreating back.

'You are too easy with him, Mistress Cromwell,' Annette Harrison remarked as I greeted them. 'If he were my son I would have cuffed his ears.'

'He is not your son, Mistress Harrison, nor mine. He is new to our home and as yet unused to it.' I waved to the cushioned benches by the window. 'Do sit, ladies and I shall send for cakes and a sweet cordial.' It was July and the weather was hot, the room stuffy and though I should take them into the garden, I would not. They might linger overly long. I was not fond of Annette Harrison, a mean-faced silversmith's wife, and Mistress Watt looked even more miserable.

'None the less,' Annette Harrison said, her tone as sharp as her long pointed chin. 'Spare the rod and you make one for your own back.'

I said tersely, 'Quite so, Mistress Harrison.'

'How are you feeling, Elizabeth?' Joanna said politely, in contrast to her mother's rudeness. 'Not long now. Does the child quicken? I saw you at the Drapers' Feast. What an exquisite gown you were wearing too.'

'What, she is out and about!' the woman with Annette Harrison said, raising a pair of scraggy eyebrows, clearly shocked. I had seen her before at St Gabriel's Church but had never conversed with her. She lived in our parish and was someone's widow but I could not recollect whom. I thought her husband might have sold undyed wool.

189

'This is Margaret Watt,' Joanna said, introducing us, and adding, 'My mother and her friend are interested in your new draperies.'

I inclined my head to Mistress Watt, who had spread her shirts and was making herself comfortable on the cushioned settle. 'I shall show you once we have taken refreshments. You must be thirsty.' I rang the bell by my sewing chair. Immediately, Meg appeared. 'The tray, Meg,' I said. 'The ladies might like strawberry cordial and ginger biscuits. And can you fetch the samples book from my chamber.'

Meg nodded to me and retreated into the corridor that led to the kitchen at the back of the house.

Margaret Watt was studying my painted hanging. She remarked. 'Our own Tudor roses. Pity the King has no living child.' Her eyes shifted from the hanging to my projected belly. 'I wish you better luck than Queen Catherine. When do you retire into seclusion, Mistress Elizabeth? Soon, I should think.'

I had not wanted to be shut up for a whole month in my chamber and had already determined that I would not call for the midwife until my travail began. I dared not say this to that sharp-faced matron. If I did, it would be all over the parish within the day, so I said instead, 'Late September, I believe.'

When she clicked her tongue, I was prepared for another caustic comment. Concern showed on Joanna's face, for the mayor's wife was a kindly woman, and clearly did not approve of Widow Watt's sharp tone. We were rescued by Meg who hurried in with the refreshments, an immediate distraction; my guests descended upon the pewter cups at once. Margaret Watt held hers up to the window glass.

'Fine pewter ware. Fortunate you are, Mistress

Cromwell, to afford pewter.'

'A wedding gift from my sister-in-law and her husband.'

She pursed her mouth and sipped her strawberry cordial, thankfully too thirsty to comment further. She reached out her cup for Meg to refill it. However, she was not of restrained tongue for long. As I served them the biscuits my gown caught in my chair and as I pulled it free I saw three pairs of eyes stare at the bright silk of my underdress. My petticoat showed.

'I would not have thought that permissible, Mistress Cromwell,' Mistress Watt remarked, pointing to my crimson underskirt. 'I suppose if it is well-concealed who would know about such secrets.'

I tugged my linen gown over the underskirt. 'It is just a remnant, an old piece of silk, not worth selling. It expands as does my girth, thus it's comfortable.' I said evenly. 'I am sure I can be forgiven for wearing it in my parlour. I would never think to wear scarlet abroad.'

'Your husband will not want any slur to touch him, if he hopes for success in the City courts. Let us hope no one else sees that kirtle.' She sniffed and added, clearly not able to resist slighting Thomas, 'Though I expect you can easily afford the fines.'

Joanna Butler and her mother exchanged concerned glances.

I felt myself redden to the shade of my petticoat as I passed around the biscuits. For the rest of their visit I felt extremely uncomfortable. Only Joanna, whose husband was a grocer turned merchant as times grew prosperous, ordered any of our cloth, a sombre grey wool mixed with linen. Though it was fine cloth she could have her tailor sew into a practical gown, I watched her mother's companion click her tongue against her teeth with disapproval. 'I hope you are not encouraging disobedience in others with the sale of your cloth, Mistress Cromwell,' she said rudely as she studied my samples book. She closed the book so carelessly I thought the parchment might tear. 'I cannot afford such luxury.'

I shook my head. 'I have never read of a law forbidding grey or a mix of wool and linen. If you wish to purchase cloth for yourself, Mistress Watt, I can offer you a good price.'

'No, I have no need. Let us hope you abide within the law's strictures. I would not want to think that the parish wardens would have our mayor's wife investigated.'

'I am sure no one can fault the grey mix,' I said evenly.

Those likely to mind would be Joanna's mother, Annette Harrison, and her friend. When they rose to leave, I felt relief.

Once they were ushered out, I could not settle to my embroidery so I hurried out into the garden in search of pleasanter air. I determined to pull the weeds growing around the hollyhocks - a clutch of invasive, spiky thistles that the gardener had previously missed. The act would cool my irritation with the unbearable Mistress Watt.

Mistress Butler sent to Cornhill for the fabric to be delivered to her house which stood four storeys high, secluded behind tall walls in a street close by. After that, I heard nothing more from the mayor's wife. I wrote her a short note thanking her for her interest in our cloth, suggesting that I inform her when more became available. She replied saying that would be suitable, and wished me well with the birth of our child. She made no mention of her mother or of Margaret Watt. I assumed that other than in St Gabriel's I was unlikely to encounter Mistress Watt again.

Chapter Twenty-two

MY TIME WAS DRAWING near; yet the closer it came, the more I loved to work in the garden. The earth smelled of autumn, apples and late roses. A gentle breeze blew. A pleasant September sun was shining and I wanted to feel the softness of the day, to be in the open air. I glanced up, beyond the rooftops, to where the sky held scudding clouds soft as duck down. There were still a few weeks left before the expected birth of the child I longed for. I would not harm the child with an hour outside.

Mother and Catherine had both come to stay, to help, they said. If Mistress Webster and my mother had their way, I should have been closed away in my chamber by now, covers over the windows and a charcoal brazier burning night and day. I certainly would not be out in the garden gathering pennyroyal, hellebore and madder, herbs would that ease my labour when it came to my time.

I was placing a clump of pennyroyal in my basket when the sharpness of the thrusting pain took me by surprise. It coursed through me, shaking me up, and throwing me down as if I were being cast into Hell's darkness. I dropped the basket, doubled over, my hands cupping my fallen abdomen. 'It's coming,' I shouted over the herb beds, desperately hoping that I could be heard.

Meg, who was throwing washing over a hedge, came running towards me, followed by Mother and Cat exiting the still room, their skirts flapping in the breeze.

'Send for Mistress Webster at once, Meg,' my mother said with reasonable calm. She turned to me. 'Lean on me. As well we were nearby. You should not be out in the garden at such a time. To the bedchamber with you, Elizabeth.' She helped me straighten up and to lean on Cat and herself.

I groaned. 'It is only the beginning, Mother. It could be hours yet.'

'Maybe not,' Cat said gently, taking my other arm. 'I'll send for Thomas. He's in the Guildhall with Smith and Master Wright, the mercer, today. Barnaby can run over and fetch him.'

As Mother and Cat helped me through the house, servants appeared in doorways, anxious and flustered. We passed through the corridor to the staircase that led up from the hall without difficulty. Somehow I hauled myself up the stairway, Mother and Cat supporting my considerable weight, managing to hold me upright until we reached my bedchamber where I collapsed onto the bed. Cat removed my shoes and loosened my clothing. Mother called down the staircase for Bessie, who was amongst the gathering of retainers below, to bring a brazier up at once. I groaned. The pain was excruciating.

'No need. It's warm enough,' I complained, feeling sweat trickle down my back.

'It is dangerous for the child, and besides we need to heat water.' Mother was adamant. All would be done as she decreed.

As I lay down on my bed another tortuous pain gripped me. I climbed out again and stood clutching the edge of my oak coffer, waiting for the next pain to descend. Servants came running with the draperies and baskets of straw for my chamber. I was hardly aware as Mother and Cat and the maids hung linen drapery over the window, lit candles, thickly scattered straw over the floor. Mother drew the ominous-looking birthing stool she had brought from Putney from an alcove where I had concealed it under folded linen.

I raised my arm imperiously and pointed to it. 'I can't use that!'

'When the time draws nearer, you will be glad of its support, Lizzy.'

'Mercy is right,' Cat said. 'As well it is here. You said the baby was due after the end of September, not so early in the month.'

'I made a mistake. I did not want to be suffocated in here for weeks,' I grumbled. Two servant girls carried a brazier into the room. 'And I don't want that either,' I cried between groans of increasing agony.

'Foolish, foolish daughter; fortunate indeed we are with you,' Mother crooned in her best soothing voice.

They loosened my smock ties and undressed me where I stood clutching the oak chest, the Virgin smiling down on me from a painting on my alcove wall. Her halo seemed to glow fiercely through the dimness of the chamber. She was encouraging me. I fancied I saw her nod at me. Mother drew a soft linen smock over my head. All of a sudden, another pain grasped me and my waters broke in a great gush over the straw. They had covered the bed with fresh sheets, so now they prised my hands from the coffer and drew me back to it. I lay down on the cool linen, glad of them since the chamber was stifling with the charcoal brazier and the windows closed and covered. The green satin coverlet had been removed to the room where Thomas was sleeping. Instead, a red flannel cover appeared. The pains were more regular and I knew it would be soon.

Voices accompanied footsteps treading up the stairs. I recognised the midwife's and another whose I did not know. I raised my head and, squinting, saw the mercer's wife in the doorway with the midwife. Agnes Wright, whose husband Thomas had been with today, swept into my chamber and I was too immersed in waves of pain to protest her presence.

'Your husband is waiting below,' the plump woman said quietly. 'I have helped Mistress Webster before. May I help you, Mistress Cromwell?' She looked closely at me. 'I think this will be over sooner than many I've seen of late.' She smiled. 'Now, what can I do?' Her voice was soft and kind.

'The baby's linen is in the small coffer. You could air it for me,' I managed to reply.

Her expensive skirts swished as she crossed my spacious chamber and began to organise swaddling and the cradle in readiness.

Meg offered me an infusion of pennyroyal laced with honey. 'I rescued your herbs,' she whispered. 'And, in any case, I had a supply ready waiting. Drink it all if you can. It will hurry on the travail.'

As I slowly sipped the sweet liquid, Meg wiped my hot brow with a cool cloth moistened with lavender water. The scent, drifting into my nostrils, was momentarily soothing.

Mistress Webster efficiently took control of my chamber. As I drifted through waves of pain all afternoon, she issued instructions to my mother and Cat which they seemed to follow without a word of complaint. She applied a mysterious sweet-smelling ointment containing oil of almonds to my belly and calmed me with soft words. I had not warmed to her brisk bossy manner when she had called on me early in my pregnancy, but now I welcomed her.

Mother lifted up some items lying on the coffer. ''Tis time for these.'

196

I possessed a good luck stone and had borrowed the Virgin's childbirth belt from St Gabriel. Mother hung my eagle stone, a stone within a stone from the east known to preserve the safety of my unborn child, about my neck, gently lifted me and tied the Holy Virgin's plaited girdle loosely above what had been my waist. There must be a magical supply of these for every parish church in the land seemed to possess such precious items. Thomas had snorted at the practice when the cincture arrived on loan from St Gabriel's Church, calling it a ridiculous and superstitious nonsense. It is a comfort to us women, no matter its origin; it was a solace that day as my agony drew towards its climax.

As the City church bells rang for Vespers, I screamed. 'She's coming.' More than ever now, I was sure that I was having a daughter.

Meg and Cat helped me down onto the straw and over to the birthing chair. As I reached down to clutch onto it I could feel Mistress Webster lifting my linen shift and probing about my secret parts. I caught a whiff of oil of lilies from her hands. 'The child has crowned, Elizabeth,' I heard her say, 'Push.' I pushed so hard I thought I must die, as Cat and Agnes Wright supported me by my arms.

'Again, once more, Elizabeth,' the midwife said. 'Nearly there.'

I pushed again with all my might. Moments later there was a lusty cry. Tears coursed down my cheeks. Our daughter entered the world.

'Is my baby whole,' I gasped through tears of exhaustion.

'St Paul, be blessed. Our city has another healthy child. Indeed, she is complete,' Mistress Webster said. 'A girl child.'

Mine had not, in truth, been such a difficult birthing. Many women died. I had survived. I whispered a prayer of thanks to God and touched the Virgin's belt.

'I caught her,' my mother cried, looking up at me. 'And Lizzy, she is healthy. She is dainty too, like her mother.'

'Thank you,' I whispered towards the still-smiling Virgin in the shadowy painting. We are calling her Anne,' I said, turning my attention to Mother and Cat. Cat supported me as momentarily I leaned back on the birthing chair exhausted.

They cut the cord, cleaned the baby of birth mucus and gave her into my arms. 'Anne,' I said. I was too entranced by my tiny daughter to feel the discomfort that followed as Mistress Webster delivered the placenta, cleaned me, bathed me, gently placed and tied linen clouts about me, removed my sweaty shift and replaced it with a clean shift. Mother and Mistress Webster helped me to lie down on the sweet lavender-scented linen.

'May we show Anne to Thomas now, Elizabeth?' Cat said, leaning over me. 'He is waiting in the hall.'

When I nodded, the midwife scooped Annie up and left me to sip a healing draught of camomile and honey that Meg prepared. Mother wiped my brow and Cat gently brushed my hair. Agnes Wright fell to her knees. 'It is by God's grace that you are safely delivered of such an angel, Mistress Cromwell.'

I nodded towards the painting. 'The Madonna smiled on me today,' I whispered.

Agnes Wright's rosary beads clacked as she knelt before the painting of the Virgin that still hung behind my oak chest. I crossed myself and whispered my thanks to the Madonna with her rounded belly and her plump, oddly grown up looking holy child. The room filled with our murmuring as we joined Agnes's prayers of thanks.

Cat and Mother tiptoed out of the room. The birthing straw was removed and the birthing chair cleaned and stored away. It would not, I hoped, be needed for a long, long time again. I demanded the removal of the brazier since it was a warm September evening and a fire was not necessary.

Mother and Cat both insisted that it stayed. 'You are not out of danger yet. Think of the baby,' Cat insisted.

'If I must,' I said because, short of rising from the bed myself and shifting it, I knew that it would have to stay until Tom took care of it later.

The linen drapes were swiftly removed. My chamber smelled of fresh herbs and lavender. Closer to me by my pillow lay a tiny swaddled Annie whose baby scent was as delicious as Meg's sweetest milk caudle laced with honey.

Thomas came lumbering into the chamber to be with me as soon as the band of women had descended the stairs to a supper laid out in the parlour. I lay in bed, glad to be alone with my husband at last, as Annie nestled against my breast. Thomas lifted her tiny fingers and studied them. 'She is enchanting,' he said. 'Just like her mother. Perfect.' He added after a moment of thought, 'She will be christened on Friday. It is Mistress Webster's privilege to carry Anne to the font. She has done well today.'

'Thomas, I am well enough to attend.'

'Not before you are churched.'

I knew I could not fight tradition, and, giving way, lay back against the pillows. 'Who did we agree will be her godparents?'

'My sister and your sister and also as gossips, if you will consider him, my sister's husband.'

'I like it well. Who will fetch Joan if it is to be so soon?'

'Your father has already sent for her. Cat must return to her family soon. Would you like Joan to stay with us for a month or so to help you organise the household?'

'Joan?' What help could Joan give me? What did my difficult sister know about keeping order with the servants or managing the cook? 'Would she be capable?'

'She seemed competent when I visited Surrey in July. She is grown up now, past her eighteenth birthday, old enough to be wed.'

'I hope you are right about that, Thomas, because if she starts complaining, upsetting the servants, or otherwise behaving inappropriately, she will be sent back to Surrey on the first river boat available.'

'Of course, my love, but don't you think we should give her a chance?'

I sighed. 'If Joan behaves, then she must have her chance.'

I was only too aware that a young clerk had caught Joan's eye and that he was often a visitor to our home. Joan must be kept so busy she would have no time to upset anyone with her outspoken tongue, nor would my little sister display forward behaviour when Master Williamson spent time in Thomas' offices behind the hall.

A round moon peered through the thick-hazed window glass, bathing us in its pale soft glow. I cast Joan from my thoughts. Meg tapped on the door with a dish of broth for I had not eaten since morning- nothing but potions and caudles. I sipped it as Thomas cradled our daughter. Later, he leaned down, kissed me and then laid a kiss upon our baby's head. 'Thank you, my wife, for this day; for making us a family,' I heard him say, as he rose to return to work in his office. He slipped away while I drifted into an exhausted sleep.

200

Chapter Twenty-three

1516

JOAN CAME TO STAY and was, I was happily surprised to discover, grown-up and helpful. She had also grown darkly beautiful, like our mother. Two of her charges were being placed in other households, and my mother considered I had a greater need of her. In truth, Mother hoped that her second daughter would learn to mix with city wives, and benefit from exposure to the people we knew. Within weeks Joan had integrated into our family and I began to enjoy her sisterly company. We attended services together in St Gabriel's and she gradually learned how I conducted our household affairs. That autumn and winter our lives settled into a pleasant, busy, domestic routine.

By February of the next year, 1516, Joan had become a devoted nursemaid to five-month-old Annie. In turn, my tiny daughter loved her aunt. Annie smiled, cried, fed and soiled her clouts with equal regularity. Yet my sister humoured her because she liked children, always happy to even change the baby's swaddling. If Annie became fractious, it was Joan who would happily sing to her, for hours rocking the cradle with her foot.

Perhaps, it was I, too, who was changing, since I was less critical these days, less retiring, content in myself and with my family. I had a small circle of friends amongst the merchants' wives and Thomas' friends. Most of all, I enjoyed Cat's company, and always that of Mother who could draw me out and make me laugh at the stories she would gather from friends at court, tales which never ceased to entertain Joan and myself when she visited Fenchurch Street.

Romance was evolving between my sister and handsome young Master Williamson. It blossomed during the Christmas revels and by February they sought out each other's company when he visited us.

Joan carried her small frame more erect than ever she had before, smiled with genuine warmth glowing from her dark eyes and she always wore a crisp clean linen cap over neatly plaited hair; it was tied perfectly below her chin, showing just a little gleaming dark hair at her broad forehead. Joan was serious as well as beautiful. She either sat listening intently or spoke up with intelligence and charm when we invited Thomas' humanist friends to supper, those who believed in questioning and debate.

I am not sure this new thinking was Mother's intent for Joan. Rather, it was the London goodwives' company that Mother considered important to furthering my sister's education and with their connections a suitable husband from a merchant family. Unbeknown to my mother, Joan was becoming an intellectual asset to our household, a self-assured, interesting young woman, learning from those discussions about history that brightened our chill winter evenings, the excitement of discussion reverberating about the parlour for days after our visitors departed. Moreover, it was clear to us all that John Williamson adored her.

Thomas was determined to help the young couple. I have always been aware, even now, years later, that he had a particular motive for his encouragement, other than just liking them. It was one he never spoke aloud during our conversations concerning Joan's future. Thomas wanted to bind John Williamson to our family. John, who was intelligent and good-looking, with thoughtful eyes and a ready smile, came from a family of builders. He had been given an education at St Antony's School, which Thomas found encouraging.

'John Williamson might soon become an agent in my employ, and he must study the law,' he said.

Thomas believed that a closely-knit, loyal family with close friends had great value. It was as if he was creating a loyal clan, one akin to family kingdom of old.

'But we must guard Joan's virtue because Father will aim higher for her. She is growing too close to our impoverished Master Williamson.'

'Humph, you are right, of course, Lizzy, and they are much in each other's company. I shall keep him busy, and well away from her,' Thomas conceded with a grunt. He turned to a new book he had purchased that day, opened it up and began to study it.

'What are you reading?'

'Herodotus.'

The subject of Joan was closed.

A happy event occurred early that year which lulled us all into temporary forgetfulness of our own lives. On a February day, just as we finished our morning prayers, and were breaking our fast in the hall with our household, church bells began to ring voraciously all over the City. They were always ringing for something- births, deaths, weddings, the chiming of the Angelus, services and even city fires. London was a city of bells. At first, we thought nothing of it. After a pause, the pealing began again, more insistent than before.

Joan leaned over the table towards me, her eyes bright with excitement. 'Must be for the Queen this

203

time. She has given birth.'

We laid down our knives and spoons and listened to the bells that, across the City, were echoing and pealing, one set after the other.

'They continue. The baby lives,' I cried out.

The celebration would continue for hours. I felt a sense of great excitement race through our hall, from Thomas at the head of our long trestle to the maids gathered close together on the bench at the lower end. They proclaimed Queen Catherine's birthing of a healthy child.

I called to Barnaby, 'Go out now. Ask the first crier you see if it is a boy.'

Barnaby did not wait to pull his cloak down from a peg by the hall door. He clambered over the bench, raced past the maids and out of the hall entrance into the bitterly cold yard.

Moments later he was back, his teeth chattering as he cried out the news. 'It's a girl.' He brushed a light covering of snow from his jerkin.

'But the King wanted a boy.' John Williamson, who had stayed late into the night before, and had slept in the hall by the fire, spoke up. He shook his head, his loose fair hair waving from side to side. 'King Hal should be grateful for a living child, but I bet he won't be. Only a boy will do. That's what everyone says.'

'Hush, John. Of course he wants sons,' said Thomas. 'And there is time yet for them.' He glanced at Annie who lay happily in her cradle by my chair. 'Look at how precious *she* is. I'm sure King Henry will love his daughter just as I love mine.'

'So many dead babies though.' My sister visibly shuddered. 'The Queen's babies never live. This one might die too.' She rose from her bench, reached for the jug and poured us all buttermilk. 'I hope the girl-child lives. Then, one day, we might have a woman to rule England.'

'Joan, you are outspoken,' I said. 'It's a crime to even think of the King's death.'

'But I was not,' she answered me pertly, 'I love our King and wish him a long life with many sons to follow him and Queen Catherine about their grand palaces. But a woman can rule as well as a man. Queen Catherine's mother ruled Castile.'

'I do not think England would agree to that,' said John Williamson. 'The people like a king and they love King Hal.'

'The Queen may yet have a son,' I said pragmatically, ending the discussion.

Annie began to whimper so I lifted her from the cradle. She ceased crying momentarily but started up again, her little head nuzzling at the laces of my gown. 'I think she is hungry.' I rose to carry my baby to where we could be private. I did not employ a wet nurse for Annie but fed her myself, enjoying the intimacy of it. However, that February morning was cold and on that bitterly cold morning, I hoped that there was a fire already lit in the parlour.

Meg rose to accompany me. 'No need, Meg. Sit and finish your oatmeal.'

'I'll carry Annie's cradle through to the parlour for you, Lizzy.' Joan plonked the milk jug down crossly in front of John Williamson, and before I could stop her had lifted the cradle, adding, 'If the parlour is warm Annie may as well take a nap in there.'

'I'd better be getting on with the cloth. Come on boys,' Gerard Smith said, rising to his feet.

I did not miss the long-faced, longing look he threw Meg. I was sure she had cooled towards him, assuming she had ever been interested, though they had danced together and joined in the games at Christmastide. It was apparent that Smith still liked her very much.

My household throbbed with the hint of romance all winter, unrequited and requited love. I smiled to myself as I followed Joan into the parlour holding Annie close and humming to myself. It was harmless surely.

Joan excused herself, saying she had to help Cook with a pudding and bustled into the passageway.

I expected a visit from Joanna Butler that day, who sent me a message saying that she was so pleased with the grey fabric she had bought from us before Annie's birth, she wished to see my latest samples. I was pleased because I now had possession of new fabrics that Thomas' agent had purchased in Norwich. The bays used weft of lamb's wool, and the perpetuanas were a delicate wool and silk mix. They were all woven in beautiful shades of blues, greens and soft pink, interwoven with a slightly darker diamond patterning. These latest fabrics were so light in weight they promised to be perfect materials for over-gowns once winter passed. Thinking of the profit they would bring us, I longed for a lightweight blue gown for summer and had promised my sister one in a deep rosy pink as a thank you for her help.

I held Annie to me and drew my shawl close against the early morning nip in the air. When, at last, she was sleeping, I called for a maid to be her rocker. As the girl rocked the crib, she could mend a pile of hose. It was as if a hosiery puck was set loose in my household that year, since there always was a great basket of darning to be done. For a moment, I listened to the chiming sounds in the street beyond the parlour and above this the excited shouts of citizens who were cheering. The bells rang on and on, then stopped. The maid glanced up from her rocking, 'Another one dead,' she said in a morose manner, her expression hang-dog.

'Surely not,' I replied, holding my breath until they started their clanging again. 'No, not this time.'

The maid shrugged. 'Daughter or son, Mistress, babies are fortunate to survive. Queen and peasant are evened up, Mistress. Our maker does not discern. We are all equal in His sight.'

'Finish the mending by dinner hour. Call me if you need me for Annie,' I said sharply and returned to the hall and to my breakfast.

Thomas rose from his chair after I arrived, and pushed it back saying, 'The King may have a child today, but my work cannot stop. Cousin Robert has news for me.' Thomas was smiling. I suspected he was keeping a secret and determined to discover it later. He turned towards little Ralph Sadler. 'And you, Master Sadler, will continue your Latin lessons despite the King's good news. If Master Matthew decides to take another holiday because of it, I still want to see that translation of Cicero done on my return. Do you hear me, lad?'

'Yes, Master Cromwell.' His dark eyes twinkled mischievously.

Thomas placed his hand on John's shoulder, 'Why don't you be my companion today, John. The Merchant accounts can wait. We're off to York Place this morning. Archbishop Wolsey is now Cardinal Wolsey so you are to visit a Cardinal, my boy.'

Delight caused John's face to glow with pleasure. He fetched their warmly lined cloaks. My veins pulsed anxiously as my blood ran faster. York Place. Was Thomas to be employed by the Cardinal? He lived as well as a king, it was said. He lived off taxes that guildsmen paid for the good of the Church.

'We'll dine with Cousin Robert,' Thomas called back over his shoulder, as he pinned his cloak at the neck and pulled on a furred cap that covered his ears. 'We'll be back for supper.' He lifted a torch from a bracket by the hall door saying that they would take horses from the stable and ride with it being snowy outside.

By late afternoon, Joanna had not arrived and my sample book lay forlornly on the bench. 'Joan, go and find Wilfrid. I have a note for Mistress Joanna.' Joan raised a dark eyebrow, but left her sewing and diligently went to do my bidding.

When Wilfrid slouched into the parlour, I handed him a note wishing Joanna well, saying what wonderful news the City had received that day. And I reminded her of our appointment.

Wilfrid hurried off, grumbling that it was unfair that he was to go out into the bitterly cold afternoon when he was busy cutting fabrics. 'You will go and quickly,' I snapped, and glared at his back, wondering if it was on account of the King's news that Joanna Butler had not come. It was remiss of her not to send us word.

We had been given a mechanical clock as a New Year's gift by Antonio Bonvisi, a merchant friend. This wonderful object sat on our wide oak mantle and for over an hour my eye was drawn to it. It was a dainty, filigreed object in shiny gold-plated casing that had hands moving around its face, always reminding us of time's passage. By the time Wilfrid returned, note in hand, I had given up all hope of Joanna's arrival.

I waited until the apprentice had departed, carefully broke her seal, and unfolded a piece of parchment which I read slowly by the firelight, as by now the day was dimming.

'I'll light the candles,' Joan piped up and scurried around the room lighting it up.

Dearest Elizabeth, I read, *I fear I am unwell and cannot come to you this afternoon. My dear, I must send you a warning, however. Mistress Watt complained about your cloth to the parish wardens a month since. She says that your cloth contravenes sumptuary. When John raised this with me yesterday, I assured him the cloth I purchased from you was not breaking the law. I reminded him that Mistress Watt's brother was a wool man and that it might be a jealous and somewhat zealous complaint but, dear Elizabeth, do take great care where you sell your new fabric.*

I folded the letter and slipped it into my sewing purse. Thomas must see this.

'So why did she not come?' Joan looked up from her embroidery and lifted a skein of black silk and her scissors.

'She is unwell,' was all I said.

'Mistress Butler should have written sooner to you.'

'She has apologised of course and excused herself and she will come another day,' I lied.

'Oh,' Joan said, and threaded her needle.

Annie began to grizzle. I lifted her from her cradle and let her suckle, finding her closeness such a comfort in the unpredictable world we find ourselves passing through.

Thomas returned home shortly after Vespers, accompanied by John Williamson and also by Jon Woodall, a clerk in the Exchequer. My husband was in high spirits.

'Another guest for supper, Elizabeth; go and order Cook to put out his best meats tonight and a plum pie if he has one, and the malmsey. We have the Princess' birth to celebrate, and I have news from Cousin Robert. Great news that I shall tell you over supper.' He laid his hand on Woodall's arm. 'Jon was on his way from the Tower when I met him on the street. Rather than him taking supper alone on such an important evening, here he is.'

I put Joanna's warning from my mind. Another warning took its place, for I was sure that Thomas' news was connected to Archbishop Wolsey. I would rather that Thomas worked for anybody but a lofty clerical cheat. Wolsey was not popular and I disliked this association.

'Of course,' I said, curtseying to Jon Woodall. 'You are welcome, sir.' I indicated the benches placed by the hall fireplace where a great blaze burned. 'I shall tell the maids to lay supper out in the parlour.' I turned to John Williamson. 'You will be staying for supper too?'

'Thank you, Mistress Elizabeth.' Williamson bowed and when he rose, I noticed his eyes flit towards Joan who coyly turned on her heel. She set off towards the kitchen to find a maid to set our supper table and another to care for Annie who was soundly sleeping against her shoulder.

Master Woodall too, to my surprise, was also watching my sister. He was a portly man with humorous, slightly bulging hazel eyes and brown hair cut at his chin in an old-fashioned pudding bowl style. He dressed neatly in plain brown worsted, his boots polished and his linen tunic spotless. He was unmarried and a few years older than my husband, well into his third decade. 'Wives are expensive,' he was inclined to say. 'They eat up your credit.' It was unlikely that he could be interested in Joan, who liked to spend the allowance Father gave her on pretty things. If he knew.

Woodall was very attached to his widowed mother and I assumed that she was responsible for the perfect care of her son's clothing. A wife to Master Woodall would have high standards to keep. As both men watched Joan's retreating back, I wondered if Woodall was lonely without a wife. My pretty sister did not lack suitors and Jon Woodall, despite his protestations about expensive wives, admired her.

Thomas' good news arrived between pigeon pie and a custard tart. He pushed his plate towards me and said, 'Now, Elizabeth, leave off serving us and sit yourself down to listen to what I have to say.'

I wondered if my premonition was right, all thoughts of Mistress Watt gone from my head.

'Our fortunes are set to improve,' Thomas began to say. 'Until it is absolutely confirmed I want not a word beyond the parlour door.' Thomas glanced from me to Joan to John Williamson. I discerned excitement in his fidgety posture.

I sipped my cup of malmsey patiently. 'Don't prolong the suspense, Thomas. Tell us. What is the news?'

We all sat absolutely still waiting for him to speak. Thomas rose and closed the parlour door, which was slightly ajar. The fire hissed as snow fell down the chimney, dropping onto burning logs. I could hear the wintry wind rattling the casement and dogs barking beyond our walls. Thomas smiled, a gesture which was unusual when he was about to impart anything relating to himself. He *was* pleased with himself tonight.

'Some time ago, Cousin Robert proposed to Cardinal Wolsey that I took over the stewardship of York Place. The position is now vacant.'

I felt my eyes widen. The atmosphere in my parlour shifted from one of jovial, good-hearted friendship to one of awe. Thomas would be close to Wolsey. I could not voice my distaste for the Cardinal. I could not pour my concern out and quench Thomas' happiness with his new important position. All I could hope was that he did not sail too close to the prelate and the courtiers Wolsey mingled with, other than to further his legitimate legal opportunities. Thomas lifted my hand and clasped it. 'And,' his voice lowered into a velvet-like softness. 'Robert thinks it possible that the Cardinal will be the next Lord Chancellor of England.' He turned to Master Woodall. 'Could it be so, Jon?'

'I have heard such a rumour in the Exchequer, Thomas, and a more canny man England has not known in that position since the days of Saint Thomas Becket himself.'

'Let us hope he does not share Becket's fate, or I shall be out of a job,' Thomas replied in an amused tone.

'Have you met him already?' Joan spoke up.

'Yes, I confess yes, indeed I have, some weeks ago, but only to say that if the post were available I would take it.'

'You never said this to me.' I felt slightly annoyed that he had not. A candle spluttered. Immediately, I regretted my petulance. I must control my possessiveness because it would never be possible to own Thomas. His work possessed him.

'Until these things are settled, one never says anything, not even to a wife, my sweeting,' Thomas said, breaking the silence.

Although his voice was kindly, his eyes were determined, steely grey, and still. I wondered what else my husband kept close to his heart. Had it been me, I could never have kept such a meeting as one with the great Thomas Wolsey, the King's confidante, Cardinal, and maybe future chancellor to the King, secret from my husband. This kind of fortune greeted ordinary men rarely and I shuddered because I could not help thinking that it

212

was a fortune born on an ill wind. It was a position held in high regard by men. In our world it was considered that Lady Fortune smiled on women if we married well, for although many of us possessed good sense, often better sense than our husbands, we were always in the shadows.

'Thomas I'm pleased for you and glad for us.' I said with generosity and in front of everyone kissed his forehead. 'I am fortunate in my husband.'

He smiled, 'And I am pleased for us too. All this is for us, my sweet wife.'

Jon Woodall raised his cup. 'A toast to Thomas and to the Cardinal and to our new Princess.'

We raised our cups three times. Thomas rose again. 'God bless our good King Henry. May he have a long and happy life.'

'And Queen Catherine,' I said pointedly. 'May she live long.'

Later, after Jon Woodall had departed, John Williamson said he too must return home that night. I remembered the warning from Joanna Butler.

After I told Thomas about Joanna's letter and Mistress Watt's accusations, we shared a last cup of wine, looking up at the sky above our casement window. We could see a hazy moon's light peer from behind the clouds. Snowflakes drifted down, batting gently against the window leads where they melted on contact.

'Look at how beautiful it is, Lizzy. It reminds me of the Alps, a first snowfall during an early winter crossing. The sky was filled with snow and we were in a hurry to reach our journey's end before it caught us out.' He took my hand, lifted it to his lips and kissed my chilling fingers one by one. 'Forget Mistress Watt, Lizzy. She is unimportant in the bigger shape of things.' He looked at me thoughtfully. 'I shall visit John Butler tomorrow. We shall both pay Mistress Watt a call. I shall put an end to this nonsense. The fabric is a mix. Joanna will not break with sumptuary by wearing it.'

'But the colours?'

'Are patterned, and there is no purple or gold, though, admittedly, the saffron has a golden sheen. I defy any warden from the drapers' court to say it breaks the law.'

'If you are sure,' I said, not really looking forward to visiting hard-faced Mistress Watt to tell her so, though with Thomas by my side I was not afraid of her sharp tongue either.

'I am sure. Now, to bed, Lizzy, before we catch our death.'

I glanced at our sleeping daughter as we undressed, climbed up into the high bed and pulled our Italian counterpane up over a great heap of plain, warm blankets. Annie slept peacefully in her crib as if her parents' concerns were but dandelion fluff in the breeze, none of her concern, and unlikely to ever disturb her serenity. I lay down, leaning my head on Tom's shoulder, and as he gathered me into the cradle of his arms, I felt that we were indeed the happiest family in the City, happier even than Queen Catherine, though she must be very happy, too, to have her daughter safely birthed.

Chapter Twenty-four

MISTRESS WATT'S HOUSE LOOMED up out of a fresh snowfall. It was a solid, substantial merchant's building, situated on Bread Street, its overhanging upper storeys constructed of timbers, wattle and daub. If I had expected, and I did, to find perfection and a bustling wealthy household inside, I was to be surprised.

When Thomas rapped an iron knocker, cast in the image of St Catherine, wheel included, the door was opened by a smut-faced, shivering, skinny, dull-eyed little maid clad in a grubby thin woollen kirtle. Her dress looked as if it needed washing and, despite the cold weather, the girl smelled stale.

Ignoring her surly look, Thomas said, 'Tell Mistress Watt that Thomas Cromwell wishes to speak with her.'

The maid glanced at us suspiciously, heavy-lidded eyes darting from Thomas to me and back again. Softening my husband's terse introduction, I said in a gentler tone, 'I assume Mistress Watt is at home this morning.'

'In the parlour,' the girl replied. I peered beyond her thin shoulders into a hall with an old-fashioned central hearth where she had clearly been trying to light the fire. The hall was filling with smoke which explained the smuts on her cheeks. We shook snow from our boots onto the rushes closest to the entrance and followed her into the smoky room. I began to cough and raised the neck of my cloak across my mouth.

'Wait here,' she said, lifting her hand to stop us entering the corridor off to the side.

We stood at a distance from the failing fire and waited. Thomas folded his arms patiently. Meantime, I studied the hall, or rather what could be seen through drifting smoke. It was a miserable place and as no other servants were evident, I assumed that Mistress Watt could not be quite the wealthy widow she purported to be. A clutter of dirty pots lay littered by the hearth and old rushes on which we stood would have harboured all sorts of vermin were it not so cold. Some time passed before the maid reappeared.

'Mistress will see you,' she mumbled.

We followed her through a low door that led into a narrow corridor and to the right, the parlour. It was warmer in the parlour, which had clearly been added onto the ancient, smoky hall recently because a brick fire-place was set deep into a stone wall where logs were burning brightly and with ease. I tried not to breathe too deeply because after my first breath I realised that the parlour, while not smoke-infested, contained the rank smell of Cheape tallow candles. There was little furniture to be seen - no chests, tables, hangings, cushions or the family ornaments that normally would make a wealthy widow's home comfortable. This, I recognised, was a home fallen on hard times.

On seeing us enter, Mistress Watt rose from an arm-chair by the fire. Thomas bowed and I curtsied. In an imperious tone, ignoring our good manners and not returning them, Mistress Watt said acidly, 'Master Cromwell, what brings you here on such a bitterly chill day? A cloth issue, perchance?' There was more than a hint of sarcasm in her tone. She had certainly come to the point, or so I had thought.

'Not entirely, 'Thomas said in a deceptively gentle

216

manner. 'May we sit? We have something else to discuss, Mistress Watt.'

What else was there to discuss? Thomas had not spoken to me of other matters.

The widow waved her hand towards a bench by the other side of the fire. I noted that she looked utterly miserable, her eyes rheumy and her mouth down-turned, very different to the confident women I had met during the previous year. I would have felt sorry for her, had I not been so angry at her trouble-making.

'Well then,' she said, studying me closely, her eyes flickering up and down my person as if she were assessing the value of my clothing. 'Why are you here?' she said as she turned from me to Tom.

'Mistress Watt,' he said in his soft-spoken voice, his look as cold as Italian marble and every bit as smooth. 'There is, Mistress Watt, a debt owing after your husband's death to one of the Drapers' Company, a Master Strong. Interestingly, Master Strong has sought legal advice from me on the matter and I understand that if you do not pay him the outstanding monies you will be visited by bailiffs before the calends of February.'

Surprise dropped upon me as if a pigeon had suddenly fallen down the chimney. Tom did not even mention sumptuary laws. He had already, he told me afterward, settled that matter with the Drapers' Company, the parish and with Mayor Butler, himself, on the previous day.

'What is this to you, apart from your legal advice, that is?' the widow snapped, looking aghast, then furious, her deep-set eyes challenging. 'What is in it for you, Master Cromwell?'

'My fee, for a start.' Thomas leaned his chin on his folded hands and waited for a moment, moved his hands to his lap. 'You see, Mistress Watt, I can be of assistance to you because I can lend you the amount you need to pay the debt. I believe you own a piece of land in Stepney. I shall take promise of it as surety of repayment.' The widow's eyes looked set to leap right out of her head. Thomas' face grew increasingly earnest as he carried on, 'You would be wise to consider my offer. Your deceased husband's debts were considerable. His wool business was failing.' He paused, before saying, his voice quiet but firm, 'There are others who demand payment.' The dagger now twisted, for he calmly shook his head and added. 'I am surprised that Mistress Joanna and her mother do not know of this situation. Once the calends come this month, secrecy will be impossible.'

Mistress Watt's mouth opened and closed shut again. She stiffened in her chair. At length, she spoke, 'Are you saying you will lend me the complete sum, Master Cromwell?' She frowned, her forehead creasing into furrows, a hint of fear displayed on her countenance. 'How long would I have to repay the debt?'

'Your son is wasting money in gambling taverns. He mixes with low life, those who prey on innocent citizens south of the river.' Thomas looked straight into her eyes. 'You must be firm with him. His irresponsible behaviour must stop.' Leaning back, as if considering his next words, he said after a moment, 'As for the debt, let us say five years. He will have money to purchase the new season's wool. The business, I believe, passed to you but you will have to oversee all, protect your interests. He must reinvest profit from the wool. You, Mistress Watt, will make sure it is profitable because if the business does not pay, if he cannot sell his wool to the Merchant Adventurers for a suitable profit and the debt is not paid, I shall take over the land. There will be an interest payment of five per cent on the loan, less, I imagine, than that

218

others will offer you.' Thomas paused again. The widow's eyes narrowed as if she was calculating her next response. He said, 'I suggest you move into your son's house. Keep watch over him.'

'He is my only living child. He lives here with me.'

'Where is he?'

'In bed today with a chill.'

'Convenient,' Thomas muttered under his breath. 'The business passed to you and you know what you must do, Mistress Watt. Do you accept my terms?'

'Yes, but I ask that this remains between us. I don't want others to know.'

'You, Mistress Watt, will assure me that you do not intend to say any more about the sale of our draperies. They are mixes and, moreover, the colours are not forbidden. They are patterned.'

The widow turned as pale as the linen on her coif. 'Sir, I do not see a difference, but I have no option.'

'Then, Mistress Watt, I wish you good day.'

Thomas rose. I stood beside him, wondering at his cleverness with the widow. I had not said a word but I thought of Thomas' money-lending. It bothered me. This was a business involving interest, one that I was sure the Church, while not forbidding the practice, would not approve either.

He bowed. 'I expect to see you, Mistress Watt, and your son in my office at my home in Fenchurch Street tomorrow at ten o'clock.'

'I do not possess a clock, Master Cromwell.' Opening her hands she looked around the chamber. My eyes followed hers. 'I sold everything I possess so that we could eat.'

'Mistress Watt, you can hear the bells chime out the hours like most citizens. As for your son, get him out of his bed and working.'

Thomas bowed again and led me from the parlour. I could not like the woman but I hoped that she would get her son to work. Never had I seen him in the Drapers' Hall, though before his death his father had occasionally sold wool to the Adventurers. The elder Watt had been a quiet man, and not sharp like his wife. I had hardly noticed him, and I had rarely seen his wife before Joanna had introduced us. Perhaps, it was envy that had caused her to stir up trouble for us, that, or deep-rooted unhappiness.

On our return to Fenchurch Street, everyone had finished dinner. Joan was minding Annie and had just put her in her crib for a nap. She said she had work to do in the still room.

'Wrap up well then,' I said, wondering what she was concocting. She answered my question before I spoke it.

'I won't be long, I promised Master Williamson a tincture of honey, lemon and sage for his mother's cough.'

'That is thoughtful of you, especially on such a bitterly cold day.'

'I shall bring it round to her as soon as it is done. Bessie has promised to mind Annie.'

We took our dinner privately in the parlour by the fire. The snow fell steadily against the window and I watched it for a while, thinking of how cleverly Thomas had handled the widow Watt. I thought of the loan.

'Do you think it is right to lend money?'

'Would you borrow money, if you must?'

I had contemplated this after I had lost all. 'Yes, I would.'

'It's not a sin to lend to someone in need. Our King

borrows money from the City. He'll be borrowing more now for the new princess' household.'

I hoped that we would never lend money to King Henry, for I feared that if we did, we would never have it returned to us. Relieved at the outcome from our visit to Bread Street, I let the matter rest. Joanna Butler's custom would be reinstated and therefore that of her friends too. Mistress Watt was successfully silenced on the matter of the ever-changing sumptuary. Thomas, cleverly, had placed her in his debt.

Chapter Twenty-five

THE ROYAL PRINCESS WAS christened Mary, and by God's good grace she survived. I gave prayers up daily for Queen Catherine, before my bedroom altar with its miniature plaster images of the holy family. The altar had been an addition since Annie's birth, one that we had positioned in our chamber's alcove below my beloved Italian painting of the Queen of Heaven.

I attended St Gabriel's Church regularly, where I prayed that a healthy son would, by the Grace of God, follow the birth of Princess Mary. Occasionally, I saw Mistress Watt in the church nave, but if she saw me coming she turned away and hurried off to pray at another saint's shrine, usually that of St Sebastian, pierced with arrows. That martyr's statue was placed at the furthest corner from the church's main door, far from my favoured position before a small altar to Saint Elizabeth, John the Baptist's mother. I was glad not to have to speak with Mistress Watt.

On a chill March Wednesday, a ragged wind tugged at my skirts as I pulled open the door into the still room. Annie suffered from a cough and Joan, who was never ill, lay in bed with an upset stomach and was refusing food. Meg reported that she vomited clear bile. Many of our servants had caught colds so at first we thought nothing odd about Joan's sickness. We were distracted. Our household was on edge, concerned, that a plague would descend on us.

I warned my mother and father ,who were to come to us at Eastertide, to stay away, suggesting in a note that we celebrate Pentecost in Putney instead. By then, our household should be well. *Perhaps by Pentecost*, I wrote, *Thomas can take a few days' needed holiday*.

I folded it up and sealed it with wax and my personal imprint with an image of St Elizabeth. I never mentioned Joan's illness as I did not want to worry my mother but sent a servant boy with my note to Father's premises on Cornhill.

The still room door blew closed behind me. I secured it against the gusting wind, and began to hunt along the shelves for a small jar of syrup of figs and honey for colds. Further along the shelf, sat a jar of willow bark tablets that we had procured from the apothecary in Fenchurch Street before Christmas. I placed both in my basket. I lifted down a bunch of dried camomile flowers to mix with milk and honey into a posset. Joan complained of a stomach ailment, not a cold. A posset might soothe it. I found the honey and stood with my hands on it, ready to add it to my herbs, wondering about my sister, thinking that Joan's behaviour had been more secretive than usual. She kept disappearing, saying she was going to Church to distribute alms. Joan did take a basket of day-old bread to St Gabriel's for the poor. She was supposed to be accompanied by a servant, but did she always take a servant? I was unsure of it. I thought that she sometimes went alone as St Gabriel's was so close.

Momentarily distracted, by my suspicious thought, I heard voices rise beyond the partition. I listened. Barnaby and Wilfrid were cutting the pieces of linen and silk mixed fabric that I had requested for my new summer fabrics book.

The still room was part of a long barn that we had broken up into several rooms. Next door to where I kept my medicines and dried herbs, we had made a room where we stored cloth samples and the apprentices kept records of our stock in a great cupboard that took up one wall. Listening carefully, the honey jar still in my hands, I heard the rustle of cloth and the snip of scissors. There was another snip, followed by the rattle of scissors being laid down on a bench and I caught a snatch of their conversation. Surprised at what they were saying, I placed the honey in my basket on the bench and laid my ear to the partition wall; all thought of Joan flew out of my head.

'Never liked that son of Mistress Watt's,' Barnaby was saying. 'Gore-belly of a man too.'

I felt myself smiling. Master Watt did have a large paunch. He came with a servant to see Thomas and not liking him, I kept out of his way.

Wilfrid spoke up, 'Have you seen the scar on the servant's face and his yellow eyes. Looks evil, that man. Barnaby, what does it remind you of?'

There was a pause. Barnaby spoke again.

'The one who was waiting with the horses when they came to see the Master yesterday? No, never seen him before.'

'Aye, me neither. He looked at me when I bade him my "Good morrow", as if I were evil, not him. He glared at me fierce as a Turk, and crossed himself. Is that not peculiar? And you know that scar.' There was a pause. 'Made me think of Toby. Barnaby, do you recollect what Toby said about a man with a scar...'

'That were long ago now. All but two year now. There is more than one man with a scarred face in this city.'

'As well that Toby is safe in Lincoln. I wonder what he is doing now.'

224

'Learning to be a knight.' Barnaby laughed. 'And charming the ladies as ever.'

'I pray 'tis so,' came Wilfrid's voice from beyond the partition.

I lifted my basket and hurried out of the still room, firmly closing the door behind me. Anxieties crowded into my mind and took root. What if Master Watt's servant *had* been involved in the attack on my Wood Street storehouse those two summers ago? What if he *was* the man who had attacked Toby? I determined to tell Thomas of the apprentices' conversation that evening at supper. The fire on my property had upset my household and nearly destroyed my business. Those responsible had never been apprehended. They were at large in the narrow dim streets. I felt myself shudder.

I forgot all about Joan.

After supper, I told Thomas what I had overheard. Thomas pulled off his boots and stretched his feet towards the fire. 'No my dear, they will not dare. I have the Watts' loan sewn up tightly. William Watt is setting off to Witney tomorrow. He wants to repay the loan with wool sales. Came to my office yesterday morning to seek advice and to ask me to call in on his mother while he was away.' He opened his hands. 'Come, Lizzy, be rational, There are many scarred men in England back from the war with Scotland. This servant seemed humble enough. He wore a cross.'

'Wearing a cross means nothing.' I wanted to say that it could have been devout men who had attacked Toby, thinking he was my first husband's lover, but we never spoke of my husband's unnatural behaviour, so I said, 'It is just that Wilfrid had been so sure.'

'Then I shall question the boys. Toby is the only

225

witness and he is far away. If it gives you peace of mind, next time I am in Lincoln I shall make a point of calling on his family.'

'I do not want anything to threaten us.'

Having spoken my piece, I lifted up the embroidery I was stitching on a partlet for my sister.

I placed the stitch-work on my lap again and watched the fire flames dance in the grate, for a moment wishing that I could see a safe and prosperous future for us in the flames, a future without danger. 'Is it necessary to deal in usury, Thomas? You will endanger us if the client cannot pay the interest and loses everything he owns to you. London traders can be jealous. Jealous men can turn to evil ways to protect their own interests.'

'Elizabeth, leave this unpleasant work to me. Stay your attention to your fabrics and threads. I am generous in my terms. Think about it. If I did not help Widow Watt and her good-for-nothing son, they would lose everything.'

There was no answer to that so I nodded and lifted my needlework again. I drew the black silk in and out of the white linen finding a settling calm in the ordinary, rhythmic action of sliding thread through fabric.

'I shall ask Barnaby and Wilfrid about this man. If I am not satisfied by their answers, I shall investigate the devil with the scar until I am.' He leaned forward and kissed my cheek. 'Now I must leave you. I have accounts to see to, and I am for the Cardinal's palace tonight.' He rose from his chair and asked about Annie's cough.

'She is with Meg and she is improving. The syrup helped ease her cough.'

'Where is Joan?'

'She is unwell too.' I did not voice my suspicions about my sister's illness.

'Joan is healthy. No doubt she will be up and about

226

soon.' He stretched his hands towards the fire. 'Meanwhile, I must find out John Williamson's intentions. He is wandering behind me these days like a boy in mourning rather than one in love.'

If Thomas thought that this would bring a smile to my face, he was wrong. I had become very fond of Joan. My concern now was my parents' loss of trust in my care of her. A betrothal was one thing but a girl already with child was another, particularly since she was in our care. 'So you will help them?' I said aloud. If what I suspected was true, marriage between the lovers was a solution, although Father might not think so, since he had hopes for a wealthy merchant.

'Yes, my dear. I certainly see John's potential. I shall train him for the law,' Thomas said, kissed my head, and gathering his dark-hued cloak about him set off for his closet off the hall.

I knew Thomas would work long into the night. I would not see him before morning if he was off to the Cardinal before dawn rose. If Thomas was not settling land disputes for gentlefolk, he was busy on cases brought before the Drapers' Court or attending to the stewardship of York Place which had already taken him on many chilly journeys to the river.

The next morning, when Joan lay under her coverlet staring at the bed canopy, eating little and heaving up what she had managed to eat, I knew I was right to suspect her. Before I had the opportunity to go to her, and confront her with my suspicion, Meg came to the parlour.

She closed the door and lowered her voice. 'Mistress Elizabeth, I must speak to you in confidence.'

'About Joan?'

'Yes.'

'I see.'

We sat together on the cushioned bench.

'I know what you are going to tell me, Meg.'

She nodded. 'Mistress Joan is with child.'

'Are we sure?'

'As sure as you are sitting there, white as your coif, Mistress Elizabeth.'

'Does she even know what is wrong with her?'

'None of her linens have been soiled for two months.'

I leaned my head into my hands. How could Joan be so stupid? They would have to marry. How had they found the opportunity? The visits to St Gabriel's. In our busy household, where John was practically one of the family, there had been opportunities. I thought back over the past busy months. They sat together over chess games during the past winter. During the snowy weather they had gone into the walled garden to look at its wintry beauty. We had thought nothing of it.

I looked up at Meg again. 'Two months, Meg, and you never said?'

'Marigold had charge of the linens last month. Still, at least it means she has not got a contagious disease.'

'As well it is not.' I let out a resigned sigh. ' I'll go to her now. 'But she has not said?' Those last words were half-hopeful.

'No, she has not.' Meg looked down. 'But I am right,' she added, looking up again. 'Sure as day turns to night.'

'I wonder have they pledged troth, because, if so, they are as good as wed. Master Williamson has been with his mother and sisters but he will return to us tomorrow. ' I took Meg's hand. 'It could be worse. They are in love, Meg. I hope she will be happy with John, because unless she chooses a nunnery that is her future.'

Meg crossed herself. 'May God bless them both and

bring them happiness.' Ever practical, she added, 'Mistress Elizabeth, she needs a brew to ease the sickness. I'll go and make one now.'

I steeled myself to confront my sister.

***

She confessed to me, saying wretchedly that she loved him and that he loved her. They were secretly betrothed. She opened a small silver box where she kept her treasures and showed me a small silver ring set with a pearl he had given her. It had a pretty engraving of miniature marigolds. 'Pearl for purity,' I could not resist saying. I asked her if he knew.

She hung her head and when she looked up her eyes glistened with tears. 'No, John does not know. Until last week I did not realise it myself. I feel so wretched.'

'You have spent so much time with Alice and her children, her so often with child, and you did not recognise your own symptoms?'

'I did not want to see it,' she whispered.

My heart went out to my sister. I took her hand. 'It will come right, Joan, you will see.'

She began to sob. 'I don't want to go to the nuns.'

I nodded. 'You must not be sad for your lot. You must be happy, not regretful. You know you love children. We shall look after you. You will not have to go to the convent. You are betrothed. He will be happy if you are.'

'You promise.'

'Yes, I give my word.'

They possessed nothing of their own. I glanced over at her clothing pole. Joan's unworn new Easter gown, rose pink shot with silver threads, would be her wedding gown.

I did not want the servants to hear our trouble, even

229

though I suspected they most likely knew already. When I had spoken with Joan that morning, her sobbing had been loud enough to alert the whole household, so I told Thomas that we must speak privately after we had eaten. He raised an eyebrow and an anxious half-hour followed as we finished supper in silence. The two kitchen maids serving us that evening tiptoed around us. I attended to my plate, anxiously pushing pastry and gravy about, eating little morsels only. My appetite was as poor as that of my errant sister lying above us in her feathered bed. I felt both sorry and happy for her. Sorry because this should not have happened and happy because she said that it was what she wanted.

When we were alone, I told him.

'I am good at watching out for secrets.' Thomas' face was thunderous. 'Yet I did not see that one, and under our noses at that. They were devious.'

'But you wanted them to wed even though I thought Father would disapprove the match,' I reasoned. 'If they are formally betrothed by Pentecost, they can marry by Midsummer. She'll have been carrying the child for five months by then, but many a bride is five months gone before the wedding, and she may not show her state until a month after that. They are betrothed.'

'Betrothed indeed! Who witnessed their betrothal?'

'No one has, but she has a ring.'

'Not legal. I'll speak with young Williamson first thing in the morning.' He raised his fingers, counting aloud, 'One, two, three; a formal betrothal in May and then three weeks to call banns and we'll have them married in June.'

'Father will be angry, and Mother too,' I said.

'Not as angry as I am at their deceit, but the boy has a bright future. He has a good sense of the wool trade. I can train him up on the legal side as an agent for me. She

230

could do worse than wed into my business.'

'His uncle is a master builder,' I said.

'He is not. He needs to earn money sooner than later if he is to look after a wife and child. I can further the lad's education. He is already coming out and about with me.'

'We must help them set up house.'

'I could give them a loan.' Thomas frowned at me. 'I suppose you disapprove.'

'No, Thomas, we will give them a home as a wedding gift.'

Thomas scratched his head and paced the closet to where we had retreated to have this conversation. When he stopped pacing, he sank into his chair. 'I shall have to speak with your father.'

Pale-faced, puffy-eyed and humbled, the following afternoon, Joan slid into the closet to stand beside John in front of the Italian cedar-wood inlaid desk. Thomas told her in a perfunctory manner that she had behaved foolishly and that they had betrayed our trust. The pair hung their heads and had the grace to beg our pardon.

Since Thomas had planned to speak to John Williamson about his intentions before he knew that Joan was with child, I considered that it was not their secret coupling and betrothal that was the crime. Thomas had been infuriated because they had sneaked around us, and at Joan's concealment of her pregnancy, and, most of all, because he had not seen it.

I accompanied Thomas to my father's building on Cornhill. We spoke kindly of John Williamson and convinced Father that Joan was as well wed.

'I like Williamson, though with Joan's looks and

learning, we could have found her a rich merchant,' Father said.

Like you did for me, I thought sadly to myself.

He grunted and slammed his fist down on his table. 'The wench can be married as soon as the banns are called in St Gabriel's. Since she is living in your parish, have her wed from your house, Thomas.'

Convenient for you Father, I thought, and less expense.

'My thoughts precisely,' said Thomas, without hesitation. 'We shall provide her wedding feast and help them to rent a house I know of in St Swithin's Lane. I shall lease it for them myself, and he can pay me a nominal rent. The boy is a hard worker. Father was a builder. The older brother inherited his business. The uncle is a master builder too, but for now young Williamson can learn some legal business. He reads and writes a good hand. I can employ him.'

'The wedding can be held after Corpus Christi.'

And so my sister's wedding was agreed. It would take place in May. My cooks would provide her feast. The apprentices would be delighted at the diversion. The maids would clean the house with vigour. Joan and her husband would lodge with us until building work was completed on the house in St Swithin's Lane. The old building needed a scullery and buttery. John's brother would see to the works.

My mother lamented Joan's short betrothal. I think she wished her second daughter's wedding could have been a large event with her many relatives, merchant friends and the Lord Mayor attending. The compensation for Joan was that she would soon afterwards move into her own house. A short betrothal and modest wedding suited the occasion, and all my sister could think about was having John to herself and her own home to arrange. We had permitted Marigold to be her personal maid and since Marigold was devoted to Joan already, the arrangement pleased my sister and the maid both.

When we had told her, Joan was delighted.

'I promised it all would come right,' I said.

'He loves me and I love him, and that is what matters most,' she said. 'Thank you, sister.'

I felt something had happened to us, a new bond and, at last, something resembling genuine sisterhood had emerged between us. I glowed with joy as she laughed again, stitched, hemmed, and sang her happiness.

We travelled by Father's river boat to Putney. The farmhouse was festive, hung with garlands of spring flowers.

We sat together, a joyful family, to eat dinner in Mother's hall, Annie crawling under our feet and my sister talking excitedly about her forthcoming wedding, occasionally proudly patting her own belly, even though, she would not show her pregnancy for a few more months.

After the initial terror of her illicit pregnancy, Joan was brim-full with excitement. Everyone liked Pentecost. If they liked Pentecost they enjoyed a betrothal even more. Yet, although it was a festival we all loved, the religious holiday held a sad memory for me, because it was just after Pentecost that Tom Williams' mother, who had been kind to me after I had come to live in her household, had died.

That long ago year, the holiday had fallen at the end of May.

As well as being a day of religious observance, Pentecost was a time of games and processions. Before

233

joining the St Alban's Church Ale that evening, we had all set out from Wood Street to watch the guilds' Pentecost procession walk from St Pauls through the City streets. A crowned statue of the Virgin was carried by four men clad in draperies. Twelve guildsmen dressed as the twelve apostles followed the statue. We were especially proud that year because St Simon, the fisherman apostle, was Tom, my husband, who had been chosen to represent the Drapers' Company.

The sky was a hazy blue suffused with soft spring sunshine, not a cloud to threaten rain. We took up a good position on the route and waited. The processing guildsmen rounded the corner and proudly came closer to us. Tom's mother's pale face lit up with admiration as Tom smiled on seeing his mother as the procession passed us. Richard Williams' chest puffed out with pride as if to say, 'See there, that man who is St Simon is my only son. Look at him.'

They had not known the truth about their son. Tom would never have frightened them by revealing it; nor could I speak of it, so I had kept the secret deep inside me though my heart ached with the weight of it.

As we stood amongst the crowds watching the procession, we had no idea on that beautiful sunny morning that Tom Williams' mother would not live to see another day. She contracted the sweat by afternoon and died soon after the midnight Angelus.

The sweat was as frightening as the secrets I guarded, so as I sat listening to my mother and sister chatter about Whitsun and weddings and pageants, I determined to enjoy every happy moment in my life. Today's joy may be snatched from us by the morrow in the time it takes to say a Paternoster.

'Perhaps Ralph Sadler could be your attendant, Joan,' I

said, casting away my moment of sadness.

'I would like that, and I can have musicians to accompany us to the Church,' she said, joyfully relishing being the centre of attention. John Williamson looked on, his blue eyes soft with love.

'Yes indeed. Thomas and Father will see to it.'

She touched her belly. 'And just to think Annie will soon have a playmate.' She looked up. 'Lizzy, maybe you will soon be with child again too.'

Mother looked me with a hopeful gleam in her lovely eyes.

'Well, soon, I hope,' I said. 'There is no great hurry.'

I did not want to conceive too quickly again. Secretly, I used an age-old method to prevent it - a cotton pessary soaked in vinegar. I dared not speak of this, because that was another heresy to add to the one of which I was already guilty.

Thomas sipped his ale and studied me, a knowing smile twitching about his mouth. 'There is plenty of time for us to make another child, Lizzy.'

He knew and he didn't mind.

'Annie is enough for now.' I scooped my daughter from the floor where she was crawling after a little black and white kitten. She teased it too hard and it lashed out and spat at her. When she began to howl, I withdrew from the company to comfort her, and seated on the cushioned settle by a fireplace over which hung one of Joan's betrothal garlands, filled with greenery, celandines and tiny cornflowers, then fed her a little moistened cake. As Annie settled and the sweet scent of spring flowers soothingly wafted down on us, I smiled to myself, pleased with this happy outcome for my sister.

On her betrothal day, Joan looked beautiful in her rose

gown, its laces incorporated into a new bodice panel, let out a little to accommodate her swelling breasts, her dark hair loose and her skin glowing, now that her first months of pregnancy had passed.

Joan's wedding followed on the first Saturday after Corpus Christi at St Gabriel's on Fenchurch Street. It was as happy an event as had been our own wedding of three years before. Ralph Sadler proudly carried her flowery wedding crown before her procession. As was the custom, musicians escorted her to the church with cymbals and viols. My brother's children threw flowers at her. My father shed tears and my mother, too, mopped at her eyes with a square of linen. This time, Joan led the dancing with her husband and all that day there was nothing but praise for her and John. I don't think I have ever seen such a happy bride since. Theirs was a true love match and I knew that I would miss her when she moved to her new home in St Swithin's Lane, but since it was only a short distance away, I hoped we would often enjoy their company in our hall.

They shared a marriage bed in our best second bedchamber behind the parlour. Italian damask curtains hung about the bed. New linen sheets scented with lavender were laid over the feather mattress. As I escorted her to the chamber and set out wine and cakes, my eyes lit upon her cedar-wood marriage coffer which my mother had brought to us from Putney. When Joan lifted its curved lid and drew out her bridal night-gown, I saw the exquisite needlework my sister had been busily stitching. Lying on the top of the carefully folded linen lay a tiny christening garment that she had embroidered with acanthus leaves stitched in silver thread. I trailed a finger over this perfect and delicate embroidery, and, to my surprise, I found myself longing for a brother or sister for Annie.

Joan smiled as she saw me gazing upon it. 'It will be my first heirloom.'

'And may you have many little ones to be christened wearing this.' I embraced my little sister, just as Mother and Cat entered the bed chamber to help her undress.

'God bless you, sister,' I said softly, as moments later I tiptoed from the chamber. 'May your future filled with joy.'

Chapter Twenty-six

1517

JOAN SETTLED INTO HER new home and her baby was
born in the October of 1516. She had a healthy boy and
they named him William. Thomas was growing wealthy
working for the Cardinal, as a merchant and on his own
lucrative legal issues. I continued to look after my
household and make up sample books. Joanna returned
and brought other merchants' wives to look at these and
purchase cloth. Business thrived. Annie grew into a
delightful, babbling child as she approached her second
birthday. I wanted another baby.

The following summer, Thomas travelled to Rome on
behalf of the Boston Stump to request the renewal of their
right to sell indulgences. If business was concluded
quickly he thought that he could return home by the
calends of September.

Before Thomas set out, I dispensed with my cotton
pessary, soaked with vinegar. I wanted yet another part of
him in case he never returned to me. Who knew what
dangers lay on an arduous journey over the high Alps and
down through the dangerous Italian kingdoms?

As we lay in our high bed on the night before he set
out, he tried to set my mind at ease. 'I'll be travelling with
Geoffrey Chambers from Antwerp. Don't frown so,
Lizzy. Geoffrey is wise and wealthy. The Boston guilds
are paying dearly for our protection. We are to be escorted
by guards from The Hanseatic League, same as last time.'

'Even so I worry, my love,' I said, rolling across our bed towards him, looking into his eyes provocatively. I thrust my hand through the slit in his nightgown and began to stroke his manhood.

He leaned over and kissed me, his ridiculous night cap falling off his freshly washed, and, that night, sweet-scented hair. Within moments he had removed my night gown and his own. My concerns for his safety on the long bandit-ridden overland route through the Alps were forgotten as if they had not existed, while the silken coverlet slid to the floor. We made love as passionately as when we had first wed.

Before I drifted into sleep in his arms, he whispered how he had wanted this adventure, his mastery of Italian necessary in their bid to persuade Pope Leo to grant the Church in Boston the right to sell indulgences, even if his own judgement of religion was unlikely to impress the Holy Father.

He added drowsily, 'My sweet, the truth of it all is that I must see what the artist Michelangelo has done in the Sistine Chapel. He had only begun the work when I was last in Rome. I might even see Pope Leo's private apartments this time. Raphael will have painted those by now and I might view his frescos.'

Thomas admired all things Italian. Yet, though he admired beauty in finely made objects, tapestries and in paintings, he would say that I was his own great beauty, his *grande bellezza*, his silver-haired mermaid who slid in and out of his arms like a creature of the sea as slippery as our green satin cover, casting enchantments.

I sat straight up. 'Thomas how can I stop you from going? I can't. It is your heart's desire, but take great care. Once they have the indulgences granted, promise, swear to me that you will return. If you don't come home before Christmastide, you could be trapped on the other side of the Alps by snowfalls and avalanches until spring.'

He raised himself and leaned against the pillows. 'I promise, my love. I shall send you letters with merchants travelling to England.' He held my face in his hands, which though plump were soft and gentle and as white as a pigeon's breast. 'Elizabeth, watch over my business during my absence. You must send me word of any disaster. And, make sure that Ralph attends to his lessons.' He removed his hands. 'Time will hurry by us. It always does, especially in summer when you are busy brewing ale, making simples, creating jellied fruits.' He folded his hands on the cover. 'Ah now, jellies, well that gives me an idea.'

'What is it?'

'I must beg some of those jellied fruits you made last week to take with me to Italy. Send me a box to Antwerp.' He hugged me close.

I wriggled from his embrace and looked down on him. Of course, he must take all the jellied fruits I had so carefully made, comfits for his long journey, and I said so. Meg would pack the sweets carefully in a small wooden casket for him. I thought of Thomas enjoying them, licking the sugar from them, remembering his wife who concocted such delights. And, my heart filled with pride, too, that he trusted me to safe guard his affairs during his absence. Tears gathered behind my eye but I blinked them away. 'Anything else, Thomas, which you wish me to take care of while you are away?'

He pulled me down into his arms and kissed me, a long deep kiss that would be our last kiss for many months. 'Yourself, my love. I have set a guard on our house. A scar-faced wretch will never threaten you,'

240

I still had occasional nightmares though Thomas had questioned Wilfrid and Barnaby and was convinced they were wrong about Master Watt's servant. However, he knew that my suspicions of the servant never totally left me. The servant did wear a crucifix and he was deeply religious, but he was not, Thomas had decided, the man who had attacked my Wood Street home. His scar was a war wound.

Thomas had placed guards for another more ordinary reason. The City was a dangerous one filled with jealousies and evil-doers. He wanted to ensure my safety. 'Be aware, Elizabeth, that there will be those who are not our friends, even though they may profess friendship. Trust family and proven friends only. Ask Cat or your mother to stay from time to time. That is all.' His grey eyes were earnest, so I nodded. I had felt foolish for listening to the apprentices' speculations. 'Come here, my sweeting, for I want to savour your beauty one last time. When I am travelling through the Alps, I want remember you as you are tonight. Remember this always, I love you well, my Elizabeth.'

'And I thee.'

We made love again and fell asleep in each other's arms exhausted by our love making, and on that night, we conceived our second daughter.

Thomas had gone by the time I awoke the following day. Annie climbed into the place beside me that was still warm from where Thomas had lain.

'Papa gone,' she said.

'Yes, but he will return,' I replied, gathering her to me, enjoying the fresh smell of her nightgown and the camomile scent of hair that was as pale as my own.

The following day I organised the casket of jellied fruits and asked that John Williamson find a courier to deliver them to Antwerp. It was done with such efficiency and speed, that I thought they would reach the port before my husband.

***

By August I knew I was pregnant. I had twice missed my courses and was constantly tired. Since Thomas had left me to watch over things, I checked our accounts and, setting aside my exhaustion, visited Father concerning our mutual cloth interests. On one of my visits to Cornhill he asked me if I would oversee a batch of fabrics that had to be examined at the Drapers' Guildhall for imperfections before he could price it up for the foreign markets. He could not attend the Hall himself because he was off to Oxfordshire to purchase cloth near a village called Filkin.

'Good weave and good price,' he said. 'We cannot miss out on it.'

I agreed, and looked forward to being a cloth merchant once again.

'How long will you be away, Father?'

'September. Maybe October. Can you manage without both myself and Thomas?'

'I have Smith and the apprentices.'

'Good, you are a sharp businesswoman, Lizzy. That husband has taught you a thing or two. He may be ruthless but he is clever and he is devoted to his family, as he should be.'

I smiled at Father's praise for us both. Too little, too late, I thought to myself, but said nothing.

When the day arrived for my attendance at the Drapers' Guildhall, Cat Williams arrived in the courtyard, saying that she would keep me company. She had brought her daughter with her, another Catherine, of a similar age to Annie. The child's pert nursemaid followed her in from

242

the stable yard, her nose held high and her eyes watchful. A servant boy carried a large leather travelling coffer and their bundles.

'Put the luggage in the chamber beside the parlour,' I said to him.

If only they had sent a messenger forward to warn me of their visit, I could have delayed them by a day. Meg, a little flustered at the sudden visit, hurried into the parlour with fresh linen and an ewer of water for the visitors to wash after their journey. I sent the servant boy to make himself useful to cook in the kitchen.

I led Cat into her chamber. 'Cat, forgive my rush today but I must see to business at the Draper's Hall,' I said. 'Make yourself comfortable and we can have a long talk over supper.' I patted little Catherine's head. 'Annie will be so pleased to have a playmate. Smith and my apprentices are waiting for me in the yard.'

Cat pulled out two jars of pickled cucumbers from her luggage and presented them to me. 'I brought you these.'

I had confided my pregnancy to her a month before and she knew I enjoyed pickles. I stood awkwardly holding the two jars.

She smiled serenely. 'Why don't I come with you today?' she asked; her grey eyes were lit up at the thought of an adventure.

'Oh Cat, no, you would hate it, and the City is filthy. It is September and it's hot and smelly.'

'I like it, I mean the City, not the smells.' Though she wrinkled her nose, I recognised her determined look. I would have to give in or be further delayed.

I shook my head. 'Not wise.'

She smiled again at that and lifted her cloak from the bed where she had thrown it down. She knew she had won.

Resigned, I said, 'If you insist. Let me send the

243

children into the garden with their nurses first.'

I hurried out with the cucumber jars, handed them to a chamber maid to take down to the kitchen, and hurriedly snatched up two small sunbonnets from one of the hall chests. When I returned, I placed them on the children's heads and hastily tied the ribbons under their chins. Within moments, I had I dispatched our two little girls and their nursemaids into the garden.

'What would Morgan think?' I hissed at Cat. 'Surely my garden has more appeal for you, too, than the Drapers' Guildhall.'

She folded her arms across her chest. 'If Morgan did know, I doubt he would much mind. Our children will be content with their nursemaids for the day.'

'Are you sure you have the energy for this, Cat?' I said, genuine anxiety creeping into my voice. Cat had been in delicate health since the birth of little Catherine.

'So people keep saying, and now you are saying it too. I do have the stamina. How are we to travel?'

'By wagon with Father's cloth. It is to be checked for blemish. He's in Oxfordshire. We'll bring the ells of stamped cloth back to the Cornhill premises, but since we'll miss dinner, we'll have to eat the pies I've had cook pack for me. Supper will have to become dinner tonight.'

Cat nodded enthusiastically. 'I like the plan well. The sooner we are on the way, the sooner we can return,' she said brightly, snatching up her hood.

We arrived late but, thankfully, in time for the inspection. Once inside the great hall, cool with its high-vaulted ceilings and opened windows, Smith and his apprentices laid our cloth out on the inspection table where the lengths were to be checked and the quality carefully inspected. Cat stood patiently beside me, smiling graciously at

244

everyone who passed.

We were greeted as if we were merchant royalty- a very changed situation to that I had found myself in after Tom Williams had died when I had to fight for recognition as a female trader, since other merchants had only accepted me grudgingly until Thomas Cromwell had championed me. Thomas still worked on legal cases, mostly disputes and land transactions for the drapers as well as selling cloth, so when I introduced Cat as Master Cromwell's sister, cloth merchants bowed low over her dainty gloved hand respectfully.

As we conversed with others who were, like us, waiting for inspections, a draper, acquainted with Cat's husband, Morgan, approached, bowed with a dramatic sweep of cloak and engaged her in conversation. I glanced around at the other draperies on display. I loved the bustle of the Hall, the variety of fabrics laid out, the smell of new wool and that of cloth just dyed, the textures of the various weaves and the gleam of freshly bleached linen. It felt good to be back in the inspection hall. I was enjoying myself and felt accepted and at home amongst the great swathes of cloth.

This building had been where Thomas asked me to plight my troth to him. Its courtyard knot garden always held a special place in my heart. My thoughts had begun to dwell on how far we had journeyed together, on how I had enjoyed many social dinners, and the plays and pageants held here in the upper rooms of the great hall, when out of the corner of my eye I observed a figure in a merchant's gown make his way towards us, pushing others aside as he propelled himself forward.

I looked around for Smith because I liked not the stranger's strident haste as he came closer. Smith and the apprentices were examining cloth further along the hall, studying the competition, talking with the other merchants who were showing their fabrics to Cat. My eye returned to the approaching merchant and, as he came closer, with a thump of my heart, and in an instance of recognition, time tumbled backwards to a late autumn afternoon in Wood Street four years before. Edward Northleach, for I was sure it was he, a shadow of his former self. Thomas' efforts to locate him had ended fruitlessly, yet now here he was in the Drapers' Guildhall hurrying towards me.

His dark hair, once lustrous was dull and shorter. His face was deeply lined and his skin wore a sallow hue, though his brown eyes were grown great, because his face had lost so much flesh. Gone was the fashionable tunic nipped in at the waist. Today, he wore a shabby dun-coloured, loose, stained gown. This was a man fallen on hard times, but I could manage no sympathy for him. How would he account for my father's lost cloth and his disappearance?

My pulse began to race faster. He was looking at me in a calculating and determined manner, his hovering smile hinting of cruelty. His mouth with those flashing teeth flew opened and his words smoothly issued forth, nay, glided at me, as if he were a slippery snake - which he was. Before any accusations could fall from my lips, he breathlessly forestalled them.

'Why, Mistress Elizabeth, I had hoped to discover your whereabouts soon, and here you are, even more beautiful than you were four years ago.'

He was as arrogant as I remembered him. My voice felt trapped in my throat and my throat was constricted. I glared at him, thought him a weed to trample upon and recovered my tongue. A moment later I said, with a calm I truly could not feel, 'Surely, Master Northleach, it is my father whom you must see, not I. There is a matter of outstanding business. You sent us no word these past years, nor did you return with the profit due to my father, and which, sir, you still owe to him. How come you are here today?'

He shook his head. 'Ah, Mistress Elizabeth, mine is a sad tale. I do indeed intend seeking out your father. I had thought he would be here today.' He opened his hands in a pleading gesture. 'I have been imprisoned and now that I am free again and have returned, my first thought has been to find your dear father and explain my absence. Forgive me, my dear Elizabeth, but, you see, I was beset upon by enemies in the year I set sail for the Low Countries, and have spent time since imprisoned in a French dungeon, praying for rescue. I endured the greatest of misfortunes, for your father's wool was stolen when I was robbed.' He lowered his voice. 'But our betrothal, dear lady- that still stands. I have returned to claim you and make amends.' He seized my hand and raising it to his mouth he laid a damp kiss on it.

I tugged my hand from his grasp. Northleach grinned, his teeth as large as ever except now he was thrusting his face down towards mine, and I saw that his two bottom teeth were missing, giving him a sinister, and even more piratical appearance.

'Never, ever did I accept you; we were not betrothed,' I said as firmly as I could manage. I glanced around, wondering if anyone had heard. Cat was still too busy talking to Smith to notice anything amiss. Other merchants were involved with their own conversations.

I folded my arms, took a deep breath and said, 'Master Northleach, I am married this' three years and more. My name is Mistress Cromwell. I suggest that you speak with Father about the debt you owe him, and pay it forthwith.' – in my confusion, I forgot that Father was in

Oxfordshire. I stiffened my back and stared him through. 'Good day, sir. Seek out my father concerning your debt.'

The inspectors had reached the trestle closest to my own. They would be at mine within minutes. I could not believe Northleach's audacity. If he had been a prisoner of the French, which, in truth, he may have been for some dubious reason, I felt no sympathy. I suspected he was lying.

'Your father is in good health I hope, Mistress -'

'Cromwell. Good day, Master Northleach. Please go.'

Smith turned from Cat, came over to me looked at Northleach and raised his eyebrows, as surprised as I had been to see the middleman again. He growled, 'A bad coin turned up once again. Be on your way, Master Northleach, or I'll call on the bailiffs to remove you.'

Northleach glared at Smith, spat onto the tiles and moved off.

'Thank you, Smith,' I said, breathing evenly again.

The inspectors were approaching us, their servants carrying scales, a great glass that magnified and their seal. Northleach beat a hasty retreat, sweeping back through the hall towards a group of merchants I knew to be Italians.

'I don't think he wants to tussle with the inspectors. I wonder where he has appeared from,' Smith said.

'I'll tell you later.'

'Who was that?' Cat asked.

'A middleman, so he claims. He owes my father money, though I doubt he will ever pay it.' I did not mention his alleged claim on me, though I remembered, as I looked down at our cloth, the silver cross which I had once accepted from him and which now lay in the bottom of one of my jewel coffers.

The inspectors arrived by my table. I put on my best

face, smiling a smile I did not feel.

'Mistress Cromwell, it is good to see you here,' a tall, bearded inspector said pleasantly as they set about the business of checking our wares. As I had expected, Father's cloth was successfully measured, checked for imperfections, passed and stamped. None the less, I was relieved when they finished, passed a few words with Smith, bowed to Cat and myself and moved away. We could escape. The airy hall I had been so happy to visit felt oppressive.

Longing for my family, I suggested that we visit Joan and eat our picnic in her garden. Joan's little son, William, would be a year old in November. Since Joan lived in the same street as the Drapers' Guildhall, and since I wanted to shake off the unpleasant encounter with Edward Northleach, a visit to Joan and William seemed a good idea. I asked Smith if he would mind.

'Not at all, Mistress Elizabeth. Pity neither your father nor Master Thomas are here to watch over you. I do not trust that man, Northleach.' He glanced about the hall and over at the group of Italian merchants, as did I, looking to see if he was still about, but Northleach was gone.

Smith turned back to me, his eyes earnest. 'Barnaby will accompany you, after we load the cloth onto the wagon, Mistress Elizabeth. It is not too far to walk, and I shall collect you on the way back to Fenchurch Street by when the church bells strike five again. You mustn't walk the streets without protection.'

'Thank you, Smith.' I reached out and held his arm for a moment. 'Thank God for you.'

'Master Northleach may try to scare up trouble. Do not leave the house without Barnaby or Wilfrid or both.'

I slowly nodded, reluctant to be so confined but not a little afraid of Northleach, at least until Father returned and we knew his intentions.

After we helped Smith with the stamped cloth, I gave him a reed basket with a flagon of ale and a pie for himself and Wilfrid. Taking the larger basket with us, we set off for Joan's house, Barnaby trailing behind us, saying he was hopeful of a cool cup of buttermilk when we arrived.

'We all need a drink, Barnaby,' I said snappily. 'Today it is, indeed, hot, but if we must wait so can you.'

Barnaby, usually good-natured, scowled but remained silent.

Joan was pleased to see us. She ushered us through her small hall and out into the fragrant cool garden that lay behind the new kitchen and parlour and sent Marigold to bring us cool beer.

That afternoon, seated on stools under an apple tree, we whiled a pleasant hour away with Joan and William. Her garden was shaded and sweetly scented, filled to its edges with herb beds and fruit bushes. We shared our pies and we gossiped, my anxious thoughts retreating now that I was safely in the company of women. Joan jumped up, hurried off and a little later returned with dishes of cream and cold stewed quinces sweetened with honey.

'Ah, if only every day could be as pleasant as today.' Cat sighed and leaned back against the tree trunk, her linen bonnet loosened and her curling hair escaping from its pins.

'Joan, you have made this a peaceful home. You can forget the world here,' I said. 'I can hardly hear the street, just the hum of bees and the rustling of leaves.'

'You do love gardens, Lizzy.' She nodded towards a flower patch. 'My purple daisies are out in time for Michelmas, and the apples are ripened already.' She stretched contented as a purring puss and smiled, 'Ah yes, we all must do this more often.'

A year and a quarter of marriage had made my sister content. Motherhood had enriched and ripened her. It filled Joan with pride that Thomas had left her John to look after the stewardship of York Place during his absence in Rome. My once awkward sister was glowing with happiness.

Smith collected us from Joan's small courtyard. He never spoke the whole way back to Fenchurch Street. I think he was concerned about Master Northleach's appearance though he never referred to it again that day. Barnaby, however, chattered on to Wilfrid about how he admired Marigold, Joan's maidservant. She had the prettiest blue eyes he had ever beheld. She had shared buttermilk and seed cakes with him in the cool of the small buttery behind Joan's kitchen. Suspiciously, I wondered if that was all they had shared that afternoon.

Barnaby's apprenticeship would soon end; he was restless but he had a few years left before he could graduate to journeyman. I made a mental note to ask Smith to lay a close eye on him. We had had one near-scandal in our household already, though it ended well enough.

Smith was soon to marry himself. At long last, it had been agreed that before Christmas this year he would wed Meg and this was an event we all looked forward to. Not wishing to lose either of them, we had already offered them two rooms at the top of our busy house. Without hesitation they accepted. I sensed that soon more changes lay ahead of us all. The last thing we needed as this year drew in was trouble from Edward Northleach.

Cat and I enjoyed a further week together. The stinging encounter with Master Northleach faded a little as we sewed and attended services at St Gabriel with a male servant accompanying us. I prayed to St Elizabeth for protection, falling to my knees, trying hard to hide sudden attacks of anxiety, I found that I was nervously telling my beads as I recited my prayers over and over. We made sure never to be alone. If we went to the Cheape to shop for spices, a servant accompanied us and carried our parcels home for us.

We visited Joan again and she came to us to help us gather my modest fruit harvest. The apples and pears were ripening on my two trees. My bramble hedge was lush with ripe blackberries which we gathered and had made into a blackberry and apple pie.

We had finished every crumb and had dabbed our mouths with our napkins when there was a diffident rapping on parlour door. I opened it to discover Smith standing awkwardly in the passage reluctant to disturb us though his countenance reflected his anxiety.

'Mistress, I must speak privately with you.'

Cat politely offered to see to the children. She had promised them ginger bread before they went to bed.

'Whatever this interruption is about, Smith, it is clearly urgent.'

'Mistress Elizabeth, I am sorry to interrupt you on Mistress Catherine's last evening together, but it is important.'

'Northleach?'

He nodded. 'It is.'

I bade Smith follow me to the closet off the hall, struck a flint we kept by the door leading into the office and lit a large candle and a wall sconce. The candle flickered, spat and, despite my nervous hands, took fire. I firmly closed the door.

We moved to the window looking over the courtyard, away from the hall door and the ears of passing servants. Church bells rang out the ninth evening hour. A dog barked, then another and another. A full moon was rising through the foggy darkness.

'Gerard, what is it?'

Smith stood by the casement watching the shadowy guards who moved about our gates. Silence hung between us for a moment and I knew whatever it was, it was unpleasant. At last, he said quietly, 'It is as well we have those lads out there.' In the candle's glow his pale eyes appeared thoughtful. He looked down at me. 'Northleach, Mistress Elizabeth, means trouble.'

'You have seen him again?'

'He was lying in wait this morning at the Cornhill shop, looking for Master Wykes. When I told him that the master was away in the country and I knew not when he was returning, he insisted that he must speak with him.'

'Perhaps he means to pay his debt?' I said hopefully, though I feared it was not so. Smith was too anxious for that to be so.

'When I asked him his business, he laughed in that arrogant way he has and said that his visit was to do with a marriage pre-contract that existed between yourself and himself, Mistress Elizabeth. He spoke it loudly, as if he wanted all the world to know the lie. The man is out of mind and I fear that he is dangerous too.'

'Was Father's assistant and the two guards there?'

'No, they were all inside readying wool for sale.'

I took an intake of breath and steadied myself by

holding on to the table edge before replying. I tried to keep calm.

'What a lie. I am a married woman with a child and, Smith, there's another child on the way.'

'I reminded him that you are wed to Master Cromwell. I spoke to him of his debt to Master Wykes. First, he said that he did not care who you were married to. You were pre-contracted to him. He shouted that the courts would give him satisfaction and he claimed that he did not owe any money since it was his right to claim a dowry. The profit from that cloth was to be your dowry, Mistress.'

'But, Gerard, I never signed any pre-contract, nor did I ever agree to marry that man.'

'Mistress Elizabeth, I know it, but, could it be possible that your father had given him the notion that he agreed to a pre-contract on your behalf?' Smith looked down at his feet. He looked up again. 'It is not my business, Mistress Elizabeth, but I feel I must repeat his words. He said that a pre-contract existed between you both. He insisted that you had accepted a token from him, and that you had pledged your troth to him. He says he has two witnesses to prove it.'

I sank down onto Thomas' chair, fearful, as Northleach was mad and God only knew what he intended now.

'Well, I am sorry he has involved you, Gerard. He wants to stir trouble for us.' I felt angry at the thought of our servants witnessing such lies. 'How can he have witnesses? If there was a marriage agreement between him and Father, it would be void without my agreement. I was a widow when Master Northleach came to visit and in total control of my own destiny.'

I sat still. The air around me chilled. Gerald Smith looked uncomfortable. I closed my eyes, feeling a migraine coming on. I pressed my fingers to my temple. At last I looked up. 'Who could these witnesses be? Did he say?'

Smith shook his head.

'There is nothing to be done until my father returns. Not a word, I have to get to the root of this. It is best that no one knows about his absurd lies. Witnesses indeed!'

A thought slid into my mind as I spoke. Susannah of course. The servant girl had left my house just before we moved to Fenchurch Street. I could not remember where she was gone or whom she had wed, but she had been in the garden on the day Edward Northleach had called to ask me to marry him.

'No, Mistress Elizabeth,' Smith was saying. 'I would not say a word.'

I hardly heard him because I was trying to remember Susannah and another person who had been in the garden morning. I had it - a boy sweeping.

'The sooner Master Cromwell returns, the better,' Smith added. 'He has his own methods of dealing with cheats and scoundrels.'

'Yes,' I said thoughtfully.

There would be no written pre-contract, but what if Susannah and the gardener's boy were his witnesses? Could Northleach have found them and persuaded the pair that a small silver cross was a betrothal token and that they had been witnesses to our betrothal? Why was Northleach so determined to destroy my marriage - his debt to Father, his need for money, obsession, insanity? A terrifying thought gripped hold of me. Was he obsessed? Had he imagined a betrothal, and he really had been robbed and imprisoned and was his mind twisted?

'Smith,' I said. 'Do you remember a girl called Susannah, one of the maids we had when we lived at

Wood Street?'

He pulled his hand through his straw coloured hair. 'Aye, she was after Master Toby, but he soon tired of her pestering, whoring ways.'

'Do you remember a gardener's boy we had that time?'

Smith laughed. 'That lazy wretch! Marcus was his name. Why?'

'I think they are the so-called witnesses. You see, Master Northleach did give me a gift, but it wasn't a token. It was a mourning gift, a silver cross because Tom Williams had died. Northleach had said that it belonged to his dead wife. At the time, I thought it touching.'

'Innocent, but naïve if I may be so bold to say, Mistress. May I sit for a moment? I need to think.'

I waved my hand to the bench by the fireplace. Smith sat down, leaned on his lanky legs and scratched his head. 'Susannah married that Marcus, true enough. I think they live over the river.'

'Near the stews?'

He glanced up with a half-smile. 'They use maids there too. Likely they dwell amongst the Winchester geese. Plenty of pots in those haunts to empty, linen to change, gardens to weed, allotments to tend.' Smith laughed. 'And a barrel full of poverty too.'

'If Northleach has found them there, we can too,' I said decisively. 'Thomas will be home soon, before the calends of September the last messenger said, and that is end of this week. I shall tell him. Father will be hopeless but Thomas will silence Northleach.' I gave up a silent prayer to St Elizabeth that Tom would not think my behaviour of all those years ago foolish and that Father had not made promises he could never deliver.

Smith rose from his bench. 'We shall double the guard

on the gate. I shall have Northleach followed, if he shows again.'

'Who is to follow him?'

'A street rat that I'm training up as a carter. He knows the warren over the river. I'll have him watch Northleach if he shows up.'

'What reason will you give the boy?' I asked.

'Money owed to myself, and that is not far from the truth.' He grinned showing a mouthful of small even teeth, so unlike those Northleach liked to flash, unfolded his long legs and stood, ready to be dismissed.

'Thank you, Gerard, for coming to me so quickly.'

'Never worry, Mistress Elizabeth. His deceit will come to nothing.'

How could I not feel anxious?

***

Cat returned home. I had enjoyed her visit. Northleach's leering face caught me at unexpected moments after she had gone. I darted glances into the shadowy corners beneath the overhangs of buildings every time I ventured out to the street. I always made sure that a guard accompanied me. My irrational fear of a servant with a scarred face was replaced by Northleach's grinning teeth. The former may have been a figment of my imagination, but Northleach was dangerous, capable of circulating gossip that could be construed as a truth. Spinning out a half-truth can be the most dangerous kind of slander.

There was no news of Susannah or Marcus that week. Smith shook his head when I sought him out and asked.

'If I do not find them, Master will root them out when he returns.'

'I hope you are right,' I said, aware that Thomas had his own spies. 'And Northleach, have you heard news of his whereabouts?'

257

'He has vanished again.'

I sighed with relief, but I knew Northleach would return to haunt me, just as surely as the vision of a scarred face man had the year before.

Chapter Twenty-seven

A MESSENGER TROTTED INTO the courtyard with news of Thomas' imminent return. Thomas had docked in the Kentish port of Dover. He had business in Canterbury but would be with us soon.

'Madonna, your servant offers you her grateful thanks,' I whispered to my little statue of the virgin after I had sent the bringer of this good news to the kitchens for refreshment.

I shook off an obsessive melancholia that had descended upon me that week and set about cleansing our Fenchurch Street house. Under my supervision, maids bustled through the house, sweeping, dusting, washing windowpanes with vinegar, and polishing the leads until they shone. I swept from parlour to hall and back to parlour to inspect that all was ready for Thomas' return. I wanted him to see his house with its new possessions gleam and smell sweet.

The servants dusted a buffet that sat on stout legs in the parlour, an exquisite cupboard, its oak carved with wolves and bears, beavers and strange birds with spreading wings. Thomas had purchased the cupboard Antwerp on his way south and had dispatched it to me by merchant cargo ship. Once it had safely arrived in Fenchurch Street, I put it to use, proudly displaying a pair of elaborate gilt candlesticks from Italy with vines climbing up them and two plump angels, wings spread at the top. This marvellous cupboard possessed a ladder of further shelves on which I showed off our pewter plate.

I walked purposefully through the hall glancing around at its furnishings, checking for dust as I trailed my fingers over freshly polished surfaces, inhaling the scent of lavender and beeswax. I paused by a pair of chests he had sent me from Italy. They stood on golden hued matting, purchased purposely to show them off. As I trailed my hand over lids that depicted *The Garden of Eden* and *King Solomon's Court*, I thought how fortunate I was to have a husband who noticed, admired and enjoyed such exquisite carvings. Logs in the wall fireplace glowed, casting warmth into the hall's recesses and over the new coffers. Instinctively, I plumped up a red velvet cushion on Tom's particular chair. It had been empty too long.

Cook bustled into the hall. 'A word, Mistress, there is a line of victuallers at the gate.' He swept a floury hand across his brow.'

'Yes, yes, I shall pay them, Cook. Send them to me in the closet. Now go before you drop a trail of flour everywhere.'

'Yes, Mistress.' He sped off, his hands buried in his great apron.

As basket after basket of vegetables, fish and meats and fowls arrived at the kitchen door, I paid off butchers and mercers, and as my cooks began cooking, the comforting smells of pies and spiced puddings drifted through the house soothing me, lulling me into a false sense of harmony. I tucked my fears, Susannah, Marcus and Northleach deep into the recesses of my mind.

Thomas arrived home on a late September day, just after the noon Angelus bells chimed through the City. The gates scrapped open and two overloaded carts trundled

260

into the yard. I had no eyes for the treasures the wagons contained. I saw only my husband, a sun-browned, solid, dark headed man wearing a russet coloured linen bonnet with gleaming pins and a feather; my husband, a wind-burned handsome merchant dressed in a brown riding cloak, sat atop a prancing roan. I raced forward to greet him as if I were Guinevere welcoming Arthur back to Camelot after campaign. Annie came toddling behind me like my retainer, her hand firmly clasped in Meg's.

Thomas swung his leg over his horse and slid down by my side. He drew me to him, kissed the top of my head and held me close. 'Mine own Elizabeth,' he said, before releasing me. 'I am so glad to be home. What's for dinner?'

'A veritable feast, sir.' I clasped his hands for a moment, then snatched up Annie and offered her to him for a father's kiss. 'See how she has grown.'

'Oh, my sweet Annie. 'Tis good to be home,' he said as he hugged his daughter to his breast.

I had invited Master Woodall and John Creke, another of Thomas' good friends, to join us for supper that evening, a small gathering in the parlour to welcome Thomas home. I knew that I had to tell him about Edward Northleach's return to England after our supper when we were private. It would best to tell Thomas the good news first. After that, I must speak of the bad.

'Jellies! You won over the Pope with English jellies and a three-part song, Thomas?' Master Woodall laughed heartily. 'I had no idea you were of such perfect tune to hypnotise a Pope with song. What secrets you keep. My, my, I would hear it now. Can you sing it for us?'

'No, because I employed three English singers for the purpose. Elizabeth had made the jellies. The Pope loves

261

sweets but, even more, he likes the unusual.'

'My sugared fruits. They lasted all the way to Rome. They were for the Pope's table?'

'Yes, and they were as delicious as when you made them. I gave them a fresh dusting of powdered sugar.'

'Did you provide the instruments too?' John Creke asked.

Thomas' grey eyes twinkled with mischief. 'Oh a dulcimer, but the three young singers were clad in multipart hose - finely turned legs, naturally - which the Pope ogled, and short capes trimmed with ermine. They looked and sounded superb. They had no need of any accompaniment, and certainly not me.'

'And where did this event take place?' Creke pushed back his dish of pears and cream. He momentarily turned from Thomas to me. 'Ah, Mistress Elizabeth, that was such a feast.'

I smiled and thanked him. I wished them both gone, for, although they were Thomas' dear friends, I desperately wanted him to myself.

Thomas laughed, his small mouth pursed. 'Creke, it was in woods, just outside the City. You see, the Pope enjoys hunting, so we bribed his guards and servants, and we appeared outside his pavilion just as the sun was setting. It was perfect timing. He was in a mellow mood.'

'And you were successful with the indulgences? It was worth the effort, I gather? The Boston guilds must be pleased.' There was just a small hint of sarcasm in Creke's tone. Master Creke did not believe in indulgences, claiming that these only served to enrich the Church as others starved. I had once overheard him say that they were a bundle of false hopes, a ludicrous promise, a nonsense.

'I was very successful in my mission.' Thomas,

seeming self-satisfied, pushed back his plate and lifted his wine. He let it touch his lips and laid the sparkling Venetian glass back on the table. The heavy red wine gleamed richly in the goblet. 'The Boston guildsmen are delighted to have such a grand source of revenue returned to them.' He became thoughtful, his round grey eyes fathomless. When he spoke again, he lowered his voice. 'Listen, Creke, I am not an evangelical but I, too, find the whole business of indulgences worrying. I like not the Vatican's greed. I do not like the corruption in our church. The Curia is no example. It is worse than ever it was, worse even than on my last visit. Nor do I like the vicious insincerity I observe amongst Pope Leo's Vatican disciples.'

I was sure that Thomas muttered 'foolish fools' under his breath, and so I said quickly, 'Hush, Thomas, do not say such things.'

'I agree with Thomas and Creke, Mistress Elizabeth,' Woodall said, his plump lips pursed in protest, for an instant making me think of a virgin's small useless pouting rebellion on being deflowered by her newly wed spouse. ''Tis a waste of time. You really cannot buy God's forgiveness for your sins. The Church needs cleansing. There are monasteries, even inside our city gates, that are the haunts of greedy and foolish monks who lie with nuns.'

'Hush,' I hissed, and lowered my voice into an anxious whisper, never forgetting that I could still be accused in some church quarters of guarding my first husband's heresy. 'There are always ears at the door ... servants ... have a care, please, sirs.' I gave Jon Woodall a hardened look. 'You may be our friend, Master Woodall, but there are those could wish us and yourselves ill.' I folded my hands. 'The Church knows best,' I added primly. I thought I noticed Thomas' eyes momentarily dart towards the parlour door as Woodall shook his somewhat large head and cast his eyes upwards, but said nothing more on the subject of indulgences.

Thomas patted my hand. 'I read Erasmus's Latin translation of the New Testament on my long journey home. In fact I learned it by heart.' He looked at Woodall. 'Elizabeth has a little book of wisdoms scribed by Erasmus, given to her by the Holy Prior of Austin Friars some years past, do you not, my love?'

I smiled at that. We were on safer territory now. 'I keep it by my bed and read it sometimes before I snuff out my candle, even though it is in Latin,' I said, proudly reminding them that I could read the language.

Creke gave me one of his lofty looks. 'Latin indeed! You are as clever as Queen Catherine herself. I would prefer that the Gospels were printed in English, so that anyone who would read them, could.' He sniffed. 'Not all have the Latin. Most people don't. You could say anything to the people. They would believe any old superstition.'

'Yes, a Bible in English so that anyone could listen to God's words in his own tongue would be no bad thing,' Thomas remarked quietly. 'St Jerome's Vulgate is very old.' I noted a change in his countenance as if he knew something he could not say. His face was serious and determined.

No good would come of this evangelical talk in our home. Thomas, usually so guarded, had shared several bottles of Italian wine with Creke and Woodall and, unusually, he had spoken his mind that night, or at least something of it. I wondered what was left unsaid. If Thomas held challenging thoughts deep in his heart, they must out, and most likely at an unfortunate time and probably in the wrong place. Someone, one day, would hold him to account. We lived in dangerous times. Things we thought were laid to rest often returned later to haunt our thoughts. I could never forget that there had been a fire in my Wood Street dwelling and that had it had been no accident. The culprits had not been discovered. And there was Northleach.

That evening, as we supped with Masters Creke and Woodall, I felt a dark shadow flit in front of me as if it were pulling us forward into a dangerous future.

Thomas touched my hand. 'You are pale, Lizzy. What is it?'

'It is nothing.'

He took my hand between his and held it. All would be well, now he was home. Within a heartbeat, the shadow was gone and I let out a sigh of relief.

'Mistress Elizabeth, you are tired and I must be gone. It is late,' Woodall said, rising to his feet. 'I'll walk the length of Fenchurch Street with you, Master Creke, as far as St Benet's Church. Our friend and his wife should be left in peace.' He pushed back the bench, bowed and gave me a kindly smile as he kissed my hand. 'That, Mistress Cromwell, was the best pigeon pie I have tasted in many a year.'

I stood, murmuring my thanks. Walking to the door, I called for the maids to clear the table and snuff out the parlour candles. Tom led his friends from the parlour, through the hall and out to the gate. I glanced out of the parlour window to watch them pass and waved before closing the shutters for the night.

When Thomas returned to me, holding hands we walked out into the garden because the night was so soft, and the moon was like a silver boat hanging above us. I confessed I wanted to tell him something. I told him about Northleach first.

He listened carefully, occasionally putting me back over my account.

After I told him how I had seen Northleach at the Drapers' Guildhall and how he had accosted Smith with lies outside Father's business premises and about Susannah and how we had tried to find her, he said, 'Lizzy, I shall root this evil out sooner than later, if I can find him. When is your father returning?'

'Any day now.'

'He owes us money, and he is slandering my wife. With no written and signed betrothal contract, his accusation is fatuous. He has been abroad these three years and will have foreign associations. The Italians won't win him friends in the Guildhall. The drapers are hurting because of the King's harsh punishment of our English apprentices who attacked foreigners last May Day. King Henry took the foreigners' part. He wanted the money from their trade. Remember how, before I left for Italy, the City Fathers were being most harsh on foreign merchants, insisting on new legislation. Foreign merchants must now have English apprentices and many have suffered loss of trade.'

An owl hooted, making me start. I remembered only too well how because of the riots that May we had locked our gates for two whole days. We had felt besieged within our own courtyard because the City guilds wanted the foreign merchants banished. They were undercutting trade. I instinctively put my hands over my ears, still hearing the City apprentices marching up Fenchurch Street shouting and banging on gates with great hammers seeking out foreign victims. We merchants had shuddered inside our halls.

266

On May Day, I had sent the servants to their beds and waited up for Thomas to return home, anxiously pacing the hall. I tried to concentrate on my embroidery but failed miserably. That night, I kept opening the hall door, longing for the sound of his boots on the cobbles and his bridle's jingle. Every now and again, I would see one peer out through the hatch in the gate's door until eventually, Thomas arrived home after the midnight angelus.

I watched from the entrance as our two guards dragged the gate opened and Thomas shouted to the stable lad, 'Take the horse and stable it, and my friend's mount too.'

One of our Italian friends, Antonio Bonvisi, slid from his horse onto the cobbles. He hopped towards me, clutching onto Thomas' arm. Blood poured down his leg into the yard straw.

He had been stabbed.

'Oh, my good Lord,' I said. 'Get him inside.'

'I found him on Hert Street,' Thomas told me as I pulled the door opened so he could help the Italian into the hall. 'He was trying to reach the Tower.'

The terrified Master Antonio babbled in a mixture of English and Italian. Thomas translated, 'He says it is not a deep wound.'

Thomas helped him into his great chair while I ran to the still room to find vinegar, water, cloths and a paste of turmeric. I cleaned his wound, which was only a surface cut to his leg. Once he was bandaged, I put him to rest in the chamber behind the parlour and closed the door. Thankfully, his wound healed.

We could hear the clashing of swords all that first night and far past Prime of the next day. On the day following his arrival, the riot died down. The City apprentices were punished after the King's guards were set loose on them. Antonio was safe with us for we kept our doors bolted for five days while he remained with us in case the riots started up again.

The King wanted revenue from foreigners' trade and punished the guilds. He hung apprentices and fined their masters. As quickly as the trouble had begun it blew over, leaving the guilds furious. Successful merchants like Master Antonio determined to leave the City. The London guilds were insisting on trade protection. New laws would soon be passed restricting foreign merchants' trade in favour of home trade and foreigners were being watched.

Thomas was probably right when he said that Northleach could be working for a dubious cloth merchant who had remained in England that summer. Sly dealings in France and Italy could explain Northleach's long absence abroad.

'Lizzy,' Thomas said, holding me, his hands on my arms. 'No one will take you from me. I shall find this evil creature and once I discover his weakness, I shall destroy him.'

'Susannah and Marcus? What about them?'

Thomas' eyes darkened. 'It was foolish of you to accept a token from a man seeking your hand, one whom you did not intend to wed.' He looked at me sternly, 'Until I get to the root of this you must not leave this house. Do you understand? The streets are dangerous when men such as Edward Northleach are loose. As for Susannah and Marcus, if they are innocent of lying they can be left alone. If not, there are ways to deal with them. I shall find that pair. Now come to bed. It has been too long.'

He led me from the garden and up to our chamber. When he had undressed me down to my shift, I told him my other news.

268

Laying his hand on my stomach, he said softly, 'If it is a girl we shall call her Grace, but I would like us to name him Gregory if he is a boy. When will it be?'

I counted on my fingers, thinking Grace such a gentle name, though I liked Rosamond. 'October, November, Christmastide... after the year turns,' I said.

He climbed the two steps up into our bed, lifted up the embroidered cover, and drew back the crisp linen sheet. 'Come, my love; how I have missed you.'

'How I have longed for you to return to me.'

I climbed in beside him and glanced down at his still firm, though now slightly stout stomach. He had dined well in Italy. 'You do believe me, Thomas, don't you, when I say there was no agreement between Edward Northleach and myself?'

His response was to draw me into his arms and whisper into my ear., 'If that wretch of a merchant, so-called, returns to bother us, Elizabeth, he shall soon disappear again. Trust me in this and do not leave the house until I find him.'

I heard him draw breath. 'There is something else you should know.'

'What?'

'Though I did not speak of it tonight, I have helped a man of the new faith. I am not an evangelical nor do I care for them, but I think well of this person and I will acquire papers for him to leave the country.'

'So he is an evangelical?'

'Possibly. I think he is. He was staying in an inn I stopped in on the Canterbury road, a printer who wants to get to Flanders.'

'What does he print?'

'Poetry. Now he hopes to print prayers in the German language. We talked long into the night and I promised to try to get him papers to travel with cloth to Antwerp.'

'Where is he now?'

'Lodging by the Walbrook. The house with the green door.'

I drew in breath and slowly exhaled. 'You have put him in one of Cousin Robert's properties.'

'I am looking after the lease for Cousin Robert. I have a key. I told the porter that my guest was going on business to Bruges and was waiting for a travel permit. I shall get him the pass and send him on his way.'

'He is a heretic?'

'Some would say so. He has been questioned once. Next time he could be tortured. They say Thomas More has instruments of pain in his gatehouse. He thinks to extract confessions and save souls. Surprising for a man of the new learning.'

'Thomas, you cannot be associated with evangelicals,' I said firmly.

'I am not, but I find that I cannot turn my back on them either. All my learning, the way religion was once in England when the Bible was scribed in our own language, speaks to my very soul. Besides, this is a good man and a very learned one.'

'His name?'

'Ah, my sweeting, this information is not for your ears. He will be sent as my agent to Antwerp. I have chits for the Merchant Adventurers which he can carry for me on one of the wool ships. If he is discovered to be a heretic, I shall deny all knowledge of his beliefs. By then he will be in Heidelberg.'

I learned against his chest, listening to the calm, even beat of his heart. I prayed a silent prayer to the Virgin that no ill would touch Thomas.

270

Chapter Twenty-eight

FATHER ARRIVED IN OUR yard on the second Monday of October with three pack horses, two servants, several guards and a frown on his face. I could see that he was unhappy, despite the amount of cloth he carried in his packs from the Gloucestershire weavers.

'Clearly you have not been to Putney.' He shook his head, his face as long as a shovel. I took his arm, steadying him, and added, with concern creeping into my voice, 'Tell me, Father, what troubles you.'

'Later,' he said.

Sagging great bags hovered below his eyes. He was pale, almost as white as the alabaster statue of the virgin in our hall. Father was too old for these journeys, but, it was more because I was sure that something unpleasant had happened on this expedition. His bearing was not that of a man who had just made a successful trip into the country to purchase cloth.

Holding onto his arm, I took command. 'Father, you must bathe first and rest for the night with us. Your men can sleep in the hall. Tomorrow, Smith will take the goods to be checked for sale.' His men had unloaded the goods and were carrying them into our lock up store by the stable. I followed his watchful eyes. 'By the look of the number of packs on those horses, you have done very well.'

'If Smith could have the cloth weighed and measured,

it would be a help. I have no desire to go to the Drapers' Guildhall this week nor, indeed, any time soon, Elizabeth.' He wiped away the sweat that glistened on his brow, and handed his reins to our stable boy.

Anxiety churned up the insides of my stomach. I was sure he must be ill.

'Come inside and I'll send a maid to the chamber behind the parlour with ewers of hot water. Do you have clean clothing or do you want the loan of fresh garments?' Father was of a similar size to Thomas.

'Thank you, Lizzy, fresh clothing please, hose, breeches and coat. Where is Thomas?'

'At York Place; he will be pleased to see you back safely. We all are.' I stood on tiptoes and kissed him. At last Father's face broke into a warm smile and he held me close for a moment.

'Not very safely, as it happens, but I shall explain shortly. Drink, food, bath, in that order. My dear, Mercy must wait until tomorrow for her husband's return.'

What could be so important that it could not wait until he had returned home first, I wondered.

Thomas returned for supper, took one look at Father and expressed concern.

'Something has happened, Henry. Won't you speak of it?'

'Later,' Father said. 'It is not a pleasant tale.'

We had to wait, and there was also the matter of Northleach. It promised to be an uncomfortable evening. We dined with very little conversation.

After supper, we retired to the parlour with a pewter jug full to the brim of hippocras, and a dish of sweet almond cakes. It was a misty, cool autumnal evening, so we sat around a log fire, as much for Father's comfort as for warmth. He smelled astringent from the cleansing herbs that the maids had mixed in with his bath water, and, at last, he appeared more relaxed.

He told us about the Oxfordshire weavers and the cloth he had purchased. He answered Thomas' interested queries about life in the wool towns, describing how he travelled about clusters of cottages seeking out the finest weaves. Many of the larger towns were wealthy from their trade. This, Father said, was reflected in large churches and the handsome, tall, glass-paned windows that adorned men's houses. He spoke of monasteries and abbeys that nestled in sunlit rolling hills, and of mills that stood by fast flowing rivers. I was transported by my father's English villages just as I had been a week earlier by Thomas' descriptions of Italian towns, and, for a time, as he talked of wool, he seemed happy and fulfilled.

'So, Father, you have had a pleasant journey, a successful one apparently. What happened to upset you?' I could wait no longer to find out why he had not returned to Mother before coming to us.

'That rogue Northleach happened,' Father said, his voice raised, veins standing out in his face.

'What,' I said. 'Northleach found you in the wool towns? I -'

Thomas placed a hand over mine. 'Hush, Elizabeth, Henry first. Tell us, Henry.'

Father had encountered Edward Northleach that morning just as he had entered the City gates, as he was crossing the Fleet River to Ludgate.

Thomas shook his head. 'We knew Master Northleach had returned. Lizzy saw him at the Drapers' Guildhall in August. That was what she would tell you, but how he knew you were on your way to the City is a mystery.'

Father looked from Thomas to me quizzically. He said,

'Well, somehow, he had discovered that I was on my way home from Oxfordshire and waylaid me on the Fleet Bridge. He followed me through the gate, riding a great dark stallion.' Father gripped the chair's arms. 'If he can afford that sinister beast, he can afford to pay me what he owes me.'

'What did he say?' Thomas asked.

'He did not mention that he had seen Lizzy at the Drapers' Guildhall. He greeted me as if I was an old friend whom he had, by happenstance, bumped into. "By St Christopher's holy bones,' he said. "If it is not Master Wykes with whom I have wanted to speak these past weeks." I stared at him, shocked at his greeting and his appearance.' Father shook his head. 'He was not the man we had known. He is thinner and hard-faced.

'Anyway, he insisted we spoke in an inn close by the gate. We retired there. I was surprised to see him and I was hungry too. We set down in The Angel's Gate and ate dinner, settled down in a private corner room, a fowl and oyster stew, which I bought for us. Horses were watered and fed, including that dark stallion of his. He called him *Beaumont*, a fancy Frenchified name, rolling the name smoothly off his tongue, as if it were a delicacy like marzipan or spun sugar to be savoured. I asked him what his business was with me and,' Father paused. 'I asked about the fabric he stole from me over four years since.'

'What did he have to say about that?' Thomas looked grim, and I felt my own eyes widen. I suspected the rest.

'He did not speak of it, except to say his delayed return was because he was imprisoned in a French dungeon for years. He had been attacked; was in an affray; a man killed by his sword, though, naturally, our friend Northleach was only defending himself. He claims he was wrongly accused of causing it. He said he lost everything. "You seem to have made good again, Edward, to afford a stallion," I said. He grunted and claimed that he worked for a Nicolo Duoda. The Italian provided him with work, horse and roof.

'I said to him that it is a dangerous business working for the Italians these days. He replied, "I carry my protection under my mantle and I watch my back." He moved his cloak to show an Italian stiletto in his belt.'

'Well, well,' said Thomas. 'You have discovered more in an hour than I found out in a week of enquiry. Duoda indeed. That Italian's business is suspect. This I do know.'

'He was with Italians at the Guildhall,' I ventured. 'They were in a group of their own.'

My father lifted his cup to his lips and drank deeply. He shook his head. 'So Edward Northleach is working for aliens?'

'Not all Italians are crooks, Henry. Let us be clear on that. But Duoda is a crook and he was one of the merchants the apprentices attacked on May Day.'

'Ah.'

'Duoda was using Italian apprentices, untrained, and was undercutting our merchants and other foreign merchants. One of his untrained workers was murdered in the riot.'

'And, by law, he must use English apprentices?' I said.

'Yes, he should, and the law will be stricter as soon as Parliament is in agreement with the City's requests. In future, foreign traders will only lodge in houses owned by Englishmen and be answerable to Englishmen. Duoda will know this. It will be why he is using Northleach. He will have placed Edward Northleach's name on his house lease and continued to use untrained apprentices. By Christmas you'll see changes. The Flemish, French and Italians will be enforced to sell cloth within two days of arrival and

275

they must sell wholesale, and not just cloth, Henry, but leather and even pots and pans. No free trading, no cheating.'

'This may be so.' Father drew breath. 'But this was not all Northleach wanted to speak of. The cur had the temerity to suggest was that I had contracted him to Elizabeth and that Lizzy had agreed. She accepted a token from him to seal it, he claims. There is no written contract, of course, but tokens indeed? Was there a verbal contract, Lizzy?'

I gasped my protest at my father. 'None.'

Thomas narrowed his eyes. 'I believe this man is obsessed with my wife. He wants her so badly that he is determined to use any means - bribery, lies and nonsense! I have ordered Lizzy to remain at home until I discover his whereabouts.'

'Of course, he lies, Father. He gave me a funeral token which I accepted; a small cross on a chain that had belonged to his dead wife.'

'And although I permitted him to woo my daughter, Thomas, it went no further.' He turned to me. 'He said he had witnesses, Lizzy, and I said "produce them."'

'What happened then?'

'He closed his eyes, smiled, and pushed back his plate. "Thank you for dinner, Master Wykes. Yes, indeed, I can marry your daughter. As she is pre-contracted to me, her present marriage is null. I owe you no debt. You owe me your daughter."' Father paused at last. His words had tumbled from his mouth. 'What do we do, Thomas?' He turned to me. 'Are there witnesses to the token, Elizabeth?'

'I had a maid then, Susannah, who may be witness to the gift, along with Marcus, a gardener's boy. How can we stop his lies?'

My husband's grey eyes had grown cold as ice on the

river in winter. He turned to Father. 'Henry, go home to Mercy and stay there. I shall destroy this falsehood and its bearer. Keep away from the City and rest. You look tired.'

'I shall if Smith watches the business.'

Thomas agreed to take care of everything. He had a plan, though I knew that he would not be questioned about it. This would be as secret as the acquisition of papers for an English heretic who was to travel to Antwerp.

Smith's boy discovered Susannah a week later in a stew where her husband had put her to work as a whore. Marcus had apparently turned from bad to worse. He rarely worked. Thomas ordered the pair brought to the house secretly that October night. He took dense, concealing woollen cloaks from them, threw these over his chair in the hall and ushered the terrified pair into his closet.

They stood awkwardly before us, frightened and bedraggled. Smith once again took up a position by the window, wearing a look that could only be described as menacing. I wondered what had been done to them before they had been brought to Fenchurch Street to scare them witless. Yet, the evidence showed on their faces. A crimson bruising covered Marcus's left cheek and a chastened Susannah looked down at her muddy clogs. I noted that her cloak, though serviceable, was patched and her gown brown and plain. Her brothel clothing, assuming she possessed a fancy gown, had remained in whatever stew they had discovered her in.

'Do you understand why you are here, Susannah?' Thomas began.

Susannah hesitated and then looked up at us and nodded dully. Her once bright eyes looked dull. She was as thin as a sparrow. Susannah's marriage had clearly not brought her the happiness she had hoped for. Thomas caught my eye and said, 'My wife has questions for you, Susannah, concerning Master Northleach, who I believe has given you coin to lie for him.'

She looked tearful. Marcus shifted about on his feet. He began to open his mouth.

'Be silent,' Thomas snapped. 'You have been the cause of enough trouble.' He looked at me. 'Elizabeth, you have questions?'

I came to the point. 'Susannah, what did you see on the day Master Northleach visited my Wood Street House?' I ignored the pathetic wretch who had ruined her in the four years since she had left my service.

She stammered a response. 'I meant no harm, Mistress, but I did see him give you that token. I did, Mistress Elizabeth. I saw you two walking together and I saw you sitting close as lovers together on the garden seat under that mulberry tree. I did, and he a fine gentleman asked you to marry him. Marcus heard that.'

'Master Northleach?'

'Aye, Mistress, 'twas he, Master Northleach, I mean.'

'Then Marcus would have heard my refusal.'

Marcus could not keep his mouth closed. He burst out, 'Mistress, I heard him ask you and I saw him give you a gift and I saw you look kindly upon Master Northleach.'

I drew the chain and cross from my purse and held it up.

'You saw this, Marcus?'

He nodded.

'And, you will remember that my first husband had died that midsummer?'

He nodded.

'You see, this is a memento mori. That is all - a cross

278

on a chain that Master Northleach gave me to express his sorrow on the death of my first husband.' I did not say it had belonged to his dead wife and that this had evoked my sympathy. I had said enough. Still, I could not resist adding, 'And you will have heard me decline Master Northleach's attentions.'

He whispered, 'I could not hear your words exactly, Mistress.'

Thomas then said, 'So, you did not hear my wife's words of refusal, nor any words of acceptance either. You will return to Southwark, and if you lie again you will be dragged by my men before magistrates before you can spit onto the floor straw.

'You will not speak of this meeting to Master Northleach. If he comes calling, you will let me know immediately. Dicken will be watching you from the Pig and Whistle. Note his name. His is a prize fighter too.' Thomas looked from one to the other. 'You have concocted lies and slander. Observe well that I am more powerful than that slanderer Northleach. You won't have lives worth living if you ever speak of what has been discussed here tonight to anybody. If there are plots yet to be spun and business to be conducted, you are my creatures now.'

Thomas paused and drew breath before saying, 'I will leave your miserable lives alone. Report to Dicken when Northleach comes to find you, and I shall protect you.'

Marcus grovelled. He bowed low, and coming up said through the dirty hair that flopped over his narrow eyes, 'I am sorry for our mistake, Master Cromwell. He promised us coin if we spoke up. We are fallen on hard times. All we want is to save what we can to get us out into the country where I can work as a shepherd and so Susy here does not have to work as she does.'

'Well we shall see how this goes, shall we?' Thomas turned to me.

'Susannah, you were greatly mistaken.' I glared at her pathetic husband. 'You have perjured yourselves.'

I hoped that Thomas would get them away from the City once Northleach was silenced. I wanted nothing here to remind me of Northleach's lies, certainly not two creatures such as these.

'Go,' I said, glancing over at Smith who leaned back against the window sill, his face expressionless. 'You can keep the capes we have given you in case you need them again.' I turned my back, slid the silver cross back into my belt purse and walked away from the closet. Smith and Thomas could get rid of the pair, for I could not feel sympathy for them.

Chapter Twenty-nine

WE HEARD NO MORE of Edward Northleach during the following fortnight, nor did we hear from Susannah or Marcus. If I thought the problem had gone away though, I was wrong.

Thomas had acquired a travel pass for the personage he was sheltering at Cousin Robert's house. He promised that he would deliver it soon. Some days went by, but still Thomas did not deliver it.

When I asked about it, he said, 'When the ship is ready to sail.'

'When will that be?'

'This week.'

A messenger from the Court of Requests hurried breathlessly into our hall on Tuesday morning as we were breaking our fast. Before I had time to say good bye to Tom, he had left his ale cup unfinished and rushed off muttering, 'They are putting Master Farrar on trial a day early. I left the papers over at the Guildhall. Must fetch them.' Moments later I heard him trotting out of the yard on his jennet, shouting at the messenger to request a delay on the Farrar hearing until after noon. Moments later the messenger mounted his horse and was off.

I found the printer's passport lying on the parlour table, in full view, beside some other bills. Curious, I examined it. The pass was for one William Tyndale of Norfolk, to travel to the Low Countries on the cloth merchant Thomas Cromwell's behalf, with three dozen ells of stamped woollen goods to be sold in Antwerp. The pass should not wait.

Thomas had intended to take it to him. I pondered it for a moment and reasoned that I could deliver the pass myself for Thomas, who had clearly forgotten it. A consignment of our wool was to sail from London to Antwerp with the *Juniper* on Thursday morning. Today was Tuesday, and if this Tyndale was a heretic, I wanted to make sure that he was on that ship and out of our lives by Thursday. I bit my lip. The difficulty was that I was still supposed to stay at home for my own protection. The pass should not wait. I wickedly smiled to myself. Surely Thomas would be pleased to be rid of this man's pass. If I was careful, he might be glad of my help.

Yet, taking the pass smelled of deceit. I bit my lip hard again and tasted blood. I am not by nature deceitful, though surely my husband, who had left me to watch over affairs in his absence in the past, would thank me for my foresight. I would be careful and, after all, Thomas was busy.

It was Thomas' carelessness, a most unusual occurrence, which finally drove me on to deceit. Simply, we must remove the reformist from our lives. He could not miss the ship. I would make this right and Tom would thank me for it. I was caught between the devil and the angel, and, that day, the devil won.

Breathing deeply, I made my decision. I needed threads. That would be my excuse. I was no inexperienced simpering maid who should be kept behind closed doors for her own protection. I had a secret pocket in my kirtle where I kept household notes. Without further thought, I slipped the pass into the lining of my overskirt. I would go alone. No one must know. I could not trust anybody.

Annie was with her nurse. Meg was making simples in the still room. I told the servants that I was spending the morning making up a pattern book and that until the dinner hour, on no account, was I to be disturbed.

Cousin Robert's house by the Walbrook had several respectable lodgers, looked after by one of Cousin Robert's distant relatives, a widow who took in washing. Threadneedle Street was close to the Walbrook. I would have an hour to purchase threads *and* plenty of time to deliver the passport.

I secured my purse onto my belt and stole down the empty stairs and through the quiet garden hardly daring to breath. My heart was rushing faster than an incoming river tide. When I reached the pear tree without encountering our many servants, I glanced down at my feet. In my haste, I had not changed my footwear and was wearing my favourite thin leather shoes. Too late. I could not risk returning. A scatter of puffed up little clouds breezily floated through a deep blue sky. If the day remained sunny, there would be no mud to ruin them. I shrugged and, without further hesitation, unlatched the back door into the alley that ran behind our house into Lyme Street. Moments later, I stood by the graveyard gate into St Dionis Back Church. There would be no retreat.

'Good morning, Mistress Cromwell.'

Mistress Watt was advancing on me from the churchyard, the last person I expected to see that morning. Habitually, she was to be discovered at St Gabriel, not in St Dionis's churchyard.

'Why the haste?' She looked at me curiously. It was unusual for me to leave our house by the garden gate, and, without doubt, Mistress Watt, who was a source of all knowledge concerning the habits of others, would know this fact.

'Good morning to you, Mistress Watt. It is an urgent matter of gold thread since I am working a new embroidery for Saint Elizabeth's altar. It must be finished by Christ's Mass.' I asked her how her son, Master Robert, fared, though I knew that all was not well with him. He was gambling. We thought he could not afford a servant any more, for the man with the scarred face was never in Master Robert's company.

'He is purchasing wool in the country, Mistress Cromwell.' She took an abrupt step away from me. Clearly, I had touched a defensive spot in her prickly sensitivity and for a moment I regretted my hasty words. She would, however, now leave me in peace, in case I asked more pertinent questions.

'I wish him success,' I said.

'God does not like the idle. I must be on my way,' she snapped back, angry as a hissing adder. My regret lessened. 'I have a dinner to cook,' she added. 'Not all of us can afford a kitchen staff. I am surprised to see you without your guard to protect you.'

My regret flew off. 'My servants are busy this morning, Mistress Watt. May the Virgin Mary watch over you and bring Master Robert safely home,' I said quickly and hurried on along the church wall, glad to escape.

On entering Gracechurch Street I paused, with an uncanny premonition that I was being followed. I glanced over my shoulder. There was no one behind me so I hurried on. The street was busy so I wound my way around two beggars with cups by a lane that led into All Hallows, Green Church. One was missing a leg, the other a hand. Both cried out with toneless synchronicity, 'Have mercy, for the sake of God, have pity, Mistress.' I tossed them two farthings, which they immediately descended upon, scrabbling about their three feet with stiff, awkward hands trying hard to scoop their treasure up from the dirt.

I thought how sad it was that they were so poor while we were wealthy. The Church should provide alms for them. It was, as they leaned back against their wall, that I caught sight of a saffron-cloaked goblin-like figure ducking into the churchyard behind me. He was too small of stature to be Edward Northleach, but his quick action unsettled me because I was sure that this little creature was watching me.

Considering my next move, I looked carefully around the street that was crowded with rumbling carts and travelling personages coming up into the City from the river. It should be possible to lose him on such a busy route way. I was small. I was also adept at concealment, though as I glanced down at the bump that stretched my kirtle I was not so sure that I could be very fleet of foot.

I decided to deliver the passport first because there were several streets on the way to Cousin Robert's houses with shops, stalls and small alleys amongst which I could hide if I saw the creature again. After I had made my delivery, I would continue to the haberdasher's which lay on Threadneedle Street, beside the Merchant Tailors' Hall. I thanked God that the Broad Street Ward was a hectic place, always occupied with traders and traffic.

I hurried on up Gracechurch Street, winding through carts and horses, and pushing through a band of white nuns who were tripping down the centre of the street towards the great city bridge. I wondered absurdly if they were from St Helen's Priory and clad in our wool. When I moved into their midst, their wimples aided my ploy and concealed me. It was a great relief when I veered to the

285

left of them and turned the corner at Lombard Street. I could not see anyone following me and was able to gain Poultry Street without further misadventure. Marion, the elderly widow whom Cousin Robert supported, did the washing in a huge copper kettle in an outhouse. On fine days her washing was draped over the hawthorns between her house and the stream. I suspected today was one such day since the sun was hot and the breeze gentle and warm.

It was only a matter of moments before I was by the Walbrook stream, where washing dried on the hedges and Marion was exiting the green door with a basket laden with wet linen. She set it down by a bramble bush.

'Marion,' I called, not thinking about any who might happen past us. 'Is Master Tyndale at home today?'

Her response was to spin around and to look startled. Placing a finger on her lips, she gestured with her other hand towards the house's overhanging top storey. I shook my head and approached the basket of washing.

She folded her arms. 'Elizabeth, dear, why are you here?'

'I have something for *him.*' I glanced to the house. 'It's from my husband.'

'Deliver whatever it is quickly and be gone.' Marion lowered her voice. 'If Robert knew that your Thomas had asked me to shelter a travelling preacher he would be furious and so would the Cardinal.'

Marion was frightened, as if the inquisition was about to descend on us that day. Her wide kirtle flared out to match her anger. Her apron stiffened as she stood beside me. 'He said it was only for a few days. It is a few days over long. There are spies everywhere looking out for preachers with peculiar notions.'

'Did he say he was a preacher?' I said, feeling my nerves rattling like bones shaken up in a knacker's cart. 'I thought he was a college man who only wanted to learn printing. I thought Thomas is helping him to travel abroad to learn more about the craft.' I lied, for did I not know that Tyndale was an evangelical.

'He *is* a preacher, Elizabeth, and one of the dangerous sort. When I took him his supper, he told me things I would not repeat near a priest, not even in the confessional.'

'Such as?' I was frightened now, and curious.

'He says God will not forgive us our sin if we purchase an indulgence. That is buying forgiveness. God would not like that, he says. We have to accept the Lord into our hearts. If we do, only then He will forgive us wrongdoing. Only God, himself, can forgive us with his Divine Grace. The preacher says God's word should be taken from the Latin and put into English and that we should all read it for ourselves.' She laughed. 'If we could read, indeed. I cannot read, nor can I write. He speaks heresy, I say. There is no comfort in this world without relics and indulgences.'

'Listen, he will sail on the *Juniper* to the Low Countries on Thursday. I have his pass for him. I want him gone too.'

'A good riddance. You go on up those stairs over there and be quick about it,' she insisted. There was no offer of a glass of ale to quench my thirst, nor a finger of her fine ginger cake. She turned her broad back on me and commenced to layer her washing over the hawthorn bush. I was dismissed.

I hurried through the opened door and flew up the staircase; my nerve weakening as I stood outside Master Tyndale's chamber. I gathered up my courage, took a deep breath and knocked twice.

'Who is there? Friend or foe?'

'Friend.'

'A woman alone,' he said, opening the door with a dramatic flourish. He did not look like a man who was frightened of authority. He did not look like a travelling preacher either, and he certainly did not look like a devil heretic, though I did not, in truth, know what a real heretic was supposed to look like; perhaps they were like the devils painted on the wall of St Gabriel's Church. This man had the appearance of a scholar recently come down from Oxford. William Tyndale was young, in his early twenties, with a high brow and a long face that possessed a healthy colour. His hair and wisp of a beard were brown. His eyes were penetrative and dark as chimney soot. He wore a plain black cap that covered his ears and long, flowing dark gown of good worsted wool.

'Well then, who are you?' He glanced down at my thin shoes. My eyes followed his. My feet were very dusty. 'You wear a lady's slippers and, in truth, should not be abroad alone. This is my suspicion.'

'No, I should not. May I enter a moment since I have something for you? I must be gone with haste.'

He raised an eyebrow and stood to one side, his hand lingering on the door knob. There was a table and a chair in the chamber and a door that led to his second chamber. Glancing through, I observed an unmade cot and a pile of books resting on a plain wooden stool. I pulled the passport from my belt and placed it on the table. 'You have a pass to travel to Antwerp, Master Tyndale. You are on cloth business there and before you attend to what business you have of your own in Antwerp, I ask that you see my cloth is placed safely with my representatives who will meet the *Juniper* – that is the ship. You will lodge at Master Vaughan's house in Antwerp. It is on Grosmarketstrete.'

He turned the document over in his hands and studied it for a moment with intensity. Looking up and laughing, he said, 'Your cloth business. So you are Mistress Cromwell. Why has your husband sent you and not come himself?'

'My husband is away on other business. We ask you not to speak of religious matters, while you are on board the *Juniper*, because if you do, you will put us all in danger.' I lifted my hand. 'I do not want to know your persuasions for I have no interest in them.'

I turned on my heel and fled downstairs. He called after me, 'When on Thursday?'

I stopped. Of course he needed to know this. 'By noon, be at Deptford. The ship docks there. Take a river boat and at Trinity House ask for Master Peter of the *Juniper*. A pilot will take you to the ship.'

I felt him laughing at me again when he said, 'My grateful thanks, Mistress. Take a care for those shoes and please, in your haste to be away, do not trip on the stairs.'

I looked back and said, 'Take a good care of yourself, Master Tyndale. I think you must be a brave and clever man, but think carefully about the words you speak lest they talk heresy. These are dangerous times for one who thinks differently to others.' I meant my words, for I could not help but like him, and I knew what it was to live fearful of heretical accusation. I understood now why Thomas had cared about his safety.

'I am indeed warned. I am travelling to Antwerp to see for myself the business of printing. Christ be with you, Mistress Cromwell. May he dwell in your heart and in that of the innocent child you carry.'

'I am guided by my priest as to where God may dwell,' I said, feeling prickly, and left him standing looking a little puzzled at the head of the staircase.

Marion was not in sight and I thought it best not to seek her out. As I hurried away, feeling unsettled by my encounter with Tyndale, who flew close to an ill wind. I *did* think in my heart that it could not be sinful to read God's word in our own language and I pondered on this as I walked towards the Taylors Hall. If this were the young man's reason for learning printing abroad rather than here in London, I could understand his reasoning and even hoped that one day I could read the Bible in English.

My walk home was pleasant. I even had time to stop at our parish church of St Gabriel. Kneeling at the statue to the Virgin, I prayed to her for guidance. Surely it was not wrong to purchase an indulgence since the money went to the Church. How could our parish help its beggars and its poor and pay to feed its priests if we did not buy God's pardon? But the beggars I saw that morning had *not* been helped by the Parish. The priests ate well, even on fast days. They wore fine woollen habits provided by merchants such as us, while others had nothing.

The thought occurred to me that you can purchase a pardon but can you really be sure of God's forgiveness? It was a dangerous thought, and I, who had once lived with danger, could not afford to risk my life or my soul again. I decided to boldly walk back inside through the front gate and found that I had returned in time for dinner.

'Just look at the dust on your best slippers, Elizabeth. Where have you been?' Thomas was puzzled as we sat down in our hall to eat. I had not been at home on his return from the Appeal Court.

'I did not think you would return for dinner today.' Lowering my voice to a whisper, I said, 'I found the passport for the man who is travelling with the Antwerp cloth on Thursday where you left it lying on the parlour table.'

'I wondered where it was. I had meant to deliver it this evening. You did what with it?' Thomas replaced his eating knife and stared at me. 'Where is it? Where have you been? Not...'

'Yes, you had forgotten to take it. Since I needed thread and I was going that way to Threadneedle Street, I thought you would be pleased if it was delivered.'

'What,' he repeated, all colour draining from his face. 'You could send a servant out for thread. As for the pass -'

'I wished to save you an unnecessary journey.'

'Were you followed?'

'No,' I lied. 'I think I was not.'

'Elizabeth, you do not know what you are doing. You are meddling. I shall speak with you later, not now.' His grey, hazel-rimmed eyes looked angry.

We had kept our voices very low. Thomas looked down the board. Many of our household had joined us for dinner that afternoon and I could see by their downcast faces that they knew all was not well. Once the maids had served us, I lifted my knife and spoon and tried to eat. Thomas spoke not another word to me. My appetite was gone.

After the dinner hour he pushed back his chair, threw on his cloak, ignored young Ralph, whom he always reminded about his learning, and marched out of the hall door without waiting for the fruit and cheese that he usually enjoyed after our midday meal.

That night, Thomas returned home beyond the third hour after midnight. I had gone to bed early feeling extremely unwell but couldn't sleep. Eventually I drifted into an uneasy dreaming long after the midnight angelus bells had sounded. A day that had started so well had ended badly.

I woke up of a sudden. He stood in the bedchamber, by the bed looking down on me. I felt his anger descend upon me like a cannon shot crushing me. Sitting up, I pushed back the embroidered counterpane. 'What is it? Northleach or Tyndale?' I said bravely, I thought.

'It has taken me all night to undo what you did today, Elizabeth. You were followed by Edward Northleach's man. He had been watching this house. And, moreover, he worked out that you had visited what he has described as an evangelical. He questioned Mistress Marion after you left and easily squeezed Tyndale's name from her, she was so frightened. How could you say it in the street? He heard you, and wanted to make sure before he carried it to his masters that he had heard correctly. That was fortunate because Marion, out of self-preservation, had the sense you lack. She hid Tyndale in her washing shed.'

'Where is he now?'

'He is on his way to Flanders on a different wool ship.'

'Which.'

'I think it best that you don't know. We'll have a visit from the parish warden once it gets out that I helped an evangelical leave the country, and that I sheltered him in Cousin Robert's house. If we *do* receive a visit from the priests or from anyone else interested in heretics, you will not be here. Get up now, Elizabeth.'

'Why?'

'You, Meg, Annie and her nurse, are off to your father's tonight. I have a cart and horse waiting in the yard. Pack all you need for a three-week stay. I don't want you here while I finish this business. This is for your own safety. Smith will escort you to Putney. You should arrive by morning.'

292

I wanted more explanation, to know what he was planning and, above all, I wanted his forgiveness. He said, 'Hurry. You have an hour. By the cock's crow, you will be with Henry and Mercy.'

'And not by the early river boat?'

'Smith has a hidden route to follow. You will sit amongst bails of wool where you must remain as silent when he dives the wagon through Aldgate. On no account can you look out. Annie, too, must be quiet. Meg can ride up front with Smith.'

With that Thomas turned his back on me. He spoke nothing more that night. Meg came in and gently helped me to dress. Sleepily, Annie clutched her poppet. She was already dressed. Her nurse, Lucy, a plump, obedient and very capable girl of twelve years, helped me to pack our essentials into a travelling bag. Thomas told her that he had heard a rumour that a new plague was about to assault the City. His pregnant wife was going to her parents just in case of danger to her and the child she carried. Lucy was glad to leave Fenchurch Street and hurried about gathering up mine and Annie's belongings.

He reminded Annie that she was not to say a word. Annie, thumb in mouth, solemnly nodded as Thomas knelt down in the yard, took her in his arms and kissed her. We all crawled to the back of the wagon, where we were concealed by the bails of wool. Once we had settled into a corner of the wagon, I sheltered Annie in my arms. Leaning on my travelling case, I wept silent tears as the cart rumbled over the cobbles through our gate and we left Fenchurch Street behind.

Thomas did not bid me farewell.

Chapter Thirty

MOTHER OPENED THE PORCH door herself that morning. She was pale, exhausted and anxious. 'You have come so quickly, Lizzy. Thank the Lord.'

'What is the matter?' I asked.

My mother was wringing her hands and crying. She made no sense; her distress was clear.

'Your father. He is ill, dying,' she managed at last.

I threw off my cloak and sent a very shocked Lucy with Annie to the kitchen. 'Find Annie something to eat,' I said.

Meg took Mother and sat her by the fire in the parlour. She sent a maid for an egg posset, Meg's cure for everything.

'Tell me all, Mother,' I said as she sipped the warm drink.

The manor house was in a pass of profound disquiet. My father had been ill since his return from Oxfordshire. Mother had called a physician in and she had sent for me early that morning. I had been packed off to Putney before her messenger had arrived at Fenchurch Street, unaware that Father was ailing.

The physician's diagnosis followed later that day. Father's heart was weak. He was exhausted. He had spent too long tramping around weaving villages that past summer. His meeting with Northleach had tormented him, my mother whispered to me after the physician left.

'I am so glad that you are here, Lizzy. You can have your old chamber and Meg and Lucy can have Joan's chamber. And Annie…'

'Annie will share my bed until Meg returns to Fenchurch Street,' I said firmly.

Meg returned to the City with a report on Father's ailing health. However, Father was cheered to see me and, with bed rest, he made a brief recovery, but it was clear to us all that he was not fit to return to the business. He had developed an ailment in his lungs.

'Rest in bed until you recover, Father. Smith is more than competent,' I reassured him.

'And that rogue, Northleach?' Father grunted from his pillows.

'Thomas will see to that business,' I said, not confessing that I was, in fact, here with such haste because Thomas had sent me away. It was a small deception because I did not want to worry him, nor did I want to mar the joy my parents took in having Annie and myself to cheer their sad household.

We passed quiet days during November. Trees became denuded and spiders spun their dripping yet taut silvery webs between fence posts. We brewed ale and hung cheeses made from sheep's milk in the dairy. A pig was slaughtered and Mother and I supervised the preserving and pickling that followed. Father slept much of the month away exhausted by his weak heart and hacking cough. Daily, he grew thinner and thinner, his face collapsed and pale; he was now a shadow father, not my determined father of old. His will to live was leaking away. Mother grew more and more anxious.

In early December, Thomas came to see us. We

greeted each other affectionately. I was relieved to see him. Annie hugged his legs and had to be unwound from him. She insisted her father greeted her new kitten, named Spike, on account of his fur that stood up straight every time he encountered one of the family hunting dogs.

He had been working hard in the courts and for the Cardinal, his time stolen from him by others. He had travelled north in November on business, he said. Was all truly well between my husband and myself? Something was not as it had been and I felt that it was more than what had happened with the pass for Master Tyndale. Thomas seemed abstracted after he mentioned his journey north.

'What were you doing in the north?' I asked.

'Legal work,' he said, but would not meet my eye.

'What legal work?'

'Land transfers. Do not concern yourself with it, Lizzy. It is lucrative and that is all you need to know. You must not worry about my travels.'

'Yes, you are right,' I said. I wanted to ask him about Tyndale but Thomas was not forthcoming so I waited. I ignored my suspicions that Thomas was not as affectionate towards me as before, thinking that perhaps he was still angry with me.

Our concerns those days were for Father's hopeful recovery, though he seemed little recovered once he saw Thomas. Thomas was reassuring to my mother, calm as was his way, even though it was clear he concealed his anxiety for my father's recovery.

We shared my bed, but when on his last night, I broached the subject of my return to Fenchurch Street, Thomas said wearily, 'Not now, Elizabeth, it is best you remain here, help Mercy and do not fret. Your father may not have long left on this earth. Give him what comfort you can. Do not fret.'

He failed to trust me and I felt empty. He turned on his side and fell into an exhausted slumber. How could I not fret when my father was ill, my mother out of her mind with worry, and when I did not know if Northleach was still plotting?

When Father asked about the merchant, Thomas said, 'Northleach is long gone, Henry. Forget him.'

When I asked, Thomas told me nothing. 'Forget he ever existed.'

The morning of Thomas' return to the City came too soon. We walked through the apple orchard, a short cut to the river, Thomas carrying his tiny leather travelling bag, a reminder of how brief his visit had been. I wanted to know about Northleach. I could not ignore it as Thomas wished Father to.

'He has gone and that is all you need to know, Lizzy,' Thomas said, and looked straight ahead into the dripping trees.

I was sure he was concealing the truth.

I grabbed his arm. 'Tell me or I'll have no peace of mind. Is he alive or dead? He harassed Father all of September. Northleach had me followed. If he found out about the preacher Tyndale, that is my fault, too, so I must know.' I folded my arms across my chest, leaned against a wet gnarled tree and said stubbornly, 'Tell me. So much for honesty between man and wife.'

Thomas shook his head. 'It is not about honesty between us. There have been repercussions.' His tone was chilly at my accusation. He had, in the past, prided himself on openness between us. 'Stay here. Mercy needs you.'

'What repercussions?'

He shook his head and sat his travelling bag down and

opened the orchard gate. I swept past him, feeling miserable as we walked silently along the river bank. All I could hear were rustlings in the winter trees and the swish of oars on the river.

With each day that passed, Father was sickening and weakened. His heart was giving out and my only consolation was that I had been here in Putney for Mother. I stared over the grey water that stretched far into the distance. There was a mist that morning. It hovered over the water so that I could not even see the opposite bank. A fleet of starlings cut through the fog, dark specks in formation in the gloomy sky flying south. I still heard the plash of a boatman's oars.

'He is dying,' I said.

'Do not lose hope,' Thomas said thoughtfully, taking my gloved hands in his. 'Henry may yet recover.' He looked down on me sternly. 'Stay safely here until the baby is born.'

I said, 'There is another thing, Thomas. Meg is to marry Smith this month. I don't think we should postpone it or she might change her mind and that would disappoint him.' I pulled my hand away. 'Meg and I have known each other since she was a child, but I won't be there for her wedding if I must remain here.'

'Lizzy. Return to us for a few days; after that your mother will need you. And remain cheerful, it will help your father recover more quickly.'

I did not hear hope for Father's recovery in Thomas' voice, which was as flat and dreary as winter. I watched him watching the starlings fly along the river to be lost in fog. I whispered, 'Tyndale? What repercussions, Thomas.'

After a few moments he said, 'The preacher is safely in Antwerp. I was questioned and was able to satisfy all the questions I faced from Wolsey's questioners on the matter of a certain pass for an evangelical travelling on a wool ship with our cloth.' He dropped my hands and looked studiously at me. I noted concern in his eyes. 'We do not have dealings with evangelicals, Elizabeth. You said it, yourself. You were right, my dear, when you said it was dangerous talk.' He took a breath and exhaled. 'I was rash.'

'You were rash and so was I.'

'The preacher had sailed with our cloth on one of Cardinal Wolsey's own ships; the King's ship. Unfortunately, his pass was for the *Juniper*.' Thomas frowned. 'You should never have taken the document to him. There were many, many difficult questions about that - *who*, *how* and *why* sorts of questions. I said that he was my agent and needed in Antwerp, and that I had paid well for the cloth transport on the King's vessel which we had already agreed would make money carrying wool transports over the channel. I claimed that the pass mistakenly said the *Jupiter*.'

His voice hardened. 'Understand this, it was a very difficult business. You were not questioned because I said you were in Putney with your family because your father was unwell. The Cardinal's questioners were satisfied and Tyndale travelled to the Low Countries.'

'On King Henry's old ship.' I laughed at that and shook my head. 'I am sorry. It is just ironic. Will you pass Christmas with us if I return here after Meg's wedding, which I must?'

He smiled at me. 'I shall join you for Christ's Day and St Stephen's Day.'

'And you won't say what happened to Edward Northleach,' I ventured.

'It is better that you don't know.'

299

I had to accept this answer or open up bad feeling between us again, so I let it lie. I nodded. 'I trust we are safe. You can tell me this.'

'You are safe.'

He climbed aboard the wherry for the City, the only passenger that day. As the boatman pushed off from the small wharf, Thomas waved back to me. 'Take care, Elizabeth. Take care of our unborn child and watch over Annie. I shall send Smith for you next week. After their wedding I go north again.'

'Go safely, my love,' I called into the misty fog, hoping he *was* my love.

As I watched, his boat became smaller and smaller. The wherry merged with other river traffic and was gone, disappearing into the still river mist. My heart was heavy, for our quarrel, in part, remained unresolved. Thomas kept secrets close and I must accept it. That cold December morning, I had learned that my husband did not forgive easily and I could not forgive myself for the impulsive action that had nearly cost him his livelihood. I instinctively touched my belly and, feeling alone, turned back along the river track.

I returned to Fenchurch Street briefly for Meg's marriage and supervised the wedding supper. Two days later we were back in Putney. Thomas and I were not as happy as we had once been. Our levity had gone to sea with Northleach and Tyndale, and he was overburdened with work.

Thomas took on Father's cloth business, as well as other calls on his time including legal work for Cardinal Wolsey and help with the King and Queen's Christmas celebrations. In between he made his visit north to Chester, on the Cardinal's land evaluation, he said.

'If all fails with the Cardinal, there is still the cloth and legal work for the Adventurers,' he said pragmatically.

'I am glad to know it,' I said. 'Must you keep travelling north?'

'If the Cardinal needs land transfers, I must.' His lips were pursed. His eyebrows heavy, his eyes inscrutable. His tone was edgy. Once again, I felt a distance between us.

My husband placed a band of underlings in charge of our joint cloth trade, all of them directed by Smith. Since he was now married, it was only natural that Smith would look to his own future. My journeyman would be a cloth man and, after all, he understood the English markets more than any of us. He and Meg would, in time, have their own household to care about and possibly, God willing, children. For now, Smith would continue as our cloth man and Thomas increased his wage.

Chapter Thirty-one

JOAN AND JOHN WILLIAMSON and their son came up the river to Putney a few days before Christmas Eve and Harry visited with Alice and the children. Joan greeted them with her old affection for her nieces and nephews. It did not change the fact that Father was dying. Ours would be a solitary and private family Christmastide.

Thomas arrived by river on Christmas Eve. He had returned from a week in the north and seemed thoughtful. He often walked out on his own during his short visit, to wander through his childhood haunts. He was brooding and moody. Wellifield and Eliza had moved away to their own manor near Harrow. Catherine and Morgan had leased a merchant's house outside the City walls, close to Lincoln's Inn, set on Chancery Lane, which was an up-and-coming place to live, especially if you were a law man.

'We must carry on with the feast,' Mother said with forced brightness. 'We won't invite the villagers to wassail this year.'

'Or the boy bishop? The children will be disappointed,' Joan remarked.

'We can make it a family occasion,' I said. 'They can perform a play as before. Planning it will distract them and cheer Father.'

Joan brightened. 'Me too.' She hugged me tearfully.

'He may yet recover. We shall pray for that,' my mother said unconvincingly and quickly crossed herself.

She hurried back from the hall to Father's chamber where she had hung a little mistletoe branch, though it was unlikely that he would rise from his bed and kiss her beneath it.

Mother tried to be brave. I regularly found her touching Father's cloak that hung from his clothing pole, her eyes brimming tears. She tried to tempt Father with junkets and jellies but he had no appetite for them. As her cooks stuffed the goose and cooked meats, Mother and I retired to the parlour. We sat together and embroidered flowers on my altar cloth, using for their hearts the gold thread I had purchased that unfortunate afternoon in Threadneedle Street. Her concentration was poor and her hands fell idle into her lap. She often sat looking into an empty space, as if seeing nothing, but remembering and speaking of little incidences they had shared. Although she tried to interest Father their shared memories, he slept for most of the day. It was as if he had left us already.

Thomas and I remained partially estranged. None but us knew it, not even my mother who, of course, had her own problems. I thought time alone together would break the chilliness that frequently hung between us like air on a cold day, unseen but ever present.

On Christ's Day, I asked Tom to walk with me along the river again, hoping to snatch just a little time to ourselves. He pulled his heavy worsted cloak down from the peg in the hall and without a smile for me, wrapped himself in it. I drew mine close as the day was bitter. Frost crunched under our boots as we stepped out of the orchard onto the river path. I was heavy with child so Thomas guided my arm. He had not touched me since our last walk here. I was surprised and comforted by his steadying hand on my arm, hoping that this simple familiar action had heralded the commencement of a lasting thaw.

303

Standing by the water for a moment, we watched a pair of swans glide close to the bank and take flight, one after the other.

'They mate for life,' Thomas remarked.

I remembered those words later. Did we love for life, or did we simply find within marriage an angle of repose.

I drew a deep breath and exhaled, watching it make a white cloud. 'Thomas, please speak to me. Tell me what happened? I know that you are still angry with me.'

He stared down at me, lips closed, his mouth tight.

I shook my head. 'It will not do. Please explain. How did you rid the City and us of Northleach?'

Our relationship could not heal properly unless we could talk openly to each other and unless this was concluded. I wondered if this was the sum of it. His lack of affection, his aloofness, his attention to my care, but not my heart, bothered me.

As he breathed, his white puffs united with my own, birds pecked at the hard earth and I patiently waited.

He spoke at last and at length. 'I was observing his movements since your father had revealed Northleach's relationship with the Italian. After we spoke with Susannah and Marcus, I found him and observed him closely. Northleach was meeting with corrupt wagon drivers. The Italian was running stamped cloth out of London to Southampton where, just before the gates, he concealed half of the cloth in corn sacks on these wagons to avoid the export tax. Southampton is lax and no one searched his grain sacks. They were cheating our King and the cloth guild by avoiding export duties. Since Northleach was stealing, I had him arrested by the guild sergeants on the day after you left Fenchurch Street. Unfortunately, the Italian fled the country.'

'Northleach was accused of the theft?'

'He was also accused of murder. He cheated at cards and was in an argument with a cordwainer in the yard of the Eagle's Egg two days previous. I found witnesses who would testify to his involvement. I was bringing them in when you decided to break your promise to stay safely in the house and rashly set out with a passport for an evangelist preacher.'

I gasped at this revelation; this as well as Tyndale, all of it linked. '*Did* Northleach commit murder?'

'As good as. It was a brawl. He provoked it and was the only one with a sword. Either Northleach must leave England immediately and for ever, or his life was forfeit. I told him this when I had him arrested by the wardens and placed in the Cloth Hall cellars - the wardens who arrested him were in my pay - that night, I told him that he would swing. He countered this with Tyndale, accusing me of aiding known evangelicals to leave England. I advised Northleach that this was none of his affair because, I told him, I was watching Tyndale. Since he knew me to be a lawyer he believed me, though he was confused because you had visited Tyndale. I said it was unwise to know about my dealings with Tyndale. He was so frightened that he believed this too, but that was fortunate. Yet, who would believe the word of a rogue? Certainly not Thomas More's men, nor Cardinal Wolsey's men either. He was cheating over the cloth. The cards were stacked against him.'

'And?'

'The victim is buried in the pauper's graveyard. Edward Northleach is gone to sea. He did not deserve a pardon.'

'What do you mean *gone to sea*?'

Thomas' eyes were stony. He said nothing. I knew then that Northleach was gone for ever.

305

'Susannah and the gardener's boy?' I asked after a stretch of silence. 'What of them? Have they…gone to sea as well?'

'In the country. I know those in the north who can train him to work as a shepherd. She has a position as a servant on a farm.'

I drew my cloak tightly about me. So this was why Thomas did not elaborate on his visits north. He had removed all evidence of our association with Northleach from the City. While I was glad that Susannah and Marcus were in the north and had a new start, I recognised that my husband was ruthless. When I asked again what he meant by *gone to sea* his lips curled. He turned away and began walking quickly back to the manor house, leaving me to follow him up the path.

Christmas Day was a sad occasion, despite our determination to remain cheerful. The children's nativity play was muted this year. All that mattered to my father was his own family's presence. I think his illness had made him forget Northleach, or perhaps he had decided to leave all that to Thomas. Not wishing to cause him upset, we never mentioned Northleach's demise. Nor did Father, or indeed Mother for that matter, know about the evangelical whom Thomas had helped to travel to Flanders.

That night, Father worsened. On St Stephen's Day, our physician told Mother, 'Mistress Wykes, your husband must make his peace with God. Call your family together.' Though we knew he had not long to live, to hear it from the physician broke our hearts.

My father drew us to his bedside separately. He gave us all, one by one, his blessing. When it was my turn, he stared at me through his rheumy eyes and said, 'Sorrow not for me, Elizabeth, my silvered angel-child. Remember me fondly. God bless you all the days of your life, my Lizzy.'

I guarded my tears and said, 'Father, I love you so.'

He held my hand in a weak grasp. 'Lizzy, take care of Thomas. He will rise in the world, but ambition may lead him a step too far. One day, he may stumble amongst the wolves and be gobbled up. Be happy and live as best a life as you can, my child. Now, send Joan to me.'

His hand dropped to lie amongst my mother's embroidered roses. I stumbled from the room and called for Joan.

We all were present when Father Christopher closed his eyes.

On a frosty, sunlit Wednesday, between Christmas and Epiphany, we made a sorrowful procession to St Mary's Church. Father's illness had been sudden and final. Our futures are so uncertain and our lives are as fragile as leaves tossed about in a sudden autumn gust. My father had been too tired to live on.

On the funeral night, our chambers were packed with female relatives who stayed at the manor house. There were pallets everywhere, even in the passage ways, tipping us up as we tried to negotiate our way to the chamber pots through the winter darkness. One large pot, placed on the landing knocked over into a screen, over-turning it with a great bang. We laughed helplessly as Meg relit a candle and ran to clean it up. It was ridiculous but it brought a momentary relief to the tension we had lived under that Christmas. We were family and we felt that bond.

Thomas departed on the following morning for business in the City. We said a gentle enough farewell to each other, having decided that I would stay with Mother until our second child was born. He sat with me in the parlour where we ate a small breakfast of baked eggs.

'Elizabeth, I shall be much away on the Cardinal's business because I still have land transfers in Lancashire to work on.'

'I expect he is a very rich man with all these land transfers,' I said with cynicism.

'He is closing some small monasteries.'

'Monks will be made homeless and the workers of their lands will have no fields to till, cows to milk, or bees to keep.'

'The monks will have other houses to go to. No monk or his abbot will be turned out to beg a living. As for the agricultural labourers and the villagers, all they get is a change of landowner. They won't even notice the difference.'

'But if their monastery is gone, Thomas, they will notice. The monks took care of their sick and the poor. They provided lessons for the children.' I was shaking with anger. 'This is about greed. What about the relics they have, and what about the statues and glass and altar cloths?'

'Stay calm, Elizabeth, please. The Cardinal will make provision for the statues and altar cloths. Those monasteries are unprofitable.'

'Life is not all about profit.'

'Let us not quarrel again, my dear. If I do not see to the closure and transfer, I will lose the Cardinal's trust and, with that, the greater part of our income.'

I glanced down at my swelling belly and sighed. 'It is wrong that we profit this way, but God go with you, Thomas, and may he keep you safe. I shall pray for you and think of you every day until you return to me.'

He gathered up his script. 'May God keep you safe until I return; Annie and our unborn child too.'

For now, I decided that I should not worry about anything other than my pregnancy and my widowed mother's welfare. Meg parted with me later that day when she and Smith returned by wagon to Fenchurch Street. My home needed her firm hand as housekeeper during my absence. She patted my hand and told me not to worry. I was tired of being told this, as if I were a petulant child.

As the year turned and everyone else left us, the house felt sad and empty. I missed Father deeply, despite our past differences. I had loved him. Mother grieved and retreated into herself. She lovingly packed Father's clothing into chests along with bags of lavender and fennel, saying she would distribute them come the spring. A sadness descended on the old gabled manor house as deep as the January snow that was falling in soft wet flakes. I trudged along the snowy lane and prayed daily in our village church for the safe birth of our second child.

Chapter Thirty-two

Midsummer 1526, The Oriole

AFTER THE NOON BELLS ring, I enter the oriole, a tiny store room, on the third floor, looking for a table cloth, aware that I must hurry. The maids will be setting the table and before the dinner hour I need to put on the yellow gown I have left lying on my bed.

Austin Friars is a large house where many small rooms are hidden, appearing as large cupboards, alcoves, bays, orioles. Its many corridors and rooms are a place to lose oneself, presenting sudden revelations to any visitor who might stumble upon these miniature chambers filled with the old things of our lives; some discarded and others that remain safely wrapped, stowed away in linen and silk cloths with fennel to protect them from moths. My best table coverings are safely stored in this little place.

The oriole is one of my favourite rooms in Austin Friars. I savour it for a moment, throw open the window with its pretty hexagonal leaded panes and lean out to watch three green finches take flight, one after the other. I know that a swallow has nested above in the creeper. I keep absolutely still and enjoy watching it fussing about its chicks. The garden is empty now. Thomas must be with Gregory in the study. From the distance I hear our daughters happily playing with their poppets, scolding them for soiling their clothes. I think that Annie has set up a pretend school and she is the teacher. I hope they have their gowns ready and are washed too. Thomas told us yesterday that we must look our best today because he has a surprise for us later. He refused to be drawn on it.

I search through several chests for a table covering I had once embroidered with a hem of marigolds and which will delight the girls today. Raising the lid of the coffer nearest the window, I easily discover it, wrapped in soft old linen. I draw it out and set it by a pile of matching napkins. Ah, I want to touch it once again. It is here, I know. My hand finds its way into the painted chest again. This time, I lift out a silk wrapped package that contains the veil I wore for my churching after Grace's birth. I shake off fennel and bits of dried lavender and hold it to my nose to inhale its sweet scent. It was used thrice, for Annie, for Grace and finally for Gregory. I discover another linen package containing my children's christening gown. How unusual it is for a mother to attend her child's christening, for we are impure, bleeding creatures after another child's birth.

The quicker a christening follows a birth, the better, for, after all, where would my child's soul be should she have died after her entry into this world? The soul would live in limbo. I think of Queen Catherine, and I remember how fortunate I am to have three healthy living children. For a moment I remember, birth, christening and purification. I think of Grace's birth on a cold, damp February morning in Putney.

Chapter Thirty-three

1518

THE CHURCH BELLS RANG the hour of Prime on the twenty-eighth day of February when Grace slipped into the midwife's hands after a painful drawn-out night of labour. I thought I might lose her but she cried lustily, for such a fragile creature. The cord was severed and the midwife wrapped her in swaddling and gave the child into my arms. 'I shall call her Grace,' I said, remembering how Thomas liked the name.

Some hours after my baby's birth, and the afterbirth was safely expelled, sheets changed, I was bathed, and wearing a clean night rail, I was sitting up in bed. Even though I was exhausted, my heart was filled with love for the whole world. The girdle of prayers I had worn during my labour would be returned to St Mary's to protect another pregnant mother to place above her swollen belly as she laboured. For now, as with my first birth, it hung suspended above the bed post like a strange papery creature that belongs to maps or at the end of the world, reminding me that God had given me and the child I bore, life. I closed my eyes and whispered thanks to St Margaret for bringing me so easily through my travail. I promised that Grace will be well-loved by her grateful mother all the days of my existence.

Midwives bustled around, helped me to give the baby

suck, and then satisfied, they discreetly removed themselves to stools in the alcove. Turning their backs, they lifted the ancient swaddling that my mother had once used for us. These good dames watched the rain drizzle down the small leaded window as their needles rhythmically slipped in and out of linen, mending rents in the soft baby wrappings.

Mother announced that we were ready to receive visitors. She hurried from the birthing chamber to fetch Annie and Thomas. My husband arrived with a smile on his face, excitedly tiptoeing in with Annie. Grace, who promised to be a contented child, lay sleeping peacefully in my arms. Mother drew Annie back towards the door for a moment and allowed Thomas to approach us first. I presented Grace to him, as if I were offering him a gift more precious than our own lives, which she surely is.

'Our child is healthy,' I said.

Thomas leaned down and kissed his second daughter's tiny head, looking up at me with tears in his eyes.

'She is beautiful, like her name,' he whispered. Carefully, as if she were made of gossamer, he gave her back into my arms and turned towards the door where Annie patiently waited in the thin winter light. 'Annie, come here now. Say hello to your sister. Come.' He held out his hand to Annie. Thumb in mouth, she drew close to us.

'Her name is Grace,' I said.

'When shall she be christened?' Annie said.

'Tomorrow,' my mother quickly said, lifting Grace and holding her so Annie could look upon her. 'It can't wait. If Grace dies before she is christened, the Devil can claim her for his own.'

'She is not going to die, Mother. Let us wait a few days.'

'Saturday it is,' Thomas said. 'I must be in the City tomorrow. I shall return. Alice, Henry's wife, and my sister Eliza can act as godparents, and Henry as godfather. They need a day at least to come to Putney.'

My mother nodded agreement. 'As you wish, Thomas. My son and his wife will be true godparents.'

'Your sister *Eliza*?' I said, raising myself up, feeling a protest slide from my lips.

'She will consider it an honour. Eliza is happier now, and I am fond of our nephew, Christopher. In fact, Lizzy, I was thinking that we could take him into our household.'

I reached over and took his hand. 'On this, at least we are agreed. Christopher is a loving child. Very well, Eliza will stand as godmother, and Christopher will join our household when he is of suitable age. Anything else I do not know?'

He looked down on our joined hands, and I thought for a moment that I noticed anxiety in this gesture.

My mother placed Grace back in my arms and we were distracted. 'Come, Annie, sweeting,' she said. 'I promised you we would bake gingerbread this afternoon.'

'But I want to stay with Grace,' our three-year-old declared, her face stubborn.

'You can come back later, sweeting,' I said. 'Papa would love some of your gingerbread for supper.'

She looked at Thomas who stood up, grabbed her, lifted her so high I caught my breath, and swinging her around, said, 'I would indeed like to eat a cake baked by my own daughter.' He placed her down gently on the rushes.

Annie placed her thumb in her mouth, looked seriously at the baby, removed it again and said, 'Would Grace like some too?'

Mother smiled. 'No, I think not, but your mama might,

and your new poppet might like to watch you bake.'

She nodded, happy to trip off with her grandmother to the kitchen. I looked from my departing daughter to the midwives who were sewing by the window and smiled to myself. We were a company of women. Thomas was outnumbered. He sat with me for a little longer and told me about home. How I longed for my own home. As I drifted into sleep, I heard him say, 'You should return home, Lizzy, as soon as you are churched. Your mother can manage now. I need you, and I have missed you.'

My churching followed a month after the christening when I was considered well enough to leave my chamber. We usually enjoyed it and looked forward to the female gathering that followed in the warmth of the parlour; a time for feminine gossip.

My sister slipped the creamy silk veil over my head, wrapping it around me so that my head and shoulders were totally concealed beneath the covering. I wore a white woollen kirtle and carried a purse filled with coin for the priest. I was accompanied by my female companions to the Church where the senior midwife handed me my candle as I entered. Mother lifted Grace from my arms and we stood in a joyful group before the priest, close to the font, all except for Annie who clung to my mother's skirts, not fully understanding what was happening.

Father Paul sprinkled me with holy water. Cat, Joan, Mother and Eliza waited with Grace and Annie as I followed the priest forward into the nave. He recited psalms and reminded me of how fortunate I was to have a safe deliverance from the perils of childbirth. I thought him kinder than the sharp priest who served at St Gabriel, who had frightened me

315

witless with stern warnings about the sins of women when I was churched after Annie's birth. With my head bowed over my candle, I said the usual prayers of thanksgiving and presented Father Paul with a velvet purse containing silver pennies. It was over and as we came out into the March sunshine, I felt uplifted, at least, until we returned to the manor house.

**

On our return, we dined on wine and sweet cakes, little pastries and jelly-covered fruits. As we nibbled the fruits and sipped wine, Eliza, who was rarely tactful, remarked that she hoped that Thomas and I had made up our quarrel and that he would permit me to return home to him.

Cat frowned.

Joan, glaring, said, 'What a lie that is, Eliza. Curb your tongue.'

Mother snapped, 'Really, Elizabeth Wellifield, I do not know where you picked up such a lie. Thomas brought Lizzy here because an old suitor was making himself troublesome and that is now dealt with.' She took my hand. 'Lizzy remained with me because her father was ill and, of late, has been recovering from her childbed. Thomas is often away on the Cardinal's business. I have been glad of her company.' Mother turned her eyes on me. 'Lizzy, I do think though that now you are churched, I must not be selfish and the moment Thomas comes back from Lancashire, you must return home. You need to manage your own house again.'

'Thank you, Mother.'

If I had thought Eliza changed, I was wrong. Turning to her, I said firmly, 'There is no quarrel between my husband and myself.'

Eliza had the grace to glance down at her worn shoes and I almost felt sorry for her. Wellifield was a gambling man and not the best of husbands, and this was, I reasoned, why she wished others ill.

'I must go and find Christopher,' she said quickly. 'It is time we were going.' She kissed Grace who was lying in her cradle, swaddled and sleeping peacefully. She came over to me and bowed her head. 'I am sorry. Forgive me. My words were uncalled for, Lizzy. Grace is so beautiful, as is Annie. Thank you for allowing me to be a godparent. I humbly beg pardon.' Her eyes filled with moisture.

I nodded. 'You are forgiven, Eliza.' I kissed her, but was not sorry to see her hurry off to find Christopher, her maid and the servant who would drive her cart home.

Cat patted my hand after she had gone. 'Never mind. Eliza never thinks before she speaks.'

'I have forgotten it already,' I said brightly, and we fell to gossiping about ordinary things, including a recipe for a cake and our needlework projects. But I could not forget it and I felt angry and hurt. Eliza's cruel words had strung me.

Thomas fetched me during the first week of soft April sunshine.

'Meg has dusted winter away and cleaned every chamber. We are all pleased that you are returning home. Everyone has missed you.' He patted my hand. 'I have missed you, even though I have been often with you here.'

'Not enough, and I need my old life, our life,' I replied. 'Mother can manage now.' I did not speak of his sister's cruel words to me on my churching afternoon. I tried to put them behind me, but often I wished that I had not agreed that Eliza be Grace's godparent.

My heart sang because my husband smiled down on me without pain in his eyes. Whatever demon he had carried about with him that winter, he had laid it to rest. I would not pry. I would not allow suspicion or anger to blight our happiness. I determined not to complain of the Cardinal or question his actions and hoped that I could keep my resolve, for I still disliked the Prelate.

As we passed through Chelsea, Thomas pointed to the chimneys of a grand house that stretched up from a house by the river. 'That is Thomas More's house. I dined there last week.'

I felt a tinge of jealousy since I had not been included. It was irrational since I never would be asked to dine with Thomas More. More was a devout Catholic who disliked evangelicals and loathed heretics. Tom admired his intellect and the fact that More was a member of the King's Privy Chamber in equal measure. If he still harboured the slightest evangelical sympathies, he kept them close and was inscrutable. 'Thomas, did you ask him how Queen Catherine is?' I asked.

He shook his head. 'I do not think he would speak of the Queen to me, Lizzy.'

I did wonder about our queen. The King's affairs had been discussed at my churching party. King Henry had a mistress called Bessie Blount, one of the Queen's own ladies, and she was with child. I thought that if my husband took a mistress, I would find forgiveness difficult.

'If only Queen Catherine could have another child,' I said holding Grace close to my breast.

'He wants a son,' Thomas said. 'Nothing will do for him but a son and yet he has only little Princess Mary, who might never be accepted as a queen.'

'It must be a great trial to be married to a king and feel such responsibility,' I said as I looked down on my beautiful girls. Grace was asleep in my arms and Annie was leaning against me, fast asleep.

Part Three

Austin Friars

Now we have loved and love will we
This fresh flower, full of beauty
Most worthy it is, as thinketh me
Then may be proved here anon
That we, three, be agreed in on.

Roses, A Song for Three Voices

Chapter Thirty-four

Austin Friars, Midsummer 1526, The Bedchamber Again

WHEN THOMAS FIRST SAT in Parliament four years ago, he rose to be called Thomas Cromwell, Gentleman. I am called Elizabeth Cromwell, Gentlewoman. Despite the strict laws passed by Parliament, I may wear expensive fabrics. The embroidered sleeves I shall wear today drape from the elbows in a graceful bell-like fall, and are trimmed with red squirrel fur. I, who once sold sleeve decorations to noblewomen, can wear a little fur, damask, silk and even velvet without complaint.

'Bessie, hurry up, my dear, and lace me into my gown,' I call down the staircase.

I catch the sound of her feet tapping on the tiles below, and her voice speaking to the maids setting the table for dinner. I linger over my jewellery casket, trying to decide on jewels for today. I look hard at an opal in a filigreed setting that hangs on a silvered chain. Lifting the dangling chain, I hold the jewel up to the sunlight that glints through the casement. Almost opaque, it catches the chamber's reflections as I move it around, threading it through my fingers, bringing it closer to the window; rose, gold and silver gleams.

I hesitate. My hurt whispers to me and catches at my heart when I least expect it. This beautiful jewel is associated with a sorrowful time. Forgiveness has been difficult, but I have, at last, granted it. It was after Grace had been born and I had returned to Fenchurch Street that I became suspicious of Thomas. He made many journeys to the North, to Lancashire and to Cheshire. He said he had cloth business there or that he was working for Cardinal Wolsey but he was always brooding on his return; for a time he seemed unloving, then he was as loving as ever he was. Our lives resumed as happy as they had ever been. I was pregnant again and Gregory was born. I felt our family to be complete and I promised myself that I would not permit suspicion to eat into our marriage.

Waiting for Bessie to mount the staircase, still holding the silky smooth jewel in my hand, I listen to whinnies rising from the courtyard and in through the chamber's casement. Between the neighs, I catch the sound of Thomas' voice as he talks to his jennet, Mercury. It is as well this sturdy little horse is walked about the yard for otherwise he would remain restless in the stables all day long. I listen to the fall of hooves and hear an answering whickering from my palfrey. The sparrow hawks we keep in the stable send up their calls. I am laughing now as a cacophony of sound invades our chamber. As if in protest, hunting dogs begin to bark. The animal life of Austin Friars longs to be in the fields beyond the City. I throw away sad thoughts of the past and contemplate our happy future. Since we moved to this house we have been content with each other and our children. I thank God for this.

Tomorrow Thomas will leave off the Cardinal's business for a second day and we shall join the Midsummer Chase in Chelsea with Thomas More and Master Roper. I am pleased that Thomas will be away from Cardinal Wolsey's company and I consider that I am privileged because I have received a coveted invitation to visit Mistress More, a woman of whom I have heard nothing but good, and I am as excited about this visit as I am about Thomas' mysterious surprise.

With a tap on my chamber door, Bessie arrives, apologising for her tardiness. Master Jon has arrived to dine with us. He is in the study with Gregory. She tells me that the maids have spread the cloth and already they have placed our silver knives and spoons on the table.

I drop the pendant back into the casket. 'Find my pearls, Bess,' I say to her.

'Yes, Mistress, the pearls.' She finds my long string of black pearls and lays them on a side table for me.

Bessie laces me into my yellow gown. The creamy underskirt swishes as I move. It is as pleasing a garment now as it was when I wore it to the Drapers' feast years before. It recovered well from the storm; mud cleaned away and skirts brushed. It is enhanced by new sleeves. I make a small turn, allowing my skirts to flare out and my gold silk petticoat reflects early afternoon sunlight as I lift my overskirt and make a few happy dancing steps.

'Mistress Elizabeth, you are so beautiful today. Master Thomas will be very proud of you. Indeed he will.'

'I hope so, Bess,' I say. 'Now, go and see if the girls are ready for dinner. Send a boy for Master Cromwell. The stable lads can finish the exercising the horses.'

She bobs a curtsey and vanishes out through the door, forgetting the pearls. She has only one thought today and that is her Betrothed.

I set them about my neck and place a French hood with velvet streamers on my head and I am ready to go to the study to fetch Gregory and Master Woodall.

Chapter Thirty-five

Fenchurch Street, 1523

GREGORY, OUR SON, WAS born early in 1520. By then, Tom's clients included goldsmiths, grocers, tailors, drapers, and not only in England. He had new clients abroad and contacts in Paris, Augsburg and Florence. Thomas represented members of the King's court, such as Lord Grey. Lord Grey was a relative of King Henry. This was a great honour and his legal work for his lordship introduced Thomas to the aristocracy. This brought increased business. As our wealth grew, we agreed to sell our cloth business to Gerard Smith.

Meg and Gerard had a son whom they had called Matthew. Matthew was a tow-headed child with darting brown eyes, and was born in the same year as Henry Fitzroy, the king's son by Bessie Blount. Following All Hallows, after Gregory's birth, they moved from Fenchurch Street to the premises on Cornhill. We added a spacious hall to the property and a comfortable kitchen with a great fireplace. In return, they paid us a substantial, though fair, rent.

Thomas entertained clients and took on new secretaries. Our household grew prosperous and fat with servants, children and visitors. Soon we would have to move to a larger house.

During the summer of 1523, Thomas sat in Parliament, as a member of the Commons. This was a huge honour for him, as this position was manipulated by the Duke of Norfolk. Thomas was drawing closer and closer to life at Court and, as ever, I feared for him, for the Court was dangerous.

There had not been a Parliament in some eight years. This time, Thomas said that the King sought money for a war with France. King Henry, ever the imaginary knight in pursuit of a chivalrous cause, still planned to claim France as was his ancient right. Thomas considered this was a poor policy, even though the strategy had been originally been advanced by Thomas Wolsey who wanted to please the king, his master.

I wondered though, if, having planted the idea of a warrior king in King Henry's imaginative and suggestible head, Thomas Wolsey had changed his mind. I suspected that the Cardinal, whom I have always considered wily, was using Thomas, who could be very persuasive and was a brilliant speaker, to curtail the King's notion to have another war with France.

Thomas rarely returned home on those days of Parliament before the Angelus bells sounded. Week after week passed without us exchanging our usual daily news. By the time he came to our chamber late at night, I was sound asleep. Then, on the evening preceding May Day, he returned from Parliament in time for supper. The May holiday had begun and I was glad of it. Parliament was in recess. The King and his courtiers would be celebrating at Greenwich, the Cardinal would be with the King and Thomas would be ours again. I hoped in vain.

'The weather has turned,' Thomas said, throwing his cloak to a maid who caught it laughing. 'Not a spot of rain today. It promises to be a glorious May holiday.'

I bade him sit down to supper which had been laid out in the parlour for one person- me. I sent the maids to fetch more food, bread and cheese and an eel pie, always one of Thomas' favourite dishes.

'I must see the children first,' he said, as a servant set out a second place with cup, plate, knife, spoon and napkin.

He hurried off to say good night to the children and on his return, we enjoyed our first supper together since Parliament had opened in March. I talked of the household's daily life and he described how Norfolk looked that day, hooded eyes and arrogant bearing, making me laugh as he was a good mimic and he afterwards spoke kindly of the witty Thomas More who as always was masterful as Speaker.

I laid down my spoon and knife and lifted my cup of Burgundy wine. I drank a few little mouthfuls, and in keeping with the mood that had settled on our evening, tried to look my most alluring as I said, 'We may as well retire early, my dearest, because I suppose we won't see you for days again.'

With a twinkle in his eye, he leaned over the table and answered, 'In that case, Lizzy, let the maids come in to clear away now. I shall tell you the rest of my news in our chamber.'

Thomas took me by the hands as if we were young lovers and, with an impatient rustle of dark gown, and with the glint in his eye that I adored, he drew me to the stairway.

He poured us each a cup of malmsey wine. Nursing his cup in his hands, leaning against the bolster, one shapely leg thrown over mine, he turned to me and said, 'Good news, my love, because I am to accompany Wolsey to Greenwich tomorrow, to court.'

I protested, 'I thought we would go a-Maying with our children.'

'Not this year, my love. I cannot, sweeting. I am to help the Cardinal with the pageants.' He sipped his wine and looked at me with determined coolness. 'We are not stopping here, Lizzy. One day I shall labour for the King, himself. One day you will be a lady and I, a lord.'

I shook my head at his words. 'Thomas, I won't see you for days and I don't want to be a lady. I am happy to remain Elizabeth Cromwell, gentlewoman.'

He laughed at that, drew me closer and kissed my head. 'Your hair, still so beautiful, Elizabeth, like a silvered waterfall.'

'You are distracting me with compliments and trying to appease me, Thomas.'

'You will make a very beautiful lady one day.'

'I am happy as we are.'

I sipped my wine slowly, feeling a little sad. Wealth was one thing, happiness and peace of mind another. Never mind that the King was infatuated with one favourite one day and that same favourite could be out of favour the next. Recently, I had heard rumours of his many infidelities to the queen he had once loved with the devotion of an honourable knight.

I whispered, with a catch in my throat, 'Beware of the insouciance of kings. I like not the way he treats Queen Catherine. The merchant wives love her dearly and they dislike how he has set up Henry Fitzroy as if he is a true-born son.'

'Lizzie, the King needs a son and it seems that the Queen will never give him another child. It is why he loves this little boy. The Cardinal says that the baby looks just like the father.'

'Cardinal Wolsey has seen him?'

'I helped the Cardinal to arrange the child's future household.'

'*You* have seen him too?'

'No, I am not so privileged.' His grey eyes had hardened in the candlelight.

I turned towards the painting of the Virgin that still hung in our bedchamber alcove. 'I remember the Queen every day in my prayers. I pray for Princess Mary too.'

'As well you do. She is a beautiful, clever child, and, according to the Cardinal, my master, the King is devoted to her.'

'That is something,' I said. 'But be careful of the nobility.

327

You know they are untrustworthy.'

'Some are, others aren't, Lizzy. I am always cautious.' His eyes shone with chill determination.

If eyes are a route into the workings of a man's soul, that night I saw naked ambition in Thomas' soul.

The King wanted money for a war with France. He wanted glory. So much for the Field of Cloth of Gold of three years before, a peace to last between our two countries, a bond of friendship between our King and King Francis. Thomas said King Henry should focus on our borders with Scotland, make those safe rather than seek wars with France. I agreed.

'The talk in this Parliament all goes around and around like a whirlpool.'

'An undecided pool.'

'Aye, Lizzy, and nothing is clear or agreed. Thomas More must be fed up with them all.'

'Be careful, Tom,' I warned again, concerned that somehow he was being used by the Cardinal to whose service he was devoted. I thought this devotion odd because Thomas had on many occasions voiced his cynicism at the greed of churchmen and he Cardinal was the greediest of them all. Somehow, he was exempt from Thomas' censure. Perhaps it was because the shrewd, ingenious, self-made Cardinal was not of noble birth. His father, like my Thomas' father, had been a tradesman. The Cardinal was ambitious and I had to accept that my husband was, too.

As the sun climbed the cloudless sky, Thomas helped us carry boughs of yew and spring flowers into the house to decorate the hall and parlour. I bustled about my morning tasks of folding linen and supervising the cooks and maids set the trestles, enjoying the scent of lilac that came wafting through the hall, determined to enjoy this day. Before the dinner hour, Thomas set off for York House to help transport costumes and props along the river for the pageant that the Cardinal was organising at Greenwich for the King and Queen's pleasure.

Our household was as excited as children receiving treats at Christmastide. May was a much beloved holiday. A Fair would stretch as far as the eye could see all along the Cheape and our girls, dancing around the trestles in anticipation of treats, were hardly able to eat their dinner. I had promised them a trip to the Maypole where the Cheape joined Cornhill to watch the dancing and sword fighting, followed by supper with Meg at the Cornhill house.

We would dine on rennet and moulded cream hedgehogs stuck with slivered almonds as a special treat, and sugar, rosewater and Russian isinglass, which when left to cool and set firm could be cut into squares. Meg gilded these shapes with little gold flowers and served them with thickened cream. It was a great May Day treat. How my own sweet tooth craved a bite of these dainties, and just thinking of them I could taste the gold flowers melting in my mouth. She promised fools, fruits swirled into mounds of cool cream, and pastries.

After our servants cleared away our dinner, I said, 'Bessie, help the children's nurse get them ready. Make sure they wear their boots. The streets are full of muck after the April rains. Come up to my chamber. I'll need help with my bodice laces.'

I removed my blue kirtle and bodice from my clothing pole, and searched for a suitable over-gown. At length I saw one, a green flowery over skirt which hung amongst Thomas' tawny velvet coats, the ones he wore for the Cardinal's work. As I lifted away the over dress, a small book poking out of a wide pocket that Thomas always had set into the fabric of his velvet coats tumbled out. I scooped it up and placed it on the chest below the window wondering if it contained poems. With teaching the children their letters every day, I had been too busy to read for my own pleasure. I would look at it later.

Bessie arrived, glanced at my choice of gown and appraised it. 'Very fine, Mistress Elizabeth. You will look a treat in that gown.'

She helped me into it and found me a pair of contrasting sleeves.

'Hurry, Bessie,' I said with impatience. 'We will miss the sword-fighting, and I promised Gregory.'

'Here, you're done, Mistress Elizabeth.' She tied the last ribbon and stood back to inspect me.

In my haste to dress, I left my linen work cap lying on top of the book. I changed my slippers for stouter shoes and set the slippers on the chest beside it.

Richard, my nephew, and Barnaby, who was now a journeyman, both accompanied us to Cheape Street. Barnaby carried my young son on his shoulders. Gregory happily chattered away, waving his miniature sword about, slaying imaginary dragons. We wound our way through the narrow streets and holiday crowds towards the Maypole that was covered with laurel branches and entwined with spring flowers. Cymbals clashed and bagpipes blasted out feet-tapping tunes.

'Hurry,' Annie said, on hearing them, tugging at Grace's hand.

'With speed,' three year old Gregory shouted, his sword waving madly, a danger in the narrow crowded street.

'Put up your sword, Green Knight,' joked Barnaby, and Gregory lowered his wooden weapon.

The tense smell of anticipation was pervasive. By the time we had pushed into the gathering by the flowery Maypole, there was a pause in the dancing. Pie sellers and hawkers weaved through the waiting throng calling out their wares. A band of Spanish Benedictine monks watched from under a silversmith's awning as a grand empty ring was created by uniformed yeomen around the Maypole. I could not help noticing a tall, slim, bald-headed man clad in a black tunic standing with them, a scabbard hanging from his broad belt. He leaned down and conversed with the closest Benedictine monk.

A swordsman, who by his strutting, arrogant bearing obviously thought he could fight as well as any of the King's yeomen, stepped forward into the ring. Nervously, I bit my lip so hard that I could taste blood. If ever I watched sword-fighting, even when contestants were supposed to fight with blunted swords, I would always become gripped by fear. I could not forget how my first husband had perished, so how could I not feel concern for the safety of the May Day swordsmen?

The King's yeomen liked to parade their skills for us ordinary people to admire. Courageous contestants hoped that their skills would be noticed at the May Day sword contests. After all, a talented young man might, if fortunate, be offered a coveted place in the King's Guard. The King's yeoman lifted his sword and bowed to us. As if in agreement, the crowd drew breath in unison. I forgot the peculiar stranger who had been deeply in conversation with the Spanish Benedictine monks, and the way he had glanced speculatively at the ring. The children shouted with excitement. 'Bravo!' The sword fights were about to begin. Gregory waved his little sword higher. Bessie, who was standing with Annie, gasped and let out a shriek.

She grabbed my arm. 'It can't be, Mistress Elizabeth.'

'What is it, Bess?'

One hand flapped over her mouth, and she let go Annie's hand. She pointed into the ring created by the water conduit for the contestants. 'Look who it is.'

'Who?'

'Toby,' she shrieked.

We were very close to the front of the gathering. I peered hard around a couple in front of me, trying to see whom Bess was pointing to. The first contestant, a blond-haired young man, wearing brown hose and a loose cream linen shirt had just entered the centre of the ring, carrying a sword. At first, his back was to me, but as he spun around to face his opponent, a yeoman of the guard, there was no mistaking him. I found my heart leaping.

The opponents kissed their swords and began to circle each other. I knew that the contestant was indeed Toby, whom we had thought lived safely far from the City's dangers. Thomas had never been sure of his actual whereabouts. On the one occasion he had enquired, he had been told that Toby was living with his uncle in Nottingham. This Toby was not a boy any longer.

Grace clung to her nurse, stuck her thumb into her mouth, and stared at the circling swordsmen. Bess grasped Annie's hand again. I watched dumbstruck with shock. Vendors stood still, the smells of their pies drifting through the crowds of excited spectators.

Toby moved like lightning that descended without warning from a summer sky. He fought well. The crowd was stunned into silence by the speed with which he had his opponent on the ground and his blunted sword at his foe's chest. A moment later they both rose and bowed. The audience cheered. Barnaby leaned down to me and said one word. 'Toby.' His face was bemused. 'Where has he sprung from?'

I nodded. 'By the sainted virgin, it is indeed he.'

Annie looked up at me. 'Mama, who is Toby?'

I protectively drew her close to me. 'Someone we knew long ago before you were born, sweeting.'

Another guardsman challenged Toby, moving into the

centre of the ring, as the crowd cheered him on. The crowd was mesmerised by the way the pair parried, ducked and exchanged places over and over. The playacting had begun all over again. This rival was more challenging competition and we could see that Toby was tiring.

'He won't win this time,' Richard said from Barnaby's other side.

'At least the swords blades are blunted,' I remarked.

Toby swiftly side-stepped his opponent. He fought bravely. From the corner of my eye, I saw the tall bald-headed man step from the gaggle of monks by the silversmith's shop. They turned into a clattering of dark jackdaws as they egged him on. Touching his scabbard, the swordsman slid serpent-like through gaps in the mass of people, and advanced on the ring. I saw him glance over straight at us as if he knew whom I was. A curl of a smile played about his thin lips. I felt fearful. Who was he?

Memory is evasive but I was sure that if I had known that man before I would recollect him. As I searched through my memories, an inner voice seemed to whisper to me, 'As you sow, so shall you reap.' Realisation descended. It was the fire in Wood Street. He was the cloaked man who had spoken to me in the yard as we watched my property burn and who had vanished without trace. Today, his appearance and raiment was that of the nobility. It had been dark with smoke that night and the man who had whispered to me had been shadowy. Glancing back over my shoulder towards the Silversmith's, I wondered why the foreign monks were forming a clerical retinue for him. As he reached the edge of the ring, the monks began to frantically converse again, their looks sliding from the bald-headed man to Toby as he waited his turn.

I concentrated on the sword play. After another round of dodging and attacking, Toby had the yeoman up against the maypole with his sword at his throat. The yeoman raised his arms and dropped his blunted sword. The clang of metal on the cobbles was followed by a great cheer. Toby had again earned the crowd's appreciation. An aproned innkeeper ran forward and thrust a pitcher into Toby's hands. Toby drank thirstily. At once, the dark-clad man stepped boldly into the ring, withdrawing a sword from his scabbard. He removed his scabbard and belt, throwing them to the ground. There was no sword-kissing ceremony this time. Toby's new foe hardly gave him time to draw breath or even hand the pitcher back. He silently stalked him.

It all began over again, but this time Toby really appeared tired, and his opponent was clearly an accomplished swordsman. He moved stealthily. As he raised his sword to strike Toby, I observed what I had always feared to see on such occasions, a sharpened blade gleaming in the sunshine as it was raised. Everyone else saw it, but nobody stopped the fight. Nobody could. It was all happening too quickly. This time the fighting was intense and faster than before, a whirl of weapons with clashes that pierced the fetid air every time the blades made contact.

Annie clung to Bess and me, clutching both of our skirts; Grace cried out and ducked behind her nurse. Gregory screamed. Even he felt the crowd's horror as they realised that this fight would not end until one of the adversaries died. The fight went on and on with grunts and shouts. I prayed hard for God to spare Toby's life. This swordplay was unfair and it was a cruel turn of fate that Toby was disadvantaged rather than the stranger.

Toby was fighting for his life, caught in a never ending repetitive spiral of evading and deflecting. This was becoming a cruel dream. His opponent knew him and I wondered if Toby recognised his enemy. The man in black was playing cat and mouse with him.

Blood spurted Toby's arm where the sword's point had

nicked through his shirt. A moment later, Toby was down, crawling about in the dirt, trying to scramble to his feet. Sword raised, his adversary waited. He was laughing.

Toby regained his feet, and the cruel dance was about to begin all over again. I heard a shriek as a most peculiar event occurred. A hooded man, standing behind Richard, deliberately let a dog off a leash and with a command sent it for the bald-headed swordsman. The dog hurtled forward, almost knocking Richard over, barred his teeth and, within the moment it took for Toby to call out a warning, had barrelled into Toby's enemy, causing him to lose balance and fly onto the cobbles, knocking his head hard on the maypole as he fell and once again as he made contact with the cobbles.

Toby dropped his sword and knelt to help him. He cradled the man's head in his arms, looked up into the spectators and called out for help. The dog had vanished as if it had never been, racing along Cheape Street and into an alley. I instinctively glanced around. There was no sign of its owner. Barnaby thrust Gregory into Richard's arms and pushed through the couple standing in front of him. The sinister-looking foreign monks elbowed the crowds out of the way and flowed forward, their dark gowns sweeping rubbish along the dusty street like besoms as they raced forward shouting 'Murder' and 'God spare Sir Antony!'.

Sir Antony was dead. Barnaby called for an apothecary and a warden. Both came running, pursued by two parish sergeants. The apothecary knelt down in the dust and a moment later, he confirmed Sir Antony's death. The sergeants set off to search for the dog and its owner, who had disappeared. The warden began to question those nearest to the circle as to what they had seen. It was clear that Toby was not responsible and he was free to leave. He had not been fighting with a sharpened blade.

The blow to the head had finished Sir Antony quicker than

any sword fight would. Barnaby lifted his opponent's sword up in both his hands and called to the crowd, 'He had a sharpened sword.' There was a collective murmur of agreement. Gradually, the watchers began to disperse. The Benedictines murmured prayers over the body. Their superior shouted for cloth. When, moments later, a draper hurried forward from his shop, as with one movement, the black shrouded clergy silently created a cradle and lifted Sir Antony into it. They placed his sword on his breast. There was a shout from the few remaining spectators: 'He does not deserve such an honour.'

The Benedictines remained silent. They moved off along Cheape Street like shades, pointed hoods pulled up to cover their heads, processing with the body cradled between them towards St Mary Le Bow. No one followed. Sir Antony was not well-liked and neither were these Benedictine monks.

Once the Spanish Benedictines were gone from the Maypole, Barnaby threw his arms about Toby. He drew him away from the Maypole. As they pushed through the departing crowd, men slapped Toby's back and praised his courage. Barnaby guided Toby into to our small company. Toby's face was drained of colour.

'Toby,' I said, my eyes still wide at the horror we had witnessed. 'What are you doing here?'

He shook his head. I clutched both girls to me. Richard comforted Gregory, who was too dumbstruck to even set up a protest.

Barnaby said in a quiet voice, 'I think we must get Toby away. I don't trust the Spanish Benedictines. They may seek revenge. We should take him to Cornhill.'

I nodded and reached out to Toby who seemed unable to find his voice. 'It's best that we disappear, in case the monks send someone after you. They have long arms and longer memories. Did you know your adversary? I think, he was familiar to both of us.'

Toby shivered visibly. Richard gallantly removed his short cloak and draped it around Toby's shoulders. Toby spoke at last. 'I ...had remembered him once he faced me.' He stared at the backs of the departing monks.

The sergeant of the yeomen stepped in front of us, bowed to me, 'Mistress Cromwell,' he said, bowing and recognising me. 'Good day to you.' I nodded. He turned to Toby, 'Had he killed you, he would have been held responsible.'

'As well he did not. He was a superior swordsman.'

The sergeant crossed himself. 'God intervened ... a cheat, a good riddance ... a cruel man. Claims he is of the knightly class. If ever evil has walked this earth, Sir Antony was that. Those Spanish Benedictines are intent on finding heretics. They would bring Castile's inquisition to England. Those whom they accuse are innocents.'

Toby shuddered. The yeoman continued, 'And well you may fear them for they are hated here. If you want to join the Yeomen, I have a place for you at Westminster. Seek me out ... your name?'

'Tobias de Bohun,' Toby said. I started, for I had never heard Toby's full name.

'A noble name.' The Sergeant bowed, clearly impressed.

Colour flooded back into Toby's cheeks. 'A very, very minor branch of a noble family. To join the King's Yeomen Guard is my dream.'

'The name, none the less, carries honour. Report to me tomorrow by the noon bells. Ask for Justin St Clare.'

'I shall, Master St Clare. Thank you.'

I shook my head and said firmly, 'To be a yeoman of the guard is a deadly occupation. I should know, and you, Toby, should return to the country. London is a cruel place. Anyone from outside is an alien.'

'All life is dangerous.'

337

Disheartened, I said we'd best be on our way, adding brightly, 'Wait until Meg sees you. She lives in the Cornhill shop now.'

'Mistress Elizabeth, you may be an angel, but I am not running away again.' He glanced down at my little ones. 'And these must be your children.' The children stared blankly up at him. He turned to Barnaby then, 'Barnaby, you remember the fire in Mistress Elizabeth's stores, over in Wood Street?'

'How could I forget it?'

'That man was one of the arsonists.'

'It was nearly ten years since,' Barnaby said. 'I had just begun my apprenticeship.'

'They have long memories.'

'It would seem so,' I said, feeling anxious.

'I want to see the dancing, Mama,' Grace said, and I was glad of the distraction.

'You promised,' Annie whinged.

'Later. Let's find Meg and have a bite of supper first. Are you hungry, sweetings? You never ate your dinner.'

Both girls nodded. Bessie smiled and simpered, all huge eyes for Toby. She had been a chit of a girl when she had first known him, only twelve years old. Now she was a young woman of twenty-two and my own maid, risen high in our Fenchurch Street house since Meg had become a married woman. As for Toby, he was some years older and likely to have a wife, or at the very least a betrothed. Poor Bessie, I thought. She is besotted.

As we walked along Cheape Street and up Cornhill, lumbering carts passed us on their way back down the hill; tradesmen's apprentices called out their wares; cooking smells from the bakers' shops accosted our noses speeding us forward. Glancing up at the sky through gaps in roofs, I made the hour to be the fourth after midday already. A group of townspeople bearing baskets with miserable angry crowing cocks peeping out of them passed. I hurried us on. Cock fights distressed me and they were best avoided.

'Pity Master Smith is not with Meg today, Toby. He was called away to help Thomas with the Cardinal's pageant.'

'They are wed, he and Mistress Meg?' Toby asked with a bemused smile.

'Yes and they have a child, a boy, a year older than Gregory. There would be a place for you, Toby, in the cloth business, I am sure, if you were interested. Thomas would happily train you to be a clerk.'

'No, Mistress Elizabeth. I know my future now. Thank you all the same.'

I murmured a silent prayer for Toby. We could never know our futures in such a fragile world as ours, as delicate and intransient as a butterfly's wing.

'May the Lord and all his saints be blessed, it's never Master Toby,' Meg declared on opening her door to our knocking. Her eyes just flitted past us to Toby's laughing face. 'God bless us all. What are you doing here and with the mistress too?'

Her son slid behind her skirts at the sight of the tall young knight, and ran off along the corridor towards the kitchen.

He hid behind the wood pile until the girls persuaded him out into the parlour with promises of play. As Meg's maid laid the parlour table with our May Day supper, the children withdrew into the window alcove and played with a collection of wooden novelties that Meg kept stored in a small coffer. They played happily until we called them to the trestle. They gasped with delight at Meg's feast, but, after their first moments of joy, my girls contained their greed with agonising restraint. Our children understood the importance of good manners. They did not dare to speak at table unless addressed.

All through supper, Toby entertained us with tales of his

adventures, how his uncle exploited him and wanted him to wed an alderman's shrew-like youngest daughter so he could better their family's connections.

'Not for me, not a life as a merchant with my uncle, and I could never live with a hen-pecking wife. There is as yet much to discover in life,' he said, his mouth full of plum tart. He reached for one of the delectable isinglass squares. 'Should we really be eating these? They are too beautiful to munch away to nothing - like church windows.' He sat it on the wooden dish, his eating knife placed beside it, wiped the crumbs from his mouth with his napkin and said, 'I shall just admire these, Mistress Meg.' He was, as ever, charming us all, even Meg, who had not loved him well.

Meg had developed a business weaving patterned ribbons and silken braids. She had promised Annie and Grace small May Day fairings of silk ribbons. The girls, excited by their fairings, insisted that Bess took them up to one of the two sleeping chambers above the large parlour to plait their hair with their new ribbons. They reappeared, visions in colourful silk carefully threaded through their braids. We all had to admire the result, and Meg's weaving skills.

Bessie smiled at Toby when he admired her hairdressing and he smiled back, his blue eyes bright and sparkling. She had grown into a beautiful young woman with wide-set green eyes and golden curling hair. They complimented each other, two golden angels. I wondered if Toby would resist her charms. Annie and Grace ran to the window where they looked out at the street longingly and waited patiently for us to take them back to the Maypole. From time to time they would reach up and finger their silken braids.

Meg's little maid and Bessie cleared the table. Gregory had fallen asleep, his face smeared with cream. The children's nurse wiped the mess away with her napkin and said that she would carry him home, if there was company to walk with her. I said that if the girls wanted to watch the dancing for a little while, I would take them back to the Maypole. Richard offered to accompany us. Toby stood, stretched and said, 'I have lodgings in Gracechurch Street. I can walk Master Cromwell and his nurse home. I have had enough for today.' He bowed. 'Remember me to Master Thomas, Mistress Elizabeth. We are almost neighbours.' Turning to Meg, he said with smiling charm, 'I thank you, Mistress Meg. Remember me to Master Gerard.' He chucked Meg's son under his chin. This time the boy did not hide from Toby behind his mother's kirtle.

Meg said, 'Master Toby, we are always here if you need us. There will be a bed for you.'

'As if, after that feast, I ever would forget to visit.'

Meg wrapped up a loaf of her bread in a cloth and two meat pies in another. 'Take these in case you are hungry later.'

Toby gratefully accepted the gift.

As we left to walk in opposite directions, the Church bells began to ring marking the Vespers hour, the fifth after midday. We waved Toby goodbye. Bessie ran back to him with a little faring, a plaited lavender and yellow silk braid that Meg had given her. He slipped it through his belt and threw her a kiss. For some reason, I remembered the small printed book I had left lying on top of my chamber linen coffer that morning. Like a sombre cloud tarnishing the azure sky, marring what had been a day of happy reunion, without warning, a shadow settled about me, tightening my chest. As the last church bell rang out, I fingered the jet beads hanging from my waist, and whispered an Ave Maria.

Chapter Thirty-six

THE SMALL LEATHER-BOUND BOOK lay unopened on top of my linen chest until Thomas sent me a message from Greenwich saying he would be home in a few days' time. I sighed because Parliament would reconvene once the holiday passed and I would not see him again for weeks.

I picked the little volume up intending to place it into the bookshelf in his closet off the hall, but I could not resist satisfying my inquisitive mind. There was something about this book that made me feel uneasy. Carefully, I opened its stamped leather covers and, at once, felt the same gloomy presentiment I had felt on May Day when I first discovered it, a thought I had shaken off as absurd. I must not be suspicious. Surely it was nothing but my imagination playing tricks with my mind. Thomas was always purchasing new books in Paternoster Row close to St Paul's for his growing library. Why would a book give off a sense of foreboding- unless, perhaps, it contained heretical teachings?

The flyleaf innocently displayed the title: *Flores*. Thomas enjoyed our small garden. He particularly liked roses, whereas I preferred herbals and plants we could eat, use in recipes or infuse with varying ingredients to make medicinal potions which I carefully labelled and stored in the still room.

I had been about to turn over the page when my eye

scrolled below the title to where I found inscribed in a feminine hand *For Thomas*, and then, *From Jeanette with my enduring love. Christmastide, 1518.*

Stepping backwards, I sank onto my bed, the book opened on my lap. I could not fully absorb what I was reading and so I read the words over and over until I knew them by rote. I looked at the date again. 1518, so long ago now. I had given birth to Gregory since.

I felt all colour drain from my face. I studied the elaborate signature. She had drawn the pansy below it, that flower which significantly we so often called heartsease. Who was this Jeanette? I reasoned that if the volume of flowers was a lover's gift, Thomas would not have left it in his cloak pocket. I frantically flicked the pages over to see if there had been anything penned in the margins that might reveal who this Jeanette was. The book contained wood cuts showing familiar flowers: the Christmas Rose that flowered to honour the birth of our Lord Jesus Christ; Our Lady's Keys, the flower of Our Lady; Our Lady's Eyes, and Foxgloves that were Our Lady's gloves.

I turned back to Heartsease, the Herb Trinity because of its white, yellow and purple colouring. I glanced up at the painting of Our Lady that hung in the alcove, my long-ago betrothal gift. Her gown was blue and there were white, yellow and purple flowers in the painting, all of these the colours of heartsease.

I sat worrying until the Vespers bells began to ring. I closed the little book, but instead of taking it to the closet shelves, I replaced it on top of my coffer. Slowly, I climbed down the staircase into the hall where Bessie was seated by a window embroidering a belt purse.

343

'Bess.' She started. 'We are attending Vespers this evening. Fetch our cloaks.' I was more snapping than was fair. Bessie jumped at my command, tucked her needlework into its linen bag and ran to fetch our summer cloaks.

The sky was spread as blue as Our Lady's mantle but I had no joy of it. I walked at such a fast pace to St Gabriel's, Bessie could hardly keep up. She trotted behind me uncomplaining, like a princess' faithful lap dog. We entered the nave as the priests were beginning the service. I genuflected. Bessie followed my lead. After a quick glance around, I drew her away from the main aisle since the nave where most people stood was filled with merchants' wives, pewterers' wives, ironmongers' wives, bakers' wives, and city merchants who all wandered about quietly forging deals following their day's work. In the midst of the women who stood nearest to the doorway, I spotted Mistress Watt. I whispered, 'Bessie, hurry, Mistress Watt is over there by that pillar.'

Bessie nodded and we slipped into my favourite alcove, approached an altar to Our Lady and knelt at a distance apart. When I heard Bessie's beads clacking, I knew she was reciting prayers. I had given her a small illustrated Book of Hours as a New Year's gift and Bessie, to my surprise, already knew many of its verses by heart. As a ray of sunshine shafted from a high window, scattering light over her, I saw that she was beautiful as she knelt lost in her prayers and I wondered, and I am ashamed to admit this thought, if I had lost my fine looks, and if Thomas had tired of me.

I collected myself and turned my thought to the prayer for the innocents of Bethlehem. That upset me too. I could not help my errant mind, for I wondered if I was suffering

344

a terrible betrayal. My thoughts revisited occasions when Thomas had returned from the north in a state of restless anxiety and how I had banished my suspicions on those occasions. Recollecting the roses and heartsease and that telling inscription in the book, I wondered could I ever forgive my husband if he had taken a mistress. But, had Thomas taken a mistress? Surely my suspicions were unfounded and without justice?

At length, as I prayed for guidance, my distress lessened. If Thomas had taken a mistress, was it such a terrible thing? Was it, if he still loved his Elizabeth? Many a woman welcomed the removal of a husband's physical attentions. But I was not one of these tolerant wives. Anger and jealousy, not admirable emotions, haunted the very thought that Thomas might have given his love to another.

I rose just as those gathered in the nave were making their way towards the great west door. To my relief, I couldn't see Mistress Watt amongst them, rather a group of women gossiping. I heard them mention Queen Catherine. I reached my hand out to stay Bessie and paused momentarily to listen.

'My husband says King Henry has taken a new mistress. No one knows who she could be?'

Another snorted. 'How do you know?'

'She has received a gift of a brooch, a ruby set in silver from the King. My own husband was commissioned for its making. He carried it to Westminster for her himself, in a silver casket.' She lowered her voice. 'And it has been paid for by the King. It was a May Day gift. We have a receipt for it.'

There was a collective gasp. One of them nastily said, 'I expect my husband will be asked to provide her, whoever she is, with a striped yellow bonnet.'

'Hush, Alison. Such words could be treason one day. The King will not have ill spoken of his women. They are not common prostitutes. They are of the highest nobility.'

'Poor Queen Catherine. How can she bear it? Men cannot be trusted. They think with their shafts.'

'Shush! What a thing to say. Poor Princess Mary. I hope she knows nothing of her father's women.'

'She will know who Henry Fitzroy is.'

They moved away. I waited for a few moments and followed them out into the sunlight, Bess's clogs clattering on the pavement behind me.

My husband was not like King Henry, spoiled and greedy. But then, how was I to know. Thomas was rising. He was becoming an important man in the City. Important men considered themselves differently to ordinary people. They kept mistresses and their wives ignored their infidelity. Wives had no choice, unless they chose to enter seclusion. I wondered if Queen Catherine would choose a convent to life at court. She was a queen and queens did not easily relinquish their thrones. There had been talk about her previous marriage to the King's brother, Arthur. It was said amongst the City merchants that the Pope had granted them a dispensation, so her marriage to King Henry must be a true marriage. So deep in thought was I, as I walked home with Bess by my side, I never noticed Mistress Watt sidling up to me.

'My son says Master Cromwell is in Parliament now. I hope that since he mixes with the great in the land, he will forget that debt my son owes him.'

I said sharply, 'I do not know anything of that part of my husband's business, Mistress Watt. I suggest you petition him yourself.'

'Petition him now, is it? I would, if I could, but he is never at home, is he, Mistress Cromwell?'

'He is in Parliament. Good day to you, Mistress Watt.'

We had reached the gate into the courtyard. I hurried through it with Bessie closely behind me, looking like a hound this time rather than a lap dog. I could sense her bristling as Mistress Watts slid off, her heavy cloak draped about her shoulders despite the warmth of a May afternoon.

That evening, Thomas lifted the book from the coffer. 'Where did you find this, Elizabeth?'

'In your cloak pocket. I was looking for an over-gown. It fell out.'

'I see.'

He stood, deep in thought, by the casement. Uncomfortably, I waited.

After a while, he turned to me; too long, I thought. His look was sad and his grey eyes were glazed over with tears. I had never seen Thomas weep before, yet a tear rolled down his cheek. He looked away and for a moment I felt sorry for my husband. I was fearful of what he might be about to say. He stared from the window into the lemon sunlight, the book in his palm unopened and I wondered what he saw out there in that strange light.

When he turned back from the casement, his eyes were dry. He frowned. 'Have you looked through this book, Lizzy?'

'Yes,' I said quietly. 'I have. Who is she? Why has she given you a token?'

'Elizabeth, you must not question me in this way. Nor should you investigate my cloak pockets. There are things a husband and wife do not share. If others find certain things of mine and carry them to the wrong person, it could cause trouble for me and for you too. That is one reason why you must not pry.' He looked stonily at me. 'I

347

must be sure that I can trust you not to meddle. You must not try to find out more than I tell you.'

'I wasn't prying. That little volume is just a book of flowers, though the hand that wrote your name is that of a woman called Jeanette.' I took a deep breath. 'Who is Jeanette, pray?'

He held my questioning look with a cool glare of his own. His face had become inscrutable again. 'I do not wish to speak of her, but rest assured, Elizabeth, she is of no worry or threat to you; nor is she of interest to you.'

He gently lifted the book from the coffer and left me sitting on swirling embroidered tendrils and flowers stitched on silk. There would be no further explanation forthcoming today. His eyes had filled with tears, and this aroused my suspicion. Our bedchamber which had been filled with lemon sunshine now held dark shadows, and amongst these dwelled secrets as deeply stitched as the leaves on our silken counterpane. Even though the secret I kept for Tom Williams had been a furtive and dangerous one, it was one I knew about. In guarding Tom's confidence, I had not felt excluded from his life. It had been an unhappy marriage. I had not loved him but the agony of betrayal was less because he never had been a recipient of my love. Now, I was overcome with a sense of loss because Thomas Cromwell, whom I loved with all my being, had refused me his trust.

A chill descended about me during the rest of those summer months. Thomas was in Parliament daily. After that day, despite my cold response to him, he behaved towards me as if there was nothing amiss between us.

Ralph, who had accompanied him to Greenwich, returned with tales of court. He had watched events unfold from the side where he had helped with scenery for the Cardinal's play. The Boleyn sisters are the most popular ladies at court, especially Lady Anne who has recently arrived from France. Her sister, Mary, is married but she is not.

'Is Lady Anne pretty?' Bessie asked one evening after supper as we sewed in the hall and the servants cleared the tables. Thomas had not come home from Westminster and Ralph was our only male companion that evening.

'She is striking and speaks with an affected French accent. She is petite and charming. The courtiers like to dance with her best. Even King Henry chooses Lady Anne to partner. He likes her best.'

'What does the Queen think of this?' I say. 'Can you tell?'

'Can anyone tell? She sits and smiles at him. I think she loves the King. She dotes on him as if he were an indulged child.'

I snorted. 'Sooner Lady Anne is married and away from court the better.'

'And her sister who *is* married should be gone too,' Bessie said firmly and held the purse she was stitching up for us to admire. 'Do you think Toby will like it? I made it for his birthday?'

I left the sample book I was working on and examined her needle-work. 'Very good, so neat, but how do you know his name day?'

'He told me when he came to see the master last week. It is in July.'

'Oh,' I said. 'I had forgotten it.' I wondered if Toby had been recruited as one of Thomas' spies but I knew better than to ask.

Ralph headed for the hall door. He threw a parting

comment over his shoulder. 'It is better if the Queen's ladies are married. They are less trouble married.'

I thought of the book again and the mysterious Jeanette. Was *she* married?

Thomas arrived home late one evening, his gown sweeping the parlour's turkey carpet and his chest puffed out with confidence. He came over to my chair where I sat stitching a cushion covering, yellow celandines with golden hearts. He kissed my head. I did not look up.

'How calm you look,' he remarked, looking at my work.

I glanced up at his praise but did not smile. 'My final speech on the war was a success. I spoke against it. I think they listened at last.'

'I should hope they would,' I said in a non-committal way and slipped my needle into the fabric again. 'The Cardinal has used you as his tongue. He has used you to say what he will not say. You will become a courtier yet, Thomas.'

'How could I become a courtier? I am a commoner. It is the Duke of Norfolk who manages the King. They are his own kind.'

'The Cardinal was once a commoner and look at how he has risen.' I said crossly.

'The Cardinal rose through the Church to become the King's chancellor. That is different.'Why are you always so angry these days, Elizabeth?'

I shrugged my petulance and bowed my head further over my embroidery, childishly refusing to answer.

'When you are ready, Elizabeth, tell me for this will not do.'

He rose to his feet again and hurried off to his closet, calling for Ralph to come and scribe for him.

A late summer day arrived when, at last, Thomas was free of Parliament. He said it had gone around in circles and had ended as it had begun.

'The King's grandsire was paid off by the French by over a thousand a year. Think of all that extra silver filling the royal coffers- an income from the French.' We were in the closet where Thomas was sorting his papers into neat piles and labelling them. I had come in to ask him if he would remain here for dinner.

'Yes, Lizzy. Today, finally, I am free of that endless Parliament and can dine at home.' He shook his head. 'Kings are expensive and this one is very costly. Let us hope we have dissuaded him from all thoughts of a French war. *Glory* indeed. No glory when England is beggared and might not win the fight.' He paused and swiped as a buzzing fly, killing it with a roll of parchment before continuing. I hovered by the door. 'Our King Henry dwells in the lands of imagined military success - a romantic, a reader of romances, of knights in armour, of tourneys made real. There is no time for such misplaced romance in this world, no money for a war we cannot win. Save the battling to keep the Scots from our borders.'

'Then, I am glad you are done with all of this.' I softly shut the closet door.

Chapter Thirty-seven

1523–1524

'WE SHOULD MOVE TO a larger property, Elizabeth,' Thomas would say that September.

The thought of moving from Fenchurch Street lifted me out of my melancholy. I never did find out more about Jeanette that summer. Moving house would make me forget that small book of flowers.

We were taking a rare late summer evening moment together to enjoy the garden. I sat on the bench and Thomas walked about looking at his flowers. I tried not to think about that book.

'Now that Parliament is over, I am looking at properties.' He plucked a rose and gave it to me.

I found I was smiling at him. 'Yes, we keep saying it, but you are always working too hard'

'Ah, a smile at last today,' Thomas teased, frowning a little. 'We must move and we must give Smith his rein. I think he can afford to buy the business. What do you think, Elizabeth?'

'They will be delighted to take the cloth on. Barnaby has been a journeyman for almost a year. He can move to Cornhill, take over Smith's old role and perhaps, one day, he will marry.'

I felt a sense of loss but I realised I would have to let the business I had once cherished go. 'If it means we can afford a lease on a new property then I am happy that we sell the cloth business to Gerard Smith.'

'Good, I shall arrange it.' He sat down beside me and took my hand in his. 'It is a beautiful evening. I think, Lizzy, we can afford a country property as well.'

I looked into his eyes. 'One property at a time, please. Let us see if Smith can afford the business first.'

I had the children and I hoped that I still had Tom and so I agreed to lose the cloth business.

Smith settled with our cloth business by October. We were free to concentrate on moving house.

One chilly evening when I came to the study to find him, Thomas pushed back a sheaf of papers and said, 'There you are, Lizzy, I was thinking of looking for you.'

'It is time for supper. The children are waiting. They are hungry.'

'I have found us a new property. Austin Friars has a large house available close to the Church. I think we might move there. What do you think?'

How could I not be pleased? I loved the Friary and Smith still supplied cloth for the friars.

'Thomas, it is a good choice. I shall enjoy the peace of Austin Friars away from the bustle here, away from the river with its foul airs. Now come for supper. The fire is lit in the parlour. It is warmer there than here.'

He stood up. 'It is a good address. I shall see what I can do when I return from the Cardinal's business in the north.'

Thomas had not travelled north for years. I leaned against the closet's door and breathed deeply. 'When do you set out?'

'On Friday next.'

Not waiting for him, I swept from the closet, annoyed. I could not forget that perhaps Thomas had a lady called Jeanette hidden away in some northern county, but I could not ask him because I feared I would not get the answer I desired, if, indeed, there was any answer at all to be gained. Just as it had been with Edward Northleach those years before, Thomas kept many things close to his heart.

Thomas returned from the north in time for my birthday on November the fifth, the day dedicated to St Elizabeth, mother of John the Baptist..

'Elizabeth,' he said, gently drawing me into the parlour and closing the door, 'sit down please.'

I sat on the edge of my chair.

'Lizzy, there is something I need to confess.'

This was it. He was going to tell me about Jeanette. I clasped my hands tensely in my lap. 'Confess then, Thomas.'

He sat on the bench facing me. 'Things have not been right with us and I want them to be as they were, my love. I want you to forgive me for the harsh words I spoke on the day you asked me about the book of flowers.'

I sat uneasily, wondering what he would tell me. I was prepared for news I would neither like nor forgive.

'Elizabeth,' he said quietly, so quietly that I knew he was about to tell me at last. I held his eyes with my own apprehensive gaze. He said the words I had needed to hear. 'I want to tell you about Jeanette.'

I found my hands could not remain. I fidgeted with my gown, gently rubbing a tiny fold of material by my side over and over between finger and thumb. It was an old habit.

The parlour fire spat. He inhaled and exhaled. His countenance betrayed his concern. This confession, if it was to be such, was painful for him.

He said quietly, 'Jeanette was a woman of Chester, a merchant's widow, and I was dealing with her estate. Unfortunately, her husband had left terrible debts when he died. Worse still, Jeanette and her husband were French. The

Merchant Adventurers claimed his profits.'

'You said were, Thomas. Why?'

'She is no more either. She died a long time ago.' He sighed. 'Jeanette was a beautiful woman, a clever, educated woman, and had not deserved such a husband. He was as great a rogue as Master Northleach and he had dealings with the same Italian merchant.'

'Why did you not tell me? Why did you have the flower book?' So many questions tumbled from my lips all at once. I had worried about this for months and months had remained angry with Thomas. I could not help myself.

'Jeanette was with child and died some weeks after giving birth. She was close to me. I stood godfather for her child and arranged for the child to be fostered into a good family. I see the child regularly. She thrives. She, of course, will be as beautiful as was her mother. We called her Jane.'

'*We* called her Jane,' I repeated. 'Is Jane your child, Thomas?'

He looked away and back again. His eyes were steady. 'No, but I am supporting the child, and I do intend seeing her from time to time. I expect you to understand.'

'When was she born?'

'Four years ago.'

I could never prove it, and I knew I had best not try to prove it, but I could not be sure if Thomas was speaking the entire truth. Why would he tell me any of this? My silent question was answered a few moments later.

'I don't like your silence with me, Elizabeth. It's unworthy of you. I am telling you this because Jeanette was as fond of me as I was her. She gave me the book as a gift because I promised to support her daughter. I lament her death and am sorrowful because of it. Yet, had she lived, I might have been more than fond of Jeanette. I shall not deny it.' He took my hands in his. 'But, Elizabeth, I shall always

355

love you and our children as I love life itself. Trust me and forgive me the feelings I once had for another. God forgive me, I am human.'

I considered this. We are all human. It is human to feel jealous of a woman who once sought your husband's heart, even if she no longer is a threat. Although he had not betrayed me other than in thought, I wondered what would have happened had Jeanette lived. 'Carefully,' I said, for I did, despite all, love Thomas with all my heart, and though angry, would forgive him as Christ forgave us our sins. I might not excuse him, but I would grant my pardon graciously. 'I forgive you this, Thomas. I hope God can.'

He bowed his head. 'I've made an offering to the Church of St Gabriel. I have given the church a relic from a small monastery we closed, a relic which needs a home. I have also arranged a pension for the widow Watt.' He looked up, his eyes twinkling.

'Mistress Watt will be delighted, Thomas. But what is the relic?'

'A splinter of the True Cross. They are somewhat prolific, though the reliquary, itself, is valuable - gold, silver and crystal. Very handsome. No doubt it will join the Easter procession and appear on Ascension Days. It is pretty enough to be displayed on All Souls Day. The candles will reflect well off the gold and silver decoration.'

How could I not smile at his wicked sense of humour? He so disliked relics, though we now had one on display on the cupboard in the parlour beside a clock. I forgave him, but later, and I begged God's forgiveness for my jealous heart, I could not entirely believe his story. He had loved Jeanette and he still loved her memory. Despite his precious name day gift and his declaration that our love endured, I found it difficult to understand my husband's love for Jeanette and this daughter whose upbringing he was supporting. I found it hard to understand that he may have been with her when I was in Putney and he had begun travelling north.

Let it rest, I told myself. Let it rest and hope it never happens again.

Thomas presented me with an opal in a filigreed setting hanging on silvered chain, and on that day we attended service together to give thanks to St Elizabeth. That night as I dropped my name day gift into my jewel casket, I knew that I would always associate the opal with a small book that contained an elaborate signature, and which my husband had kept secretly in his cloak pocket.

I eventually forgave my husband because I am still very much in love with this burly man who favours dull colours for his garb, who possesses a brilliant memory, always has good conversation and who loves his family. As the year turned again, Thomas was only interested in working for the Cardinal. He was to oversee the furnishing of the Cardinal's new colleges, a task that would keep him far away from court, its nobles and the King.

That winter I prepared for the move to Austin Friars. I liked the fine neighbourhood and the large stone property we would lease on Broad Street, nestled safely behind its walls beside the Friary church. The archway into the courtyard was larger and grander than our small entrance that was squashed in so tightly, only the width of one cart could pass through. At Austin Friars, two could pass comfortably through that archway set into the property's front wall.

Thomas would not trust the carters we were employing to move our more personal and valuable items such as books, jewels and clocks. It took us two days to pack up the contents of his study into leather coffers. All was ordered carefully and precisely and inventoried by Tom and myself.

'Where shall I put this?' We had risen early to pack up

357

the books and objects in Thomas' closet. I lifted a small clock from the desk.

'On top of the books,' he replied. 'Hold it carefully, Lizzy.'

A row of small oak chests was lined up neatly on his desk ready for transportation to our new home. I carried books from the shelves, put them in a linen lined trunk and placed my cloth sample books lovingly next to them.

Wiping my forehead with my apron, I said looking up at Tom, 'I am sad to lose what I once worked hard for. I can't even find time to make sample books. Though, if Smith wants, I can continue with them after we move.'

'You don't have to, Lizzy. Only make them if you really want to.'

I lifted two more books down off the shelves. 'Did you know that Meg's ribbons and trims are making a small fortune? She is helping him attract trade from courtiers. They are rising in the world of merchants.'

Thomas paused with another book half way into a chest. Standing up, he smiled. 'It's good to see her business aptitude. You taught her well, Lizzy.' He reached up and affectionately tugged the ribbon that tied my linen coif. 'And you will never lack ribbons.' He bent down again and placed the book in the chest, on top of Herodotus.

'I shall continue with the pattern books,' I said, kissing the top of his bent head with affection. 'When the girls go away and Gregory is sent into another household, I'll be glad to occupy my thoughts with things other than caring for our house beside the Friary.'

I was, in truth, sorrowful to see my cloth business finally sold off, but the changes in our lives had left us with no choice. I was busy supervising the household, entertaining our friends, and teaching the children. Gregory, a solemn boy, had joined my morning lessons now that he was fast approaching his fourth birthday. I had to start all over again with him and that made the girls a little impatient and Gregory frustrated. He was always striving to catch them up. They were, all three, more than compensation for the loss of our cloth business. Now, I would have an enormous house to care for and a new garden to fill with plants as well as teaching the children.

My children would not always remain with me, since it was the tradition to place children from great homes in other's homes. As ever, this was about forging important helpful connections for their future.

'We shall keep the girls with us,' he said, closing the closet door on our conversation. The maids were up at last and were moving and setting the trestles for our morning meal.

'I am glad of it,' I said. 'Because I think they will learn as much from me as from others. Perhaps we can find a tutor for our daughters.'

He looked thoughtful. 'They should be educated like their mother,' He reminded me of how Thomas More had his girls educated in his own house at Chelsea.

'A wise man,' I remarked. 'I think we can stop to break our fast now.' I stretched my back and pushed back my escaping locks under my coif.

'I shall be with you in a moment.'

He was placing his papers in a chest ready for transportation, as I hurried out to supervise the household breakfast.

We had arrived in Fenchurch Street with little, and after ten years, during which Thomas had collected a library of books and many valuable objects from abroad, we would leave with much. Our goods were inventoried and sent daily to Austin Friars where we had guards watch over the vacant property. Meg gave up her valuable time to establish the kitchen, the many bedrooms, the hall, parlour, still room, and quarters for the servants in the attics.

I supervised most of packing for our removal from Fenchurch Street, the tapestries, linens, valuable Italian paintings, the globe of the world, two mechanical clocks, a set of gilded Italian chairs and stools, benches clad with velvet padding, embroidered velvet cushions, silver and pewter, and strangely, the relic in its delicate and beautiful crystal case, an almost invisible St Thomas' finger nail, which Tom said amused him. I sent for a great number of carts to transport our goods. Thomas was involved with work for the Cardinal, closing monasteries to furnish the new colleges, his stewardship, a new post in Middlesex and his legal business, so it fell to me to organise many things.

We planned a goodbye supper. I carried my portable desk into the hall where I drew up a list of those I wanted to come and set out invitations.

'Don't forget young Wyatt,' Tom said, on discovering me seated by the fire on his best chair in the almost empty hall, intently scratching with charcoal on a scrap of parchment.

'I wish Cat could be with us,' I laid the charcoal aside and sighed. I felt a tear trickle down my cheek. I dabbed at it with an end of my kerchief. Cat was unwell. Richard, who carried reports to us of his mother's illness, would be with us for the last supper party at Fenchurch Street. His sister and father would remain at home.

Thomas sank down on a cushioned bench, one of several still remaining in the Fenchurch Street house, leaned over and took my hand. There was nothing to be done, nothing more to be said. She had not long to live and it broke both of our hearts. We sat still for a moment holding hands. I was glad of the reassuring warmth of his great hand holding my tiny one and the pressure in my breast lessened.

'Perhaps she will make a miraculous recovery.'

'I think not. Be prepared, Lizzy. She won't last the spring.' After a few moments he said, 'Still, do invite Thomas Wyatt. His father has asked me to watch over his son. It is time to introduce young Wyatt to our household.'

'That will be an honour,' I said, looking up at him, tears for Cat still clouding my eyes. I blinked them away. 'The supper is on Saturday next.'

I added young Wyatt's name to my list and wrote out the invitation on a small sheet of Italian paper that was edged with gilding.

During the evenings of the previous summer when Parliament sat, Thomas had entertained others in our house or he was entertained in theirs. He did legal work for Henry Wyatt, the boy's father, and, as requested, had taken this clever but unhappy young man, Thomas Wyatt, under his wing. My husband was already like an uncle to him, and he had visited us. I liked this courtier because he wrote poetry of such beauty that tears came into our eyes.

The house was swept. The supper evening arrived. A great fire crackled in the hall's hearth. Guests were seated and fed with fish and pastries, jellies and custards, cheeses and soft white bread, for it was the Lenten season and we did not eat meat. Thomas' friends took their leave by nine of the clock but my family lingered, as did young Thomas Wyatt.

Just as, long ago, my mother had told us tales that had been carried from a cousin close to the court, Thomas Wyatt now brought us stories of the lady who was, he declared, the most intelligent of the Queen's ladies.

'Alas, her engagement to an Irish lord has long been broken,' he said as we sat crowded around the trestle, the

361

remains of our feast before us. 'She has another admirer. He is Lord Percy and none can compete with him. She will have him without a doubt, though I think Lord Percy will not be permitted her attentions for much longer.' He lowered his voice. 'He is engaged to Mary Talbot and his father will not have La Boleyn. They are above her.' He picked at his nails. 'And, though, it is not common knowledge, the King likes her.'

'I thought her sister was his mistress,' I said.

'Not any more. She is with child again.'

'Whose? The King's?' I asked.

'No, probably her husband's. The King has not looked at her since last April.'

I remembered the conversation I had overheard back in the summer. The King had sent Anne Boleyn a gift, not her sister. I said nothing of it because Thomas never smiled and I gathered from his lack of comment that he knew something of this business and was not prepared to reveal what he knew. After all, young Percy was in the Cardinal's household.

My sister raised an eyebrow. Joan enjoyed gossip, the tastier the better. My mother, who liked very much any tales of Court, tut-tutted and smiled. She looked glorious in burgundy wool trimmed with velvet and with fashionably wide sleeves. Her dark hair shone where it peeped out from her French hood. She had remarried some years before and was ecstatically happy.

Sir John Pryor, her cheerful and plump new husband, laughed and remarked, 'So the King will be piqued by young Percy.'

The candle flickered as he spoke. I reached up to steady it.

At that moment, my girls ran into the hall. On seeing Sir Thomas with a plum half way to his mouth, they curtsied.

Annie loved to dress up in a tall steeple hat that she had made for St George's Day and to play ladies and knights. Grace was her companion in this game and she, too, wore a tall pointed hat which sat enchantingly askew on her long pale curls.

Thomas Wyatt made a small bow to the two delighted girls.

With a whoop, Gregory galloped up to our supper table on a hobby horse, shaking his sword in the air. We all laughed. To complete the chaotic tableaux, their nurse bustled after them, complaining at the noise they made, insisting that it was time they were in bed. She swept them up out of the hall and back through the house. We listened for a moment to her scolding and their answering squeals of laughter.

'They are beautiful children and of such a charming nature. Ah, now, what was I saying?'

'Lady Anne?' Mother said.

Wyatt finished his plum and wiped his mouth with a napkin. 'Henry Percy will be sent up north and married off to Mary Talbot. Alas, Lady Anne is impoverished in comparison. She may be clever and have beautiful black eyes but she is not of the highest nobility in the land. The Percys are proud people.'

'I think perhaps you love the lady yourself,' I said in a teasing manner, seeing longing in his wistful eyes.

He pulled a long face. 'Nay, not love. Admire perhaps, but then I have known her for quite a long time. Our estates in Kent adjoin, you see. And, Mistress Cromwell, the lady is untouchable.' He dramatically placed a long delicate hand across his heart. 'I, unlike Lord Percy, would never place my heart in such danger. Besides, I have a wife, though she dislikes Court. She stays in the country.' He looked sad.

'Percy is in Cardinal Wolsey's care. I suspect the

Cardinal has already summoned his father,' Thomas said.

'Then, Master Cromwell, they will make Percy marry that rich heiress without doubt,' Thomas Wyatt remarked. 'Another miserable marriage, I would say.'

'Maybe, maybe not,' my husband said quietly.

'Mother, we still have the lute here. Will you play for us,' I said, changing the conversation to something happier.

Mother shifted in her chair and I fetched the instrument. 'Will you sing for us, Sir Thomas,' she said.

'It would be a pleasure.' He rose and bowed.

Their voices mingled as my mother played a ballad and then another. They were happy songs, songs of the countryside, of knights and ladies, of wooing and weddings, of March hares dancing and of swans mating on quiet, shaded rivers.

'They mate for life, my sweet Elizabeth,' Thomas whispered into my ear below the strains of the melody.

'They do,' I whispered back. 'As shall we, my love.' My jealousy and frustrated anger of the previous summer had finally faded.

Chapter Thirty-eight

1524

OUR MOVING DAY DAWNED with drips of rain hanging like tear drops in the hedgerows. They dropped with splashes from the empty branches of the pear tree that stretched its arms across the wall and tunnelled down the roof tiles. It was as if everything, even the plants in the garden, was saying 'goodbye'. Rooms were emptied as if waiting for ghosts to move in, rather than a master tailor's family. My footsteps echoed in a lonely manner, as I crossed the tiled floors. In the nursery Grace had shared with her brother and sister, I scooped one of her poppets from the floor. It had dropped from the basket we had filled this morning with the children's playthings, chalk sticks and slates.

I would not linger. I wanted to be away, for I felt like an intruder in the silent house that had once bustled with activity. There would be another garden to love and plant; another house to make my own.

Barnaby and Wilfrid stood waiting for me in the yard beside a horse and cart. I had stowed a huge basket of laundry, my own clothing chests and my needlework in it. I tucked the poppet into the cart beside a box of toys and treasures.

'Ah my horse is waiting, I see,' I said and climbed into the saddle.

'Can we go now, Mistress?' Wilfrid asked.

I nodded and my apprentices, now cloth men in their

365

own right, took their places on the seat in front of the cart and flicked the palfrey's reins. It plodded forward clattering over the cobbles. The watchman waited to padlock the gate behind me for the final time as I sat erect on my mare and followed the rattling cart out of the gates.

Half an hour later, I rode in through the gates of Austin Friars, a house built of stone, and gave over my palfrey, Sapphire, to Wilfrid. The young men would stable the cart and horse and then go to the property in Cornhill. Barnaby and Wilfrid were already living betwixt and between Cornhill and Fenchurch Street. They had completed their apprenticeships but stayed on as journeymen. I would miss them but we had new apprentices training to be Thomas' legal assistants, two of whom were Ralph and Richard. One day, Thomas had said, Ralph Sadler would be my secretary.

Meg welcomed me, sweeping me into the kitchen where Cook was now preparing our dinner. The delicious smells of a broiled salmon and green herb sauce floated from the handsome new brick oven set into an outer wall and close to the fireplace. Something sweet-smelling bubbled in a cauldron over the fire. I went over and dipped the stirring spoon in. Cook had concocted a delicious spicy barley stew filled with vegetables and dried fruits.

'Lenten food, but delicious,' I said, replacing the spoon on its hook by the fireplace.

'How do you like your new kitchen?'

'Very well, Mistress.' He grinned, obviously pleased with this move. 'I am still arranging it. We shall need more spit-turners.'

'We'll employ them.'

'We have the parlour set for dinner,' Meg said. 'The maids have set the table. It has benches enough and the two cupboards, the one from Fenchurch Street and the new one Master Thomas has just purchased.'

'I look forward to unpacking and placing our silver on it,' I said. 'Meg, where are the children?' We were walking through an airy corridor towards the parlour.

'Exploring. They can come to no harm and there is much to explore.'

'Is Thomas in his study?'

'Yes. Dinner will be ready.'

'I have so much to do afterwards. Will you stay Meg, for another few days?'

'Until Friday. Gerard is going to Antwerp. I must be back in Cornhill by then.'

'Thank you.' I hugged her, for I was grateful for her help.

I hurried away to look for Thomas, leaving Meg to oversee the last of the unpacking in the grand tiled hall, a hall in which to receive visitors rather than the hurly-burly of everyday living.

I discovered Thomas sorting out his new study, a spacious room on the first floor. He was supervising a table he had ordered to be placed where the light would be most advantageous, looking out towards the garden. A secretary was stacking his books into shelves. Thomas turned around to instruct him where each should be placed, and saw me watching him from the doorway.

'Come in, Lizzy, and look out of the window.'

I crossed to a huge diamond-paned window and looked out into our new garden. The clouds had cleared and a rainbow hung in the sky. 'Thomas,' I said with delight, 'the sun is casting a rainbow over the garden. It's a good omen.'

'This will be our home for the rest of our lives,' he said, coming to stand beside me. 'Never shall we move house again, though I do have my eye on a new property in the country. I bought the land owned by Master Watt when I gave his mother a pension.'

'You did?'

'He paid off his debt and didn't need the land; his mother has a pension and I can see it would be to our advantage to build a house on it.'

'We are to become property owners as well as leasing this house?'

'Land is the best asset we can have for Gregory to inherit.' He put his hand on my shoulders. 'And for you and for our daughters as well. One day, they will want dowries.'

'I like it well,' I said looking up at him. His face was caught in the setting sun's rosy glow. I reached up and plucked out a grey hair. He smiled down on me and on the stiff grey hair I held between finger and thumb.

'And Lizzy, this is a new beginning for us. Ghosts are laid to rest, do we agree?'

'Yes, we agree.'

He leaned down and laid a kiss on my head. I glanced behind me in case the servant was listening, but we were now alone in the study. The desk was in place. The books were in their shelves and the secretary had slipped out, leaving us to ourselves.

'Have you seen our bedchamber?'

I shook my head.

'Go and look before dinner.'

The servants would have chambers of their own at the top of our new house. No one would ever have to sleep in the hall again other than a watchman. And, as well as the servants' attic rooms, the house had five bedchambers.

A new Turkey carpet was spread over the wooden boards of our bed chamber. My slippers sank into its deep pile. It was thicker than those we had hung on the chamber's walls. Thomas had purchased new cushions and a bench of pale wood that leaned against the foot of our great canopied bed. I touched the fresh bed curtains that Meg and my maids had carefully hung. They had been beaten of dust and, to my pleasure, the whole bed chamber smelled of roses. I had chosen the bed's new hangings myself the previous year before having had them made from a damask mix, burgundy with a pattern of creamy lilies through the weave. I had not used them and now hung in this gracious chamber they looked handsome. It was truly a new beginning.

I glanced around the spacious bed chamber and saw that the painting of the Virgin and child had already been placed on an alcove wall. Empty spaces by the other walls waited for clothing coffers. I opened the great cupboards on the wall to the left of the bed. We would never have enough garments to fill them. Softly closing these, I ran to the window. I could see beyond the courtyard into a second garden. This time, I saw trees, quince and pear, cleverly trained along the side wall separating the far garden from that of the Austin Friars.

Once we were settled in, I would visit the Friary and ask for Prior Lawrence. I would ask if could I see the library and I considered that I might procure a Latin tutor from the Friary for our daughters. Full of joyful thoughts, I descended the stairway to join my family in the parlour.

The dinner bell resounded throughout the house. I heard footsteps running towards the parlour.

'Stop running, children,' their nurse scolded.

The children were seated demurely around the table with their nurse, Bessie and Meg. Thomas took his place at the head of the table and we were served our first dinner in Austin Friars.

A week later, a breathless Toby came to visit us with news. We hurried him into Thomas' study where he told us that a man - he was sure it was the one who had been with those two who had attacked my Wood Street warehouse, the man with the scar on his face - had been arrested for attacking a King's guard.

'I saw him, Mistress Elizabeth. He was one of the Spanish monks. I think he was following me. He mistook another guard for me. He cut him and left him for dead in St Gabriel's churchyard.'

'How can you be sure?' Thomas said.

'My friend survived to tell the tale.'

'What was his tale?' I said anxiously.

'When he was attacked, it was my name the monk spoke. He gabbled a load of nonsense about heretics and how I had escaped God's wrath once but I would not this time.'

'How did they find the attacker?' My fears were not laid to rest by the monk's arrest. I still feared the Church's judgement all these years later.

Toby smiled. 'The monk had made the mistake of saying that he was a member of the Benedictines of Grace Church Street. It was not difficult to locate him.'

'Will his accusations hold?' I said anxiously.

'No one likes those particular Benedictines. They smack of Spain's cruelty. He will be sent back to whence he came.'

Thomas laid a hand on my arm and said, 'Lizzy there is no danger that the monk will dare to make further mischief. I'll see that he is sent back to Spain.'

'But Queen Catherine is from Spain,' I remarked.

'Yes, and, thankfully, she doesn't subscribe to their ruthless methods. Besides, she has her own concerns these days and those are at court. Times are set to change,' Thomas said.

'How?' I said.

'There's talk that the King wants to annul his marriage to Queen Catherine and that he's consulting with Wolsey over it. He claims it was no true marriage.'

'Don't let the Cardinal draw you in.'

'I'm involved in legal issues only, not the affairs of the great ladies and gentlemen of the court; mostly property. This is what brings us our wealth. I'm not drawn into the King's marital issues.'

Not yet, I thought.

And there the discussion rested. Toby hurried off to seek out Bessie, and we, not wanting to worry further that evening about the Spanish monk and his mischief-making, began discussing what we would plant in the garden this spring.

Chapter Thirty-nine

April 1525

THE FIRST YEAR IN OUR new home flew past without
event. At Eastertide, I made one final visit to the Wood
Street graveyard where my first husband was buried. I laid
a bunch of evergreens on his grave. As I prayed for his
soul, a blackbird hopped about the mound that was Tom
Williams' resting place. It studied me with curious eyes
before flying off.

How far I had come since the day of Tom Williams'
funeral. How far would life's journey take us, my family
and myself, in future years? As I began to rise from the
cold ground, my rosary beads rattled insistently. I knelt
again and whispered another prayer, this time for Queen
Catherine, with whom I would not exchange places for all
the Orient's silks.

After I had risen again, I thanked God for Thomas
Cromwell, for everything we shared and the children we
both loved deeply. A chill wind blew into my cloak and I
drew it tighter about my neck. My servant waited at the
gate to accompany me home. As we walked along Wood
Street, I thought of the fire and the Benedictine monk who
I hoped had by now, as Thomas had promised, returned in
disgrace to Spain.

The presentiment I felt as I crossed the City was nothing
to do with the Benedictine monk's arrest, as I had at first
wondered. On my return home, sad news awaited me.

Thomas' sister Cat, after a brief recovery and another a year of illness, was dying. He had left already to be with her. I had ridden on Sapphire to her home near the law courts to visit her several times during the past winter. We all knew that God would claim her for his own before summer.

As I sat out that evening for her home in Chancery Lane, riding my palfrey, the manservant following on one of Thomas' jennets, I noted grey-blue clouds passing slowly across the stars. It might rain. I paused as we approached Morgan's cobbled yard, and as I dismounted I heard the nearby church bell toll. It was announcing a death. When I hurried inside Morgan's hall, I knew that Catherine, my dear friend, was already dead. Thomas was kneeling in the hall with Morgan, Richard and the servants. The priest was praying with them.

So as not to disturb them, I slipped past and softly climbed the staircase. Joan and Elizabeth were in Cat's chamber, by the bedside, their eyes red from weeping. The women were already washing her body and dressing her in her shroud. Candles were lit about the bedchamber and a vigil was about to commence. The women nodded to me as I approached. Little Catherine was standing by her mother's corpse like a sentinel, a miniature version of her mother, pale and dark, huge and solemn eyes stared at her mother. Her dark hair reached her waist in a long plait, secured with a black ribbon. She was such a little creature, so fragile, and, in that sad moment, I longed to protect her. The funeral candles flickered, casting shadows into the dark corners. It was a sorrowful scene. My eyes filled with tears.

'Catherine,' I whispered later, standing by her side and taking the little girl's hand. 'I am so sorry, my sweeting, for I loved her too.'

She looked up at me with huge frightened eyes. 'Where is Mama now? Is she with the angels?'

'Yes, my sweet, she is, for she is so good that angels will want to take her straight to Heaven.'

'I shall miss my mama.'

'You shall, and that is the way of things, but she has no pain now. She is at peace. In time, you will remember her with joy, little one.'

Catherine was only five years old, too young to lose her mother to a recurring canker.

'I have ordered gloves as funeral gifts. I knew she was dying,' Morgan said that evening.

'We all knew she was dying,' Tom said in a choked voice.

'I had already sent to a haberdasher's for them. Black lace gloves for the women and plain ones for the men. Do you think that wise? She loved gloves, Lizzy.'

'I think you chose as she would have wished,' I said quietly.

'I had candles ordered too. I want all to be proper.'

'It is, Morgan. It is proper and very sad.' I felt my voice crack and bowed my head. It is hard to lose those you love. Life's passing is but a fluttering in the great cosmos. We must try to live it well, I kept reminding myself that evening. It is the best we can do.

We promised that we would help Morgan however we could. Richard was already one of our household and if little Catherine would like to join our household too, I was happy to raise her as one of our own. Morgan said he would think about it. 'Not yet,' he said. 'But if the offer remains open, when she is older, yours would be a fine and happy family for her to grow into womanhood. For now, we shall grieve together and recover.'

374

After Cat's funeral, I wrapped my black lace gloves in silk and kept them in a drawer, but I often thought of her that summer. I had lost one of the few close friends in my life. She was irreplaceable. Eliza, her sister, had softened as the years passed and she often came to visit us with Christopher, who became a companion for Gregory, but never could the sharp Eliza replace Cat in my heart.

Gradually, we came to know our neighbours, merchants and humanists alike. It was an enlightened parish. When we attended our new parish church on Easter Sunday the priest asked Thomas if he would honour the parish by standing as a parish warden. He would, of course. It gave him more important connections, as the Broad Street Parish was a wealthy parish.

My mother and Sir John visited us to share our festivities on St George's Day of 1525. We dressed up in our best finery and the children wore their queens' and knights' costumes. That afternoon, our house was filled with the laughter of children and of adults. The girls danced about our new hall in their steeple hats, the same they had worn for Thomas Wyatt over a year before. Joan was with child again and John Williamson attended to her every need. The children tried to make her dance but she was too cumbersome, she said. Life goes on, I thought sadly, thinking of Cat, only weeks before laid in her mossy grave.

We wore masks which we had spent days before creating from scraps of fabrics. The children chose a king. They chose Thomas who acted his part well, teasing us all and ordering us about in play in a way he never did in reality. Thomas always got what he wanted, but his methods more subtle than demanding. He used reason that

375

usually was so sound no one challenged him, which was why the children picked their father. They adored him and I rejoiced that we were a happy family, for many families were not.

Hired musicians played long past the midnight angelus. We cleared back trestles and started the dancing. After the sorrow that surrounded Cat's death, the dancing that night lifted our spirits.

'I think one day, Lizzy, we must have our own resident players, musicians and actors.'

'What, Thomas, here, at Austin Friars? Next you will be telling me that one day you will be a peer of England.' I had long resigned myself to his ambition and recognised that nothing would stop him becoming closer to the king if this was where ambition led him. My dislike of the Cardinal had never lessened but I could not change what was. I could not dictate Thomas' life.

He smiled at that. 'One day, I may be granted such favour, though that is unlikely. I am happy as we are, for now.'

'Good,' I said firmly.

We glanced over at our children who pranced about in a circle with children belonging to our relatives. They were all wearing variously decorated dragon masks, growling and blowing out pretend smoke.

'May God protect them from all the world's evil, Lizzy, for they are truly innocent,' Tom remarked as we turned around each other in the dance.

'Amen to that,' I said, as Gerard Smith reached out, caught me and twirled me around and around over and over again.

Chapter Forty

Midsummer 1526, The Hall

WE HAVE COME FAR in our twelve years of marriage.

I glance around at the company of family, friends and senior servants seated at our dining table in the great dining room at Austin Friars. Our side-boards are laden with food. The expensive Italian and Brussels tapestries that grace the walls make me feel proud. A warm sun creates lemon pools of light as it shines through long mullioned windows. I lift a spoonful of Midsummer tart to my mouth, allow it to graze slowly past my lips for a moment, thinking that some things, like my mother's delicious Midsummer tart, never change.

Others do. Our lives thrive on change. We are thrusting upwards and forwards, ever hopeful of discovering the best way to live, hoping to discover our life's purpose and happiness.

For now, all is peace in our lives. We feel the rumbles at court - the King's pursuit of the Lady Anne, who has no hope of the happiness she sought with young Harry Percy, that gentleman long ago sent home to bleak Northumberland to marry a more suitable bride. The King desires the lady. With desire follows pursuit. The City goodwives say that he has no taste, this one being worse than the sister and maybe the greater threat. Poor Queen Catherine remains hopeful that her husband's latest infatuation will pass.

Thomas says that Lady Anne has good sense about religious matters. He has told me more than once that to the best of his knowledge, she is broad-minded, cultured and enlightened. Like our humanist friends she follows the notions of new learning; to question and to discuss scripture; to study history and art; to find out interesting things; to explore Heaven's firmament and earth's boundaries, whether by voyages to new lands or by listening to travellers' stories about the distant islands that are recently added to our maps.

From what I hear, the Lady Anne is intent on the King's interest and encourages him. She is flirtatious, young Wyatt informs us. Thomas, I think, must not allow himself to be seduced by her intellect, the talents she has with music and dance, or by her affected French words in conversation, because she will entrap him within her ambition. Let us pray that such things will never come to pass and that Thomas, now closer to affairs at court, will have good sense and keep his distance as he rises within the Cardinal's council. It is dangerous to become involved in the King's private matters.

At last dinner is over and we set off to see the Midsummer processions. Jon Woodall bows and wishes me a good day and Happy Midsummer. He sets off to find other companions with whom to make merry but Vaughan will remain with us.

'Down to the river,' says Thomas, grabbing his bonnet from the peg in our porch. 'We may be in time to enjoy the King's journey up river to Westminster.' He glances down at our three excited clustering children and at Meg's son. 'Would you like to see the boats and their pennants?' They squeal with delight. A mischievous grin crosses his countenance. He winks at me. 'Would you like to go out on the river today?'

I raise an eyebrow. 'Why so?'

'We have been granted the Cardinal's own barge. He is with the King. It is waiting for us by the bridge wharf, on the other side so as to avoid the rapids close to the bridge. I said

378

we would be there by four in the afternoon. That is the surprise.' He hurries into his light wool cloak. 'Just think, Lizzy, we can become part of the river pageant instead of watching it pass.' He glances at the hanging clock. 'Vaughan, have you fetched down your cape? Meg, you and Bessie keep the children together. Ralph and Richard, carry the basket with our masks.' He chivvies us out into the courtyard. 'And did I say that the Cardinal's cooks are providing our supper?'

Stephen Vaughan groans. 'I cannot manage another bite today. The pasties, the beef, the Midsummer tart - Meg, Mistress Elizabeth, this year it has been better than ever.'

'My mother's recipe,' I remind him, though this is not the first time Stephen has been with us at Midsummer. Absent from our table are Barnaby and Wilfrid, since they have travelled to Flanders with Smith. Since they have both now graduated to journeymen and will be allowed to become members of the guild later in the year.

Everything changes. Nothing can remain as it is for long.

'Thomas, is it sensible to accept such a gift from the Cardinal?' I say with anxiety creeping into my voice.

'It would be foolish to refuse and we shall enjoy it.'

'I hope we are not out too late. Remember we are to join Thomas More's hunt tomorrow.'

'And I am on holiday,' says Thomas taking my arm. 'You have me for two whole days.' He smiled. 'So let us enjoy the afternoon.'

I note, when we reach the barge, that servers are rushing about, setting our supper on a table covered with a crisp linen cloth. We admire the silver and the dainty dishes and confections that grace the Cardinal's golden plates. Our fingers lightly touch the crystal drinking vessels he has provided for us to drink from tonight.

I sink onto a cushioned seat in the boat's prow and the oarsmen push off. There are rowing boats and barges as far as the eye can see and a late afternoon sun gives all a soft pinkish saffron glow. The oarsmen guide us through the river traffic until we are part of the King's procession. We pick out his barge because it is golden with embossed figures and carvings. The red Welsh dragon flutters high above it more proudly than the many other royal banners. The children are as delighted as I had been so many years ago when I travelled by river boat to watch the King and Queen's coronation procession through Cheape Street and Cornhill; the day Queen Catherine sheltered from the rain under our awning.

That had been a day of great optimism for it heralded their new reign and Queen Catherine was beautiful. I had envied her long red-gold hair and was delighted on that far off day to be the recipient of her smile. It was a smile that spilled kindness on all receiving it. I wondered if we would draw closer to the King's barge and if I would be able to catch a glimpse of her again.

At that moment, Gregory shrieks because a band of puppeteers appeared as if summoned magically from one of the boat's striped awnings. 'Puppets,' he called. 'We have our own puppet masters, Mama.'

We do, I thought to myself.

The children, thrilled, become engrossed in the puppet show, a story of Robin Hood and the Mistress Marion. Painted scenery depicts a forest with trees and flowers and a musician who makes appropriate noises when the Sheriff of Nottingham appears. There is even a miniature castle with a bower for Mistress Marion. When Friar Tuck appears, jiggling a very fat belly, he makes them laugh. Robin Hood and his puppet outlaws attack and take possession of the castle of Nottingham. They rescue Lady Marion. Now the

380

children cheer.

As the show ends, we draw closer to the King's barge, so close that we could hear his musicians' music float over the water. The tall pinnacles of King Henry III's great abbey church rise up to our right.

'We have passed Westminster,' I say with surprise because I had thought that would be our destination. 'Where are we going?'

'To the Cardinal's palace.'

'At Hampton?'

'Yes, but worry not, for we are turning back soon enough. We are only travelling part of the way.'

The Cardinal's barge is now closing in on the King's vessel. Other boats have made way for the gilded craft, recognising its fluttering banner with cross, cardinal's hat, crossed keys and Tudor rose flanked by two cockerels. The grey velvet-uniformed oars men plough steadily through the traffic, passing the many vessels out on the wide river. I see the Queen. For a time, I cannot not lift my eyes from her. She remains as elegant as ever, her garments rich and her face serene. She is larger and more commanding in appearance than on that long-gone day of their coronation. The King too has broadened. He wears cloth of gold and a large blue velvet bonnet below which his hair falls as golden as it ever was. My eye rests upon Princess Mary, a slender lovely girl with red hair that flows like a waterfall over her green silk gown. She is crowned with a coronet of pink roses, and sits close to the Queen on her own golden chair.

'Look at the Princess,' I say to our children who have been trailing their hands in the water and have been exclaiming at the pennants and the glittering ladies and nobles who accompany the royal couple and their daughter.

'She looks lonely,' Annie remarks.

'She might be a queen one day,' I answer. 'Being a queen is lonely because you cannot be too familiar with anyone.'

'I wish she had a friend,' Annie says. 'There are no other girls with her.'

'Or a brother,' Gregory remarks. 'I would make a good brother for her.'

I laugh. 'I have no doubt of it, but you, Gregory, are not noble. You should be thankful, for one day like your father you will be a great lawyer.'

Gregory does not yet know much about his father's work though he makes us laugh, saying earnestly, 'I am learning Latin and soon I shall know as much as Father.'

'You have much to learn yet, Gregory,' Thomas says, ruffling our son's hair. He looks again towards the King's party.

Stephen Vaughan remarks, 'The lady is not there today.'

'Apparently not,' Thomas says. 'She is not at court this Midsummer.'

The Cardinal rises from the King's side. Gazing about the river he spots his own vessel now gliding just behind the King's party. He waves, and as my husband waves back, I observe the watchful King studying Thomas. King Henry smiles and leans down to speak into the Cardinal's ear. They are speaking of Thomas. I am sure of it, and for an intake of breath, I feel as if a north wind has risen over the river, the glittering pageant, and us. For a moment, a cloud obscures the sun. The King inclines his head in our direction. It is as if an invisible finger has singled Thomas out and summons him closer into King Henry's orbit. Thomas rises and bows. Yes, we are fragile moths, compulsively drawn to the royal candle where, if we are not careful, we shall be singed.

Thankfully, we slow down as we reach a bend in the river and a distance opens up between us and the King. It is time for us to turn back towards the City.

Epilogue

1528, Summer

WHEN I ARRIVED AT Austin Friars I knew that my life would change and change it did. Thomas guarded carefully the time he spent with us, his family and friends. He also passed many long weeks on his horse, travelling up and down Oxfordshire, closing another group of small monasteries. The Cardinal long wanted to build new colleges and the closure of these monasteries meant that he grew wealthier and wealthier. He built his colleges and Thomas has overseen this work.

As the Cardinal became wealthy from the closures, we benefited. There were bribes to persuade Thomas to go easier on the monks. Sometimes he did. I do not question the source of our recent wealth and the new properties my husband has purchased. After all, he is the Cardinal's director of works and he has been meticulous with his attention to detail. Perhaps he deserves recompense, but I have thought it sad to close down any monasteries.

The years passed and I did not conceive again. After all, I am in my thirty-seventh year. Yet, I feel youthful still, and there are but few white hairs amongst the silver on my head. The King is more determined than ever to set Queen Catherine aside. He hopes to marry the Lady Anne and have a son off her.

Of late, the Lady Anne has shown a dislike for the Cardinal, whom she says is not on her side in their great matter. It has not gone so well for Cardinal Wolsey. If the

Cardinal falls where will my husband be? Thomas says he has more and more legal work from courtiers, the noble and the great. They all respect his talent, even the hook-nosed Norfolk. He is the cleverest lawyer who ever lived in the realm, they say. If the Cardinal falls, Thomas will survive because he serves others. My husband may be a loyal servant to his Cardinal, but he is pragmatic also. He is ambitious though cautious.

My mother's new husband died a year since, and she has come to live with us. She says she will never remarry - two husbands are enough in one life-time - and I am glad of her company. Our friends adore her and our family is complete now that she dwells in Austin Friars. Though she enjoyed Sir John Pryor's company, he never replaced Father in her affections and her saddened heart has healed again. She teaches the girls to sew and to play the virginals. Some afternoons, as I listen to them play I wish that time would stand still for us all. I wish we were a moment captured in a painting, and that the moment will last for ever.

Only a few weeks ago, Toby married Bess. They will move to Lincoln to claim his inheritance. He has given in his notice as a guard because they have an estate to manage. Meg and Smith thrive, as does their cloth business. I make sample books, several every year, and am paid in silk ribbons and new fabric. Sometimes I take a servant and walk to Cornhill just to gaze on and feel the silk material caress my fingers and to select my favourite silk mixes for gowns for the girls and myself. Thomas still favours dark grey velvets or expensive black silk. When I see him in a colour, which he will wear on pageant days, or the forester green he wears for the hunt with his hawks, my heart lifts. Just as my jewellery coffer fills with bright gems, my being swells with pride for what my husband

384

has accomplished. We are so happy that I feel I shall burst like a peach that has received too much sunshine.

I must hurry along the passage to the kitchen because a friend of Thomas has shot a doe while hunting and has promised to send it to me as a gift. I shall speak with cook as to its destiny, for we shall dine well on princely meat.

A frown creases my brow. Is that another bell I hear, yet another death? I pause and listen, anxiety knocking at my breast, making my heart beat so fast that I fancy I hear it echo from wall to wall. The bell tolls on and on. This summer, the sweating sickness has returned to our city, seeping along the river, virulent, stealing of our lives as if they must be blown away like the pollen on Tom's roses. The bell's sombre toll is close. It is tolling too close to us and I fear that the sickness will catch us up. I whisper a small prayer. I lightly touch an amulet, the St Christopher that I wear on a long, thin chain of gold, praying for protection. 'God save all our souls,' I whisper.

I hear horses neighing in the courtyard and the clip of their hooves on the cobbles. Thomas is home. His voice calls out, 'Elizabeth' and I hurry to greet my well-beloved husband. The low pealing bell, the cook and the deer are forgotten in my haste to see him, Thomas Cromwell, my well-beloved, loyal-hearted husband.

Author Note

First of all, thank you, readers, for reading this story. I hope that you enjoyed it and can forgive the inventions that exist alongside the few known facts about Thomas and Elizabeth Cromwell's marriage. Although this is the nature of historical fiction, I do acknowledge a responsibility to stay with recorded facts where they exist, and have done so. Although this book is thoroughly researched, I would though remind the reader that it is a work of historical fiction.

Not much at all is known about Elizabeth Cromwell. She was previously married to Tom Williams who was supposed to have been a member of the King's guard. The couple did not have children. Elizabeth was allegedly a wealthy widow by the time she met her second husband. It is suggested in most sources that the Cromwells married circa 1514. Elizabeth's father was a cloth merchant from Fulham, and it is likely that Thomas Cromwell's father, who owned a fulling mill (to refine cloth before it was dyed), knew Elizabeth's father. As a girl, Elizabeth may have known the boy Thomas Cromwell.

Cromwell was a commoner, not necessarily impoverished at all, as was Thomas Wolsey. He lived on the continent in his youth and may or may not have run away from home to seek his fortune. He did say in later life that his father was violent. His father, Walter, owned land and property and Thomas, as a late child of the marriage, may have been formally educated, at least until the age of fourteen. It is recorded that Walter had been in trouble circa 1513 with the law over issues regarding brewing - for, in addition to his other businesses, he owned a public house and a brewery close to the river in Putney.

The characters in both families were researched as far as it is possible to research them. Their spouses were named as in the story. There is no suggestion, according to my research, that when Elizabeth died Thomas Cromwell had an affair with Elizabeth's sister, although I cannot say conclusively that he did not. After Elizabeth died from an outbreak of sweating sickness in 1529, Thomas Cromwell never remarried. There were frequent outbreaks of this illness in London during this period. It is suggested by historians that the sweat was carried from the continent by Henry VII's mercenaries during the Cousins' War. It was a deadly disease, although there were survivors, but sadly not in Thomas Cromwell's family. The sweat took all classes of people, rich and poor.

Thomas mentions a child, Jane, who dwelt near Chester, in a will he had drawn up in the early 1530s after the deaths of his two daughters, Anne and Grace, from sweating sickness. Jane is documented as having married a wealthy farmer and, interestingly, she was a Roman Catholic all her life. I found Jane's existence intriguing, thus that aspect of the story is from my imagination, not the records of history. Cromwell's son Gregory survived and in the late 1530s married Jane Seymour's sister. He was related by marriage to royalty.

Mercy Wykes, Elizabeth's mother, remarried after her husband Henry's death. Either she moved into Austin Friars alone in the middle to late 1520s or along with her second husband. This part is evidenced fact.

It is also fact that Thomas Cromwell was a humanist, which I found profoundly interesting, and the friends mentioned in the story were indeed his friends. Humanists questioned rather than accepted and were interested in Classical Roman and Greek texts in particular. Cromwell was a Renaissance man. He spoke several languages fluently and loved everything Italian. He also admired the works of Erasmus and Machiavelli. He was different in the detail of his religious beliefs to Thomas More, who was a devout Catholic and believer in all the trappings of Roman Catholicism.

Thomas Cromwell, I believe, genuinely questioned aspects of the Catholic religion from 1517 onwards. He had travelled that year to Rome to obtain permission for the Boston Stump to sell indulgences. Thomas More and even the decadent, outrageously wealthy Cardinal Wolsey saw faults in the Church and advocated some reform, but they absolutely would not question the Pope's authority or Transubstantiation. They would have accepted traditional beliefs and the ancient Latin Vulgate Bible. Cromwell was responsible for Tyndale's English translation of the Bible being placed in Churches during the 1530s. Sources tell us that he learned Erasmus' translation of the New Testament into Latin from Greek by heart. This indicates a man who cared about religion, although he did possess a relic, which is recorded in the Tudor-era inventory for Austin Friars. His interest in humanist thought and in older writings suggest to me that he admired the Gospels written in Anglo-Saxon, as they were scribed in the vernacular prior to the Norman Conquest. I speculate in this novel that Cromwell was aware of Tyndale much earlier, as early as 1517, and I believe that, although I invented this section of my story, it is plausible. It contains my personal favourite scenes in the novel.

I was interested in looking at Thomas Cromwell's early career as a merchant, as a lawyer and as an employee of Cardinal Wolsey. I believe that before he became involved with Henry VIII he was upwardly mobile and ambitious but that at this earlier point in his personal history, since he was not placed in the extremely ruthless position he later embraced, he may have been an interesting and likeable person who loved family and cared about the dispossessed. I suggest though that one reads Machiavelli's *The Prince* to understand Cromwell's mind set. He was a strange, complex character. He was totally devoted to the notion of family and he was extremely loyal to his masters. He had a formidable memory and he was extremely intelligent and resourceful. He was good company and sociable. He was witty, fun-loving and he loved to entertain. He was also a workaholic and could be very stern. In later years, of course, he was a king's henchman and a brilliant negotiator.

Looking at Cromwell through Elizabeth's eyes has, for me, humanised a person who possesses a very nasty reputation within the traditional historical record, although this reputation is being more fairly re-examined by many historians. He lived through cruel times, growing wealthy and important during a

388

period of great societal change that involved men, and some women too, rethinking men's place within the world. The middle classes were increasing, and London possessed a very wealthy cloth merchant class. New draperies, as referred to in the story, were the latest thing in fabrics and probably made a nonsense of sumptuary laws that existed throughout the sixteenth century. Foreigners were suspected of taking away Englishmen's livelihoods and laws were issued to curtail their trading in cloth. The London May Day riots did happen as described in 1517.

Women had businesses, though they were usually widows, so I decided to give Elizabeth a degree of independent thought for a woman of her time. Her husband's difficult secret was my own invention, as was the fire to her property. The story needed to be cohesive. The themes and ideas I have explored in the book: those of the merchant class, Tudor London and guilds, humanism, women as housewives and merchants in early Tudor England, cried out for a story frame that would allow these themes to show through the text. I allowed Elizabeth to worry about her first husband's soul in an accepting way. I think that the fictional Elizabeth is resourceful. She is conflicted about any challenging religious atmosphere that enters her home. I saw their personal story as a love story, despite the unanswered question over whose daughter Jane really was. I invented Jeanette and her gift to Thomas. There is no existing record of Jane's mother.

Importantly, in *The Woman in the Shadows*, I wanted to give a flavour of the atmosphere of the period and a sensory portrait of London during this era. I hoped to give a sense of birth, marriage and death rituals in the early Tudor period and a sense of daily life inclusive of the major seasonal festivals. We know much about important men and royal women. This time, I wanted to explore the everyday life of an early Tudor woman married to a man who became one of the most famous men of Henry VIII's court, and I wanted to consider the speculated-upon, intimate side of this particular marriage, particularly because, after Elizabeth died, Thomas Cromwell, the king's loyal servant, never remarried.

Carol McGrath

A Short Bibliography

The following may be useful for a reader interested in further reading and research. Here listed are a small number of the books that I consulted when writing *The Woman in the Shadows*.

Ackroyd, Peter, *London*, Chatto & Windus, 2000

Ackroyd, Peter, *Thomas More*, Vintage, 1999

Borman, Tracy, *Thomas Cromwell, The Untold Story of Henry VIII's most faithful Servant*, Hodder, 2014

Bowden, Peter J, *The Wool Trade in Tudor and Stuart England*, St Martin's Press, 1962

Cavendish, George, *The Life and Death of Cardinal Wolsey*, 1815, 1959

Cressy, David, *Birth, Marriage & Death, Ritual, Religion and the Life Cycle in Tudor and Stuart England*, Oxford University Press, 1997

Goodman, Ruth, *How to be a Tudor*, Viking Press, 2015

Hutchinson, Robert, *Thomas Cromwell: The Rise and Fall of Henry VIII's Most Notorious Minister*; Weidenfield &

Nicolson, 2007

Loades, David, *Thomas Cromwell, Servant to Henry VIII*, Amberley Publishing, 2013

Lipscomb, Suzannah, *A Visitor's Companion to Tudor London*, Ebury Press, 2012

Manchester, Peter, *A World Lit by Fire*, Little, Brown, 1992

Power, Eileen, *Medieval Women*, Cambridge University Press, 1975, 1997

Schofield, John, *Thomas Cromwell, Henry VIII's Most Faithful Servant*, The History Press, 2011

Sim, Alison, *The Tudor Housewife*, Sutton Publishing, 1998

Sim, Alison, *Pleasures and Pastimes in Tudor England*, Sutton Publishing, 1999

Snow, Joh
n, *A Survey of London 1598*, Sutton Publishing, 2005

These are only a few of the books, articles, blog sites, Tudor houses, etc., I visited while writing the novel.

Acknowledgements

Many thanks are due to those who helped to bring this story from my pen into the world. Thanks go to my superb editor Greg Rees, whose comments were invaluable and who thoughtfully helped to shape the book's content. I would like to thank Eleanor Dryden, my publisher at the Headline Group and Rosanna Hildyard, her assistant, for giving this book new energy and for their guiding the updating of the original cover art. Thanks are due to Jane Judd, a friend in the publishing world, who suggested I write this novel. Jane, I am glad I listened to you; the book was a labour of love and a delight to research and write. My husband Patrick, to whom this novel is dedicated, has, as ever, been supportive and helpful. My writing group in the Greek Mani, where I can be found in summer, were enthusiastic and helpful during the early stages of the book's conception. Particular thanks go to Sarah Bower and Deborah Swift, my generous beta readers; your input has been observant and valuable. Finally, thanks to you, my readers because you, of course, are most important of all. Without you books cannot thrive. Thank you for reading *Mistress Cromwell*

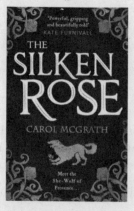

For the latest news, updates and exclusive content from Carol McGrath, sign up to her newsletter at: www.CarolCMcGrath.co.uk

You can also find Carol McGrath on social media . . .

Like her on Facebook: facebook.com/mcgrathauthor

Follow her on Twitter: @carolmcgrath

And follow Headline Accent: @AccentPress

ACCENT